PENGUIN  CLASSICS

JACQUES THE FATALIST

DENIS DIDEROT was born at Langres in eastern France in 1713, the son of a master-cutler. He was originally destined for the Church, but rebelled and persuaded his father to allow him to complete his education in Paris. For most of his twenties and early thirties, Diderot remained nominally a law student, but in fact led a rather precarious and Bohemian existence. He read extensively during this period, and this is reflected in his early works such as the *Pensées philosophiques* (1746) and the *Lettre sur les aveugles* (1749) which show a keen interest in contemporary philosophical issues. During the early 1740s Diderot met three contemporaries of great future significance for himself and for the age: d'Alembert, Condillac and J.-J. Rousseau. In 1747 Diderot embarked on the most important task of his life, the editorship of the *Encyclopédie*, whose publication he oversaw until its completion in 1773. Diderot's boldest philosophical and scientific speculations are brilliantly summarized in a trilogy of dialogues collectively known as *Le Rêve de d'Alembert* (1769). With *Le Neveu de Rameau*, begun in 1761, and *Jacques le Fataliste*, written between approximately 1755 and 1784, Diderot produced his greatest works of prose fiction, works which are highly original and daring, both in their form and in their content. Towards the end of his life, by now one of the most famous French writers, Diderot visited Saint Petersburg at the invitation of one of his most powerful admirers, the empress Catherine the Great, to whom he had promised his extensive library in return for her financial assistance. He died in 1784.

MARTIN HALL was born in 1946. He studied French and German at Christ Church, Oxford, and is at present a lecturer in French at King's College, London.

MICHAEL HENRY was born in 1954 and read French at King's College, London, graduating in 1977. His radio adaptation of this translation was produced by Radio 3, directed by John Theocharis. He now makes a living as an entertainment lawyer.

DENIS DIDEROT

JACQUES THE FATALIST
AND HIS MASTER

Translated by Michael Henry
with an Introduction and Notes
by Martin Hall

PENGUIN BOOKS

PENGUIN BOOKS

Published by the Penguin Group
Penguin Books Ltd, 27 Wrights Lane, London W8 5TZ, England
Penguin Books USA Inc., 375 Hudson Street, New York, New York 10014, USA
Penguin Books Australia Ltd, Ringwood, Victoria, Australia
Penguin Books Canada Ltd, 10 Alcorn Avenue, Toronto, Ontario, Canada M4V 3B2
Penguin Books (NZ) Ltd, 182–190 Wairau Road, Auckland 10, New Zealand

Penguin Books Ltd, Registered Offices: Harmondsworth, Middlesex, England

This translation first published 1986
7 9 10 8

Copyright © Michael Henry, 1986
Introduction copyright © Martin Hall, 1986
All rights reserved

The publishers gratefully acknowledge permission to base this translation upon the text of
Jacques le Fataliste edited by S. Lecointre and J. Le Galliot, Editions Droz, Paris, 1977.

Printed in England by Clays Ltd, St Ives plc
Photoset in Sabon

Except in the United States of America, this book is sold subject
to the condition that it shall not, by way of trade or otherwise, be lent,
re-sold, hired out, or otherwise circulated without the publisher's
prior consent in any form of binding or cover other than that in
which it is published and without a similar condition including this
condition being imposed on the subsequent purchaser

CONTENTS

INTRODUCTION

ABOUT DIDEROT

Denis Diderot was born in Langres in 1713, leaving the town in 1728 for Paris, where he lived until his death in 1784. What little evidence there is of Diderot's life and activities during his first dozen years in the capital suggests that he led the Bohemian life of an aspiring man of letters, often forced to resort to literary hack-work, private coaching and translation to make ends meet. His family helped him out for some years until Diderot quarrelled with his father in 1743 over his marriage plans. In spite of all these difficulties, these were the years in which Diderot developed his literary and intellectual talents and became keenly interested in contemporary developments in literature, philosophy and science.

In the late 1740s Diderot was approached by a consortium of Parisian publishers and asked to take over joint editorial control with the eminent mathematician d'Alembert of a project to translate and furnish suitable additions to Chamber's *Cyclopaedia*. In October 1747 Diderot signed a contract with the publishers, and so embarked on the single most important enterprise of his life. What finally emerged over the next twenty-odd years was one of the greatest and most representative monuments of the Enlightenment, the *Encyclopédie ou Dictionnaire raisonné des sciences, des arts et des métiers*. This work – the first modern encyclopaedia – ran to seventeen folio volumes of text and eleven of plates. After d'Alembert withdrew in 1758, Diderot was left in sole editorial control. In addition to the normal tasks of an editor he also took on a major role as researcher and contributor to the *Encyclopédie*. His articles were among the best and most original and covered topics ranging from the technological to the metaphysical.

From its early days the *Encyclopédie* was at the centre of political and ideological conflict. Far from being allowed to carry on his work in an atmosphere of peace and tranquillity, Diderot had to cope with the hostility of the *parlements*, the greater part of the Catholic Church, an important party at Court and various other influential groups as well as with the threat of prosecution and censorship.

His labours and difficulties were, however, justified by the importance of what was achieved. The *Encyclopédie* brought together the leading intellectual and scientific lights of the age. More than any other eighteenth-century work it defined the consensus of liberal and progressive ideas and values which was the Enlightenment. The *Encyclopédie* made Diderot a figure of European reputation and the acknowledged leader of the militant younger group of *philosophes*. The *Encyclopédie* also gave Diderot financial security and a large degree of independence besides stimulating the development of an omnivorous intelligence which made him the greatest polymath among the *philosophes*.

Nevertheless, the *Encyclopédie* never constituted Diderot's exclusive preoccupation, nor does it contain his most interesting contribution to the literature and thought of the period. This lies in writings that remained largely unknown to the general public during his lifetime, and which were written both during and after the publication of the *Encyclopédie*. Thus, Diderot's masterpiece of scientific speculation, *D'Alembert's Dream*, was unknown until 1831. Most of his prose fiction – novels, dialogues and short stories – remained unpublished until after his death, and included such major works as *Rameau's Nephew*, *The Nun* and *Jacques the Fatalist and his Master*. One reason why Diderot published so little during his lifetime was that it was often dangerous for writers to do so under a regime which exercised a fierce, if inefficient, censorship. Diderot learnt this at first hand when, in 1749, he published anonymously a brilliant exposition of atheist and materialist ideas in a work entitled *Letter Concerning the Blind*. Diderot's authorship was soon known to the authorities, and he was arrested and imprisoned for three months. There are, however, other reasons which may explain why Diderot was reluctant to publish many of his works. For example, the content of some of his work might have offended friends, as was the case with *D'Alembert's Dream*, which Diderot suppressed at the request of d'Alembert and his mistress, who felt they had been represented in an offensive manner. Another reason may be Diderot's preoccupation with the usefulness of the intellectual to society. While this never came into direct conflict with his commitment to stating the truth, it is fair to say that Diderot sometimes felt that the public good would not be best served by his broadcasting his more heterodox flights of fancy. Finally – and here *Jacques the Fatalist* might be taken as an example – it seems likely that Diderot believed his best and most original work would not be properly understood and appreciated in his own time and consciously accepted that, for him, true recognition had to be posthumous.

Jacques the Fatalist was conceived and written over a long period between the late 1760s and 1778 – a time of intense creative activity for Diderot after the depression accompanying the conclusion of work on the *Encyclopédie*. It was partially published in the *Correspondance littéraire* between 1778 and 1780. An early and enthusiastic reader was Goethe, but, for the most part, the reception of the work tended to confirm Diderot's suspicions about the likely reaction to his most original work. Even after the novel became more widely available after its publication in 1796, reactions tended to vary from incomprehension to patronizing indifference. At best it was deemed an amusing pot-pourri, at worst obscene and unreadable. It is only recently, in the last few decades, that both specialist and non-specialist readers have begun to catch up with Diderot and discover the strange originality of *Jacques the Fatalist*.

FICTION AND REALITY

Jacques the Fatalist is a novel which refers insistently to other novels, to story-telling and fiction. The reader soon becomes aware that a powerful attack is being mounted against a particular sort of novel, and will have little difficulty in recognizing what kind of fiction is under fire – undemanding, escapist literature, full of implausible plotting and stereotyped characterization, relying heavily on a strong love-interest. In its refusal of the romanticizing exaggeration of conventional fiction, *Jacques* belongs to a long and important tradition in the European novel, a tradition which can be defined by its rejection of the tawdry resources of 'mere' fiction and its proclamation of its own adherence to the superior claims of truth. *Jacques* repeatedly asserts not only that it is not an invented story, but also that it is a *true story* referring to the *real world*.

Readers who come to *Jacques* anticipating a 'true story' might find some initial reassurance in the Narrator's repeated assurances of fidelity to the truth. This might even be reinforced by the presence in the text of some of the indicators readers have come to expect as evidence of the authenticity of the story they are being told. They are, for instance, given dates, places and proper names belonging to people who really existed. They are given explanations about the provenance of the story and its transmission via the Narrator to themselves. However, it soon becomes clear that the mere presence of these indicators does not mean that they work very successfully. A simple example is the matter of historical dates. One might imagine, on a first reading, that the presence of references to major events such as battles and great natural disasters secured the novel in a firm chronological framework. Closer examination reveals that, far from offering the reader the security of a stable historical context, dates are delusory. Jacques was wounded in the knee in 1745 at the battle of Fontenoy, and refers to himself as having limped for twenty years, thus locating the time in which he is telling the story of his loves somewhere in the mid-sixties. What then are we to make of the reference to Mandrin's gang in the final pages of the novel? Mandrin himself died in 1755. The dates appear to be contradictory. A similar situation arises when the reader pauses to consider the provenance of Jacques' life story. There seems to be a manuscript somewhere which is the basis of the Narrator's claim to be telling a true story. At the same time, there appears to be direct contact between Jacques and the Narrator ('Jacques told me . . .'). In the final pages, however, this apparatus is thrown into doubt by the sudden intervention of an 'Editor' who inevitably reduces the Narrator from being a powerful authenticatory voice to a mere fictional device.

Once the readers' suspicions are alerted they will notice more and more instances in which the seemingly secure structures of the narrative start to look shaky. Contradictions and logical impossibilities begin to crop up with alarming frequency. A widow is mourned by her husband. Jacques takes up a point made by the Narrator. A character's death is fixed by two incompatible time sequences.

As a true story *Jacques* doesn't work, it doesn't fit together. Parts of the novel may maintain an internal coherence, but even these tend to look like exercises in style and rhetoric when replaced in their context. The story of Madame de La Pommeraye and the Marquis des Arcis is the most important instance of this. Taken by itself (and it has frequently been published as an autonomous novella), the story is convincing and moving. Replaced in the inn, where it is told to Jacques and his master by the innkeeper's wife, its implausibility is easily demonstrated by two questions: Who is this innkeeper's wife who speaks so eloquently? How has she learnt the story? What might, in one perspective, seem like a true story, becomes, in another, a fictional construct.

It gradually becomes apparent that what could initially have seemed mistakes – contradiction, incoherence, incompatibility – are 'deliberate mistakes', part of a strategy of disruption and subversion that seems designed to deny the reader any easy retreat into fictional illusion. *Jacques* not only points the finger of scorn at the inadequacies and artificialities of conventional fiction, but also points to its own fictional nature. When, for the umpteenth time, the Narrator asks us what is to prevent him from giving us whatever fictional continuation he chooses, we may well cease to take this as part of a rhetorical protestation of truthfulness, take the question literally and answer 'nothing'. The reference to truth is finally self-defeating. We cannot read *Jacques* straightforwardly as a chronicle of events, but must call into question our own expectations in reading fiction.

STORIES AND STORY-TELLING

'When someone tells a tale, to a listener, and assuming that the tale goes on for some length of time, it's unusual for the teller not to be interrupted by his listener.' These lines, which open one of Diderot's short-stories, might serve as the epigraph to *Jacques*, a novel that is remarkable not merely by the quantity of tales and anecdotes that it contains but also by its dramatization of the relationship between the teller of a story and the listener or reader.

As we read *Jacques*, we are constantly made aware that the tales we are reading are being told by one person to another. Nor is this a point which we can simply take note of and then ignore: the circumstances surrounding the telling of a story almost always serve as an intrusive reminder. The innkeeper's wife, for example, finds her attempts to begin her story repeatedly thwarted by the interruptions of her husband, customers and staff. Jacques' efforts to continue the story of his loves are frustrated by the distressing tendency of his horse to bolt. At another point, he is physically prevented from continuing by a sore throat.

Stories are not received in silence, but interrupted, commented upon, interpreted and judged. The Narrator wages a running battle with the Reader over the stories he relates, provoking, teasing and bullying him to the point where the convention of authorial address to the reader ceases to be a mere convention and becomes the means to explore the complex dynamics of the story-telling relationship.

This exploration is most fully and subtly worked out in the relationship of Jacques and his master. The underlying symbiosis of the couple is expressed in the one's need to talk and the other's need to listen. At the same time, the latant antagonism of master and servant also finds expression in story-telling. Jacques is irritated at his master's interruptions and exasperated at his demands to side-track to other issues. His master in turn seeks to make of his servant an almost mechanical furnisher of tales for his satisfaction. Jacques frets and worries over the difficulties and ambiguities of story-telling, while his master, with characteristic complacency, simply tells

Jacques that the important thing is that one should tell stories and the other listen.

The dramatization of the story-telling relationship fulfils another important function: it highlights the quest for significance or meaning which the stories are intended to provoke. For instance, Jacques and his master are fascinated by the story that the innkeeper's wife tells them. They argue about the psychological coherence of the characters and how to interpret their behaviour; they argue about the morality of this behaviour and what judgement to pass on it. The Narrator then intrudes to provoke the Reader into discussion. The story has generated what might become an endless series of debates and discussions. The world of *Jacques* is not a fixed and settled one in which incidents and behaviour are easily assessed and interpreted. On the contrary, it is a world of dizzying variety and unpredictability, one which beckons its readers to embark on their own search for meaning rather than offering them ready-made answers.

THEMATIC ORGANIZATION

Is there any ordering principle to be discerned in the welter of anecdotes that make up such a large part of the novel? Certainly, readers may initially be inclined to think that they are being offered a representation of the sprawling untidiness and inconclusiveness of life itself. However, it is fair to say that, besides the major themes of master—servant relations and fatalism dealt with below, there are four other important thematic areas which can be discerned emerging from the confusion.

1. Mutability and Change

Among the great writers of the Enlightenment Diderot is distinctive by the importance which time and transformation play in his vision of the world, a world whose working can only be understood in terms of its perpetual change. This vision is evoked in one of the rare passages of high-flown rhetoric in *Jacques*, an invocation to the folly of two lovers swearing eternal constancy in a world whose every feature is witness of change. This theme of mutability emerges insistently in the motif of sexual inconstancy and infidelity and is most fully developed in the story of Madame de La Pommeraye and the Marquis des Arcis. This story also illustrates the closely related motif of jealousy, the counterpart of inconstancy, which might also be defined as the refusal of the harsh rule of universal change.

2. *Rivalry*

The second theme of rivalry, like that of jealousy, is frequently illustrated in the context of sexual relations but throughout *Jacques* there recurs a particularly bizarre figure of rivalry in the form of the compulsive duellists. The rivalry motif involves a succession of couples hardly distinguishable the one from the next and offers the reader a haunting image of inexplicability – two men closely attached to one another, unable to live apart and at the same time impelled to fight bloody and dangerous duels.

3. *Bizarreness of Human Nature*

The inexplicability of human nature, as illustrated by the duellists, is a constant preoccupation in *Jacques* which clearly reflects Diderot's fascination with the 'outsize' human character in Madame de La Pommeraye, Father Hudson and Jacques himself even. These figures, whose counterparts can be found in other works of Diderot, are distinguished by their unity of character, a hardness and autonomy which separates them from their fellows. They are those whose control over their fiery nature allows them to channel their exceptional energy into far-reaching and ambitious designs. It is not so much their contradictoriness that seems to fascinate Diderot as their irreducibility to any easy moral judgement. Admirable in certain respects they are also marked by a certain amoralism, often made manifest in their ruthless destruction of those who cross or oppose them. In the end, as in the case of the duellists, it is to the acceptance of the diversity of human nature that the reader is led.

4. *Deceit and Duplicity*

Hudson himself is the supreme deceiver, who manages not only to sustain an image of industry, piety and austerity while leading a life of debauchery but also manages to turn the tables on those sent to establish his guilt, to such effect that they, and not he, end up accused and punished. Hudson's tale is only the most striking and elaborate illustration of a theme which pervades the novel. The deceiver may end up deceived, as in the case of the Steward who sleeps with the pastry-cook's wife and ends up suffering the fate he had himself intended for the pastry-cook. Jacques' love life and that of his master offer other examples of complex permutations of deceit. This group of themes is particularly recalcitrant to explanation and interpretation. It offers recurrent images of reversal, of artifice, of the opposition of appearance and reality. It may also perhaps offer a loose symbol of the opposition of truth and fiction so insistently referred to by the Narrator throughout the novel.

SERVANT AND MASTER

The importance of the central relationship of the novel is signalled in the very title of the book, *Jacques the Fatalist and his Master*, as are its subversive implications: Jacques takes precedence over his master, Jacques has a name and his master has none. This reversal of the usual social order relates *Jacques* to a long tradition stretching back at least as far as Latin comedy, which explores the dramatic possibilities offered by bringing together two individuals, one the social superior, the other the intellectual superior. The literature of the French eighteenth century explores this relationship with particular zest and constitutes a veritable 'Golden Age' of the clever servant, whose two outstanding figures are Jacques and his first cousin and near contemporary, Beaumarchais' Figaro. The similarities between the two are numerous and significant. Like Beaumarchais' hero, Jacques is conscious of his worth and ready to assert his conviction that he is the equal, if not the superior of his master. More importantly, Jacques and Figaro both demand out of self-respect that this equality be recognized. It is no coincidence that for both men the cause of outright conflict with their master should be sexual rivalry. When Jacques' master expresses his disbelief at the idea that a woman could prefer Jacques to himself, he formulates this in a particularly offensive manner, referring to Jacques as 'A Jacques', a contemptuous and dismissive term for a peasant. What he is saying is that Jacques is not an individual and cannot be taken seriously even in something as fundamental as his sexual aspirations. A servant, a peasant, is not a man. Jacques' response is to assert the contrary, to claim equality and demand to be treated with appropriate respect. The context may seem trivial but the issue is not, and the figure of the servant asserts (as does Beaumarchais' Figaro) a rejection of any social order which defines an individual's worth by his social position.

This quarrel between Jacques and his master constitutes a high point in the novel, where the fundamental rejection of the *ancien régime* is most apparent. The subsequent patching up of the quarrel (which as the Narrator points out has occurred a hundred times before) is just as significant. The intervention of the innkeeper's wife restores the equality between Jacques and his master which constitutes the *de facto* reality of their day-to-day existence. Indeed equality is perhaps too mild a term since, as Jacques points out, he exercises effective control in the relationship, while his master has a merely titular authority. This pragmatic solution (by no means the only one of its kind in Diderot's works) leaves certain fundamental contradictions unresolved, but it does have the virtue of effectiveness; it works. It also underlines the fact that while the master/servant relationship is, in some respects, a conflictual one, it is also a profoundly symbiotic one. Much has been made by some critics of the ineptness and stupidity of Jacques' master, who appears to them the embodiment of an effete and parasitic aristocracy, while Jacques is the symbol of the valorous Third Estate. This is an exaggeration and a simplification: Jacques' master, for all his limitations, is presented as an amiable and good-natured man, genuinely fond of his servant, and capable, for most of the time, of recognizing Jacques' peculiar gifts and accepting his natural superiority. Indeed, as their relationship of story-teller and listener illustrates, each man needs the other. What characterizes Diderot's treatment of the master/servant theme is the subtlety with which he brings out both the inevitably exploitative side of the relationship and its profoundly symbiotic nature.

Jacques is the hero of the novel not simply by virtue of his dominant position in his relationship with his master, but also by the fact that it is his past, the story of his loves, that provide the principal element of continuity in the work. This means that a considerable part of the novel focuses on a social setting that was comparatively rare in the French novel of the eighteenth century, the village and the countryside. Diderot had read extensively the work of English novelists of the century and had been struck by the relative broadness of scope the English novel allowed. Defoe, Fielding and Richardson could paint on a wider canvas and represent a greater variety of manners, customs and classes than could their French counterparts, who were bound, Diderot felt, by the rather restricted range of their public's taste. In this respect *Jacques* is one of the most adventurous French novels of the century in its insistent reference to what might be termed scenes of everyday life in the village and the countryside, the traditional domain of the peasant, a social setting found only rarely in the French novel of this time. Often the episodes recounted come from an old stock of popular images and references – the farcical scene with the little village priest, the bawdy episodes of sexual initiation and the career of Brother Jean – which cannot be said to be of Diderot's invention. They belong to a popular tradition of tales, fables and jokes which after a considerable period of absence come back into the mainstream of prose fiction through *Jacques*. Indeed, it is arguable that *Jacques* is truly Rabelaisian not in its rather clumsy attempts at a literal reworking of Rabelais (as in the reference to the sacred gourd) but in a much more fundamental sense. With *Jacques*, Diderot reintroduces popular elements into the serious novel with an effect that is as liberating as it was in Rabelais' time. The egalitarian message of *Jacques* lies as much in its re-introduction of popular forms into the novel as in its celebration of the clever servant.

JACQUES THE FATALIST

The title tells us that Jacques is a fatalist, but what does this mean? Many critics have assumed that *Jacques* is about fatalism, that it is an exploration in fictional terms of philosophical issues raised by Diderot's materialist view of the world – a view which requires the universe to be explained exclusively in terms of matter, its properties and activity. Diderot was led from this position to a commitment to determinism which propounded that if the universe is explicable exclusively in terms of the organization and activity of matter, then there is no room for any 'play' in the system. Nothing is chance: all is determined.

At the same time, Diderot was intensely preoccupied by ethical problems and concerns. Resolutely hostile to what he saw as the unnatural and stultifying effects of Christian ethical teaching, he remained equally resolute in seeking some alternative foundation to ethics. But this was where Diderot's problems began, because the philosophical position he held seemed to deny any possibility of establishing a secure basis for ethics except as a form of utilitarian social engineering: if everything is determined, the argument will run, free will is a nonsense and, if this is the case, although we may attempt by means of an appropriate system of incentives and deterrents to make man what is socially desirable, we cannot make him a moral being.

Freedom or determinism? This becomes the starting-point for a philosophical reading of *Jacques*. The fatalistic Jacques is committed to a form of determinism, believing that all is foreordained, 'written up above', in his own words, yet he constantly contradicts his own viewpoint by actions and feelings which are the behaviour of a moral being. The novel can then be read as an elaboration in fictional form of the philosophical dilemma in which Diderot found himself, committed to a philosophical doctrine which denied his need for a universe in which moral choice was meaningful.

An interpretation of *Jacques* along these lines is plausible, and finds justification both in the text and in Diderot's practice as a writer (*Jacques* is not the only one of Diderot's works to explore dilemmas and unresolved tensions of his thought and personality). However, there are dangers in this line of interpretation.

First, it would be wrong to explain this strange and complicated novel simply in terms of its exposition of some philosophical doctrine. Jacques' fatalism is not really philosophical determinism but is more closely related to certain popular ideas and expressions (the idea of every bullet having its address on it, for instance, and the notion of everything being 'written up above') than to any philosophical doctrine. In so far as it relates to any philosophical doctrine the link is a tenuous one whose fallibility is underlined. Jacques' 'philosophical' ideas are derived from his Captain, who in turn derives them from Spinoza. From Spinoza to 'It's written up above' is not a route that is either obvious or direct.

Secondly, if the novel were straightforwardly 'about' fatalism one might expect that there would be some developed argument, even perhaps a conclusion reached. This is not the case. Jacques may score points off his master – as when they become involved in the question of free will – but nowhere is there any conventional elaboration and exploration of issues. In pursuing this line, one might ask whether, apart from in the amount of time and space allocated to them, there is any difference between the discussion on fatalism and that on the subject of women which the Narrator tells us could go on interminably without getting anywhere. This is not to deny the importance of the discussion, but to underline the fact that the issue of fatalism is presented in *Jacques* as part of a work of fiction.

CONCLUSIONS

If there is no conclusion offered to the alternative of freedom or determinism, it is because the novel as a whole tends towards the representation of such alternatives as fundamentally irresoluble. Indeed the figure of what might be called alternativity runs throughout *Jacques*. Do the duellists love or hate each other? Is Gousse good or bad? Is Jacques servant or master? In each case the alternative does not allow a simple resolution. We cannot decide but have to cope as best we can with the answer: 'Both at once'.

Like the great comic works that it avows as its inspiration – Rabelais' novels, Molière's comedies, Sterne's *Tristram Shandy – Jacques* is above all a celebratory work. It proclaims its delight in diversity and difference, and a fascination with the quirkiness and bizarreness of human life. Like these masterpieces it is irreducible to any fixed and limiting scheme of interpretation. *Jacques* has been interpreted as a novel of moral experience, as a critique of the eighteenth-century novel, as an attack on the *ancien régime*, and as a philosophical exploration. It is all of these things but none of them exclusively. The worst misreading of *Jacques* would consist precisely in thinking that one could offer an exhaustive interpretation of it. With due regard to the Narrator's strictures concerning allegory, we might say that *Jacques* is like the 'château' where Jacques and his master spend (or don't spend) a night. It belongs to everybody and to nobody. *Jacques* calls to the intelligent reader – not the doctrinaire one – and invites us all to write our own conclusion.

JACQUES THE FATALIST
AND HIS MASTER

How did they meet? By chance like everyone else. What were their names? What's that got to do with you? Where were they coming from? From the nearest place. Where were they going to? Does anyone ever really know where they are going to? What were they saying? The master wasn't saying anything and Jacques was saying that his Captain used to say that everything which happens to us on this earth, both good and bad, is written up above.

MASTER: That's very profound.

JACQUES: My Captain used to add that every shot fired from a gun had someone's name on it.

MASTER: And he was right . . .

(After a short pause Jacques cried out:) May the devil take that innkeeper and his inn!

MASTER: Why consign one's neighbour to the devil? That's not Christian.

JACQUES: Because while I was getting drunk on his bad wine I forgot to water our horses. My father noticed and got angry. I shook my head at him and he took a stick and hit me rather hard across the shoulders. There was a regiment passing through on its way to camp at Fontenoy,[1] and so out of pique I joined up. We arrived. The battle started . . .

MASTER: And you stopped the bullet with your name on it?

JACQUES: You've guessed it. Shot in the knee. And God knows the good and bad fortunes that were brought about by that shot. They are linked together exactly like the links of a fob-chain. Were it not for that shot, for example, I don't think I would ever have fallen in love, or had a limp.

MASTER: So you've been in love then?

JACQUES: Have I been in love!

MASTER: And all because of a shot?

JACQUES: Because of a shot.

MASTER: You never said a word of this to me before.

JACQUES: Very likely.

MASTER: And why is that?

JACQUES: That is because it is something that could not be told a moment sooner or a moment later.

MASTER: And has the moment come for hearing about these loves?

JACQUES: Who knows?

MASTER: Well, on the off-chance, begin anyway . . .

Jacques began the story of his loves. It was after lunch. The weather was very close, and his master fell asleep. Nightfall surprised them in the middle of nowhere. There they were, lost, and there was the master in a terrible temper, raining huge blows from his horsewhip on to his valet and at every blow the poor devil cried out: 'That must also have been written up above!'

So you can see, Reader, that I'm well away and it's entirely within my power to make you wait a year, or two, or even three years for the story of Jacques' loves, by separating him from his master and exposing each of them to whatever perils I liked. What is there to prevent me from marrying off the master and having him cuckolded? Or sending Jacques off to the Indies? And leading his master there? And bringing them both back to France on the same vessel? How easy it is to make up stories! But I will let the two of them off with a bad night's sleep and you with this delay.

Dawn broke. There they were back on their horses carrying on their way.

– And where were they going?

That is the second time you have asked me that question and for the second time I ask you, what has that got to do with you? If I begin the story of their journey then it's goodbye to Jacques' loves . . . They went on for a little while in silence. When they had both recovered a little from their annoyance the master said to his valet: 'Well then, Jacques, where did we get to in your loves?'

JACQUES: We had, I believe, got to the rout of the enemy army. Everyone was running away and being chased and it was every man for himself. I was left on the battlefield, buried under the prodigious number of dead and dying bodies. The next day I was thrown onto a cart along with a dozen or so others to be taken to one of our hospitals. Ah! Monsieur, I do not believe there is any wound more painful than a wound in the knee.

MASTER: Come along, Jacques, you're joking.

JACQUES: No, by God! Monsieur, I am not joking! There are I don't know how many bones, tendons and other bits called I don't know what . . .

Some sort of peasant who was following them with a girl he was carrying on his saddle and who had overheard them interrupted and said: 'Monsieur is right . . .'

It was not clear to whom this 'Monsieur' was addressed but both Jacques and his master took it badly and Jacques said to this indiscreet interlocutor: 'Why don't you mind your own business?'

'I am minding my own business. I am a surgeon[2] at your service and I am going to give you a demonstration . . .'

The woman he was carrying on the crupper said to him: 'Monsieur le Docteur, let us carry on our way and leave these gentlemen who don't want to be given a demonstration.'

'No,' replied the surgeon, 'I want to demonstrate to them and I am going to demonstrate to them . . .'

And as he was turning round to demonstrate he pushed his companion, made her lose her balance and threw her to the ground, with one foot caught in his coat tails and her petticoats over her head. Jacques got down, freed the poor creature's foot and pulled her skirts back down. I don't know whether he started by pulling her skirts back down or freeing her foot, but, to judge the state of this woman from her screams, she had hurt herself badly.

And Jacques' master said to the surgeon: 'That's what comes of demonstrating! . . .'

And the surgeon said: 'That's what comes of not wanting people to demonstrate! . . .'

And Jacques said to the fallen or picked-up young woman: 'Calm yourself, my dear. It is neither your fault, nor the fault of Monsieur le Docteur, nor mine, nor my master's. It was written up above that this day, on this road, at this very hour, Monsieur le Docteur would talk too much, my master and I would both be unfriendly, and you would receive a bump on the head and show us your bottom . . .'

What might this little incident not become in my hands if I took it into my head to reduce you to despair. I could make this woman somebody important. I could make all the peasants come running. I could bring in stories of love and strife, because, after all, underneath her petticoats this peasant girl had a nice little body, as Jacques and his master had noticed. Love hasn't always waited for so seductive an opportunity. Why shouldn't Jacques fall in love a second time? Why shouldn't he be, for a second time, his master's rival – even his preferred rival?

– Had that happened to him before?

Always questions! Do you not want Jacques to continue with the story of his loves then? Once and for all, tell me: Would that give you pleasure, or would it not give you pleasure?

If that would give you pleasure, then let us put the peasant girl back up behind the surgeon, allow them to carry on their way, and return to our two travellers.

This time it was Jacques who spoke first, and he said to his master:

That's the way the world goes . . . You, a man who has never in his life been wounded and who has no idea what it is like to be shot in the knee, you tell me, a man who has had his knee shattered and has had a limp for the last twenty years . . .

MASTER: You may be right. But that impertinent surgeon is to blame for you still being on that cart with your companions, far from the hospital, far from being cured and far from falling in love.

JACQUES: Whatever you might think, the pain in my knee was extreme. It was becoming more so with the hard ride in the wagon and the bumpy roads, and at every bump I screamed . . .

MASTER: Because it was written up above that you'd scream?

JACQUES: Undoubtedly! I was bleeding to death and I would have been a dead man if our wagon, which was the last in the column, hadn't stopped in front of a cottage. There I asked to get down and I was helped to the ground. A young woman who was standing at the door of the cottage disappeared inside and came out again almost immediately with a glass and a bottle of wine. I drank one or two glasses quickly. The carts in front of ours moved off. They were getting ready to throw me back into the wagon amongst my companions, when grabbing hold of the woman's clothes and everything else within reach I protested that I would not get back in and that, if I was going to die anyhow, I preferred to die on the spot rather than two miles further on. As I finished these words I fainted. When I came to I found myself undressed and lying in bed in the corner of the cottage with a peasant – the master of the house – his wife, the woman who had rescued me, and a few young children gathered around me. The woman had soaked the corner of her apron in vinegar and was rubbing my nose and temples with it.

MASTER: Ah! You villain! You rogue! You traitor! I can see what's coming.

JACQUES: My master, I don't think you see anything.

MASTER: Isn't this the woman you're going to fall in love with?

JACQUES: And if I were to have fallen in love with her, what could you say about that? Is one free to fall in love or not to fall in love? And if one is, is one free to act as if one wasn't? If the thing had been written up above, everything which you are about to say to me now I would already have said to myself. I would have slapped my own face, I would have beaten my head against the wall, I would have torn out my hair, and it would have been no more or less so, and my benefactor would have been cuckolded.

MASTER: But if one follows your reasoning there can be no remorse for any crime.

JACQUES: That objection has bothered me more than once, but for all that, however reluctantly, I always come back to what my Captain used to say: 'Everything which happens to us in this world, good or bad, is written up above . . .'

Do you, Monsieur, know any way of erasing this writing?

Can I be anything other than myself, and being me, can I act otherwise than I do?

Can I be myself and somebody else?

And ever since I have been in this world, has there ever been one single moment when it has not been so?

You may preach as much as you wish. Your reasons may perhaps be good, but if it is written within me or up above that I will find them bad, what can I do about it?

MASTER: I am wondering about something . . . that is whether your benefactor would have been cuckolded because it was written up above or whether it was written up above because you cuckolded your benefactor.

JACQUES: The two were written side by side. Everything was written at the same time. It is like a great scroll which is unrolled little by little.

You can imagine, Reader, to what lengths I might take this conversation on a subject which has been talked about and written about so much for the last two thousand years without getting one step further forward. If you are not grateful to me for what I am telling you, be very grateful for what I am not telling you.

While our two theologians were arguing without listening to each other, as can happen in theology, nightfall was approaching. They were coming to a part of the country which was unsafe at the best of times, and even more unsafe when bad administration and poverty had endlessly multiplied the number of malefactors. They stopped at the most sordid of inns. Two camp-beds were made up for them in a room made of partitions which were gaping on all sides. They asked for something to eat. They were brought pondwater, black bread and sour wine. The innkeeper, his wife, their children and the valets all appeared rather sinister. They could hear coming from the room next to them the immoderate laughter and rowdy merriment of a dozen or so brigands who had arrived there before them and requisitioned all the victuals. Jacques was happy enough. This was not at all the case with his master. He was walking his worries up and down, while his valet consumed a few pieces of black bread and swallowed a few glasses of the sour wine, grimacing. At this point they heard a knocking on their door. It was a valet who had been persuaded by their insolent and dangerous neighbours to bring our two travellers all the bones of a fowl they had eaten on one of their plates. Jacques, indignant, took his master's pistols.

'Where are you going?'

'Leave me alone.'

'Where are you going, I'm asking you?'

'To sort out those scum.'

'Do you know there are a dozen of them?'

'Were there one hundred, the number doesn't matter if it is written up above that there are not enough of them.'

'May the devil take you and your impertinent speech! . . .'

Jacques dodged his master and went into the cut-throats' room, a cocked pistol in each hand.

'Quickly, lie down,' he said. 'The first one who moves gets his brains blown out . . .'

Jacques' appearance and tone were so convincing that these rascals, who valued their lives just as much as honest people, got up from table without saying a word, got undressed and went to bed. His master, uncertain of how this little adventure would end, was waiting for him, trembling. Jacques returned, loaded up with these people's clothes. He had taken possession of them in case they were tempted to get up again. He had put out their light and double-locked their door, the key of which he was carrying on one of his pistols.

'Now, Monsieur,' he said to his master, 'all we have to do is to barricade ourselves in by pushing our beds against the door and then we can sleep peacefully.' And he set about moving the beds, coolly and succinctly recounting to his master the details of his expedition.

MASTER: Jacques, what kind of devil of a man are you? Do you really believe? . . .

JACQUES: I neither believe nor disbelieve.

MASTER: What if they had refused to go to bed?

JACQUES: That was impossible.

MASTER: Why?

JACQUES: Because they didn't do it.

MASTER: What if they get up again?

JACQUES: So much the worse or so much the better.

MASTER: If . . . if . . . if . . . and . . .

JACQUES: If . . . if the sea was boiling, there would be, as the saying goes, an awful lot of fish cooked. What the devil, Monsieur, just now you believed that I was running a great risk and nothing could have been more wrong. Now you believe yourself to be in great danger and nothing, perhaps, could be more wrong again. Everyone in this house is afraid of everyone else, which proves we are all idiots . . .

And while speaking thus, there he was, undressed, in bed, and fast asleep. His master, eating in his turn a piece of black bread, and drinking a glass of bad wine, was listening all around him and looking at Jacques, who was snoring, saying: 'What kind of devil of a man is that?'

Following his valet's example, the master also stretched himself out on his camp-bed but didn't sleep quite the same. As soon as day broke Jacques felt a hand pushing him. It was the hand of his master, who was calling him softly.

MASTER: Jacques? Jacques?

JACQUES: What is it?

MASTER: It's daylight.

JACQUES: Very likely.

MASTER: Get up then.

JACQUES: Why?

MASTER: So we can get out of here as quickly as possible.

JACQUES: Why?

MASTER: Because we're not safe here.

JACQUES: Who knows? And who knows if we'll be better off anywhere else?

MASTER: Jacques?

JACQUES: Well, Jacques, Jacques. You're the devil of a man.

MASTER: What kind of devil of a man are you? Jacques, my friend, I beg you.

Jacques rubbed his eyes, yawned several times, stretched out his arms, got up, dressed without hurrying, pushed back the beds, went out of the bedroom, went downstairs, went to the stable, saddled and bridled the horses, woke up the innkeeper, who was still asleep, paid the bill, kept the keys to the two bedrooms, and there they were, gone.

The master wanted to get away at a fast trot. Jacques wanted to go at walking pace, still following his system. When they were quite a good way from their miserable resting-place the master, hearing something jangling in Jacques' pocket, asked him what it was. Jacques told him it was the two keys to the bedrooms.

MASTER: Why didn't you give them back?

JACQUES: Because they'll have to break down two doors – our neighbours' to release them from captivity, and ours to get back their clothes, and that will give us some time.

MASTER: Very good, Jacques, but why gain time?

JACQUES: Why? My God, I don't know.

MASTER: And if you want to gain time, why go as slowly as you are going?

JACQUES: Because, without knowing what is written up above, none of us knows what we want or what we are doing, and we follow our whims which we call reason, or our reason which is often nothing but a dangerous whim which sometimes turns out well, sometimes badly.

My Captain used to believe that prudence is a supposition in which experience justifies us interpreting the circumstances in which we find ourselves as the cause of certain effects which are to be desired or feared in the future.

MASTER: And did you understand any of that?

JACQUES: Of course. I had little by little grown used to his way of speaking. But who, he used to ask, can ever boast of having enough experience? Has even he who flatters himself on being the most experienced of men never been fooled? And then, what man is there who is capable of correctly assessing the circumstances in which he finds himself? The calculation which we make in our heads and the one recorded on the register up above are two very different calculations. Is it we who control Destiny or Destiny which controls us? How many wisely conceived projects have failed and will fail in the future! How many insane projects have succeeded and will succeed! That is what my Captain kept repeating to me after the capture of Berg-op-Zoom and Port-Mahon.[3] And he added that prudence in no way assured us of success but consoled us and excused us in failure. And so on the eve of any action he would sleep as well in his tent as in barracks and he would go into battle as if to a ball. And you might well have said of him: 'What kind of devil of a man! . . .'

MASTER: Could you tell me what is a foolish man, and what is a wise man?

JACQUES: Why not? . . . A foolish man . . . wait a moment . . . is an unhappy man. And consequently a happy man is a wise man.

MASTER: And what is a happy man or an unhappy man?

JACQUES: Well, that one's easy. A happy man is someone whose happiness is written up above, and consequently someone whose unhappiness is written up above is an unhappy man.

MASTER: And who is it up there who wrote out this good and bad fortune up above?

JACQUES: And who created the great scroll on which it is all written? A captain friend of my own Captain would have given a pretty penny to know that. But my Captain wouldn't have paid an obol, nor would I, for what good would it do me? Would I manage to avoid the hole where I am destined to break my neck?

MASTER: I think so.

JACQUES: Well, I think not because there would have to be an incorrect line on the great scroll which contains the truth, the whole truth and nothing but the truth. In that case it would have to be written on the scroll that Jacques would break his neck on such a day and Jacques would not break his neck. Can you imagine for one moment that that could happen, whoever made the great scroll?

MASTER: There are a number of things one could say about that . . .

At this point they heard a lot of noise and shouting coming from some distance behind them. They looked round and saw a band of men armed with sticks and forks coming towards them as fast as they could run. You are going to believe that it was the people from the inn and their servants and the brigands we have spoken of. You are going to believe that in the morning they broke down their doors since they didn't have the keys and that these brigands thought that our travellers had decamped with their possessions. That is what Jacques thought and he said between his teeth: 'Damn the keys and damn the fantasy or reason which made me take them. Damn prudence, etc. etc.!'

[margin note: cursing himself]

You are going to believe that this little army will fall upon Jacques and his master, that there will be a bloody fight, blows with sticks and pistol shots, and if I wanted to I could make all of these things happen, but then it would be goodbye to the truth of the story and goodbye to the story of Jacques' loves.

Our two travellers were not followed. I do not know what happened in the inn after they left. They carried on their way still going without knowing where they were going although they knew more or less where they wanted to go, relieving their boredom and fatigue by silence and conversation, as is the custom of those who walk, and sometimes of those who are sitting down.

It is quite obvious that I am not writing a novel since I am neglecting those things which a novelist would not fail to use. The person who takes what I write for the truth might perhaps be less wrong than the person who takes it for a fiction.

This time it was the master who spoke first, and he started with the usual refrain: 'Well now, Jacques, the story of your loves?'

JACQUES: I don't remember where I had got to. I've been interrupted so many times that I would do just as well to start all over again.

MASTER: No, no. When you had come round after fainting at the door of the cottage you found yourself in bed surrounded by the people who lived there.

JACQUES: Very good. The most pressing thing was to get hold of a surgeon and there wasn't one within less than a league. The peasant put one of his children on a horse and sent him off to the nearest one. Meanwhile the peasant's wife had heated up some table wine, torn up one of her husband's old shirts and my knee was cleaned, covered with compresses and wrapped in linen. They put a few pieces of sugar they had saved from the ants into part of the wine which had been used for the bandage and I drank it down. Next they told me to be patient. It was late. The family sat down to table and had supper. Supper was finished and the child had still not come back and there was no surgeon. The father became angry. He was a naturally ill-tempered man. He sulked at his wife and found nothing to his liking. In a temper he sent the other children to bed. His wife sat down on a wooden seat and took up her distaff. He paced up and down and as he was pacing up and down he tried to pick an argument on any pretext.

'If you'd gone to the mill like I told you to . . .', and he finished the sentence shaking his head in the direction of my bed.

'I'll go tomorrow.'

'It's today that you should have gone like I told you to . . . And what about those bits of straw left on the floor of the barn? What are you waiting for to pick them up?'

'It will be done tomorrow.'

'But what we've got left is almost finished and you'd have done much better to pick them up today like I told you to . . . And that heap of barley that's rotting in the loft? I'll wager you didn't think to turn it?'

'The children did it.'

'You should have done it yourself. If you had been up in your loft you wouldn't have been at the door . . .'

At that moment a surgeon arrived, and then a second surgeon and then a third with the little boy from the cottage.

MASTER: And there you were with as many surgeons as there are hats on Saint Roch.⁴

JACQUES: The first was away when the little boy arrived at his house, but his wife had passed word to the second and the third had come back with the little boy.

'Good evening, friends, what are you doing here?' said the first to the others.

They had come as quickly as they could and were hot and thirsty. They sat down around the table which still had the table-cloth on it. The wife went down to the cellar and came up again with a bottle. The husband was muttering under his breath: 'What the devil was she doing at the door?'

They drank, chatted about the illnesses of the neighbourhood, and started listing all the people they were treating. I started complaining. They said: 'We'll be with you in a moment.'

After the first bottle they asked for a second, on account, for my treatment, then a third, then a fourth, still on account, for my treatment. And with every bottle, the husband came back to his first cry: 'What the devil was she doing at the door?'

What a scene anybody else would have made of these three surgeons, of their conversation on the fourth bottle, of the multitude of their marvellous cures, of the impatience of Jacques and the bad temper of their host, of what our country Aesculapiuses had to say as they clustered round Jacques' knee, of their different opinions, one claiming that Jacques would be dead unless they made haste and amputated the leg, the other that they should remove the bullet and the piece of cloth that went in with it to save the poor devil's leg. In the meantime, you might have seen Jacques sitting up in bed and looking at his leg pitifully, bidding it a last farewell like one of our generals being treated by Dufouart and Louis was recently seen doing.⁵ The third surgeon would have sat around gawping up to the point where a quarrel broke out between them and words then led to blows.

I will spare you all of these things which you can find in novels, the comedies of antiquity and in society. When I heard the host exclaim about his wife, 'What the devil was she doing at the door?' I was reminded of Molière's Harpagon when he says, referring to his son: 'What was he doing in that galley?'⁶ And I admit that it is not enough for a thing simply to be true, it must be amusing as well. And that is why people will always say: 'What was he doing in that galley?' while my peasant's phrase, 'What was she doing at the door?', will never pass into proverb.

Jacques did not show the same reserve towards his master as I am showing to you. He did not omit the smallest detail even though he risked sending him to sleep for a second time. If it was not the cleverest it was at least the most sturdy of the three surgeons who remained in control of the patient.

Are you not going to take out lancets in front of our eyes, I hear you ask me, start cutting his flesh, make his blood run and show us a surgical operation? Would that be in good taste in your opinion? . . .

Come, let us pass over the operation. But you must at least allow Jacques to say to his master, as he did: 'Ah, Monsieur, it's a terrible job to put a shattered knee back together again.'

And allow his master to reply as before: 'Come, come, Jacques, you're joking.'

But the one thing I would not keep from you for all the gold in the world is that hardly had Jacques' master made this impertinent reply when his horse stumbled and fell and his knee came into violent contact with a pointed stone and there he was shouting at the top of his voice: 'I'm dying! My knee is shattered!'

Although Jacques, who was the nicest chap you could imagine, was very fond of his master, I would very much like to know what was going on at the bottom of his heart, if not in the first moment, at least when he had assured himself that his master's fall would not have any serious consequences, and whether he was able to resist a slight feeling of secret joy at an accident that would teach his master what it was to have an injury to the knee. And, Reader, there is another thing which I would like you to tell me. That is whether his master would not have preferred to have been injured even a little more seriously any place other than the knee or in other words whether he was not more sensitive to shame than to pain?

When the master had recovered a little from his fall and his pain he got back into his saddle and spurred his horse five or six times, which made him go off like greased lightning. Jacques' mount followed suit because there existed between the two animals the same intimacy as between their riders. They were two pairs of friends.

When the two panting horses had gone back to their normal pace Jacques said to his master: 'Well, Monsieur, what do you think, then?'

MASTER: About what?

JACQUES: An injury to the knee.

MASTER: I agree with you. It is one of the most painful injuries.

JACQUES: When it's your knee?

MASTER: No, no, yours, mine, all the knees in the world.

JACQUES: Master, master, you obviously haven't thought about this at all. We only ever feel sorry for ourselves, believe me.

MASTER: What nonsense.

JACQUES: Ah, if only I knew how to speak the way I think, but it was written up above that I would have things in my head and the words wouldn't come to me.

Here Jacques threw himself into some very subtle philosophical ideas which might also be very true. He was trying to make his master conceive that the word pain does not refer to any real idea and only begins to signify anything at all at the moment when it recalls in our memory a sensation which we have already experienced. His master asked him if he had ever given birth.
'No,' replied Jacques.
'Do you think that giving birth is a painful experience?'
'Of course it is.'
'Do you feel sorry for women in childbirth?'
'Very much so.'
'So you sometimes feel sorry for people other than yourself?'
'I feel sorry for anyone who wrings their hands, tears out their hair and screams because I know from experience that one does not do that unless one is suffering. But as for the particular pain of a woman giving birth, I cannot sympathize with that because I don't know what it is, thank God. But to come back to a pain with which we are both more familiar. The story of my knee which has now become yours as well because of your fall . . .'

MASTER: No, Jacques, the story of your loves which have become mine as well through my own past sorrows.

JACQUES: So there I was, bandaged up and feeling a little better. The surgeon had gone and my hosts had retired and gone to bed. All that separated their room from mine was a lattice-work partition covered with grey paper on which they had stuck a few coloured pictures. I couldn't sleep and I could hear the wife saying to her husband: 'Leave me alone, I don't feel like it. That poor wretch dying at our door . . .'
'Woman, you can tell me all that afterwards.'

'No, I'm not going to. If you don't stop it I'm getting up. Do you think I can enjoy that the way I'm feeling?'

'Oh, if you're making yourself hard to get, the more fool you.'

'I'm not making myself hard to get, it's just that you're sometimes so hard . . . it's just . . . it's just . . .'

After quite a short pause the husband began to speak and said: 'Wife, admit that at the moment, owing to your misplaced compassion, you have put us in an embarrassing situation which is almost impossible to get out of. It's a bad year and we've only just got enough for ourselves and the children. Grain is so dear! There's no wine! Even that wouldn't be so bad if there were work to be found. But the rich are cutting back and the poor are idling. For every day's work there are four without. Nobody pays what they owe. Creditors are so rapacious it makes one despair and this is the moment you choose to give shelter to someone we've never set eyes on before, a stranger who will stay here as long as it pleases God and the surgeon who will be in no hurry to cure him because these surgeons make illnesses last as long as they can. And a man who hasn't got even a sou and who will double, triple our expenses. Now, woman, how are you going to get rid of this man? Well, speak, woman, give me an explanation.'

'How can anyone talk to you?'

'You say that I'm bad-tempered, that I scold you? Well, who wouldn't? Who wouldn't scold? There was still a little wine left in the cellar. God knows the rate it's going! Those surgeons drank more this evening than ourselves and the children would have done in a week. And who will pay the surgeon, who isn't going to come for nothing as you might think?'

'Oh, that is all nicely put. And because we're in extreme poverty, you're going to give me another child, as if we don't have enough already.'

'Oh no, I'm not.'

'Oh yes, you are. I'm sure I'm going to become pregnant.'

'That's what you say every time.'

'And I've never been wrong yet when my ear plays me up afterwards and I can feel it itching worse than ever.'

'Your ear doesn't know what it's talking about.'

'Don't touch me! Leave my ear alone! Leave it, man, have you gone mad? You'll regret it.'

'No, no. I haven't done it with you since midsummer day.'

'And you'll do it and the result will be that . . . and then in a month's time you'll be cross with me as if it were all my fault.'

'No, no.'

'And in nine months from now it'll be even worse.'

'No, no.'

'Well you've asked for it.'

'Yes, yes.'

'And you'll remember this time. You won't say the things you said all the other times.'

'Yes, yes.'

And so he changed from 'No, no' to 'Yes, yes', this man furious with his wife for having given way to a feeling of humanity.

MASTER: That's what I was thinking.

JACQUES: It is certain that the husband wasn't very logical but he was young and his wife was pretty. People never make so many children as when times are hard.

MASTER: Nothing breeds like paupers.

JACQUES: One child more is nothing to them. It's charity that feeds them. What's more it's the only pleasure which doesn't cost anything. At night they console themselves without expense for the troubles of the day . . .

However, the man's reflections were none the less true. While I was thinking this to myself I felt a violent pain in my knee and I cried out: 'Ah! My knee!'

And the husband cried out: 'Ah! My wife!'

And the wife cried out: 'Ah! My husband! But what about that man who is here?'

'Well? What about him?'

'Perhaps he heard us.'

'What if he has?'

'Tomorrow I won't be able to look at him.'

'Well, why not? Aren't you my wife? Am I not your husband? Does a husband have a wife or a wife have a husband for nothing?'

'Ah! Ah!'

'What's wrong with you?'

'My ear . . .'

'What's wrong with your ear?'

'It's worse than ever.'

'Go to sleep. It'll wear off.'

'I can't. Ah! My ear! Ah! My ear!'

'Your ear, your ear, that's easily said . . .'

I won't tell you what happened between them next, but after the wife had repeated the words 'My ear, my ear' several times in a low hushed voice she finished up babbling in interrupted syllables 'ee . . . ee . . . aaah' and after 'ee . . . ee . . . aah', I don't know what, which together with the silence which followed led me to believe that her earache had got better one way or another, it doesn't matter how, and that gave me pleasure, and her too.

MASTER: Jacques, put your hand on your conscience and swear to me that it wasn't this woman you fell in love with.

JACQUES: I swear it.

MASTER: So much the worse for you.

JACQUES: So much the worse or so much the better. Could it be that you believe that women with ears like hers are willing listeners?

MASTER: I think that is written up above.

JACQUES: I think that it is written lower down that they never listen for long to one man and that they are all more or less inclined occasionally to lend an ear to someone else.

MASTER: It could well be.

And there they were started off on an interminable quarrel about women. One claimed they were good, the other wicked, and they were both right; one said they were stupid, the other clever, and they were both right; one that they were unfaithful, the other faithful, and they were both right; one that they were mean, the other generous, and they were both right; one that they were beautiful, the other ugly, and they were both right; one talkative, the other discreet; one open, the other deceitful; one ignorant, the other enlightened; one moral, the other immoral; one foolish, the other wise; one big, the other small. And they were both right.

While engaged in this discussion – and they could have travelled around the entire world without either pausing or agreeing – they were caught up in a storm which forced them to seek shelter.

– Where? – Where?

Reader, your curiosity is extremely annoying. What the devil does it have to do with you? If I told you it was Pontoise or Saint-Germain or Loreto or Compostella, would you be any the wiser?[7]

If you insist I will tell you that they made their way towards . . . yes, why not? . . . towards a huge château, on whose façade were inscribed the words:

'I belong to nobody and I belong to everybody. You were here before you entered and you will still be here after you have left.'

– Did they go into this château?

No, because either the inscription was a lie, or they were there before they went in.

– Well, did they manage to leave, at least?

No, because either the inscription was a lie, or they were still there after they left.

– And what did they do there?

Jacques said whatever it was written up above that he would say and his master whatever he liked. And they were both right.

– What kind of people did they find there?

A mixture.

– What did they say?

A few truths and a lot of lies.

– Were there intelligent men there?

Where are there not some? And damned questioners whom they avoided like the plague. The thing that most shocked Jacques and his master while they were walking about . . .

– So they were walking, were they?

They did nothing but that except when they were sitting down or sleeping. The thing which shocked Jacques and his master most was to find about twenty scoundrels there who had taken over all the most luxurious rooms, where, it appears, they stayed almost all the time crowded together and pretended, in defiance of customary right and the true meaning of the château's inscription, that the château had been bequeathed to them lock, stock and barrel, and with the help of a certain number of pricks in their pay they had brought round to this view a great number of other pricks, also in their pay, who were quite prepared for the smallest sum of money to hang or kill the first man who dared contradict them. Nevertheless, in the days of Jacques and his master people sometimes dared.

– With impunity?

That depended.

You are going to say that I am amusing myself and that because I do not know what to do with my two travellers any more, I am throwing myself into allegory, which is the usual recourse of sterile minds. For you I will sacrifice my allegory and all the riches I could draw from it and I will agree with whatever you want, but on condition that you don't bother me any more about where Jacques and his master spent last night. They may have reached a big town and spent the night with whores, or they may have stayed the night with an old friend who gave them the best he could, or they may have taken refuge in a Franciscan monastery where they were badly lodged and badly fed all for the love of God. They may have been welcomed into the house of a great man where they lacked everything that was necessary to them and were surrounded by everything that was superfluous, or the next morning they may have left a large inn where they paid dearly for a bad supper served on silver platters and a bad night spent in beds with damask curtains and damp creased sheets, or they may have received hospitality from some village priest on a meagre stipend who ran round his parishioners' poultry yards requisitioning the wherewithal to make an omelette and a chicken fricassee, or they may have got drunk on excellent wine, eaten far too much and got the appropriate bout of indigestion in a rich Benedictine abbey. Although all of these might appear equally feasible to you, Jacques was not of this opinion. The only possibility was the one that was written up above. What is, however, true, is that when they had started out from whatever location you would have them start out from they had gone no further than twenty paces when the master said to Jacques, after, of course, having first, as was his habit, taken his pinch of snuff: 'Well then, Jacques, the story of your loves?'

Instead of replying Jacques cried out: 'The devil with the story of my loves! I've gone and left . . .'

MASTER: What have you left?

Instead of answering him Jacques turned out all of his pockets and then searched himself all over without success. He had left the purse for their journey under the head of his bed and he had no sooner admitted this to his master when he cried out: 'To the devil with the story of your loves! I've gone and left my watch back there hanging on the chimney!'

Jacques needed no encouragement, but turned his horse about, and because he was never in a hurry started slowly back to . . .

– The huge château?

No, no. Out of all the different places, possible or impossible, which I have listed above, choose the one which best suits the present circumstances.

Meanwhile his master continued on his way. But now, with the master and the servant separated from each other, I don't know which of the two I would rather follow. If you want to follow Jacques, take care. The search for the purse and the watch could become so long and so complicated that it might take him a long time before he meets up again with his master who is the sole confidant of the story of his loves and then it would be goodbye to the story of Jacques' loves. If, however, leaving Jacques to go alone in search of the purse and the watch, you choose to keep his master company, you are being polite but you will be very bored. You do not know that type of person yet. He has very few ideas in his head at all. If he happens to say something sensible, it is from memory or inspiration. He has got eyes like you and me but most of the time you cannot be sure he is actually seeing anything. He does not exactly sleep, but he is never really awake either. He just carries on existing simply because it is what he usually does. Our automaton carried straight on ahead, turning round from time to time, to see if Jacques was coming. He got down from his horse and walked for a while on foot. Then he remounted, went about a quarter of a league, got down again and sat on the ground with his horse's reins looped under his arm and his head in his hands. When he got tired of that position, he got up and peered into the distance to see if he could see Jacques. No Jacques. Then he got impatient and without really knowing whether he was talking or not he said: 'The wretch, the dog, the rascal, where is he? What is he doing? How could it take anyone so long to recover a watch and a purse? I'll beat you black and blue. Oh! That's for sure – I'll beat you black and blue.'

Then he looked for his watch in his fob-pocket and it wasn't there, and that was the last straw. Because, without his watch, without his snuff-box and without Jacques, he didn't know what to do. They were the three mainstays of his life which was spent in taking snuff, looking at the time, and questioning Jacques, which he did in every possible combination. Deprived of his watch he was reduced to his snuff-box, which he kept opening and shutting every minute, like I do when I am bored. The amount of snuff left in my snuff-box at night is in direct proportion to the amusement or in indirect proportion to the boredom of my day. I beg you, Reader, to familiarize yourself with this manner of speaking which is taken from geometry, because I find it precise and shall use it often.

Well then, have you had enough of the master? As the valet is not coming to you, would you rather we went to him? Poor Jacques! At the very moment we were speaking of him Jacques was sorrowfully meditating: 'So it was written up above that in the same day I'd be arrested as a highwayman, be on the point of being taken to prison and be accused of having seduced a girl.'

On his slow way back to . . . the château? No, the place where they had spent the previous night, he passed by one of those itinerant pedlars known as 'portebailes', who called out to him: 'Monsieur le Chevalier, garters, belts, watch-straps, snuff-boxes in the utmost good taste, all genuine, rings, fob-seals, a watch, Monsieur, a fine watch with engraving, double action, good as new.'

Jacques replied: 'I'm looking for one but it's not yours', and carried on his way slowly. As he was going, he thought he could see that it was written up above that the watch this man had offered him was his master's. He retraced his steps and said to the pedlar: 'Friend, show me your gold watch, I have a fancy it might suit me.'

'Indeed,' said the pedlar, 'I wouldn't be at all surprised. It's a very beautiful watch, made by Julien Le Roi. I've only had it a moment. I bought it for next to nothing and will do a good price on it. I like little repeated profits, but these are hard times and I won't have a bargain like this for the next three months. You seem a fine chap and I would rather see you profit than another . . .'

As he was speaking the pedlar had put his bundle on the ground, opened it up and pulled out the watch, which Jacques recognized immediately without any surprise, because, since he was never in a hurry, he was rarely surprised. He had a good look at the watch.

'Yes,' he said to himself, 'that's it.'

To the pedlar: 'You're right. It is beautiful, very beautiful, and I know it's a good watch . . .'

Then, putting it in his fob-pocket, he said to the pedlar: 'Thank you very much, my friend.'

'What do you mean, thank you very much?'

'Yes, it's my master's watch.'

'I don't know your master. That watch is mine. I bought it and paid for it fair and square . . .', and grabbing Jacques by the collar, he tried to take the watch back. Jacques went to his horse, took one of his pistols and held it against the pedlar's chest: 'Get back,' he said to him, 'or you're a dead man . . .'

The frightened pedlar let go. Jacques got back on his horse and started slowly back towards the town, saying to himself: 'That's the watch back. Now let's see about our purse . . .'

The pedlar hurriedly shut up his pack, put it on his shoulders and followed Jacques, shouting: 'Thief! Thief! Murderer! Help! Help me! Help me!'

It was harvest time and the fields were full of workers. They all left their sickles and crowded around the man, asking him: 'Where is the thief?' 'Where is the murderer?'

'There he is, there he is, over there.'

'What! That man riding slowly towards the town gate?'

'That's him.'

'Come on, you're crazy. That's not the way a thief behaves.'

'He's one, he's a thief, I tell you. He took a gold watch from me by force.'

These people did not know what to believe, the cries of the pedlar or the calm pace of Jacques.

But the pedlar added: 'My friends, I will be ruined if you don't help me. It's worth thirty louis if it's worth a brass farthing. Help me. He's carrying off my watch and he's only got to spur his horse and my watch will be lost . . .'

Even if Jacques was out of earshot of the shouting he could easily see the crowd, but still he went no faster. The pedlar had persuaded the peasants to run after Jacques in the hope of a reward. There was a crowd of men, women and children running after him shouting: 'Thief! Thief! Murderer!'with the pedlar following as closely as his burden would permit shouting: 'Thief! Thief! Murderer!'

They entered the town, because it was in a town that Jacques and his master had spent the previous night, I remember it now. The townspeople left their dwellings and joined the peasants and the pedlar, all going along shouting in unison 'Thief! Thief! Murderer!' and they all caught up with Jacques at the same moment. The pedlar threw himself on to Jacques, who lashed out at him with a kick which knocked him to the ground but did not stop him shouting: 'Rogue, rascal, scoundrel, give me back my watch! You'll give it back to me and you'll still be hanged for it . . .'

Jacques retained his composure, addressed the crowd, which was growing larger every moment, and said: 'There is a magistrate here. Take me to him. When we get there I'll show you that I'm not a thief, but this man might be one. I am not unknown in this town. The day before yesterday evening my master and I arrived here and we stayed with the Lieutenant-Governor,[8] my master's old friend . . .'

If I did not say sooner that Jacques and his master had passed through Conches and that they had stayed with the Lieutenant-Governor of this place, then that is because it didn't come back to me any earlier.

'Take me to the Lieutenant-Governor,' said Jacques, and dismounted. Jacques, his horse and the pedlar were in the middle of the procession. They set off and arrived at the gate of the Lieutenant-Governor's house. Jacques, his horse and the pedlar went in, Jacques and the pedlar holding each other by the lapels. The crowd stayed outside.

Meanwhile, what was Jacques' master doing? He was sleeping by the side of the road, the reins of his horse looped round his arm, and the animal grazing the grass around the sleeping figure as far as the length of the reins allowed.

As soon as the Lieutenant-Governor saw Jacques he shouted out: 'Ah! Is that you, my poor Jacques? What's brought you back here all alone?'

'My master's watch. He left it hanging on the corner of the chimney and I've just discovered it in this man's pack. Our purse, which I left under the head of my bed, will doubtless also be found if you order it.'

'If it is written up above,' added the magistrate . . .

He called his people straight away and the pedlar immediately pointed out a large rascal with a shifty manner who had recently arrived at the house and said: 'There's the man who sold me the watch.'

The magistrate, taking on a solemn tone, said to the pedlar and his valet: 'The pair of you deserve to go to the galleys, you for having sold the watch, and you for having bought it.'

To his valet: 'Give this man back his money and take off your livery immediately . . .'

To the pedlar: 'Hurry up and get out of these parts, unless you want to stay here hanging from a gibbet. The way you two earn your living always leads to a bad end . . . Now, Jacques, let's see about your purse.'

The person who had taken it appeared without being called for. She was a full-grown shapely girl.

'Monsieur, I have the purse,' she said to her master, 'but I didn't steal it. He gave it to me.'

'I gave you my purse?'

'Yes.'

'I suppose it's possible, but the devil take me if I can remember.'

The magistrate said to Jacques: 'All right, Jacques, we won't go any further into that.'

'Monsieur . . .'

'She's pretty and obliging from what I can see.'

'Monsieur, I swear . . .'

'How much was there in the purse?'

'Around nine hundred and seventeen pounds.'

'Ah! Javotte! Nine hundred and seventeen pounds for one night. That's far too much for you, and for him. Give me the purse.'

The girl gave the purse to her master who took out a six-franc piece: 'There you are,' he said, throwing her the coin, 'that is the price of your services. You deserve better, but from someone other than Jacques. I wish you twice as much as that every day, but not in my house, do you hear? And as for you, Jacques, hurry up and get back on your horse and return to your master.'

Jacques bowed to the magistrate and went off without answering, but saying to himself: 'The brazen hussy! So it was written up above that someone else would sleep with her and that Jacques would pay for it, was it? Come along Jacques, cheer up; aren't you pleased that you got the purse and your master's watch back and that it cost you so little?'

Jacques got back on to his horse and pushed his way through the crowd which had gathered round the entrance to the magistrate's house, but because he took it rather badly that so many people should take him for a thief he affected to take the watch out of his pocket to look at the time. Then he spurred his horse, which was not used to this and took off faster than it had ever done before. It was Jacques' habit to let the horse do whatever it wanted because he found it just as inconvenient to stop it when it was galloping as it was to make it go faster when it was going slowly. We believe that it is we who control Destiny but it is always Destiny which controls us. And Destiny for Jacques was everything which touched him or came near him – his horse, his master, a monk , a dog, a woman, a mule, a crow. And so his horse took him as fast as it could go towards his master, who was sound asleep by the side of the road with his horse's reins tied around his arm, as I have told you. On that occasion, however, the horse was on the end of the reins but when Jacques arrived the reins were still there and the horse was not. It would appear that a thief had come up to the sleeping figure, quietly cut the reins and led the animal away. On hearing the noise of Jacques' horse his master woke up and his first words were: 'Come here, come here, you scoundrel. I'm going to . . .'

Then he started to yawn his head off.

'Have a good yawn, Monsieur, as much as you like,' said Jacques, 'but where is your horse?'

'My horse?'

'Yes, your horse.'

The master, noticing straight away that somebody had stolen his horse, was about to belabour Jacques with the reins when Jacques said to him: 'Gently, Monsieur, I'm in no mood today to let myself be beaten senseless. I'll take the first blow, but, I swear to you, on the second I'll set spur to my horse and leave you here.'

This threat of Jacques' had the sudden effect of calming the wrath of his master, who asked him in a gentler manner: 'And my watch?'

'Here it is.'

44

'What about the purse?'

'Here.'

'You've been a long time.'

'Not too long for all that I've done. Listen carefully. I went there. I got into a fight. I stirred up all the peasants in the fields. I caused a riot amongst the townsfolk. I was taken for a highwayman and I was brought before the judge. I underwent two cross-examinations. I very nearly caused two men to be hanged. I made a valet lose his job and had a maidservant lose hers. I've been convicted of spending the night with a creature I've never seen in my life, whom I nevertheless paid. And I came back.'

'And as for me, while I was waiting for you . . .'

'While you were waiting for me it was written up above that you would fall asleep and that someone would steal your horse. Monsieur, think no more of it. It's one lost horse, and perhaps it is written up above that it'll be found again.'

'My horse! My poor horse!'

'And if you cry from now till tomorrow it won't be any the more or the less so.'

'What are we going to do?'

'Well, I'll take you up behind me, or , if you would rather, we can take off our boots, tie them on to my horse's saddle and carry on our way on foot.'

'My horse! My poor horse!'

They chose to continue on foot, the master crying out from time to time: 'My horse! My poor horse!' and Jacques elaborating on the account of his adventures. When he had got to the girl's accusation his master said to him: 'Is it true, Jacques, that you didn't sleep with the girl?'

JACQUES: No, Monsieur.

MASTER: And yet you paid for her?

JACQUES: Of course.

MASTER: Well, I was once even unluckier than you.

JACQUES: You mean you paid for it after you slept with her?

MASTER: You've said it.

JACQUES: Won't you tell me about it?

MASTER: I think that before we start on the story of my loves we had

45

better get to the end of yours. Well, Jacques, tell me more of your loves, which I shall take as the first and only loves of your life notwithstanding your little adventure with the servant girl of the Lieutenant-Governor of Conches, because although you may have slept with her that doesn't mean you were in love with her. Every day people sleep with women they don't love and every day they don't sleep with women they love. But . . .

JACQUES: But what? Well, what's wrong?

MASTER: My horse! . . . Jacques, my friend, don't get angry with me. Put yourself in my horse's shoes. Suppose that I'd lost you, and tell me if you wouldn't have thought the better of me if you heard me saying: 'Jacques! My poor Jacques!'

Jacques smiled and said:

I think I had got to the dialogue between my host and his wife during the night after my wound had first been dressed. I rested a little. My host and his wife both got up the next day a little later than they usually did.

MASTER: I can believe that.

JACQUES: When I woke up I quietly drew back the curtains around my bed and I saw my host, his wife and the surgeon in secret conference over by the window. After what I had heard during the night it wasn't difficult to guess what was being discussed. I coughed. The surgeon said to the husband: 'He's woken up. Friend, go down to the wine cellar. We'll have a drink to steady our hands. Then I'll change the bandage and after that we'll see about the rest.'

After the bottle had arrived and been emptied, because 'to have a drink' is a term of art and means to empty at least one bottle, the surgeon came to my bed and said to me: 'What sort of night did you have?'

'Not bad.'

'Your arm . . . good, good, your pulse isn't bad, there's hardly any more fever. Now let's see about this knee. Come on, mistress,' he said to my host's wife, who was standing at the foot of my bed on the other side of the curtain, 'and help us . . .'

The hostess called one of her children.

'It's not a child we need here, it's you. One false move will give us work for the next month. Come here . . .'

The woman drew near, her eyes lowered.

'Take hold of his leg, the good one, I'll take care of the other one. Gently,

gently. Towards me, a little bit more. And you, my friend, a half turn to the right, to the right, I said, and there we are . . .'

I was holding the mattress with both hands, grinding my teeth, sweat running down my face.

'My friend, this isn't going to be easy.'

'I can see that.'

'There you are. Now, dear, let go of the leg and take hold of the pillow. Bring up the chair and put the pillow on top. Too close . . . a bit further away . . Friend, give me your hand and hold me tight. You, dear, go between the bed and the wall and hold him under the arms. Marvellous. Neighbour, is there anything left in that bottle?'

'No.'

'Come here and take your wife's place so she can get another one . . . Good, good, fill it up . . . Woman, leave your man where he is and come round next to me.'

The woman again called one of her children.

'Damnation, I've already told you, a child is not what we need. Kneel down and put your hand under the calf. You're trembling, my dear, as if you'd been up to no good. Courage! Left hand under the bottom of the thigh, there above the bandage . . . very good . . .'

And then the seams were cut, the bandages unrolled, the dressing taken off and my wound uncovered. The surgeon felt above it, below it and all round it and every time he touched me he said: 'The ignorant fool! The ass! The lout! And he thinks he's a surgeon! A leg like this, cut it off? It'll last as long as the other, take my word for it.'

'I'll get better?'

'I've cured worse than you.'

'I'll walk?'

'You'll walk.'

'Without a limp?'

'That's another matter. Devil take it, my friend, what does it matter how you walk, isn't it enough for you that I've saved your leg? Anyway if you limp it won't be much. Do you like dancing?'

'A lot.'

'If you walk a little less well, you'll dance all the better. My dear, the warmed wine . . . no, I'll have the other one first. Just one more little glass and our bandage will be the better for it.'

He drank and they brought over the warmed wine, cleansed and dressed my wound, bandaged me up, laid me out on the bed again and told me to sleep if I could. They drew the curtains around my bed, finished off the bottle they had started, brought up another and the conference between my host and hostess and the surgeon started again.

PEASANT: Friend, will it be for long?

SURGEON: Very long . . . Here's to you, friend.

PEASANT: But how long? A month?

SURGEON: A month! Let's say two, three, four, who knows? The kneecap is damaged, the femur, the tibia . . . Here's to you, my dear.

PEASANT: Four months! Saints preserve us! Why take him in here? What the devil was she doing at the door?

WIFE: My friend, you're off again. That's not what you promised me last night. But just wait. You'll see.

PEASANT: But tell me, what are we going to do with this man? It wouldn't be so serious if it weren't such a bad year.

WIFE: If you wanted I could go to the parish priest.

PEASANT: If you set foot in there I'll beat you black and blue.

SURGEON: Why not, my friend? My wife goes there.

PEASANT: Well, that's your business.

SURGEON: Here's to my god-daughter. How's she keeping?

WIFE: Fine.

SURGEON: Come along, my friend. Here's to our wives, they're both good women.

PEASANT: Yours is more prudent. She would never have been stupid enough to . . .

WIFE: But there are always the Sisters of Charity.

SURGEON: Ah! My dear! A man, a man go to the Sisters of Charity! There's just one little problem about that, and it's not all that much longer than a finger . . . Let's drink to the sisters, they're good girls.

WIFE: What little problem?

SURGEON: Your husband doesn't want you to go to the parish priest and my wife won't allow me anywhere near the sisters ... well, my friend, another drink, perhaps that will give us the answer. Have you questioned this man? He is perhaps not without means himself?

PEASANT: A soldier?

SURGEON: Well, a soldier's always got a father and mother, brothers, sisters, relations, friends, someone in the world ... Let's have another drink. Leave me with him and let me see what I can sort out.

And that was word for word the conversation between the surgeon and Jacques' host and hostess. But what a different complexion could I not have put on the matter by introducing a villain among all these good people. Jacques would have been seen, or rather you would have seen Jacques, on the point of being pulled out of his bed, thrown into the highroad or even a ditch.
— Why not killed?
Killed, no. I would easily have been able to call someone to his assistance. That someone could have been a soldier from his company but that would have stunk to high heaven of *Cleveland*.[9] Truth, truth.
— Truth, you tell me, is often cold, ordinary and dull. For example, your last description of Jacques' bandaging is true, but what's interesting about it? Nothing.
Agreed.
— If it is necessary to be truthful, then let it be like Molière, Regnard, Richardson or Sedaine.[10] Truth has its interesting sides which one brings out if one's a genius.
Yes, when one is a genius, but what if one isn't?
— When one isn't one shouldn't write.
But what if one has the misfortune to resemble a certain poet I sent to Pondicherry?
— Who is this poet?
This poet ... But if you keep on interrupting me, Reader, and if I interrupt myself all the time, what will become of Jacques' loves? Take my word for it, let us leave our poet there ... Jacques' host and hostess moved away ...
— No, no, the story of the poet of Pondicherry ...[11]
The surgeon went over to Jacques' bed ...
— The story of the poet of Pondicherry, the story of the poet of Pondicherry.
One day a young poet came to me, as they do every day ... But, Reader, what has that got to do with the journey of Jacques the Fatalist and his master?

— The story of the poet of Pondicherry.

After the usual social niceties about my wit, my genius, my good taste, my benevolence and other things I didn't believe a word of even though people have been repeatedly telling me them, and perhaps in all sincerity, for the last twenty years, the young poet took a sheet of paper out of his pocket.

'Here are some verses.'

'Verses?'

'Yes, Monsieur, some verses on which I hope you will have the kindness to give me your opinion.'

'Do you like truth?'

'Yes, Monsieur, and I'm asking you to tell me it.'

'Well, you'll have it.'

'What! Are you really stupid enough to think that a poet seeks the truth from you?'

'Yes.'

'And stupid enough to tell him it?'

'Certainly.'

'Without attenuation?'

'Of course. Any attenuation, however artful, would be the most offensive of all insults. Faithfully interpreted it would mean: "You're a bad poet and, since I don't believe you are man enough to hear the truth, you're a worthless man as well."'

'And has honesty always worked for you?'

'Almost always . . .'

I read my young poet's odes and told him: 'Not only is your poetry bad but it is evident that you'll never write any good poetry.'

'Then I must write bad poetry because I can't stop myself from writing.'

'That's a terrible affliction. Can you not see, Monsieur, what abjection you will fall into? Neither the gods, your fellow men, nor the reviews have ever forgiven mediocrity in a poet. It's Horace who said that.'[12]

'I know.'

'Are you rich?'

'No.'

'Are you poor?'

'Very poor.'

'And you are going to add to your poverty the ridicule of being a bad poet. You will have wasted your entire life and before you know it you'll be old. Old, poor, and a bad poet. Ah! Monsieur, what a combination!'

'I can see that but there's nothing I can do to stop myself.'

(Here Jacques would have said: 'It was written up above.')

'Have you got parents?'

'I have.'

'What is their position in life?'

'They are jewellers.'

'Would they help you financially?'

'Perhaps.'

'Well, go and see your parents and ask them to lend you a small bag of jewels. Embark for Pondicherry and on the way you'll write terrible poetry but when you get there you'll make your fortune. When you've made your fortune you can come back here and write as much bad poetry as you want to, provided you don't have any of it printed because you mustn't ruin anyone else . . .'

It was around twelve years after I gave this advice to the young man that he reappeared. I didn't recognize him.

'It's me, Monsieur,' he said to me, 'the man you sent to Pondicherry. I went there and I made a hundred thousand francs. I have come back and started to write poetry again and here is some which I've brought you. Is it still bad?'

'It's still bad, but at least your future is taken care of and I don't mind if you carry on writing bad poetry.'

'That is just what I intend to do . . .'

And when the surgeon had got to Jacques' bed, Jacques didn't give him the chance to speak: 'I heard everything,' he told him.

Then, turning to his master, he added . . . that is, he was about to add something when his master stopped him. He was tired of walking and sat himself down by the side of the road, his head turned in the direction of another traveller who was coming towards them on foot, with the reins of his horse, which was following him, over his arm.

You are going to believe, Reader, that this horse was the one that was stolen from Jacques' master, and you are going to be wrong. That is what would happen in a novel, a little bit sooner or a little bit later, one way or another. But this is not a novel. I've already told you that, I believe, and I repeat it again.

The master said to Jacques: 'Do you see that man coming towards us?'

JACQUES: I see him.

MASTER: His horse seems good, don't you think?

JACQUES: I served in the infantry, I wouldn't know about that.

MASTER: Well, I commanded in the cavalry and I do.

JACQUES: Well?

MASTER: I would like you to go and ask that man to let us have the horse. We'll pay him for it, of course.

JACQUES: What a foolish idea, but I'll go. How much do you want to pay?

MASTER: Go as high as one hundred écus.

After having reminded his master not to fall asleep, Jacques went to meet the traveller, suggested to him the purchase of his horse, paid him and led the horse away.

'Well,' Jacques' master said to him, 'if you have your premonitions you can see I have mine too. He's a nice horse, this one. I suppose the man swore there was nothing wrong with him, but when it comes to horses all men are sharp dealers.'

JACQUES: When aren't they?

MASTER: You can ride this one and I'll have yours.

JACQUES: All right . . .

And there they were, both on horseback, and Jacques added: 'When I left home my father and mother and my godfather all gave me something, each of them what little they could afford, and I already had in reserve the five louis which Jean, my elder brother, had given me when he left on his unfortunate trip to Lisbon . . .'

Here Jacques started to cry and his master began to tell him that it must have been written up above.

JACQUES: That's true, Monsieur, and I've told myself that a hundred times. But in spite of all that I can't stop myself from crying . . .

And there he was sobbing and crying even more while his master was taking his pinch of snuff and looking at his watch to see what time it was.

After he had put his horse's reins between his teeth and wiped his eyes with both hands Jacques continued:

With brother Jean's five louis, the money I was paid on joining up and the presents of my parents and friends I had a fund – of which I had not spent an obol. It was a lucky thing for me that I had it – don't you think?

MASTER: It was impossible for you to stay any longer in the cottage.

JACQUES: Even if I paid.

MASTER: But why did your brother Jean go to Lisbon?

JACQUES: It seems to me that you are trying your best to make me lose my way. With all your questions we'll have gone round the world before we've finished the story of my loves.

MASTER: What does that matter so long as you are speaking and I am listening to you? Aren't those the two important things? You are scolding me when you should thank me.

JACQUES: My brother went to Lisbon in search of peace. Jean, my brother, was a smart lad – it was that which brought him misfortune. It would have been better for him if he had been an idiot like me – but then that was written up above. It was also written that the friar almoner from the Carmelites who used to come to our village to ask for eggs, wool, straw, fruit and wine all the year round would stay at my father's house, and would corrupt Jean, my brother, and that Jean, my brother, would take a monk's habit.

MASTER: Jean, your brother, was a Carmelite?

JACQUES: Yes, Monsieur, and a barefoot Carmelite at that.[13] He was active, intelligent, a haggler, he was the village lawyer. He knew how to read and write, and even as a young man he used to spend his time deciphering and copying out old manuscripts. He worked his way through all the jobs in the order one after the other – porter, bellringer, gardener, assistant to the procurator and treasurer. At the rate he was going he would have made all of us our fortunes. He married off two of our sisters, and a few other girls in the village, and married them off well at that. He couldn't walk down the streets without fathers, mothers and children all running up to him and shouting out: 'Good day, Friar Jean! How are you, Friar Jean?'

It is certain that whenever he went into a house God's blessing went with him and wherever there was a girl she'd be married two months after his visit! Poor Friar Jean. Ambition was his downfall. 🌟

The Procurator of the House where Jean was assistant was old. The monks said that it was Jean's plan to succeed him after his death, and that, to this end, he turned the deed room upside down, burnt all the old registers and made up new ones in such a way that on the death of the old Procurator the devil himself would have been unable to make head or tail of the community's papers. If ever anyone needed a document he'd have to spend a month looking for it and then often it couldn't be found at all. The monks worked out what Friar Jean was up to and what his aim was. They took the thing very seriously and Friar Jean, instead of being procurator, as he flattered himself he would be, was reduced to bread and water and disciplined to the point where he eventually gave up the secret of his registers to someone else. Monks are merciless. When they had got all the enlightenment they needed from Friar Jean they made him the coal carrier for the laboratory where they made Carmelite liqueur. Friar Jean, former treasurer of the order and deputy procurator, now a coal carrier! Friar Jean had a stout heart but he could not tolerate his fall from importance and splendour and he was only waiting for the opportunity to escape from this humiliation.

Now at about this time there arrived at the monastery a young monk who was accepted as the wonder of the order in the confessional and the pulpit. He was called Friar Angel. He had beautiful eyes, a handsome face, and the arms and hands of a sculptor's model. There he was preaching sermons and more sermons, hearing confessions and more confessions and the old spiritual directors were abandoned by their female congregation who flocked to the young Friar Angel. The eve of every Sunday and feast day, Friar Angel's confessional was surrounded by more and more penitents while the old fathers waited fruitlessly for business in their deserted confessionals which upset them a great deal . . . But, Monsieur, if perhaps I left the story of Friar Jean and carried on with the story of my loves, it might be more cheerful.

MASTER: No, no. Let's take a pinch of snuff, see what time it is and carry on.

JACQUES: All right, if that's what you want . . .

But Jacques' horse was of another opinion. All of a sudden it took the bit between its teeth and charged into a ditch. Jacques dug his knees into the beast's side and pulled back hard on the reins but it was all to no avail and the stubborn animal hurled itself out of the bottom of the ditch and started climbing as fast as it could to the top of a hillock where it stopped dead and where Jacques, looking around, found himself to be between the forks of a gallows.

Anyone other than myself, Reader, would not miss the opportunity of dressing up the gallows with its prey and arranging a sad reunion for Jacques. And if I were to tell you something of this sort you might well believe it because there are stranger things in life but it wouldn't be any the more true for that. The gallows was empty.

Jacques allowed his horse to get its breath back and then the animal, of its own accord, went back down the hillock, crossed over to the other side of the ditch and brought Jacques back alongside his master, who said to him: 'Ah! My friend! What a fright you gave me! I thought you were going to be killed . . . But you're dreaming! What are you thinking about?'

JACQUES: About what I found up there.

MASTER: And what did you find up there?

JACQUES: A gallows. A gibbet.

MASTER: The devil you did! That's a bad omen. But remember your doctrine. If it is written up above, then no matter what you do you'll be hanged, my dear friend. And if it isn't written up above, the horse is a liar. If that beast isn't inspired he's suffering from delusions. I should be careful if I were you.

After a moment's silence Jacques rubbed his forehead and shook his head, as people do when they're trying to stop themselves thinking about something nasty, and carried on abruptly:

The old monks held a conference amongst themselves and resolved that no matter what the cost and no matter what means they had to use they would get rid of this young upstart who was humiliating them. Do you know what they did? . . . Master, you're not listening to me.

MASTER: I'm listening. I'm listening. Carry on.

JACQUES: They bribed the porter, who was an old rascal like them. This old rascal accused the young priest of having taken liberties with one of the ladies of the congregation in the visiting room and swore on oath that he'd seen it. Perhaps it was true, perhaps it wasn't. Who knows? What is amusing is that the day after this accusation the Prior of the House received a summons from a surgeon seeking payment for medicines and treatment given to the old porter when the latter was suffering from an amatory ailment . . .

Master, you're not listening and I know what's distracting you. I bet it's those gallows.

MASTER: I can't deny it.

JACQUES: I caught you looking at me. Do you find something sinister about me?

MASTER: No, no.

JACQUES: You mean 'Yes, yes'. Well, if I frighten you we can always go our own ways.

MASTER: Come on, Jacques, you're losing your wits. Are you becoming insecure?

JACQUES: No, Monsieur. Who is ever secure anyway?

MASTER: Every good man. Could it be that Jacques, honest Jacques, feels revulsion for some crime he's committed? . . . Come on, Jacques. Let's finish this argument and carry on with your story.

JACQUES: As a result of this calumny or slander on the part of the porter, they thought themselves justified in doing a thousand wrongs and injuries to poor Friar Angel, who seemed to lose his wits. Then they called in a doctor whom they bribed and who certified that the priest was mad and needed to return to his home for a rest. If it had been simply a question of sending Friar Angel away or shutting him up the matter would have been quickly dealt with, but he was the darling of the female church-goers amongst whom there were a number of important ladies who had to be handled carefully. The ladies heard their spiritual director spoken of with hypocritical commiseration: 'Alas! The poor father . . . It's a terrible shame . . . He was the leading light of our community.'

'What's happened to him, then?'

The answer to this question was a deep sigh, accompanied by an upward movement of the eyes towards heaven. Further questions were met by a downward movement of the head and total silence. Occasionally they would add to this mummery: 'Oh God! This mortal coil . . . He still has his surprising moments . . . flashes of genius . . . It will come back to him perhaps . . . But there's little hope . . . What a loss for the Faith.'

Meanwhile they stepped up their nastiness. They tried everything to bring Friar Angel to the state they said he'd reached. And they would have succeeded had Friar Jean not taken pity on him. What more can I tell you? One evening when we were all asleep we heard a knocking at the door. We got up and opened to Friar Angel and my brother who were in disguise. They stayed in our house all the next day and at dawn the day after that they went off. They went away with their hands full of provisions and as he embraced me Jean's parting words were: 'I married off your sisters and if I had stayed in the monastery for two years longer, with the position I used to have, you would have been one of the richest farmers of the district, but everything's changed and that's all I can do for you. Farewell, Jacques, if ever we meet good fortune, Friar Angel and I, you will know about it . . .'

Then he left in my hand the five louis I've told you about, with five more for the last of the girls of the village, whom he had married off and who had just given birth to a bouncing baby boy who looked as much like my brother Jean as two peas in a pod.

MASTER (his snuff-box open and his watch back in his pocket): And what were they going to Lisbon for?

JACQUES: For an earthquake which couldn't happen without them, to be crushed, swallowed up and burnt, as it was written up above.[14]

MASTER: Ah! Those monks!

JACQUES: Even the best of them isn't worth much.

MASTER: I know that better than you.

JACQUES: Have you fallen into their hands as well?

MASTER: I'll tell you about that another time.

JACQUES: But why is it they are so wicked?

MASTER: I think it's because they're monks. But let's get back to your loves.

JACQUES: No, Monsieur, let's not.

MASTER: Don't you want me to know about them any more?

JACQUES: Of course I still want you to, but Destiny doesn't. Can't you see that as soon as I open my mouth on the subject the devil interferes and something always happens which cuts me off? I'll never finish it, I tell you. That is written up above.

MASTER: Try, my friend.

JACQUES: Perhaps if you were to tell me the story of your love life, that would break the spell and mine would go better afterwards. There's something in the back of my mind that tells me that's what we need to do. Monsieur, I tell you, it seems to me sometimes that Destiny speaks to me.

MASTER: And do you always find it to your advantage to listen?

JACQUES: Of course. Witness the day when it told me the pedlar had your watch . . .

The master started to yawn and as he was yawning he tapped his snuff-box with his hand and as he tapped on his snuff-box he looked into the distance, and as he looked into the distance he said to Jacques: 'Can you see something over there on your left?'

JACQUES: Yes, and I bet it's something else which doesn't want me to continue the story, or you to start yours for that matter . . .

Jacques was right. Since the thing they could see was coming towards them and they were going towards it, this convergence quickly shortened the distance between them and before long they could see a carriage draped in black, drawn by four black horses, in black drapes which covered their heads and hung down to their hooves. Behind them were two servants dressed in black and after them were two more servants dressed in black riding two black horses which were caparisoned in black. On the driving-seat of the carriage sat a coachman in black wearing a floppy brimmed hat with a long black ribbon which hung down his left shoulder. This coachman had his head bent forward and was letting the reins hang loose so that the horses appeared to be driving him rather than him driving them. Before long our two travellers found themselves alongside the funeral carriage. At that moment Jacques cried out and fell rather than got off his horse, tore out his hair and started rolling around on the ground, shouting: 'My Captain! My poor Captain! It is him, there's no mistaking it. Those are his arms . . .'

In the carriage there was, indeed, a long coffin under a funeral shroud. On top of this shroud was a sword with a cordon. Next to the coffin sat a priest intoning the office from an open breviary in his hand. Jacques followed behind, still lamenting. His master followed Jacques, swearing, and the servants assured Jacques that the cortège was that of his Captain, who had died in a neighbouring town whence he was being transported to the tomb of his ancestors. Ever since he had, by the death of his friend, a captain in the same regiment, been deprived of the satisfaction of fighting at least once a week, he had fallen into a profound melancholy which, after a few months, had eventually killed him.

Jacques, having paid his Captain the tribute of praise, regret and tears which he owed him, begged his master's forgiveness, got back on his horse and then they carried on their way in silence.

But you are asking me, Reader, where in God's name were they going?

And I reply, Reader, in God's name, does anybody ever really know where they are going? What about you? Where are you going? Do I have to remind you of the story of Aesop?

His master, Xanthippus,[15] said to him one summer's evening, or it may have been a winter's evening for that matter because the Greeks used to have baths whatever the season: 'Aesop, go to the baths. If there are not too many people there we'll take a bath.'

Aesop set off. On the way he met the town guard of Athens.

'Where are you going?'

'Where am I going?' replied Aesop. 'I don't know.'

'You don't know? Then you're coming with us to prison.'

'There you are,' said Aesop, 'Didn't I tell you I didn't know where I was going? I wanted to go to the baths, and here I am going to prison.'

Jacques followed his master like you follow yours. His master followed his as Jacques followed him.

– But who was the master of Jacques' master?

All right. Is anyone ever short of a master in this world? Jacques' master, like you, had a hundred masters if he had one. But among all the many masters of Jacques' master, it seems that there wasn't one satisfactory one since from one day to the next he used to change master.

– He was a man.

A passionate man like you, Reader. A curious man like you, Reader. A questioning man like you, Reader. A nuisance like you, Reader.

– And why did he ask questions?

What a question! He asked questions so that he could learn and quibble like you, Reader. The master said to Jacques: 'You don't seem to be in the mood to carry on with the story of your loves.'

JACQUES: My poor Captain! He's going where we are all going, and the only extraordinary thing is that he hasn't gone there sooner. Ahi! ... Ahi! ...

MASTER: But Jacques! I do believe you're crying!

Cry without restraint because you may cry without shame. His death has set you free from the scrupulous propriety which oppressed you during his life. You no longer have the same reasons to hide your grief as you had to hide your happiness. The same conclusion will not be drawn from your tears as from your joy. People forgive misfortune. And then in this moment one must show either feeling or ingratitude, and all things considered it is better to reveal a weakness than to allow oneself to be suspected of a vice. I would wish your grief to be unrestrained so that it might be less painful. I would wish it to be violent so that it might be less long. Remember him as he was and exaggerate even. Remember his acuity in getting to the bottom of the most profound matters, his subtlety in speaking of the most delicate, his sound good taste which made him value the most important, the fertility which he would bring to the most sterile matters. Remember the skill with which he would defend the accused. His indulgence gave him one thousand times more intelligence than interest or egoism gave to the guilty. He was severe only when it came to himself. Far from looking for excuses for the inconsequential faults which he might inadvertently commit he used to exaggerate them with all the hostility of an enemy, and he would debase the value of his virtues with all the venom of one who was envious of them by rigorous examination of the motives which had perhaps inspired them unbeknownst to him. Do not limit your grief to any period except the time it will take to heal. When we lose our friends let us submit ourselves to the order of the universe as we ourselves will submit to it when it sees fit to dispose of us. Let us accept without despair the decree of Fate which condemns them in the same way that we ourselves will accept it without resistance when it is pronounced against us. The duties of burial are not the final duties of friends. The earth that has been disturbed will settle over your lover's ashes but your soul will retain all his sensibility.

JACQUES: Master, that's all very nice, but what the devil do you mean by it? I have lost my Captain and I am grief-stricken. And you rattle off to me like a parrot a fragment of a speech made by a man or a woman to another woman who has lost her lover.

MASTER: I think it's a woman's speech.

JACQUES: I think it's a man's. But whether it's a man's or a woman's I ask you again, what the devil do you mean by it? Do you take me for my Captain's mistress? My Captain, Monsieur, was a worthy man, and I've always been a decent lad.

MASTER: Is anyone disputing that, Jacques?

JACQUES: What the devil does your speech from a man or a woman to a woman who's lost her lover mean, then? Perhaps if I ask you enough times, you'll tell me?

MASTER: No, Jacques, you must find that out all by yourself.

JACQUES: I'll spend the rest of my life pondering on that and I still won't find out. It's enough to keep me wondering till Judgement Day.

MASTER: Jacques, it seemed to me that you were paying great attention when I was speaking.

JACQUES: How could I not pay attention to such absurdities?

MASTER: Well done, Jacques!

JACQUES: I almost exploded at the bit about rigorous propriety which restrained me during my Captain's life and from which I was freed by his death.

MASTER: Well done, Jacques. Then I have done what I set out to do. Tell me if it was possible to find a better way of consoling you? You were crying, and if I had talked about the object of your sorrow, what would have happened? You would have cried even more and I would have only added to your grief. But I fooled you by the absurdity of my funeral speech and by the little quarrel which followed it. Admit that at this moment your thoughts about your Captain are as remote as the funeral cortège which is taking him to his last resting-place. Consequently I think that you can come back to the story of your loves.

JACQUES: I think so too.
'Doctor,' I said to the surgeon, 'do you live far from here?'
'A good quarter of a mile at least.'
'Are you comfortably lodged?'
'Reasonably comfortably.'
'Do you think you could make a bed available?'
'No.'
'What? Even if I pay you, and pay well?'
'Oh, if you pay, and pay well, that's a different matter . . . But, my friend, you don't seem to be in any position to pay, let alone pay well.'
'That's my business. Would I be cared for a little at your house?'
'Very well. My wife has been looking after sick people all her life, and my eldest daughter's prepared to shave all comers, and is as handy with dressings as I am.'
'How much would you charge for accommodation, food and being looked after?'
The surgeon said, scratching his ear: 'Accommodation . . . food . . . attention . . . But who will be responsible for paying?'

'I'll pay every day.'

'Now that's what I call talking, that.'

But Monsieur, I don't think you're listening to me.

MASTER: No, Jacques. It was written up above that you would speak this time and perhaps not for the last time wouldn't be listened to.

JACQUES: When a person doesn't listen to someone who is speaking it's either because they are thinking about nothing or thinking about something else other than what the speaker is saying. Which were you doing?

MASTER: The latter. I was thinking about what one of those servants following the cortège said to you about your Captain having been deprived through the death of his friend of the pleasure of fighting at least once a week. Did that make any sense to you?

JACQUES: Certainly.

MASTER: Well, it's an enigma to me and I'd be obliged if you would explain it to me.

JACQUES: What the devil has it got to do with you?

MASTER: Not much, but when you speak you apparently like to be listened to, don't you?

JACQUES: Of course.

MASTER: Then in all conscience, I don't think I'll be able to satisfy your requirements for as long as that inexplicable remark continues to vex my brain. Don't leave me in this state, I beg you.

JACQUES: Willingly. But swear to me at least that you won't interrupt me any more.

MASTER: Come what may, I swear it.

JACQUES: It is simply that my Captain, a good man, a gallant man, a very worthy man, and one of the best officers in the corps, was something of an eccentric. He had met and made friends with another officer in the same regiment, who was also a good man, a gallant man, a very worthy man, just as good an officer as my Captain, and also just as much of an eccentric.

Jacques was on the point of beginning his Captain's story when they heard a large number of men and horses coming up behind them. It was the same lugubrious carriage coming back, surrounded by . . .

– The excise men?[16]

No.

– The mounted constabulary?

Perhaps . . .

Whatever they were, the cortège was preceded by the priest in surplice and cassock, hands tied behind his back and the coachman in black, his hands tied behind his back and the two valets in black whose hands were also tied behind their backs. And who was in for a surprise? Why, Jacques, of course, who cried out: 'My Captain, my poor Captain isn't dead! God be praised!'

Jacques turned his horse around, spurred him and went as fast as he could towards the supposed cortège. He was not quite thirty feet from it when the excise men or the mounted constabulary took aim at him and shouted: 'Stop! Go back or you're a dead man!'

Jacques stopped, quite dead, and consulted for a moment with the voice of Destiny in his head. It seemed to him that Destiny was telling him: 'Go back . . .', so he did.

His master asked him: 'Well then, Jacques, what's it all about?'

JACQUES: My God, I don't know.

MASTER: Why not?

JACQUES: I don't know that either.

MASTER: You'll see. It'll turn out that these men are smugglers who have doubtless filled the coffin with contraband and been betrayed to the excise by the same ruffians they bought the goods from.

JACQUES: But why the carriage with my Captain's arms?

MASTER: Or it's a kidnapping. They have hidden who knows what, a woman, a girl, a nun even in the coffin. It takes more than a shroud to make a dead man.

JACQUES: But why the carriage with my Captain's arms?

MASTER: For whatever reason you like, but finish your Captain's story for me.

JACQUES: You still want to hear it? But perhaps my Captain is still alive?

MASTER: What's that got to do with it?

JACQUES: I don't like to speak about the living because from time to time one is ashamed of the good and the bad things one says of them – of the good things because they go and spoil them and the bad because they make amends.

MASTER: Be neither the reluctant panegyrist nor the embittered censor. Just tell the thing as it is.

JACQUES: That's not easy. Has not everyone his own character, his own interests, his own tastes and passions according to which he either exaggerates or attenuates everything?

Tell the thing as it is, you say! . . . That might not even happen twice in one day in the whole of a large town. And is the person who listens any better qualified to listen than the person who speaks? No. Which is why in the whole of a large town it can hardly happen twice in one day that someone's words are understood in the same way as they are spoken.

MASTER: What the devil, Jacques, those principles are enough to outlaw speaking and listening altogether. Say nothing, hear nothing, believe nothing . . . Just tell the thing as you will. I will listen as I can and believe as I am able.

JACQUES: And it's not just that one's words are hardly ever understood in the same way as they are spoken. Even worse than that is that one's actions are hardly ever judged in the way they are performed.

MASTER: I doubt that there can be anywhere under God's heaven another head which contains as many paradoxes as yours.

JACQUES: What harm is there in that? A paradox isn't always a lie.

MASTER: That is true.

JACQUES: We were passing through Orléans, my Captain and myself. The only talk in the town was of an incident which had recently happened to a citizen called M. le Pelletier, who was a man who was filled with such profound commiseration for the poor that after having reduced his own quite considerable fortune to a bare subsistence through excessive alms-giving he was himself reduced to going from door to door seeking from the purses of others the help which he was no longer able to give from his own.[17]

MASTER: And you think there were two different views of this man's behaviour?

JACQUES: Not among the poor, but practically all of the rich, without exception, looked on him as some kind of madman, and his relatives nearly had him declared incapable of managing his own affairs.

While we were taking refreshment at an inn, a crowd of idlers gathered round a sort of orator who was the local barber, and asked him: 'You were there. Tell us how the thing happened.'

'Certainly,' replied the local soap-box orator, who liked nothing better than being asked to hold forth . . .

Monsieur Aubertot, one of my clients, whose house is opposite the Franciscan church, was standing on his doorstep and M. le Pelletier went up to him and said: 'Monsieur Aubertot, will you give me nothing for my friends?' – because that is, you know, how he refers to the poor.

'Nothing today, Monsieur le Pelletier.'

Monsieur le Pelletier insisted: 'If you only knew on whose behalf I was asking for your charity. It's for a poor woman who's just given birth and who hasn't even a rag to wrap her baby in.'

'I cannot.'

'It's for a beautiful young girl who has no food and no work, whom your generosity might save from ruin.'

'I cannot.'

'It is for a labourer who has only his hands to live by and who has just broken a leg falling from his scaffolding.'

'I cannot, I tell you.'

'Come on, Monsieur Aubertot, allow yourself to be touched. You can be sure that you'll never have the chance of doing a more meritorious action.'

'I cannot. I cannot.'

'My dear merciful Monsieur Aubertot . . .'

'Monsieur le Pelletier, leave me alone . . . When I want to give I don't have to be asked.'

And at that M. Aubertot turned his back on him and went into his shop where M. le Pelletier followed him. He followed him from his shop and into his back room, from his back room into his living-quarters, and there, M. Aubertot, who had been driven to the end of his tether by M. le Pelletier's insistence, slapped his face.

At this point my Captain got up suddenly and asked the orator: 'Didn't he kill him?'

'No, Monsieur, does one kill for something like that?'

'A slap in the face! My God, a slap in the face! What did he do then?'

'What did he do after he was slapped in the face? He said to M. Aubertot in an amused tone of voice: "That's for me, but for my friends? . . ."'

On hearing this everyone who was listening cried out in admiration, except my Captain, who said to them: 'Your Monsieur le Pelletier, Messieurs, is nothing but a beggar, a wretch, an unspeakable coward who would for all that have been vindicated on the spot by this sword of mine if I had been there. And your Aubertot would have been extremely lucky if it had only cost him his nose and his two ears.'

The orator replied: 'I can see, Monsieur, that you would not have left this insolent man the time to acknowledge the error of his ways and throw himself at the feet of M. le Pelletier and give him his purse.'

'No, of course not.'

'You are a soldier and M. le Pelletier is a Christian. You haven't got quite the same ideas about a slap on the face.'

'The cheek of every man of honour is the same.'

'That's not what the Gospel says.'

'The Gospel is in my heart and in my scabbard, and I don't know any other.'

'Your Gospel, my Master, is I don't know where, but mine is inscribed up above. Everyone understands the good and bad done to him in his own way and perhaps we never judge anything the same way twice in our lives.'

MASTER: What happened next, you damned gossip? What happened next?

Whenever Jacques' master became annoyed, Jacques used to shut up and lose himself in thoughts, often breaking his silence only by an occasional word which was linked in his thoughts, but as disconnected conversationally as the reading of a book when one has skipped a few pages. This is precisely what happened to him when he found himself saying the words: 'My dear Master . . .'

MASTER: Ah! I see that you've recovered your powers of speech at long last. I'm pleased for both of us because I was beginning to get bored not hearing you speak, and I suppose you were bored too since you weren't speaking. So, speak.

JACQUES: My dear Master. Life is a series of misunderstandings. There are the misunderstandings of love, the misunderstandings of friendship, the misunderstandings of politics, finance, the church, law, commerce, women, husbands . . .

MASTER: Forget about your misunderstandings and try to understand that it is terribly rude to start moralizing when it's a question of historical fact. Now, your Captain's story?

Jacques was about to start his Captain's story when, for the second time, his horse slewed violently off the road to the right, carried him a good quarter league across a long plain and then suddenly stopped dead between the forks of a gallows ...

– Between the forks of a gallows? That's really extraordinary behaviour for a horse, to lead its rider to the gibbet.

'What does this signify?' asked Jacques. 'Is this a warning from Destiny?'

MASTER: My friend, do not doubt it. That horse of yours is inspired and the only worrying thing is that all of these prognostications, inspirations and warnings by dreams or by apparitions which come from on high are useless. Whatever it is will happen all the same. My dear friend, I advise you to put your conscience in order, to sort out your little affairs, and to tell me your Captain's story and the story of your loves as quickly as you can because I would be very annoyed to lose you without hearing them. If you were to worry about it any more than you are worrying already, what good would it do you? None. The decree of your Destiny, pronounced twice by your horse, will be fulfilled. Tell me, do you have nothing which you ought to give back to anybody? Confide your last wishes in me and you may be sure they will be faithfully carried out. If you have taken anything from me, I give it to you. Ask only for pardon from God, and during the long or the short time which remains to us together don't steal any more from me.

JACQUES: No matter how much I go back over the past, I can't see that I have any score to settle with the justice of men. I haven't killed or stolen or raped.

MASTER: Too bad. All things considered I'd prefer it if the crime had already been committed than remained to be, and for good reason.

JACQUES: But, Monsieur, perhaps I won't be hanged on my account, but on account of someone else's actions.

MASTER: That's possible.

JACQUES: Perhaps I'll only be hanged after my death?

MASTER: That's possible too.

JACQUES: Perhaps I won't be hanged at all.

MASTER: I doubt that.

JACQUES: Perhaps it is written up above that I will merely assist at the hanging of another person. And as for that other person, who knows who he is? Whether he is near by or far away from me?

MASTER: Monsieur Jacques, be hanged, since Fate wills it and your horse says it, but do not be insolent. Stop your impertinent conjecture and tell me your Captain's story quickly.

JACQUES: Monsieur, don't get angry. Sometimes perfectly honest people have been hanged. It's one of the misunderstandings of justice.

MASTER: These misunderstandings of yours are painful. Let's change the subject.

Jacques, who was feeling a little reassured by the diverse interpretations he had found for his horse's prognostication, said:

When I joined the regiment there were two officers who were both of more or less the same age, same birth, same length of service, and both of equal merit. My Captain was one of them. The only difference between them was that one was rich and the other wasn't. My Captain was the rich one. This similarity was bound to produce either the greatest sympathy or the most violent antipathy. In fact it produced both . . .

Here Jacques stopped, and this happened to him several more times during the course of his story, every time his horse moved his head to the left or the right. And to carry on he repeated his last phrase, as if he had the hiccups.

JACQUES: In fact it produced both. There were days when they were the best of friends and others when they were mortal enemies. On their days of friendship they would seek each other out, make a great show of pleasure when they met, embrace each other and then tell each other all their problems, their pleasures and their needs. They would consult each other on the most intimate subjects, on their domestic affairs, their hopes, their fears, their ambitions. And then the next day they would pass each other by without looking, or they would glare fiercely at each other, call each other 'Monsieur', say harsh words to each other, draw their swords and fight. If it happened that one of the two was wounded, the other would rush up to his friend crying and lamenting, see him to his quarters and install himself at his friend's bedside until he was better. Then, a week, or a fortnight, or a month later, it would begin again, and people would see from one moment to the next two gallant men . . . two gallant men, two sincere friends each facing death at the other's hands and the one who died would certainly not have been the one deserving the most pity.

People had often spoken to them about the strangeness of their conduct. I, myself – for my Captain allowed me to discuss things with him – used to ask him: 'Monsieur, what if you killed him?'

At these words he would start to cry and bury his face in his hands. Then he would run round his apartment like a madman. Two hours later, either his friend would bring him back wounded or he would do the same for his friend.

Neither my protests . . . neither my protests nor those of anyone else did any good. The only solution was to separate them. The Minister of War was informed of their extraordinary persistence in these extremes of behaviour and my Captain was given command of a fortress with strict orders to present himself there immediately and an absolute prohibition on leaving it. For his part, my Captain's friend was forbidden from leaving the regiment . . . I think this damned horse will drive me insane . . . Hardly had the orders of the Minister arrived than my Captain, under the pretext of going to present his thanks for the favour bestowed on him, left for Court, where he pointed out that he himself was rich, but his comrade had the same right to the King's graces, that the command which he had been given would reward his friend's services and add to his small fortune – and this would for his part make him very happy. Since the Minister only had it in mind to separate these two strange men and since generous behaviour always has an effect on people, it was decided . . . Damned beast, can't you keep your head straight . . . it was decided that my Captain would stay in the regiment and his friend would be transferred to take command of the fortress.

Hardly had they been separated when they realized how much they needed each other and they both fell into the most profound melancholy. My Captain asked for six months' leave to go back home for a rest. When he was two leagues away from the garrison, he sold his horse, disguised himself as a peasant and made his way towards the fortress his friend commanded. It appears that this had been arranged between them. He arrived . . . Oh, go where you like! Is there another gibbet you'd like to visit? . . . It's all right for you to laugh, Monsieur! I don't find it at all funny! . . . He arrived. But it was written up above that, despite the precautions they took to hide the satisfaction they felt at seeing each other again and the care they took to approach each other with the external appearance of deference that might be expected of a peasant in the presence of the commanding officer of a fortress, some soldiers and some officers, who were by chance present at their meeting, and who happened to know of their past adventures, became suspicious and went to warn the adjutant of the fortress.

The adjutant, a careful man, was amused by the situation but did not fail to attach to it the importance it merited. He set spies around the Commandant. Their first report was that the Commandant hardly ever went out and the peasant not at all. It was impossible for these two men to live together for a week without their strange obsession taking hold of them and this did not fail to happen.

You can see, Reader, how obliging I am. If I had a mind to do it, I could whip on the horses pulling the black-draped carriage, I could assemble together at the door of the nearest cottage Jacques, his master, the excise men or the mounted constabulary and the rest of the cortège. I could interrupt the story of Jacques' Captain and make you as impatient as I wanted to. But to do all that I would have to lie, and I don't like lies unless they are necessary and useful. The fact is that Jacques and his master saw no more of the draped carriage and that Jacques, although he was still very worried about his horse's behaviour, continued his story.

JACQUES: One day the spies reported to the adjutant that there had been a violent argument between the Commandant and the peasant and that after this they had gone off, the peasant leading the way with the Commandant following him reluctantly, to the house of a banker in the town and that they were still there.

Afterwards it transpired that in despair of ever seeing each other again, they had resolved to fight to the end. Ever conscious of the duties imposed by the most tender of friendships, even while in the throes of the most incredible ferocity, my Captain, who was rich, as I've told you . . . I hope, Monsieur, that you're not going to condemn me to finish our journey on this bizarre animal . . . my Captain, who was rich, had insisted on his comrade agreeing to accept a bill of exchange for twenty-four thousand pounds which would provide him with enough means to live abroad in the event of my Captain's death. He insisted that unless this condition was satisfied he would not fight. His friend's reply to this offer was: 'Do you believe, my friend, that I would survive you for long if I killed you?'

They left the banker's and started off towards the gates of the town where they were suddenly surrounded by the adjutant and some other officers. Although this encounter appeared to be just a coincidence, our two friends, or two enemies, whichever you please to call them, were not taken in. The peasant admitted his real identity. They went off to spend the night in an isolated house. The next day, at dawn, my Captain, after embracing his comrade several times, left him for good. Hardly had he arrived at his birthplace when he died.

MASTER: And who told you he was dead?

JACQUES: What about the coffin? And the carriage with his arms? My poor Captain is dead, I'm sure of it.

MASTER: And what about the priest whose hands were tied behind his back? And the servants whose hands were tied behind their backs? And the excise men or the mounted constabulary and the cortège heading back to town? Your Captain is alive, I've no doubt of it. Do you know nothing of his friend?

JACQUES: The story of his friend is quite a long line on the scroll of Destiny, or whatever is written up above.

MASTER: I hope . . .

Jacques' horse did not allow his master to finish. He went off like a shot, and this time did not deviate to the left or the right but followed the road. Soon Jacques was lost from sight and his master, convinced that he would find another gallows at the end of the road, was splitting his sides laughing.

And since Jacques and his master are only good when they are together and are worth nothing when they are separated, any more than is Don Quixote without Sancho or Richardet without Ferragus, which is something that Cervantes' continuator and Ariosto's imitator, Forti Guerra, have not quite understood,[18] Reader, let us chat while waiting for them to meet up again.

You are going to take the story of Jacques' Captain as a mere fiction, but you will be wrong. I assure you that, such as he told the story to his master, so did I hear it at the Invalides, in I'm not sure what year, but on the feast of Saint-Louis. I was dining with Monsieur de Saint-Etienne the adjutant of the Invalides.[19] The story-teller spoke in the presence of several other officers of the establishment who had knowledge of the facts and was a serious man who didn't seem at all like a joker. This is a timely moment for me to give you a reminder for both the present and the future that you must be circumspect if you want to avoid taking the truth for lies and lies for the truth in Jacques' conversation with his master. Now that I have warned you, I wash my hands of the matter.

They really are quite an extraordinary pair of men, you are saying to me.

Is that what makes you suspicious? Firstly, nature is so varied, especially when it comes to instinct and character, that there is nothing in a poet's imagination, however bizarre, for which experience and observation might not find a model in nature. I, who speak to you now, I have met the real-life counterpart of the *Médecin malgré lui* whom I had thought until then to be the most mad and whimsical of inventions.[20]

– What! The real-life counterpart of the husband whose wife says to him: 'I've three children on my hands', and he tells her: 'Put them on the ground.'

'They are asking me for bread.'

'Give them a beating.'

Exactly. This is an account of his conversation with my wife.

'Is that you there, Monsieur Gousse?'

'No, Madame, I am here.'

'Where have you come from?'

'From where I've just been.'

'What did you do there?'

'I repaired a windmill which was working badly.'

'To whom did this windmill belong?'

'I don't know. I didn't go there to mend the miller.'

'You're very well dressed today, contrary to your usual practice. But tell me, why are you wearing such a dirty shirt under such a clean suit?'

'That's because I've only got one.'

'Why have you got only one?'

'Because I've only got one body at a time.'

'My husband's not here at the moment, but I hope that won't prevent you from having dinner with us.'

'No, it won't, since I have entrusted him with neither my stomach nor my appetite.'

'How is your wife keeping?'

'However she likes. That's her business.'

'And your children?'

'Wonderful.'

'And the one with the nice eyes, who looks so healthy and has such beautiful skin?'

'Much better than the others – he's dead.'

'Are you teaching them anything?'

'No, Madame.'

'What, not even reading, writing or the catechism?'

'No reading, no writing and no catechism.'

'And why is that?'

'Because nobody taught me anything and I'm not any the more ignorant for it. If they've got brains they'll do as I've done. If they're stupid what I teach them will only make them more stupid.'

If ever you meet this eccentric, you don't have to know him to strike up a conversation with him. Take him into the nearest inn, tell him your business, ask him to follow you twenty miles and he will follow you. After you've employed him send him away without a sou, and he'll go away happy.

Have you ever heard of a certain Prémontval who used to give public lessons in mathematics in Paris? He was his friend . . . But perhaps Jacques and his master are back together again? Do you want to go back to them or stay with me? . . .

Gousse and Prémontval ran the school together. Among the pupils who used to flock there was a young girl called Mlle Pigeon, the daughter of that talented artist who made those beautiful relief maps of the world which used to be in the Royal Botanical Gardens and which were transported to the Academy of Sciences.[21] Mademoiselle Pigeon used to go there every morning with her briefcase under her arm and her box of mathematical instruments in her muff. One of her teachers – in fact it was Prémontval – fell in love with his student and somehow by way of the propositions concerning solids inscribed in spheres a child was begotten.

Monsieur Pigeon was not the kind of man who would quietly accept the truth of this corollary. The lovers' position was becoming embarrassing. They discussed the matter, but having nothing – and I mean nothing at all – what could be the outcome of their deliberations? They summoned their friend Gousse to their assistance and he, without saying a word, sold everything he possessed – linen, clothes, apparatus, furniture, books – got together a sum of money, and bundled the two lovers into a post-chaise and accompanied them at full gallop as far as the Alps. Once there, he emptied his purse of what little money remained, gave it to them and embraced them, wishing them good luck on their journey, and started back on foot as far as Lyons, begging alms all the way. There he painted the walls of a cloister of monks and earned enough money to return to Paris without begging.

– That's very fine.

Certainly, but because of this heroic action, you now believe that Gousse was a deeply moral man, don't you? Well, disillusion yourself, he had no more morals than you'll find in the brain of a pike.

– That's not possible.

Isn't it? I employed him. I once gave him a mandate for eighty pounds to my order. The amount was written in figures. What did he do? He added a zero and had himself paid eight hundred pounds.

– Ah! How awful!

He was no more dishonest when he took from me than he was being honest when he took the shirt off his back for a friend. He is an eccentric without principles. Those eighty francs weren't enough for him, so with one stroke of the pen he got himself eight hundred francs which he needed. And what about the valuable books he gave me . . .

– What valuable books?

But what about Jacques and his master? What about . . . Jacques' love life? The patience with which you listen to me shows what little interest you have in my protagonists. And I'm tempted to leave them wherever they are . . .

I needed a valuable book which he brought to me. A short while afterwards I needed another valuable book which he also brought to me. I wanted to pay him but he refused the money. Later, I needed another valuable book.

'Ah, that one . . .' he said. 'I'm afraid you can't have that. You've asked me too late. My Sorbonne Professor is dead.'

'What has the death of your Sorbonne Professor got to do with the book I want? Did you take the other two from his library?'

'Certainly.'

'Without his consent?'

'Why should I need that for an act of redistributive justice? All I did was find a better location for the books by transferring them from a place where they were useless to another where they would be put to good use.'

Now speculate on the ways of men if you dare! But it is the story about Gousse and his wife which is the best . . . I understand, you've had enough of this and you want to return to our two travellers. Reader, you're treating me like an automaton. That's not polite. 'Tell the story of Jacques' love life', 'Don't tell the story of Jacques' love life', 'I want you to tell me about Gousse', 'I've had enough . . .'

It is no doubt necessary that I follow your wishes, but it is also necessary that I sometimes follow my own. And that is without considering the fact that anyone who allows me to begin a story commits himself to hearing it through to the end.

I told you in the first place . . .

Now, when a person says: 'In the first place . . .' it is a way of announcing at least a second place . . .

So, in the second place . . . listen to me . . .

All right, then, don't listen to me . . . I'll speak to myself . . .

Jacques' Captain and his friend could have been tormented by a violent and secret jealousy. It is a feeling which friendship does not always extinguish. Nothing is so difficult to forgive as someone else's worth. Were they not perhaps afraid that one of them would be unfairly promoted, which would offend both of them equally? Without being conscious of doing so, each was trying pre-emptively to rid himself of a dangerous rival. They were sounding each other out for the opportunity. But how can one think such a thing of a man who so generously gave up his Commandant's post to an impecunious friend?

He gave it up, that is true, but if he had not been awarded it in the first place, he might perhaps have claimed it at swordpoint. In the army an unjustified promotion, even if it does not bring honour to the person who profits from it, dishonours his rival. But let us leave all that. Let us just say that it was their particular kind of madness. And which of us does not have his own? The folly of our two officers was for several centuries that of the whole of Europe and used to be called the spirit of chivalry. That brilliant multitude, armed from head to toe, decked out in the favours of their various ladies, on their prancing chargers, lances in hand, visors raised, visors lowered, looking at each other proudly, sizing each other up, threatening each other, casting each other down in the dust, strewing vast tournament-fields with splinters of their broken arms, were all just friends, striving jealously for the particular type of merit which happened then to be in vogue.

At the moment when, at opposite ends of the arena, they raised their lances to the ready, at the moment when they pressed their spurs into the flanks of their chargers, these friends became the most terrible enemies. They would descend on each other with the same fury they would have displayed on a battlefield. And so our two officers were nothing more than two knights errant who were born in our time with the mores of former times. Every human virtue and every vice has been fashionable for a while and then unfashionable. Physical strength had its moment. So did martial skills. Bravery is sometimes more and sometimes less well thought of. The more a thing is common the less it is valued and the less it is praised. Examine the proclivities of men and you will note some who appear to have come into the world too late. They belong to another century. But what is to prevent us from believing that our two soldiers engaged in their perilous daily conflicts purely out of a desire to find their rival's weak spot and gain superiority over him? Duels recur in many forms in our society — between priests, between magistrates, between men of letters, between philosophers. Every occupation has its knights and its lances. Even our most serious or amusing assemblies are no more than miniature tournaments into which people sometimes carry the colours of their ladies, if not on their shoulders, at least in their hearts. The more people there are present, the more lively the contest. The presence of women makes the contest extremely intense and hard fought. The shame of having been beaten in front of women is hardly ever forgotten.

And Jacques? Jacques had gone through the gates of the town and through the streets cheered on by children until he reached the edge of the opposite quarter of the town where his horse threw itself through a small low archway. There took place between the lintel of this archway and Jacques' head a terrible collision, the result of which could only be that the lintel was thrown out of alignment or Jacques knocked over backwards. It was, as you might well imagine, the latter which happened. Jacques fell, his head split open and unconscious. He was picked up and brought back to life with spirits. I think he may even have been bled by the master of the house.

– Was he a surgeon, then?

No . . . Meanwhile Jacques' master had by now arrived and was asking for news from everybody he met.

'Have you by any chance seen a tall thin man on a piebald horse?'

'He's just gone by. He was going like the devil himself was after him. He must have arrived at his master's by now.'

'And who is his master?'

'The hangman.'

'The hangman!'

'Yes, the horse is his.'

'Where does the hangman live?'

'Quite far. But don't bother going there. Here are his servants and it would appear that they are bringing the thin man you were asking for, whom we had taken for one of his valets.'

And who was it who spoke to Jacques' master in this manner? It was an innkeeper, outside whose door he had stopped. There could be no doubt about what he was. He was as round and fat as a barrel and wore a shirt with the sleeves rolled up to his elbows, a white cotton hat on his head, a kitchen apron round his waist and a large knife at his side.

'Quickly, quickly, a bed for this poor man,' Jacques' master said to him, 'and a surgeon, a doctor and an apothecary . . .'

Meanwhile the people who had been carrying Jacques had set him down at his master's feet, his forehead covered with an enormous thick compress and his eyes tightly shut.

'Jacques? Jacques!'

'Is that you, Master?'

'Yes, it's me. Look at me.'

'I can't.'

'What on earth happened to you?'

'Ahh! The horse. The damned horse!... I'll tell you about it tomorrow if I don't die during the night...'

And while they carried him up the stairs his master supervised the operation, shouting: 'Take care! Easy does it! Easy does it! Dammit! You're going to hurt him! You, yes, the one holding his feet, turn to the right. And you... with his head, go to the left.'

And Jacques said quietly: 'So it must have been written up above...'

Hardly had Jacques gone to bed than he fell into a deep sleep. His master spent the night at his bedside, the whole time taking his pulse and wetting his compress with lotion. When Jacques woke up he caught him doing this and said: 'What are you up to?'

MASTER: I am watching over you. You are my servant whether I am well or ill, but I am yours when you are ill.

JACQUES: Well, it's nice to know you're human. That's not a quality very often found by valets in their masters.

MASTER: How's your head?

JACQUES: Almost as well as the beam it collided with.

MASTER: Take this sheet between your teeth and give your head a good shake... What did you feel?

JACQUES: Nothing. The jug seems not to have been cracked.

MASTER: So much the better. I suppose you want to get up.

JACQUES: And what would you have me do in bed?

MASTER: I want you to rest.

JACQUES: Well, I think we should have lunch and leave.

MASTER: And what about the horse?

JACQUES: I left him with his master, who being an honest and worthy fellow bought him back for what he sold him to us for.

MASTER: And this honest, worthy fellow, do you know who he is?

JACQUES: No.

MASTER: I'll tell you that when we're on our way.

JACQUES: Why not now? Why make a mystery out of it?

MASTER: Mystery or not, is there any reason why I should tell you at this moment and not later?

JACQUES: None.

MASTER: But you need a horse.

JACQUES: The keeper of this inn might be only too pleased to let us have one of his.

MASTER: Sleep a while and I'll go and see to it.

Jacques' master went downstairs, ordered breakfast, bought a horse, went back upstairs and found Jacques dressed. They had lunch and left. Jacques, however, protested that it was impolite to go away without paying a courtesy visit to the citizen against whose door he had nearly brained himself, and who had so obligingly rescued him. His master quietened his scruples by assuring him that he had already well rewarded the servants who had brought Jacques to the inn. Jacques argued that the money given to the servants did not acquit him of his obligations to their master, that it was behaviour such as this which caused men to feel regret and disgust at doing good and that they were making themselves appear ungrateful: 'Master, I can hear everything this man is saying about me by thinking what I would be saying about him if he were in my place and I were in his . . .'

They were just leaving the town when they met a tall well-built man wearing a braided hat and a suit with gold braiding on the seams. He was alone – unless you counted the two large hounds which preceded him. Jacques had no sooner set eyes on him than he was off his horse shouting, 'It's him!', and was all over the man before anyone knew what was happening. The man with the dogs appeared to be very embarrassed by Jacques' caresses and pushed him away gently, and said: 'Monsieur, you do me too much honour.'

'No, no. I owe you my life and I could never thank you enough.'

'Don't you know who I am?'

'Are you not the helpful citizen who rescued me, bled and bandaged me when my horse . . .'

'That is true.'

'Are you not the honest citizen who bought back this horse for the same price he sold it to me for?'

'I am.'

And Jacques began to kiss him again, first on one cheek, then on the other. His master smiled and the two dogs stood with their noses in the air, apparently filled with wonder at a scene which they had never seen the like of before. After Jacques had added several bows to his effusions which his benefactor did not return and many good wishes for the future which were received rather coldly, he got back on his horse, and said to his master: 'I feel the greatest respect for that man and you must tell me who he is.'

MASTER: And why, Jacques, in your opinion, is he so worthy of respect?

JACQUES: Because he attaches no importance to the good works he performs and must therefore be of a naturally kindly disposition and have a long-standing habit of doing good.

MASTER: And how do you reach that conclusion?

JACQUES: From the cold and indifferent manner in which he received my thanks. He did not acknowledge me. He didn't say a word. He seemed hardly to recognize me and, who knows, perhaps at this very moment he may be saying to himself with contempt: 'Kindness must be a very strange thing to that traveller and just dealing a difficult thing for him since he is so touched by them.'

What have I said that is so absurd as to make you laugh so heartily? Whatever it is, tell me the man's name so that I may make a note of it.

MASTER: Willingly. Write.

JACQUES: Tell me.

MASTER: Write: The man for whom I hold the greatest respect . . .

JACQUES: . . . the greatest respect . . .

MASTER: . . . is . . .

JACQUES: . . . is . . .

MASTER: The hangman of   *****.

JACQUES: The hangman!

MASTER: Yes, yes! The hangman.

JACQUES: Perhaps you could tell me what the point of this joke is?

MASTER: I am not joking. Just follow the links in your fob-chain. You need a horse. Fate directs you to a passer-by, and this passer-by happens to be a hangman. The horse takes you to a gallows twice. The third time he delivers you to a hangman's home where you fall half dead. And from there, where are you taken? Into an inn, a resting-place, a common refuge. Jacques, do you know the story of the death of Socrates?

JACQUES: No.

MASTER: He was an Athenian sage. For a long time now the role of sage has been dangerous amongst madmen. His fellow citizens condemned him to drink hemlock. Well, Socrates did what you've just done and behaved as politely with his executioner who brought him the hemlock as you did. Jacques, you're a sort of philosopher, admit it. And I know all too well that philosophers are a breed of men who are loathed by the mighty because they refuse to bend the knee to them. Magistrates hate them because they are by their calling protectors of the prejudices which philosophers attack, priests because they see them rarely at the foot of their altars. And poets, who are people without principles, hate them and are stupid enough to think of philosophy as the hatchet of the Arts not to mention the fact that those poets who have indulged in the hateful genre of satire have simply been flatterers. They are hated also by the peoples who have always been enslaved to the tyrants who oppress them, the rogues who trick them and the clowns who amuse them. So you can see that I am familiar with all of the perils of your profession and am fully aware of the importance of the admission I am asking you to make. But I will not betray your secret. Jacques, my friend, you are a philosopher, and I am sorry for you. If it is permitted to read the events of the future from those of the present and if what is written up above is ever revealed to men long before it happens, I predict that your death will be philosophical and that you will put your head in the noose with the same good grace as Socrates took his cup of hemlock.

JACQUES: Master, a prophet couldn't put it better. But fortunately . . .

MASTER: You don't really believe me. But that gives more weight to my premonition.

JACQUES: And you, Monsieur, do you believe it?

MASTER: I believe it, but even if I didn't it wouldn't make any difference.

JACQUES: Why?

MASTER: Because there is only danger for people who talk. And I keep quiet.

JACQUES: What about premonitions?

MASTER: I laugh at them but somewhat nervously, I must admit. Some of them are of such striking character and we have all been lulled with tales like that from an early age. If your dreams had come true five or six times and it happened that you should dream your friend were dead you would surely go to him the next morning to find out whether it was true or not. But the premonitions which are hardest to rebut are those which come to one at the moment an event is taking place far away from one and which appear symbolic.

JACQUES: Sometimes you are so profound and sublime that I don't understand you. Could you not enlighten me with some example?

MASTER: Nothing simpler. There was once a woman who lived in the country with her eighty-year-old husband who suffered from gallstones. The husband left his wife and went into town to have an operation. On the eve of the operation he wrote to his wife: 'At the time you read this letter I'll be under the scalpel of Friar Cosmas.'[22]
Are you familiar with those wedding rings which are divided into two parts, one bearing the husband's name, and the other the wife's? Well, this woman had one on her finger when she opened her husband's letter. At that moment the two halves of the ring fell apart. The half which bore her name stayed on her finger. That which had his name fell broken on to the letter which she was reading. Tell me, Jacques, do you think that there is anyone who is strong-minded or resolute enough not to be more of less shaken by a similar incident taking place in similar circumstances? So the woman nearly died. Her fright lasted until the day the next post arrived and she received a letter in which her husband wrote that the operation had gone well and he was completely out of danger and hoped to embrace her by the end of the month.

JACQUES: And did he?

MASTER: Yes.

JACQUES: I asked you that question because I have noticed several times that there's something sly about Destiny. The first time round you think

Destiny is a liar but later it turns out it has told the truth. So, you, Monsieur, think my case comes under the heading of symbolic premonitions and, in spite of yourself, you believe me to be threatened by a philosopher's death.

MASTER: It's no good my trying to hide it from you . . . but, so as not to dwell on such a sad idea, could you not . . .

JACQUES: Carry on with the story of my loves?

Jacques carried on with the story of his loves. We had left him, I believe, with the surgeon.

SURGEON: I'm afraid it'll take more than a day to mend your knee.

JACQUES: It will take precisely the length of time that is written up above. What does it matter?

SURGEON: At so much a day for accommodation, food and my services, that'll make quite a sum.

JACQUES: Doctor, it's not a question of how much it will cost for all this time, but how much a day.

SURGEON: Twenty-five sous. Is that too much?

JACQUES: Far too much. Come along, doctor, I'm a poor devil so let's say half of that and see how quickly you can have me taken to your house.

SURGEON: Twelve and a half sous, that's hardly anything. Shall we say thirteen sous?

JACQUES: Twelve and a half sous, thirteen sous . . . done!

SURGEON: And you'll pay every day?

JACQUES: That's the condition.

SURGEON: It's just that I've got the devil of a wife who doesn't like any funny business, you understand.

JACQUES: Yes, doctor. Just arrange for me to be taken to your devil of a wife as quickly as you can.

SURGEON: A month at thirteen sous a day, that's nineteen pounds ten sous. You'll make it twenty francs, won't you?

JACQUES: Twenty francs. Done.

SURGEON: You want to be well fed, well looked after and quickly cured. Besides food, accommodation and attention there will perhaps be medicaments, linen. There will perhaps be . . .

JACQUES: Well?

SURGEON: Well, all that adds up to twenty-four francs easily.

JACQUES: All right then, twenty-four francs, but no more.

SURGEON: One month at twenty-four francs. Two months, that will be forty-eight. Three months will be seventy-two. Ah, how pleased Madame my wife would be if you could pay me half of those seventy-two pounds in advance.[23]

JACQUES: I agree.

SURGEON: She'd be even happier if . . .

JACQUES: If I paid for the quarter. I'll pay for it.

Jacques added: The surgeon went off to find my hosts and tell them of our arrangement and the next moment the peasant, his wife and the children gathered around my bed all looking happy and relieved. There were endless questions on my state of health and about my knee, praise for the surgeon their friend and his wife, endless good wishes, the most friendly affability, and what solicitude and zeal to serve me. The surgeon had not, however, told them that I had a little money, but they knew the man. He was taking me into his house and they knew what that meant. I paid these people what I owed them and I gave the children small presents which their mother and father did not leave in their hands for long. It was morning. My host left for the fields, and my hostess took her basket on her shoulders and went off. The children, who were saddened and annoyed at being robbed, disappeared. When someone was needed to help me off my pallet, dress me and put me on my stretcher, there was nobody there but the surgeon, who started to shout his head off . . . not that anyone could hear.

MASTER: And Jacques, who likes talking to himself so much, was probably saying: 'Never pay in advance unless you want bad service.'

JACQUES: No, no, Master, this was not the time to moralize, but more the time to get impatient and swear. So I got impatient and swore. I moralized afterwards. And while I was moralizing the surgeon, who had left me alone, came back with two peasants whom he had hired to carry me, at my expense, as he didn't hesitate to point out. These men helped me with the preliminaries prior to getting me to a sort of stretcher they had made for me out of a mattress stretched over two thin poles.

MASTER: Praise be to God. There you are in the surgeon's house, falling in love with the surgeon's wife, or perhaps it's his daughter.

JACQUES: I think, Master, that you are wrong there.

MASTER: Do you think I'm going to wait in the surgeon's house for three months before hearing the first word of your loves? Ah, Jacques! That's not possible. I beg you, spare me the description of the house, the description of the surgeon's character, his wife's temper, your recovery. Skip over all that. The facts – those are what matters. Your knee is almost cured. You're quite well and you're in love.

JACQUES: I'm in love, then, since you're in so much of a hurry.

MASTER: And who are you in love with?

JACQUES: A tall brunette aged eighteen, with a beautiful figure, large black eyes, delicate crimson mouth, nice arms, pretty hands . . . ah, Master . . . such pretty hands . . . It's just that those hands . . .

MASTER: You think you're still holding them?

JACQUES: It's just that you have taken them and held them furtively yourself more than once, and if they had only let you you would have done whatever you wanted.

MASTER: My God, Jacques, I didn't expect that!

JACQUES: Nor did I.

MASTER: No matter how hard I try I cannot remember either the big brunette or the pretty hands. Try and explain yourself.

JACQUES: All right, but on condition that we retrace our steps to the surgeon's house.

MASTER: Do you think that is what is written up above?

JACQUES: That depends on you. But down here it is written: *Chi va piano va sano.*

MASTER: And it is also written: *Chi va sano va lontano.*[24] And I'd like to hear the end of this.

JACQUES: All right, then, what have you decided?

MASTER: Whatever you want.

JACQUES: In that case here we are again at the surgeon's – and it was written up above that we'd return there. The surgeon, along with his wife and children, made such concerted efforts to empty my purse by all sorts of little tricks that they soon succeeded. The recovery of my knee seemed well advanced without in fact being so. The wound had just about closed. I could go out with the aid of a crutch and I had eighteen francs left. There's nobody who likes to speak more than a man with a stammer and nobody likes walking more than a man with a limp. One autumn day after lunch I planned a long trip because the weather was nice. The distance from the village where I was living to the next village was about two leagues.

MASTER: And this village was called?

JACQUES: If I told you that you'd know everything. Once I got there I went into an inn, rested awhile and took some refreshment. Night was beginning to fall and I was just about to start out on the journey back home when, from where I was sitting in the inn, I heard the piercing screams of a woman. I went out and a crowd had gathered around her. She was on the ground tearing out her hair, and pointing to the remains of a broken pitcher, saying: 'I'm ruined. I shan't have a sou for the next month, and who will feed my poor children then? That steward whose heart is harder than stone won't let me off even a sou. How unlucky I am! I'm ruined! Ruined!'

Everyone felt sorry for her, and all I could hear around her were cries of 'Poor woman,' but nobody put their hands in their pockets.

I went up to her suddenly and asked: 'My good woman, what has happened to you?'

'What's happened to me! Can't you see? I was sent to buy a pitcher of oil. I stumbled and fell. The pitcher broke and there is the oil that was in it.'

At this moment the woman's little children arrived. They were practically naked and the bad clothing of their mother showed the full extent of the poverty of this family. The children and their mother all started to cry. As I am standing here now, Master, it needs ten times less than that to move me. I was deeply moved with compassion and tears came to my eyes. I asked her in a broken voice how much the oil in the pitcher was worth.

'How much?' she answered, lifting her hands up to heaven. 'Nine francs' worth! More than I could earn in a month!'

I untied my purse straight away and tossed her two six-franc pieces, saying: 'Here you are, my good woman. There are twelve . . .' and without waiting for thanks I started on my way back to the village.

MASTER: Jacques, you did a beautiful thing there.

JACQUES: I did a very foolish thing, if you please. I wasn't a hundred yards from the village when I said as much. And half-way home I said a lot more. On my arrival at the surgeon's house with an empty purse I felt quite differently.

MASTER: You could well be right and my praise could be as inappropriate as your commiseration . . . No, no, Jacques, I come back to my first judgement. The principal merit in your action lies in the disregard for your own need. I can see the consequences: you will be exposed to the inhumanity of your surgeon and his wife. They will throw you out of their house but, when you find yourself dying on the dungheap outside their door, you will lie dying on that dungheap satisfied with yourself.

JACQUES: Master, I am not made of such stern stuff as that. I went limping on my way and I am afraid that I must admit that I missed my two écus, which didn't bring them back and spoiled the good deed I had done with my regrets.

I was about half-way between the two villages and it was quite dark when three bandits came out from the undergrowth at the side of the road, leapt on me, knocked me to the ground, searched me and were astonished to find me with so little money. They had counted on a better prey. Having witnessed my alms-giving in the village they had imagined that somebody who could divest himself of half a louis so easily must have twenty or more. In their fury at seeing their hopes dashed and exposing themselves to having their bones broken on a scaffold for the fistful of sous I had on me if I should denounce them and they were caught and identified by me, they debated for a while whether or not they ought to kill me. Fortunately they heard a noise and fled and I escaped with a few bruises from my fall and a few more which I received when they were taking my money. When the bandits had gone I withdrew and got back to the village as best I was able, arriving at two o'clock in the morning, pale and exhausted. The pain in my knee was by now extremely intense and I was suffering from pains in various parts of my body caused by the blows I had received. The surgeon . . . Master, what's wrong with you? You're clenching your teeth and getting all agitated as if you were in the presence of some enemy.

MASTER: That's exactly what I am. I've got my sword in my hand, I'm descending on your robbers and I'm avenging you. Tell me how it is that whoever wrote out the great scroll could have decreed that such would be the reward of a noble act? Why should I, who am merely a miserable compound of faults, take your defence while He calmly watched you being attacked, knocked down, manhandled and trampled underfoot, He who is supposed to be the embodiment of all perfection? . . .

JACQUES: Master, be quiet, be quiet. What you are saying stinks to high heaven of heresy.

MASTER: What are you looking at?

JACQUES: I am looking to see if there is anybody near us who could have heard you . . .
The surgeon took my pulse and found I was feverish. I went to bed without speaking of my adventure and lay dreaming on my pallet, faced with the prospect of dealing with two people . . . and what people, my God! I didn't have a sou and not the slightest doubt that when I woke up the next morning I'd be asked for the agreed daily price.

At this point the master threw his arms round the neck of his valet crying: 'My poor Jacques. What are you going to do? What will become of you? Your situation frightens me.'

JACQUES: Master, reassure yourself. Here I am.

MASTER: I wasn't thinking. I was on to tomorrow, beside you at the surgeon's house at the moment you woke up and they came to ask you for money.

JACQUES: Master, in life one never knows what to rejoice about or what to feel sorry about. Good brings bad after it and bad brings good. We travel in darkness underneath whatever it is that is written up above, all of us equally unreasonable in our hopes, our joys and our afflictions. When I cry I often think that I'm a fool.

MASTER: And what about when you laugh?

JACQUES: I still think that I'm a fool. However, I can't stop myself from crying or from laughing. And that's what makes me angry. I've tried a hundred times . . . I didn't sleep a wink that night.

MASTER: No, no, tell me what it is you've tried.

JACQUES: Not to give a damn about anything. Ah, if only I could have succeeded!

MASTER: What would that have done?

JACQUES: It would have made me free from worry, made me no longer need anything, made me completely master of myself, made me find myself just as well off with my head against a milestone on the side of the road as on a good pillow. I am like that sometimes, but the devil of it is that it doesn't last, and, however hard and rock-steady I am on important occasions, a little contradiction, a mere trifle, will often throw me. It's enough to make me kick myself. I've given up and decided to be as I am and I've realized through thinking about it a little that that is almost the same thing if one adds: 'What does it matter how I am?' It's another kind of resignation, easier to achieve and more convenient to live with.

MASTER: Oh, it's certainly more convenient.

JACQUES: In the morning the surgeon pulled back the curtains around my bed, and said: 'Come along, my friend, I've got a long way to go today, so let's be looking at your knee.'
I replied sorrowfully: 'Surgeon . . . I'm sleepy . . .'
'So much the better. That's a good sign.'
'Leave me to sleep. I don't want to be bandaged.'
'Well, that's no problem. Go back to sleep.'
At that, he shut the curtains, but I didn't sleep. One hour afterwards the surgeon's wife came, drew back my curtains and said: 'Come along, friend, I've brought your sugared toast.'
'Madame,' I replied sorrowfully, 'I don't feel very hungry.'
'Go on, eat it, eat it. It's not going to cost any extra and you won't pay any the less.'
'I don't want to eat.'
'So much the better. The children and I will have it,' and at that she shut my curtains, called her children and they all sat about polishing off my sugared toast.

Reader, if I were to stop for a while here and come back to the story of the man who had only one shirt because he had only one body at a time, I would very much like to know what you would think. Would you think that I had got myself into what Voltaire would call an impasse or more vulgarly a cul-de-sac,[25] and that I didn't know how to get out of it? That I had thrown myself into a tale dreamed up so that I might gain time to look for some way of getting out of the story I've already started?

Well, Reader, you are wrong. I know very well how Jacques got out of these straits, and what I am about to tell you of Gousse – the man with only one shirt at a time because he had only one body at a time – is not made up at all.

One Whitsun, I received a note from Gousse in which he begged me to visit him in a prison where he was being held. While getting dressed I was thinking about his predicament and I supposed that his tailor, his baker, his wine merchant or his landlord, had obtained and executed against him an order of imprisonment.

I arrived there and found him sharing a cell with some rather ominous-looking people. I asked him who they were.

'The old boy over there is a very able man who is extremely knowledge-able in arithmetic and who is trying to make the ledgers which he is copying out tally with his accounts. This is difficult and we've discussed it but I have no doubt that he will succeed.'

'And the other one?'

'He's a fool.'

'How so?'

'A fool who invented a machine for counterfeiting bills. It was a pretty bad machine, a dreadful machine with twenty or more faults.'

'And the third? The one wearing livery and playing the double-bass?'

'He's only here waiting. Tonight or tomorrow morning perhaps – because really his case is nothing – he'll be transferred to Bicêtre.'[26]

'And you?'

'Me? My case is even less important.'

After this reply he got up and put his bonnet on his bed, and his three cell-mates disappeared instantly.

When I had entered I had found Gousse in his dressing-gown seated at a little table plotting geometric figures and working just as happily as he would have done at home. Now we were alone.

'And you, what are you doing here?'

'I'm working, as you can see.'

'But who got you put in here?'

'Me.'

'What do you mean, you?'

'Yes, me, Monsieur.'

'And how did you go about that?'

'The same way I would have gone about having anyone else put in here. I sued myself. I won, and as a result of the sentence I obtained against myself and the warrant which followed I was apprehended and taken here.'

'Are you mad?'

'No, Monsieur. I will tell you the thing as it is.'

'Could you not sue yourself again, win, and by means of another sentence and another warrant get yourself released?'

'No, Monsieur.'

Gousse had a pretty servant girl who served him as other half more often than his own did. This unequal division had somewhat disturbed the domestic peace. Even though there was nothing that was harder to do than unsettle this man, who of all men was least afraid of gossip, he decided to leave his wife and go and live with his servant girl. But his entire fortune consisted of furniture, machines, drawings, tools and other moveable effects. And he preferred leaving his wife naked to going away empty-handed. Consequently this is the project he conceived.

It was to give credit notes to his servant who would pursue him for payment and so obtain the distraint and sale of his goods which would then be transferred from his home in Pont Saint-Michel to the lodgings he proposed to occupy with her.

He was enchanted with the idea, wrote out the notes, had a writ issued against himself and engaged two lawyers. There he was, running from one to the other, prosecuting himself with the utmost vivacity, attacking himself well and defending himself badly. And then he was condemned to pay the penalty prescribed by the law. In his mind's eye he was taking possession of everything there was in the house, but it wasn't quite like that. He was dealing with a very crafty hussy who, instead of obtaining execution on his effects, obtained it on his person, had him arrested and put in prison to such effect that, however bizarre were his enigmatic replies to my questions, they were none the less true.

While I have been telling you these facts – which you have dismissed as a mere tale . . .

– What about the man in livery playing the double-bass?

Reader, I promise you on my word of honour that you won't lose that story . . . but allow me to come back to Jacques and his master.

Jacques and his master had arrived at the place where they were to spend the night. It was late. The gates of the town were closed and they were obliged to stop in the suburb. There I heard an uproar . . .

– You heard? You weren't there . . . It's got nothing to do with you at all.

You're quite right. Well, Jacques . . . His master . . . there was a terrible uproar . . . I saw two men.

– You saw nothing. We're not speaking about you. You weren't even there.

That's true. There were two men at table, talking quite quietly. At the door of the room they were in there stood a woman, hands on hips, pouring out a stream of abuse at them.

Jacques tried to calm the woman down but she paid no more attention to his pacifying remonstrations than the two people she was addressing were paying to her invective.

'Come along, my dear,' said Jacques, 'be patient. Calm down. What's it all about? These gentlemen seem to be decent enough to me.'

'Decent! Them! They're brutes, people without pity, humanity or any feeling. Ah! And what harm did poor Nicole do to them for them to treat her so badly? She'll probably be crippled for the rest of her life.'

'Perhaps the injury is not as bad as you believe.'

'It was a frightful blow, I tell you. She'll be crippled.'

'You'll have to wait and see. Someone must get the doctor.'

'Someone's already gone.'

'Put her to bed.'

'She's already in bed. And she's crying enough to break anyone's heart . . . My poor Nicole!'

In the midst of these lamentations a bell rang somewhere else and a voice called: 'Hostess, some wine.'

'Coming,' she replied.

'Hostess, bring some sheets.'

'Coming.'

'What about the cutlets and the duck?'

'Coming.'

'Bring me something to drink. Bring me a chamber-pot.'

'Coming, coming.'

And from another corner of the inn a frantic man was shouting: 'Damn you, you demented chatterbox, what are you interfering for? Have you decided to make me wait till tomorrow? Jacques? Jacques?'

The hostess, who had recovered a little from her sorrow and her anger, said to Jacques: 'Monsieur, you may leave me now. You've been too kind.'

'Jacques? Jacques?'

'Go to him quickly. Ah, if you only knew the misfortunes of that poor creature.'

'Jacques? Jacques?'

'Go on. I think that's your master calling you.'

'Jacques? Jacques?'

Jacques' master was indeed shouting for him. He had undressed all by himself. He was dying of hunger and getting extremely impatient at not being served. Jacques went on up followed a moment afterwards by the innkeeper's wife, who looked really miserable.

'A thousand pardons, Monsieur,' she said to Jacques' master, 'but it is just that there are sometimes things in life which are hard to swallow. What do you want? I have chickens, pigeons, excellent saddle of hare, rabbits – this is a very good area for rabbits – perhaps you'd prefer a river fowl?'

Jacques ordered his master's supper as if it were for him, as he normally did. It was served and, while he was eating, his master asked Jacques: 'What the devil were you doing down there?'

JACQUES: Perhaps some good, perhaps some bad, who can tell?

MASTER: And exactly what good or bad were you doing down there?

JACQUES: I was stopping that woman from getting herself beaten up by two men who are down there and who have at the very least broken her servant's arm.

MASTER: Perhaps it would have done her some good to get beaten up.

JACQUES: For ten reasons, each of them better than the previous, one of the best things that has ever happened to me in my life – to me who speaks to you now . . .

MASTER: Is to have been beaten up? . . . Give me something to drink.

JACQUES: Yes, master, beaten up. Beaten up on the high road at night on my way back from the village as I have told you after having committed what was in my opinion the folly or in your opinion the good deed of giving away my money.

MASTER: I remember . . . Give me something to drink. What was the cause of the quarrel you were pacifying downstairs that the innkeeper's wife's servant or daughter should be so badly treated?

JACQUES: For the life of me, I don't know.

MASTER: You don't know what it was about and you interfere! Jacques, that's not prudent, it's not just, it's against the principles of . . . Give me something to drink.

JACQUES: Principles are only rules which some people lay down for other people to observe. I think in one way but I am unable to stop myself acting in another. All sermons are like the preamble to the king's edicts. All preachers want people to practise what they preach because we might find ourselves better off and they certainly will be. Virtue . . .

MASTER: Virtue, Jacques, is a good thing. Both the good and the bad speak well of it . . . Give me something to drink.

JACQUES: Because they both profit from it.

MASTER: And how was it such good fortune for you to be beaten up?

JACQUES: It is late. You've eaten well and so have I. We are both tired. It would be better for us, believe me, if we went to bed.

MASTER: We can't do that. The innkeeper's wife still has something to bring us. While we're waiting let's go back to the story of your loves.

JACQUES: Where was I? I beg you, Master, on this occasion and on all future ones put me back on the right track.

MASTER: I'll see to that. And to begin my duties as prompter, you are in your bed, with no money, at a loss to know what to do while the surgeon's wife and her children are eating your sugared toast.

JACQUES: At that moment a carriage drew up outside the door of the house and a valet came in and asked: 'Does a poor man lodge here, a soldier who walks with a crutch and who came back last night from the next village?'
'Yes,' replied the surgeon's wife, 'what do you want him for?'
'To put him in this carriage and take him away with us.'
'He's in that bed. Draw back the curtains and speak to him.'

Jacques had got to this point when their hostess came in and asked: 'What do you want for dessert?'

MASTER: Whatever you've got.

Without giving herself the trouble of going downstairs their hostess shouted from their room: 'Nanon, bring some fruit, biscuits, jams.'
On hearing the name Nanon, Jacques said to himself: 'Ah! It was her

daughter who was maltreated. One could get angry for less than that.'
And his master said to their hostess: 'You were very angry just now.'

HOSTESS: And who wouldn't get angry? The poor creature hadn't done anything to them. She'd hardly gone into their room when I heard her start crying – such cries . . . Thank God I'm a little reassured now. The surgeon says it's nothing but she's got two huge bruises, one on her head, the other on her shoulder.

MASTER: Have you had her long?

HOSTESS: A fortnight at the most. She was abandoned at the nearby staging-post.

MASTER: What, abandoned!

HOSTESS: Alas, yes. There are some people whose hearts are harder than stone. She almost drowned trying to cross the river which runs near here. She arrived here by a miracle and I took her in out of charity.

MASTER: How old is she?

HOSTESS: I think a little more than a year and a half.

At this point Jacques burst out laughing and exclaimed: 'Is it a dog?'

HOSTESS: The prettiest animal in the world. I wouldn't give my poor Nicole away for ten louis. Poor Nicole!

MASTER: Madame has a kind heart.

HOSTESS: I have indeed. I look after my animals and my people.

MASTER: Good for you. But who are these people who treated your Nicole so badly?

HOSTESS: Two bourgeois from the next town. They're whispering to each other non-stop and they think that people don't know what they're saying, and nobody knows what they're doing. They haven't been here for more than three hours and there's not a single bit of their business that I don't know about. It's an amusing story and if you're in as little hurry to go to bed as I am I'll tell you everything exactly as their servant told my servant, who, by coincidence, comes from the same province and who told my husband who told me. The mother-in-law of the younger one passed through here not more than three months ago. She was going, against her will, to a convent in the provinces where she didn't last long. She's dead and that's why our two young men are in mourning . . .

But look at me, I'm telling their story already. Good-night, Messieurs, and sleep well . . . Was the wine to your liking?

MASTER: Very good.

HOSTESS: And were you happy with your supper?

MASTER: Very happy. Your spinach was a bit salty.

HOSTESS: I'm sometimes a little heavy-handed.[27] You'll be well put up here, and in clean sheets. We never use them twice here.

Having said this, the innkeeper's wife withdrew, and Jacques and his master went to bed, laughing at the misunderstanding which had made them take a dog for the daughter or servant of the house and at their hostess's passion for a stray dog which she had only had for a fortnight. As Jacques tied up the head-band of his master's nightcap, he reflected on this: 'I bet you that out of all the things living in this inn that woman only loves her Nicole.'

His master replied: 'That's as may be, Jacques, but let's go to sleep.'

While Jacques and his master are sleeping I shall fulfil my promise by telling you, or rather by having M. Gousse tell you, the story of the man in prison scraping away at the double-bass.

'The third man', he said to me . . .

. . . is the steward of an important house. He fell in love with the wife of a pastry-cook in the rue de l'Université. The pastry-cook was a decent sort of fellow who watched more carefully over his oven than his wife's conduct. It wasn't so much his jealousy as his zeal which hindered our two lovers. And how did they go about removing this restriction? The steward showed his master a petition where the pastry-cook was represented as a man of low morals, a drunkard who never left the tavern, a brute who beat his wife who was the best and most unfortunate of wives. On the strength of this petition he managed to obtain an order under the King's private seal which forfeited the husband's freedom and this was put in the hands of a bailiff for execution without delay.[28]

It happened by chance that this bailiff was the pastry-cook's friend – they used occasionally to go to the tavern together. The pastry-cook would provide some of his pastries and the bailiff would buy the wine. This time the bailiff, carrying the sealed order of the King, went to his friend's door and signalled to him in the usual way. When they were both eating their pastries and washing them down with wine the bailiff asked his friend how business was.

'Very good.'

'No trouble at all?'

'None.'

Had he any enemies?

Not that he knew of.

How were things with his relations? His neighbours? His wife?

'Very friendly. Peaceful.'

'Well, how does it happen that I've got an order to arrest you? If I did my duty I'd put my hand on your collar, there would be a carriage ready and waiting and I would take you to the place specified in the sealed order of the King? Here, read it.'

The pastry-cook read it and turned white.

The bailiff said to him: 'Don't worry about it. Let's just work out together the best thing we can do for my safety and for yours. Is there anyone who goes to your shop frequently?'

'No one.'

'Your wife is pretty and a flirt.'

'I let her do what she wants.'

'Nobody's after her?'

'My God, no, unless it's a certain steward who comes sometimes and holds her hands and speaks nonsense in her ear. But it's in my shop, in front of me, in the presence of my lads, and I don't think anything's going on between them which is not decent and above board.'

'You're a good man.'

'Maybe I am but it's always the best course to believe one's wife to be honest, and that's what I do.'

'And this steward? Whose is he?'

'He's M. de Saint-Florentin's.'[29]

'And from whose offices do you think the sealed order of the King came?'

'From M. de Saint-Florentin's perhaps?'

'You said it.'

'Oh . . . eat my pastries, make love to my wife, and have me locked up, that's too evil, and I can't believe it.'

'You're a trusting sort. How's your wife been over the last few days?'

'More sad than happy.'

'And the steward, is it long since you've seen him?'

'Yesterday, I think . . . yes, it was yesterday.'

'Did you notice anything?'

'I notice very little. But it seemed to me that when they said goodbye they were making signs with their heads as if one were saying yes and the other no.'

'Whose head was saying yes?'

'The steward's.'

'Either they're both innocent or they're both accomplices. Listen, my friend, don't go back to your house. Escape to some safe place, to the temple or the abbey, wherever you want. In the meantime let me take care of it. Above all remember . . .'

'Not to show myself and to keep quiet.'

'That's right.'

At this very moment the pastry-cook's house was surrounded by spies, and police informers under all sorts of disguises went up to the pastry-cook's wife to ask for her husband. To the first she said he was ill, to the second that he had left for a celebration and to a third for a wedding. When would he be back? She didn't know.

On the third day at two o'clock in the morning, the bailiff was warned that a man whose face was hidden by his cloak had been seen quietly opening the street door and slipping quietly inside the pastry-cook's house. Immediately the bailiff, accompanied by a commissioner of police, a locksmith, a hackney carriage, and a few constables, went to the scene. They picked the lock, and the bailiff and the commissioner went quietly upstairs. They knocked on the door of the pastry-cook's wife's bedroom: no reply. They knocked again: still no reply. They knocked a third time and a voice from inside asked who was there.

'Open up.'

'Who is it?'

'Open up in the name of the King.'

'Good,' said the steward to the pastry-cook's wife with whom he was sleeping, 'there's nothing to worry about. It's the bailiff come to execute his order. Open up and I'll identify myself, he'll go away and that'll be the end of that.'

The pastry-cook's wife, in her nightshirt, opened up and got back into bed. The bailiff asked: 'Where is your husband?'

'He's not here,' the pastry-cook's wife replied.

The bailiff pulled back the curtains and asked: 'Who's that there, then?'

The steward replied: 'It's me. I'm M. de Saint-Florentin's steward.'

'You're lying. You're the pastry-cook, because the pastry-cook is the person who sleeps with the pastry-cook's wife. Get up, put your clothes on and follow me.'

He had to obey and so they brought him here. When the Minister had been told of his steward's villainy he approved of the bailiff's conduct. And the bailiff will be returning here at nightfall to take him away and transfer him to Bicêtre where, thanks to the economy of the prison governors, he will eat his quarter pound of stale bread, his scrap of meat and scrape away on his double-bass from morning to night.

If I were also to rest my head on the pillow while waiting for Jacques and his master to wake up, what would you think?

The next day Jacques got up early, put his nose to the window to see what the weather was like, saw it was abominable and went back to bed again leaving his master and me to sleep for as long as we wanted.

Jacques, his master and the other travellers who had stopped at the same resting-place thought that the sky would clear at noon. It did nothing of the sort, and since the rain from the storm had swelled the stream which separated the suburb from the town to such an extent that it would have been dangerous to cross it, everyone travelling in that direction decided to lose a day and wait. Some struck up conversations, others went back and forth, putting their noses outside to look at the sky and then coming back in swearing and stamping. Several set to drinking and talking about politics. Many gambled. The rest occupied themselves in smoking, sleeping and doing nothing.

The master said to Jacques: 'I hope that Jacques will carry on the story of his loves and that Heaven which wants me to have the satisfaction of hearing the end will detain us here with this bad weather.'

JACQUES: Heaven which wants! We never know what Heaven wants or doesn't want, and perhaps Heaven doesn't even know itself. My poor Captain, who is no longer, told me that a hundred times, and the longer I've lived the more I've realized he was right . . . Over to you, Master . . .

MASTER: I understand. You'd got up to the carriage and the valet whom the surgeon's wife had told to open the curtain and speak to you.

JACQUES: The valet came over to my bed and said to me: 'Come along, friend. On your feet. Get dressed and then we'll go.'

I replied to him from under the bedclothes which I had pulled over my head without seeing or being seen: 'Friend, go away and let me sleep.'

The valet told me that he had his master's orders which he had to carry out.

'And tell me, has your master, who gives orders to a man he doesn't know, given orders to pay what I owe here?'

'That's all taken care of. Hurry up. Everybody's waiting for you in the château and I guarantee you'll be better off there than you are here if the curiosity they all have about you is anything to go by.'

I let him persuade me. I got up and dressed and he took me by the arm. I had said goodbye to the surgeon's wife and I was about to get into the carriage when she came up to me, pulled me by the sleeve, and asked me to go over into the corner of the room, because she had something she wanted to say to me.

'Now, my friend,' she said, 'you haven't got any complaints about us, have you? The surgeon saved your leg, and, as for me, I've served you well and I hope you won't forget that in the château.'

'What could I do for you there?'

'Ask for my husband to come and bandage you. There are a lot of people there. It's the best practice in the area. The lord of the château is a generous man and pays well. It's simply a question of you doing that and we would make our fortune. My husband's tried several times to get in there, but to no avail.'

'But, Madame, is there not a surgeon at the château?'

'Certainly.'

'And if this other surgeon were your husband, would you be happy if someone was to do him a bad turn and get him thrown out?'

'This surgeon is a man to whom you owe nothing and I think you owe something to my husband. If you are walking around on two legs now it's only because of what he's done.'

'And because your husband's done me some good, you want me to do harm to someone else! Now, if the position were vacant . . .'

Jacques was about to continue when their hostess came in carrying Nicole, who was wearing a coat, kissing her, pitying her and caressing and speaking to her as if she were a child: 'My poor Nicole! She only cried once all night. And you, Messieurs, did you sleep well?'

MASTER: Very well.

HOSTESS: The weather's closed in on all sides.

JACQUES: We're quite put out about that.

HOSTESS: Are you gentlemen going far?

JACQUES: We don't know.

HOSTESS: Are you gentlemen following someone?

JACQUES: We're not following anyone.

HOSTESS: Perhaps you gentlemen stop and go according to the business you have along the way.

JACQUES: We have none.

HOSTESS: You are travelling for pleasure, perhaps?

JACQUES: Or for our pains.

HOSTESS: I hope it's the former.

JACQUES: Your hopes won't make a scrap of difference. It will be however it is written up above.

HOSTESS: Oh! . . . Is it a wedding?

JACQUES: Perhaps it is, perhaps it isn't.

HOSTESS: Messieurs, be careful. That man downstairs who treated my poor Nicole so badly made the most ridiculous marriage. Come along, my poor little animal, come here and let me kiss you. I promise you it won't happen again. Just look at the way she's shaking all over.

MASTER: And what was so unusual about the man's marriage?

At this question of Jacques' master the hostess said: 'I hear noise downstairs. I must go and give my orders and then I'll come back and tell you about it.'

Her husband, who was tired of calling out 'Wife! wife!', came up followed by a neighbour whom he hadn't seen.

He said to his wife, 'What the devil are you doing here?' and then to his acquaintance, 'Hello, old chap, have you brought me some money?'

'No, my friend, you know well I haven't got any.'

'You haven't got any? I'll make some soon enough with your plough, your horses, your oxen and your bed. Hey, you scoundrel.'

'I am not a scoundrel.'

'What are you, then? You're living in abject poverty. You don't even know how you're going to get the seed to sow your fields. Your landlord's tired of advancing you money and won't lend any more. So you come to me, and this woman, this damned gossip who's the cause of all of the follies of my life, persuades me to lend to you. I lend you money, you promise to pay me back and you fail me ten times. Oh! I promise you I won't let you down! Get out of here! Get out!'

Jacques and his master were getting ready to intercede for the poor devil but the hostess put her finger on her lips and signalled them to keep quiet.

HOST: Get out of here!

PEASANT: Everything you say is true and it's also true that the bailiffs are at my house and in a short time from now we'll be reduced to begging, my daughter, my son and I.

HOST: That's what you deserve. What have you come here for this morning? I had to stop bottling my wine, come up out of the cellar, and you weren't here when you should have been. Get out of here, I tell you.

PEASANT: Friend, I did come, but I was afraid of the reception I'd get and now I'm off again.

HOST: Good idea.

PEASANT: And now my poor little Marguerite who's so pretty and well behaved will have to go into service in Paris.

HOST: In service in Paris! You want to ruin her, do you?

PEASANT: It's not me that wants it, it's the hard-hearted man I'm speaking to.

HOST: Me, hard-hearted? I'm nothing of the sort. I never was that, and you know it well.

PEASANT: I no longer have enough money to feed my daughter or my son. My daughter will go into service. My son will join up.

HOST: And it's me who will be the cause of that? Well, it's not going to happen. You're a cruel man. As long as I live, you'll be my cross. Now let's see what we can do for you.

PEASANT: You can do nothing for me. I'm heartbroken that I owe you anything, and I'll never again owe you anything. You do more harm with your insults than you do good with your deeds. If I had the money I'd throw it in your face, but I haven't got it so my daughter will become whatever God pleases and my son will get himself killed if necessary. As for me I'll go begging but it won't be at your door. I'll not incur any more obligations towards such a wicked man as you. Make sure you get yourself paid out of my oxen and horses and implements – and much good may it do you. You were born to make people ungrateful and I don't want to be ungrateful. Goodbye for ever.

HOST: Wife! He's going away. Stop him!

HOSTESS: Come here, friend, let's try and find a way to help you.

PEASANT: I don't want any of his help. It costs too much.

The host kept muttering to his wife: 'Don't let him go, stop him. His daughter in Paris! His son in the army! Him at the door of the parish! I won't have it.'

However, his wife's efforts were useless. The peasant had integrity and didn't want to take anything, and it took four people to stop him from leaving. The innkeeper, tears in his eyes, turned towards Jacques and his master and said: 'Messieurs, try to make him change his mind.'

Jacques and his master intervened and everybody was beseeching the peasant at the same time. If ever I saw . . .

– If ever you saw? But you weren't there. You mean if ever anyone saw . . .

Oh well, all right. If ever anybody saw a man become put out by a refusal and then become enraptured that somebody would take his money, it was this innkeeper. He kissed his wife, kissed Jacques and his master, and shouted: 'Come on, quickly, let's get those damned bailiffs out of his house.'

PEASANT: But you must agree that . . .

HOST: I agree that I spoil everything, but what do you want, my friend? You see me as I am. Nature made me the hardest-hearted man and the softest-hearted man. I don't know either how to give or how to refuse.

PEASANT: Could you not be different?

HOST: I am at the age when hardly anyone corrects themselves, but if the very first people who came to me for help had snubbed me as you have just done, perhaps I would have been a better man. Friend, I thank you for your lesson. Perhaps I will benefit from it . . . Wife, go quickly, go down and give him whatever he needs . . . Devil take it, hurry up, will you, damn it, hurry up, you're so . . . Woman, I beseech you to hurry up a bit and not keep him waiting. And after that, you can come straight back to these gentlemen with whom you seem to get on so well.

The wife and the peasant went down. Their host stayed for a moment and when he had gone away Jacques said to his master: 'What a peculiar man! And what does our Destiny, which sent bad weather to delay us here so that you could hear about my love life, hold in store for us now, I wonder?'

His master, who was stretched out in his armchair yawning and tapping his snuff-box, replied: 'Jacques, we have more than one day to live together, unless . . .'

JACQUES: What you are saying is that today our Destiny is for me to keep my mouth shut, or, to put it another way, for our hostess to speak. She's a chatterbox and that will obviously suit her. Let her speak, then!

MASTER: You're getting cross.

JACQUES: Well, I like to talk too.

MASTER: Your turn will come.

JACQUES: Or not come.

I know what you are thinking, Reader, you are thinking that this is the real denouement of the *Rough Diamond*.[30] I believe it is. If I had been the author I would have introduced into this little work a character whom one would have taken as being episodic, but who would, in fact, not have been. This character would have appeared a few times, and some motive would have been given for his appearances. The first time he would have come to ask for grace, but the fear of a hostile welcome would have made him leave before the arrival of Géronte. Pressed by the bailiffs breaking into his house, the second time he would have had the courage to wait for Géronte, but Géronte would have refused to see him. Eventually I would have brought him on at the denouement, where he would have played the same role the peasant did with the innkeeper. Like the peasant he would have had a daughter whom he was going to place with a dressmaker, a son whom he was going to withdraw from school and send into service, and as for him, he would have decided to beg until he became tired of living. We would have seen the Rough Diamond at the feet of this man. We would have heard the Rough Diamond rebuked because he merited it. He would have been obliged to appeal to his whole family around him in order to move his debtor to pity to persuade him to accept fresh help. The Rough Diamond would have been punished. He would have promised to correct himself but at this very moment he would revert to his true character and, losing patience with the characters on stage, who would, by now, be exchanging civilities in order to go back into the house, he would have said brusquely: 'May the devil take these damned . . .' but he would have stopped dead in the middle of the word, and in a softer tone he would have said to his nieces: 'Come along, girls, take my hand and we'll go . . .'

— And in order that this character should be better integrated into the play, you would have made this character a protégé of Géronte's nephew?

Very good.

— And it would have been at the nephew's request that the uncle lent him money?

Perfect.

— And this loan would have been a bone of contention between uncle and nephew?

Exactly that.

— And the denouement of this agreeable play, would it not have been a repeat with the whole family in chorus of what he had previously said with each of them individually?

You're right.

— Well then, if ever I meet Monsieur Goldoni I will repeat the scene in the inn to him.

You would do well there. He's got more than enough talent to make something of it.

The hostess came back, still carrying Nicole in her arms, and said: 'I hope to give you a good dinner. The poacher's just come, which means the squire's gamekeeper will not be far behind', and as she was speaking she took a chair, 'One should always be suspicious of servants. Masters do not have a worse enemy.'

JACQUES: Madame, you don't know what you're talking about. There are good ones and bad ones and it might be that there are more good valets than good masters.

MASTER: Jacques, you are not being very circumspect and are committing precisely the same indiscretion which shocked you.

JACQUES: It's just that masters . . .

MASTER: It's just that valets . . .

Well now, Reader! What is there to stop me from starting a violent quarrel between these three characters, from having the innkeeper's wife taken by the shoulders and thrown out of the room by Jacques, from having Jacques taken by the shoulders and thrown outside by his master, from sending one off in one direction and the other in a different one so that you wouldn't hear either the innkeeper's wife's story or the rest of the story of Jacques' love life? But don't worry, I will do no such thing. And so the innkeeper's wife continued: 'It must be admitted that if there are a lot of very wicked men there are also a lot of very wicked women.'

JACQUES: And one never has to go too far to find one . . .

HOSTESS: What are you interfering for? I am a woman and entitled to say whatever I like about women without your approval.

JACQUES: My approval's worth just as much as another's.

HOSTESS: Monsieur, you have a valet who thinks he knows about everything and is not showing you proper respect. I have valets too, but I would like them to get it into their heads . . .

MASTER: Jacques, shut up and let Madame speak.

The innkeeper's wife, encouraged by Jacques' master's words, squared up to Jacques, put her hands on her hips, forgot that she was holding Nicole, let go and there was Nicole on the floor, bruised and struggling in her blanket, barking her head off, and their hostess adding her cries to Nicole's barking and Jacques adding his peals of laughter to the barking of Nicole and the cries of their hostess and Jacques' master opening his snuff-box, taking his pinch of snuff, and unable to suppress a smile. The whole inn was now in tumult.

'Nánon, Nanon, quickly, quickly, bring me the spirit bottle. My poor Nicole's dead! Undress her . . . Oh, you're so clumsy.'

'I'm doing my best.'

'How she's crying. Get out of the way. Let me do it. She's dead. That's right, laugh, you big booby, I suppose you think it's a laughing matter. My poor Nicole is dead!'

'No, Madame. I think she'll come out of it. Look, she's moving . . .'

And Nanon rubbed brandy into the dog's nose and made her swallow some and the hostess was wailing and storming about impertinent valets and Nanon was saying: 'Look, Madame, she's opening her eyes. There she is, looking at you.'

'Poor beast. How expressive she is. Who could fail to be moved by her?'

'Madame, stroke her a little, say something to her.'

'Come here, my poor Nicole. Cry, my baby. Cry if it makes you feel better. There's a Destiny for animals just the same as for people. It sends happiness to idlers, unpleasant people, brawlers and gluttons and misery to the best creature in the world.'

'Madame is perfectly right. There's no justice in the world.'

'Be quiet. Put her clothes back on and put her under my pillow. And remember, if she makes the slightest cry you'll answer to me for it. Come here, my poor creature, and let me kiss you before she takes you away. Bring her here, then, you silly girl. Ah, dogs, they're so good, they're worth more . . .'

JACQUES: Than father, mother, sisters, children, valets, husbands . . .

HOSTESS: Yes, that's right. There's nothing to laugh at. They're perfectly innocent, faithful, never do any harm, while all those others . . .

JACQUES: Long live dogs! There's nothing more perfect under God's heaven.

HOSTESS: If there is anything more perfect it certainly isn't man. I wish you knew the carpenter's dog. He's my Nicole's lover. There's not one amongst the lot of you whom he wouldn't make blush with shame. He comes as soon as day breaks, from more than a league away, to station himself under this window. And his sighs, they'd break anyone's heart. No matter what the weather is like he stays there. The rain falls down on him. He sinks into the mud so that you can hardly see his ears and the end of his nose. Would you do so much for the woman you loved best?

MASTER: That's very gallant.

JACQUES: One might also ask, where is the woman as worthy of this treatment as your Nicole?

The innkeeper's wife's passion for animals was not, however, her dominant passion. As you might imagine, her dominant passion was talking. The more that people found pleasure and were patient in listening to her, the more worthy they were in her eyes. Consequently she didn't have to be asked to carry on with the interrupted story of the strange marriage. The only condition she imposed was that Jacques shut up. His master promised silence on behalf of Jacques. Jacques stretched himself out nonchalantly in the corner, his eyes shut, hat pulled down over his ears and his back half-turned to their hostess.

His master coughed, spat, blew his nose, took out his watch, looked at the time, took out his snuff-box, tapped its lid and took a pinch of snuff while their hostess prepared to indulge in the delicious pleasure of holding forth.

She was about to start when she heard her dog cry: 'Nanon, go and see to the poor animal . . . That disturbed me. I don't know where I'd got to.'

JACQUES: You haven't said anything yet.

HOSTESS: Those two men with whom I was arguing about Nicole when you arrived, Monsieur.

JACQUES: Say – Messieurs.

HOSTESS: Why?

JACQUES: Because up to now we've been treated politely and I've got used to it. My master calls me Jacques, but others call me – Monsieur Jacques.

HOSTESS: I'm not going to call you Jacques or Monsieur Jacques. I'm not speaking to you.

'Madame! The bill for number five!'
'Have a look on the chimney breast.'

These two men are worthy gentlemen. They've come from Paris and are going to the elder's land.

JACQUES: How do you know that?

HOSTESS: They said so.

JACQUES: Fine explanation.

His master made a sign to the innkeeper's wife which led her to understand that Jacques' brain was a little scrambled. She replied to the master's sign with a sympathetic movement of the shoulders and added: 'At his age. What a terrible shame.'

JACQUES: It's a terrible shame never to know where one is going.

HOSTESS: The elder of the two is called the Marquis des Arcis. He used to be a man of pleasure, very likeable, although he is sceptical about feminine virtue.

JACQUES: He's right.

HOSTESS: Monsieur Jacques, you're interrupting me.

JACQUES: Madame, hostess of the Grand-Cerf, I'm not talking to you.

HOSTESS: The Marquis managed, however, to find one woman peculiar enough to resist his advances. Her name was Mme de La Pommeraye. She was a widow of high moral character, high birth, good breeding, wealth and haughtiness. Monsieur des Arcis broke off with all his other acquaintances and devoted himself exclusively to Mme de La Pommeraye. He courted her with the greatest possible assiduity, attempted by every sacrifice imaginable to show her that he loved her and even proposed to her. But this woman had been so unhappy with a first husband that she . . .

'Madame!'
'What is it?'
'The key to the oat bin?'
'See if it's on the nail. If it's not there look in the lock.'

. . . that she would rather expose herself to any kind of misery than the danger of a second marriage.

JACQUES: Ah! If that had been written up above!

HOSTESS: The lady led a very quiet life. The Marquis was an old friend of her husband's. He had been a visitor to the house and she continued to receive him. If one could overlook in him his unrestrained passion for love affairs he was what one would call a man of honour. The Marquis' unremitting pursuit backed up by his personal qualities, his youth, good looks, what seemed to be the truest of passions, her solitude, her longing for affection, in a word everything that makes us women yield to the wishes of men . . .

'Madame!'
'What is it?'
'The mail.'
'Put it in the green room and distribute it as usual.'

. . . had its effect, and Mme de La Pommeraye, after having resisted both the Marquis and herself for several months and having exacted from him the most solemn of vows, as is customary, finally made him the happiest of men, whose destiny would have been most sweet had he only been able to retain for the Marquise those feelings which he had sworn he had felt for her and which she felt for him. I tell you, Monsieur, it is only women who know how to love. Men don't know the first thing . . .

'Madame?'
'What is it?'

'The friar almoner.'

'Give him twelve sous for these gentlemen here, six sous for me, and let him go round the other rooms . . .'

. . . after a few years the Marquis began to find Mme de La Pommeraye's life too uneventful. He suggested that she venture out into society. She did so. Then he suggested that she receive a few ladies and a few gentlemen. She did so. He suggested that she give a dinner party and she did so. Little by little he went one day, two days, without seeing her. He would miss the dinner parties he had arranged. Gradually he shortened his visits. He had other business which needed seeing to. When he arrived he would say one word, stretch himself out in an armchair, pick up a pamphlet, and throw it down again, talk to her dog, or go to sleep. In the evenings his health, which was becoming wretched, apparently required that he retire early. This was the advice of Tronchin.[31]

'He's a great man, that Tronchin,' he would say, 'and by God I haven't the slightest doubt he will save our friend's life which the other doctors have despaired of.'

And as he was speaking he would take his hat and his cane and go away, sometimes forgetting to kiss her. Madame de La Pommeraye . . .

'Madame!'

'What is it?'

'The cooper.'

'Send him down to the cellar and have him check the two barrels in the corner . . .'

. . . Madame de La Pommeraye suspected that she was no longer loved. She had to find out for certain, and this is how she went . . .

'Madame!'

'Coming, coming!'

Tired of these interruptions the hostess went back downstairs and apparently found a way to put an end to them.

One day after lunch she said to the Marquis: 'My friend, you're dreaming.'

'You are dreaming too, Marquise.'

'Yes, and sad dreams at that.'

'What's wrong with you?'

'Nothing.'

'That's not the truth. Come along, Marquise,' he said yawning, 'tell me about it. It will relieve your boredom and mine.'

'Are you bored?'

'No, it's just that there are some days . . .'

'When you get bored.'

'You're wrong, my friend. I swear to you you're wrong. It's just that there are some days . . . Well, I don't exactly know what causes it.'

'My friend, I have been tempted to tell you something for a long time now, but I am afraid to hurt you.'

'You hurt me?'

'Perhaps, but as heaven is witness to my innocence . . .'

'Madame! Madame! Madame!'

'Whoever or whatever it is I've absolutely forbidden you to call me. Call my husband.'

'He's not here.'

'Excuse me, Messieurs, I'll be with you again in a moment.'

And now the hostess has gone downstairs, come back up, and is well into her story.

HOSTESS: 'It happened without my willing it, or even being aware of it, by a curse that the whole human race must be subject to since I myself am not free from it.'

'Ah! It's that you . . . I was afraid . . . What is it?'

'Marquis, it's . . . I'm heartbroken and I will break your heart and all things considered it would be better if I kept quiet.'

'No, my friend, speak. Do you have a secret for me in the bottom of your heart? Wasn't it the first thing we agreed that we would open up our souls to each other without reserve?'

'That is true, and that is what is worrying me. That is a reproach which is greater than the one I have to make myself. Can you not see that I am no longer so happy? I have lost my appetite. I only eat and drink because I make myself. I cannot sleep. Our most intimate gatherings displease me. At night I question myself and ask: Is he any the less kind? No. Have you anything to complain about? No. Do you have to reproach him for suspect liaisons? No. Has his love for you diminished? No. How is it that if your friend is the same your heart has changed? For it has and you can't hide the fact. You no longer await him with the same impatience. You no longer feel the same pleasure in seeing him, or experience the same anxiety when he is late. That tender pleasure, to hear the noise of his carriage, to hear his name announced, to see him finally appear – you no longer feel any of it.'

'What! Madame!'

Then the Marquise de La Pommeraye covered her eyes, lowered her head and was quiet for a moment, after which she added: 'Marquis, I expected the full scale of your astonishment and the bitter words that you are going to say to me. Marquis! Spare me . . . No, do not spare me. Say them to me. I will resign myself to listening because I deserve them. Yes, my dear Marquis, it is true . . . yes, I am . . . But is it not bad enough that the thing should have happened at all without my adding to it the shame and the scorn of being false and hiding it from you? You are the same but your friend has changed. She reveres you and respects you as much as and more than ever but . . . but a woman as accustomed as she is to examine carefully everything that happens even in the most secret parts of her heart, and to avoid all self-deception, such a woman cannot hide the fact that there is no love in her heart. The discovery is horrifying but is not any the less real. Me, the Marquise de La Pommeraye, inconstant, fickle . . . Marquis, fly into a rage, look for the most odious of names. I've called myself them all already. Call me them. I will accept them, all of them, except that of false woman, which you will spare me, I hope, because, in all truth, I am not that.'

'Wife?'

'What is it?'

'Nothing.'

'There's never a moment's rest in this house . . . even on days when there's hardly anyone here and you would think there was nothing to do. Oh, a woman in my position is not to be envied, especially with a fool of a husband like that . . .'

When she had finished Mme de La Pommeraye threw herself into her armchair and started crying. The Marquis rushed to her knees.

'You are a charming woman, an adorable woman, a woman unlike any other. Your candour and your honesty confound me and ought to make me die of shame. Ah, how vastly superior you are to me at this moment. How noble I find you and how mean I perceive myself. You have spoken first and yet it is I who was guilty first. My friend, your sincerity inspires me, and I would be a monster if it did not, and I admit that what you have said of your feelings applies word for word to mine. Everything that you have said to yourself I have said to myself, but I have kept quiet and suffered in silence. I don't know when I would have had the courage to speak.'

'Is that true, my friend?'

'Nothing is truer. It only remains for us to congratulate ourselves on having both at the same time lost that fragile illusory emotion which united us.'

'Indeed. What misfortune if my love had lasted when yours was dead.'

'Or if it were in me that it died first.'

'You are right, I can feel it.'

'Never have you seemed to me so kind, so beautiful, as in this moment, and if past experience did not make me more cautious I would believe I loved you more than ever.'

As he spoke the Marquis took her hands and kissed them.

'Wife!'

'What is it?'

'The straw chandler.'

'Look in the register.'

'Where is it? . . . It's all right, I've got it.'

Madame de La Pommeraye concealed the fierce displeasure which burned inside her, spoke again and said to the Marquis: 'Marquis, what is to become of us?'

'We haven't deluded ourselves. You deserve the right to all my esteem and I do not think that I have lost every right to yours. We shall continue to see each other and enjoy the intimacy of the most tender friendship. We will have spared ourselves all those minor irritations, all those petty betrayals, all those reproaches, all that bad temper, all those things that normally mark a dying love affair and we would be quite unique. You will recover all your freedom and give me back mine. We will go out in society. You will tell me all about your conquests, and I will hide nothing of mine from you – if I make any, which I doubt very much, because you have made me difficult to please. It will be delightful! You will help me with your advice, and I will not refuse you mine in difficult circumstances, or when you believe you need it. Who knows what might happen?'

JACQUES: Nobody.

'It is even possible, Marquise, that the longer I am away, the more you will gain by comparison and I will return to you more passionate, more tender, more than ever convinced that Mme de La Pommeraye is the only woman with whom I could be happy. After my return it is almost certain that I would stay with you until the end of my life.'

'What if you did not find me on your return? After all, Marquis, life is not always fair and it is not impossible that I might develop a taste, a fancy or even a passion for someone who is not your equal.'

'I certainly would be very unhappy, but I couldn't complain except that Fate should have separated us when we were united and brought us back together when we could no longer be together . . .'

After this conversation they started to moralize on the inconstancy of the human heart, the frivolity of oaths, of marriage vows . . .

'Madame!'

'What is it?'

'The coach!'

'Messieurs,' said the hostess, 'I must leave you. This evening after I've finished my work I'll come back and finish the story if you're interested.'

'Madame!'

'Wife!'

'Hostess!'

'Coming, coming.'

When the hostess had gone the master said to his valet: 'Did you notice anything, Jacques?'

JACQUES: What?

MASTER: This woman tells a story much better than an innkeeper's wife ought to.

JACQUES: That is true. The constant interruptions from the people of the house annoyed me several times.

MASTER: And me too.

And you, Reader, speak without dissimulation, because, as you can see, we have struck a rich vein of honesty. Would you like us to leave our elegant and prolix gossip of a hostess here and come back to Jacques' loves? I don't mind which. When this woman comes back up again, that chatterbox Jacques couldn't ask for better than to take over her part and shut the door in her face. All he would have to do would be to shout through the keyhole: 'Good night, Madame. My master is sleeping and I'm going to bed. The rest will have to wait until we come back.'

The first oath sworn by two creatures of flesh and blood was at the foot of a rock that was turning into dust. They called upon the heavens (which are never the same from one instant to the next) to witness their constancy. Although everything inside them and outside of them was changing, they believed their hearts to be immune to change. Oh children! You are still children . . .

I don't know whether these reflections were made by Jacques, his master, or by me. What is certain, however, is that they were made by one of the three of us, and that they were preceded and followed by a great many others which would have taken Jacques, his master and me up till we had finished supper, and until the return of the innkeeper's wife, if Jacques had not said to his master: 'Listen, Monsieur, all those grand phrases you've just rattled off without rhyme or reason are not worth half as much as an old fable told at harvest gatherings in my village.'

MASTER: And what fable is this?

JACQUES: It is the fable of the Knife and the Sheath.
One day the Knife and the Sheath started quarrelling. Knife said to Sheath: 'My dear, you are a hussy, because every day you allow a new knife to enter you.'
Sheath replied: 'Friend Knife, you are a rogue, because every day you put your blade into another sheath.'
'That is not what you promised me, Sheath.'
'You were unfaithful to me first, Knife.'
The discussion had started at table and he that was seated between them spake thus: 'You, Knife, and you, Sheath, did well to change, since to change gave you pleasure, but you did wrong to promise each other that you would not change.
'Do you not see that God made you to fit into several sheaths, Knife?
'And you to take more than one knife, Sheath?
'You thought that those knives who swear that they will always do without sheaths are mad, as are those sheaths who swear that they will never allow any knife to enter into them.
'And yet you did not consider that you were almost as mad as them when you swore to allow only one knife to enter you, Sheath, and you, Knife, to confine yourself to only one sheath.'

And the master said to Jacques: 'I do not find your fable very moral, but it's certainly a merry one. You'll never guess what strange idea has just come to me. I see you married to the innkeeper's wife and wonder what a husband who loves to speak would do with a wife who won't stop talking.'

JACQUES: What I did for the first twelve years of my life, which I spent with my grandparents.

MASTER: What were their names? What did they do?

JACQUES: They dealt in second-hand clothes. My grandfather Jason[32] had several children. All the family was serious. They would get up, get dressed, go about their business, come back, have lunch and then go off again without saying a word. At night they would sit down. The mother and the girls would spin, sew or knit in silence. The boys would rest and the father would read the Old Testament.

MASTER: And what would you do?

JACQUES: I would run around the room with a gag on.

MASTER: With a gag!

JACQUES: Yes, with a gag, and it's because of that damned gag that I've got a mania for talking. A whole week would go by sometimes without anyone in the Jason household opening their mouth. During her entire life, which was long, the only thing my grandmother ever said was 'Hats for sale', and my grandfather, who would always be amongst his ledgers, upright, his hands under his frock-coat, had only ever said 'One sou.' There were days when he was tempted not to believe in the Bible.

MASTER: Why was that?

JACQUES: Because of the repetitions in it which he regarded as idle chatter unworthy of the Holy Spirit. He used to say that people who repeated themselves were idiots who took those who listened to them for idiots.

MASTER: Jacques, to compensate for the long silence you kept during the twelve years you were gagged at your grandfather's and also while our hostess was speaking, perhaps you could . . .

JACQUES: Come back to the story of my loves?

MASTER: No, not that one, but another story on which you've left me in suspense – the story of your Captain's friend.

JACQUES: Oh, Master, what a cruel memory you have!

MASTER: Jacques, my dear Jacques!

JACQUES: What are you laughing at?

MASTER: At something which will make me laugh more than once. I'm picturing you at your grandfather's in your youth, with your gag.

JACQUES: My grandmother used to take it off me when there was nobody about but my grandfather was not very happy if he saw that and he'd say: 'Carry on and that child will become the most frantic chatterbox who's ever existed.'
His prediction has been fulfilled.

MASTER: Come on, Jacques, my dear Jacques, the story of your Captain's friend.

JACQUES: I'll tell it if you want, but you're not going to believe it.

MASTER: Is it that incredible?

JACQUES: No, but it has happened to someone else already, a French soldier, I believe, called M. de Guerchy.[33]

MASTER: Well, I shall reply in the words of a French poet who had written quite a witty epigram and who said to someone else who claimed to have written it: 'Why shouldn't Monsieur have written it? I managed to write it . . .'
Why shouldn't Jacques' story have happened to his Captain's friend since it certainly happened to the French soldier de Guerchy? If you tell it to me you'll kill two birds with one stone, since you'll tell the story of two people which I don't know.

JACQUES: So much the better, but will you swear you don't know it?

MASTER: I swear it.

Reader, I'm terribly tempted to insist on the same oath from you, but I will simply point out to you a strange aspect of Jacques' character which he inherited, apparently, from his grandfather Jason, the silent second-hand clothes dealer. It is that Jacques, contrary to most chatterers, although he loved talking, had a profound dislike of repetition. That is why he would sometimes say to his master: 'Monsieur is preparing the saddest future for me. What will become of me when I have nothing left to say?'
'You will begin again.'
'Jacques! Begin again! The opposite is written up above, and if I should ever begin again I would not be able to prevent myself from crying out: "Ah! If only your grandfather could hear you now!" – and I would miss the gag.'
'You mean the gag he used to make you wear?'

JACQUES: In the days when one played games of chance in the fairs of Saint-Germain and Saint-Laurent . . .

MASTER: But they're in Paris and your Captain's friend was commanding officer of a border post.

JACQUES: For the love of God, master, let me speak . . .

Several officers went into a shop and found another officer there talking to the lady of the shop. One of them suggested a game of dice to him, because you should know that after my Captain's death his friend, having become rich, took to gambling as well. So, he, or, if you prefer, M. de Guerchy, accepted. Fortune gave his opponent the dice box and he won and won and won and it seemed that it would never end. The game became heated, and they had played for simple stakes and double stakes, high and low, played finally for quadruple stakes and then all or nothing, when one of the spectators took it into his head to say to M. de Guerchy, or my Captain's friend, that he'd do better to call it a day and stop playing because there was more to it than he could see. On hearing this, which was only a joke, my Captain's friend, or M. de Guerchy, thought he was dealing with a cheat. He discreetly put his hand in his pocket and brought out a sharp knife. As soon as his opponent stretched out his hand to gather up the dice and put them in the dice box he stuck his knife in his hand, pinning it to the table, and said: 'If the dice are loaded, you are a cheat. If they are good, I am wrong.'

The dice were good. M. de Guerchy said: 'I am very sorry and I will give you whatever compensation you want.'

That was not what my Captain's friend said. He said: 'I have lost all my money and wounded a good man's hand. But, in return, I have rediscovered the pleasure of being able to fight for as long as I want.'

The wounded officer withdrew to have himself bandaged. When he had recovered, he went to see the officer who had knifed him to demand satisfaction. Monsieur de Guerchy found this request quite reasonable. My Captain's friend threw his arms round his neck and said: 'I have been so impatient for you to come. I can't tell you how . . .'

They went off and fought. The knifeman, M. de Guerchy or my Captain's friend, received a sword thrust to the body. The knifed officer picked him up, had him carried home and said: 'Monsieur, we will see each other again.'

Monsieur de Guerchy didn't say anything, but my Captain's friend replied: 'I am counting on it.'

They fought a second and third time, then eight or ten times, and it was always the knifeman who was wounded. However, they were both officers of distinction and merit. Their story was much talked of and the Minister intervened. One was kept in Paris and the other confined to his post. Monsieur de Guerchy obeyed the orders of the Court whereas my Captain's friend was very unhappy about it, and such is the difference between two men of brave character, one of whom is wise and the other slightly mad.

Up to this point the stories of M. de Guerchy and my Captain's friend are identical. They are one and the same story and that is why I have named them both, do you understand, Master? Here I shall separate them, and from now on speak only of my Captain's friend, because the rest of the story concerns him alone. Ah! Monsieur, this will show you how little we are masters of our destinies, and how many strange things there are inscribed on the great scroll.

My Captain's friend, or the knifeman, requested leave to return to his birthplace and obtained it. His route was via Paris. He took a seat in a public carriage. At three o'clock in the morning the carriage passed in front of the Opera, just as all the people were coming out of a ball. Three or four young scatterbrains, all wearing masks, decided to join the coach and go off for breakfast. The coach reached the scheduled breakfast stop just as day was breaking. And what a surprise it was for the knifed officer to recognize the man who had knifed him. The latter offered his hand, embraced him and told him how pleased he was at such a fortuitous meeting. Straight away they went behind a barn and drew their swords, the one in his frock-coat, the other in his ballroom mask. The knifeman, or my Captain's friend, ended up wounded on the ground once again. His adversary sent help to him and then sat down to table with his friends and the other people in the carriage and ate and drank a hearty meal.

The travellers were about to continue on their journey and the others to go back into town in their masks on their hired horses when their hostess reappeared and put an end to Jacques' story.

Here she is, come back again, and I warn you, Reader, that it is no longer in my power to send her away again.

– Why not?

Because she has presented herself carrying two bottles of champagne, one in each hand, and it is written up above that any orator who addresses Jacques with an introduction such as that will inevitably be listened to. She came in, put her two bottles on to the table and said: 'Come along, Monsieur Jacques, let's bury the hatchet.'

Their hostess was not in the first flush of youth. She was a tall sturdy lady, nimble, good looking, with a very generous figure. Her mouth was a little on the large side, but she had nice teeth, large cheeks, protuberant eyes, a square forehead, the nicest skin, a lively, cheerful and open face, and breasts large enough to roll around in for two whole days. Her arms were a bit brawny, but her hands superb, the kind of hands one would want to paint or sculpt.

Jacques took her around the waist and embraced her warmly. His bitterness had never held out against a good wine or a handsome woman. That was written up above about him, about you, Reader, about me and about a good many others.

'Monsieur!' she said to the master, 'you aren't going to let us drink alone, are you? I tell you, even if you've got another hundred leagues to go, you won't find a better bottle of champagne on the way,' and speaking thus she placed one of the bottles between her legs, pulled the cork, and covered the neck of the bottle with such dexterity that not a drop of the wine was spilt.

'Quick,' she said to Jacques, 'your glass, quickly!'

Jacques held out his glass and the hostess lifted her thumb a little, uncovering the top of the bottle slightly and covering Jacques' face with foam. Jacques went along with this monkey business and the hostess, Jacques and his master all started laughing. They drank a few glasses, one after the other, to assure themselves of the wisdom of the bottle and then the hostess said: 'Thank God they're all in their beds. No one will interrupt me any more and I can carry on with my story.'

Jacques, looking at her with eyes whose natural vivacity had been augmented by the champagne, said to her, or his master: 'Our hostess was once as beautiful as an angel, don't you think, Monsieur?'

MASTER: Was once? By God, Jacques, she still is.

JACQUES: Monsieur, you're quite right. It's just that I'm not comparing her to any other woman but rather to herself when she was young.

HOSTESS: I'm not much to look at these days. Time was when a man could put his thumbs and index fingers round my waist and have room to spare. You should have seen me then! People used to come four leagues out of their way to stay here. But let's not talk about all the good and bad admirers I've had and let us come back to Mme de La Pommeraye.

JACQUES: Before we do that, perhaps we could drink the health of all your bad admirers, or my health.

HOSTESS: Willingly. Some of them were worth it, even if I don't take you into account. Do you know that for ten whole years I was the officers' financial standby, everything above board. I must have helped scores of them who would have had an awful job getting themselves kitted out for the year's campaigning without me. But they were good men and I've no cause to complain about any of them, nor them of me. I never asked for pledges, though sometimes they used to make me wait. But at the end of two, three or four years my money was returned . . .

And of course that set her off on the list of officers who had done her the honour of drawing from her purse, the colonel of the †††† Regiment, Captain so and so of the ****** Regiment, and Jacques cried out: 'My Captain! My poor Captain! Did you know him then?'

HOSTESS: Did I know him! Tall man. Well built. A little thin. A severe but noble manner. A well-shaped leg. And two little red marks on his right temple. Have you seen service?

JACQUES: Have I seen service!

HOSTESS: I like you even better for it. You must have some of the good qualities of your first occupation left. Let's drink the health of your Captain.

JACQUES: If he is still alive.

HOSTESS: Dead or alive, what's that got to do with it? What are soldiers for if not to be killed? But God, it must be annoying, after ten sieges and five or six battles, to find oneself dying in the middle of that black-coated rabble . . .[34] But let's get back to our story and have another drink.

MASTER: By God, hostess, you're right there.

HOSTESS: Oh! You were speaking of my wine, were you? Well, you are still right. Do you remember where we were?

MASTER: Yes. At the end of one of the most perfidious of confidences.

HOSTESS: Monsieur le Marquis des Arcis and Mme de La Pommeraye embraced, absolutely delighted with each other, and went their ways. But because she had suppressed her feelings so much when he was there, her grief was all the more violent when he had left.

'It's only too true . . .' she cried out, 'he doesn't love me any more.'

I will not describe to you in detail all the wild and foolish things we women do when we are abandoned because that would only flatter your vanity. I have already told you that this woman was proud, but her pride was nothing to her vindictiveness. When her first furies had calmed and her mood turned to cold indignation her thoughts turned to avenging herself, and to avenging herself in a cruel way, in a way which would frighten all those who in future would be tempted to seduce and deceive honest women. She had her revenge, a cruel revenge, a public revenge, but it turned against her and served as a lesson to no one. Since that time we have not been any the less cruelly seduced or deceived.

JACQUES: That may be the case for other women, but what about you?

HOSTESS: Alas! Me even more than other women. Oh, we are so stupid! And it is not even as if these wicked men come out of it any better! But let us leave that. What will she do? She has not decided anything yet. She will dream of it. She dreams of it.

JACQUES: If, perhaps, while she is dreaming . . .

HOSTESS: Yes, well said. But our bottles are empty . . .

'Jean!'
'Yes, Madame.'
'Bring up two bottles from the special reserve at the back, behind the firewood.'
'I understand.'

Eventually, after much thought, this is the idea she had. In earlier times Mme de La Pommeraye had once known a woman from the provinces who had been obliged to come up to Paris with her daughter, who was young and beautiful and well brought up. She had learnt that this woman, ruined by the loss of her case, had been reduced to running a bawdy-house.[35] People used to go to her house, gamble, have dinner and generally one or two of her guests would stay and spend the night with either the lady of the house or her daughter, at their choice. She set one of her people on the trail of these creatures. They were tracked down and invited to visit Mme de La Pommeraye, whom, of course, they hardly remembered. These women had taken the names Mme and Mlle d'Aisnon and they did not wait for a second invitation. The very next day the mother arrived to see Mme de La Pommeraye. After paying her compliments Mme de La Pommeraye asked the d'Aisnon woman what she was doing and what she had been doing since the loss of her case.

'To tell you the truth,' replied the d'Aisnon woman, 'I am in a dangerous business which is shameful, hardly lucrative, and which revolts me. But necessity knows no law. I had almost decided to get my daughter taken on at the Opera but she only has a little chamber music voice and has never been more than a mediocre dancer. I took her all round Paris, during and after my trial, to magistrates, noblemen, priests, speculators, and they all showed interest for a while, but then lost interest. It's not that she isn't beautiful, nor that she's not pretty as an angel, and it's not because she lacks finesse or grace. It's just that there's no devilry in her, none of those talents needed for stirring jaded men from their lethargy. So these days I ask people to gamble and eat, and whoever wants to stay the night stays. But what hindered us the most is that she became infatuated with some aristocratic little abbé who is impious, unbelieving, dissolute, hypocritical, anti-philosophical and whom I won't name.[36] He is only the latest in a long line of them who in order to obtain a bishopric have taken the route which is at the same time the most sure and the one requiring the least talent. I don't know what he used to say to my daughter, but he used to come every day and read her extracts from his latest compilation or whatever he had scribbled over his lunch or dinner. Would he be bishop, wouldn't he be bishop? Anyway, thank God they fell out. My daughter asked him one day if he knew the people he was writing against and the little priest told her that he didn't. She asked him if his views were any different from those of the people he ridiculed and he told her they were not. She allowed herself to lose her temper and told him that what he was doing made him the most wicked and two-faced of men.'

Madame de La Pommeraye asked her if they were both very well known.

'Far too well, unfortunately.'

'From what I can see you don't care for your present condition.'

'Not at all, and my daughter complains daily that even the most miserable existence would be preferable to hers. She is now so melancholic that she's putting the men off . . .'

'What if I took it into my head to give you both the most brilliant future? Would you agree to it?'

'I'd agree to a lot less.'

'But first of all I must know whether you are able to promise me that you will follow to the letter the orders I will give you.'

'Whatever it is, you can count on it.'

'And will you be at my disposal whenever I want?'

'We will await your orders with impatience.'

'That is enough. You may go now and you will not have long to wait. While you are waiting, get rid of your possessions. Sell everything. Do not keep even your dresses if you have any that are even slightly gaudy. That would not fit in with my plans at all.'

Jacques, who had begun to get interested, said to their hostess: 'Perhaps if we were to drink to the health of Mme de La Pommeraye?'

HOSTESS: Willingly.

JACQUES: And the health of Mme d'Aisnon?

HOSTESS: Cheers.

JACQUES: And you won't refuse to drink to the health of Mlle d'Aisnon who has such a pretty little chamber-music voice, not much talent for dancing and is so melancholic that she is reduced to the sad necessity of accepting a new lover every night?

HOSTESS: There's no need to laugh. It's the cruellest thing. If only you knew what torture it is when you are not in love.

JACQUES: To the health of Mlle d'Aisnon, because of her tortures.

HOSTESS: Come on, then.

JACQUES: Hostess, do you love your husband?

HOSTESS: Not much.

JACQUES: In that case I am very sorry for you because he seems in good health to me.

HOSTESS: Everything that glistens is not gold.

JACQUES: To the good health of our host.

HOSTESS: You'll drink alone to that.

MASTER: Jacques, Jacques, my friend, you're drinking very fast.

HOSTESS: Don't worry, Monsieur, it's good stuff and there won't be any hangover tomorrow.

JACQUES: Because there won't be any hangover tomorrow and because tonight I'm not too concerned about my reason, my master, my beautiful hostess, one more toast, a toast which I'm very keen on drinking: To the health of Mlle d'Aisnon's little priest!

HOSTESS: Ah, no, Monsieur Jacques! A hypocrite, an ambitious, ignorant, intolerant slanderer – for that is what I think one calls people who are prepared to cut the throats of others because they think differently.

MASTER: What you don't know, Madame, our hostess, is that Jacques here is a sort of philosopher and he has great esteem for those little imbeciles who dishonour both themselves and the cause they are defending so badly.

He says that his Captain used to call them the antidote of the Huets, Nicoles and Bossuets of this world.[37] Jacques didn't know what that means any more than you . . . Is your husband in bed?

HOSTESS: He went some time ago.

MASTER: And he allows you to chat away like this?

HOSTESS: Our husbands are used to it . . . Madame de La Pommeraye got into her carriage and combed the suburbs as far away as possible from Mme d'Aisnon's quarter. She rented a small apartment in a respectable house near a church, furnished it as simply as possible and invited Mme d'Aisnon and her daughter to dinner. She moved them in on the same day or a few days after, leaving them with a set of rules they were to abide by.

JACQUES: Madame, our hostess! We have forgotten to drink to the health of Mme de La Pommeraye and the Chevalier des Arcis. Ah! That is not honourable!

HOSTESS: Go ahead, Monsieur Jacques, the cellar isn't empty . . . Here are their rules – or what I remember of them:

'You will not go near public places because you must not be recognized.

'You must not receive anyone into your house, not even your neighbours or their wives, because you must affect to lead a very secluded life.

'From tomorrow you must dress like church-goers because people must take you for such.

'The only books which you may have in your house are books of devotion because there must be nothing around you which can betray you.

'You will attend the services of the parish with the greatest assiduity, both on work days and feast days.

'You will find a way of introducing yourselves into the parlour of some convent, because the chitter-chatter of these recluses will not be without use to us.

'You will strike up the closest acquaintance with the parish priest and the other priests in the parish because we may need them to act as references for you.

'You will not allow anyone to visit you regularly.

'You will go to confession and take communion at least twice a month.

'You will resume your family name because it is an unsullied name and sooner or later inquiries will be made in your province.

'From time to time you will make small charitable donations but you will

'What! Have you really nothing to confide in me?'

'No.'

'But what about my friend the little count, who was pursuing you so avidly in my day?'

'I have shut my doors to him and I no longer see him.'

'What strange behaviour! Why did you send him away?'

'Because I don't like him.'

'Ah! Madame, I think I know what it is. You are still in love with me.'

'Perhaps.'

'You are counting on a reconciliation.'

'Why not?'

'And you are making sure of the moral advantage your blameless conduct would give you over me.'

'I believe so.'

'And if I had the fortune or the misfortune to take up with you again you would at the very least be able to take credit for the silence you would maintain over my conduct.'

'You must believe me to be extremely delicate and very generous.'

'My friend, after what you have done, there is no sort of heroism of which you are not capable.'

'I'm quite happy that you should have such an opinion of me.'

'By God, I'm in great danger from you, that I'm sure of.'

'And so am I.'

For about the next three months things were much the same, until Mme de La Pommeraye decided that the time had come to set her great schemes in motion. One summer's day when the weather was good and she was expecting the Marquis to lunch, she sent word to the d'Aisnon and her daughter to go to the Royal Botanical Gardens. The Marquis came. Lunch was served in good time. They dined. They dined happily. After lunch Mme de La Pommeraye suggested to the Marquis that they should go for a walk if he didn't have anything more enjoyable to do. That day there was nothing on at the opera or the theatre, as the Marquis remarked, and so as to make up for the loss of entertainment by an instructive outing chance had it that it was the Marquis himself who invited the Marquise to go and see the Royal Collection. The invitation was not refused, as you can well imagine. The horses were harnessed and they left. When they arrived at the Royal Botanical Gardens they mingled with the crowd, looking all around them and seeing nothing, just like everybody else.

Reader, I have forgotten to describe to you the positions of the three characters we are concerned with here – Jacques, his master, and their hostess. Because of this oversight you have heard them speak but you have not been able to picture them. Better late than never. On the left Jacques' master, in his night-cap and dressing-gown, was nonchalantly stretched out in a large tapestry work armchair, his handkerchief thrown over one of its arms and his snuff-box in his hand. At the end, opposite the door, and near the table, was their hostess, her glass in front of her. And, on her right, Jacques, without a hat, his elbows on the table, his head leaning forward between two empty bottles, and two more on the floor beside him.

HOSTESS: On leaving the Royal Collection, the Marquis and his good friend went for a walk in the garden. They followed the first path to the right as you go in near the arboretum when Mme de La Pommeraye suddenly cried out in surprise: 'I am not mistaken. I think it's . . . yes, it is, it's them,' and immediately left the Marquis to go over and meet our two saintly ladies. The d'Aisnon girl looked stunning in a simple dress, which, without attracting attention, made her the centre of attraction.

'Ah! Is it you, Madame?'

'Yes, it is I.'

'And how have you been keeping and what has become of you after all this time?'

'You know our misfortunes. We have had to resign ourselves to them and we lead a withdrawn life as befits our meagre fortune. When one can no longer continue to show oneself decently, one must withdraw from social life.'

'But me, leave me? I am not of society and I have always had the wit to see how tedious it is.'

'One of the bad things about misfortune is the suspicion it inspires. Those in misfortune are always afraid of being unwelcome.'

'You, unwelcome to me! That suspicion is a terrible insult.'

'Madame, I am innocent of it. I reminded Maman of you at least ten times, but she always said: "Nobody thinks of us anymore, not even Mme de La Pommeraye."'

'What an injustice! Let us sit down and chat. This is M. le Marquis des Arcis. He is my friend and his presence here need not disturb us. How Mademoiselle has grown! How pretty she has become since the last time we saw each other!'

'The good thing about our position is that it deprives us of everything which could be harmful to our health. Look at her face! Look at her arms! Look at what one gains by a frugal well-ordered life, sleep, work, and a happy conscience. It is certainly something . . .'

They sat down and conversed warmly. The d'Aisnon mother spoke a lot, her daughter hardly at all. The tone of each was that of devotion without being contrived or prudish. Long before nightfall our two church-goers got up. In spite of protests that it was still early, the d'Aisnon mother whispered to Mme de La Pommeraye loudly enough to be heard that they still had an office of devotion to fulfil, and that it was not possible for them to stay any longer. They were already some way off when Mme de La Pommeraye reproached herself for not having learnt where they lived and not having told them where she lived. It was a fault, she added, which she would not have committed in earlier days. The Marquis ran after them to make amends. They accepted the address of Mme de La Pommeraye but no matter how hard the Marquis insisted he could not obtain theirs. He did not dare to offer them his coach although he admitted to Mme de La Pommeraye that he had been tempted. The Marquis did not fail to ask Mme de La Pommeraye who these two women were.

'Two people who are happier than we are. Can you not see the good health they enjoy! Their serenity of expression! The innocence, the decency which governs their every word! One does not see or hear any of that in the circles we move in. We pity the devout and they pity us, but all in all I am inclined to think that they are right.'

'But, Marquise, are you tempted to become devout?'

'Why not?'

'Take care, I would not want the end of our relationship – if that is what it is – to drive you to that.'

'Would you rather I reopened my doors to the little count?'

'Much rather.'

'Would you advise me to do that?'

'Without hesitation.'

Madame de La Pommeraye told the Marquis what she knew of the name, the origins, the earlier status and the court case of our two devout ladies, making the story as interesting and as touching as possible.

'They are two women of rare merit – the daughter above all. You must admit that with looks like hers one would lack for nothing if one wished to exploit them. But they have preferred honest poverty to shameful luxury. What they have left is so little that in all honesty, I cannot imagine how they can live on it. They work night and day. Plenty of people know how to put up with poverty when they are born into it, but to fall from opulence into the direst necessity and somehow find contentment and happiness is something which I cannot understand. That is what religion does. No matter what our philosophers say, religion is a good thing.'

'Especially for the unfortunate.'

'And who isn't more or less?'

'I'm damned if you're not turning devout.'

'What's so tragic about that? This life is so insignificant when one compares the eternity to come!'

'But you sound like a missionary already.'

'I speak like a convinced woman. Now, Marquis, give me an honest answer. Would not all our riches appear to us to be mere baubles if we were more affected by the anticipation of future reward and fear of future punishment? If someone were to seduce a young girl or a woman devoted to her husband, while believing that if he should die in her arms he would be plunged immediately into endless tortures, you must admit that would be the height of folly.'

'However, it happens every day.'

'Because people have no faith, because they allow themselves to be distracted.'

'It's because our religious opinions have very little influence over our morals. But, my friend, I tell you that you are going the quickest route to the confessional.'

'That would be the best thing for me.'

'Come on, you are mad. You've got another twenty or so years of happy sinning ahead of you. Don't miss out on it. After that you will be able to repent, and you can go and parade your repentance at the feet of a priest if that is what you want ... But this is a very serious conversation. Your imagination is becoming terribly morbid and it is because of this dreadful solitude you have driven yourself into. Believe me, call back the little count as soon as possible and you will see no more devil or hell and you will be as charming as you were before. You are afraid that I will reproach you for it if ever we take up again. But in the first place, we may never be reconciled, and because of your apprehension which may or may not be well founded you are depriving yourself of the most delightful of pleasures. In all honesty, the merit of being morally superior to me is not worth the sacrifice.'

'What you say is true, but that is not what is holding me back ...'

They also said many other things which I cannot remember.

JACQUES: Madame, let's have a drink. That refreshes the memory.

HOSTESS: Let's have a drink ... After a few turns around the gardens, Mme de La Pommeraye and the Marquis got back into the carriage and Mme de La Pommeraye said: 'How she ages me! When she first came to Paris she was no higher than a cabbage!'

'You are speaking of the daughter of the lady we met on our walk?'

'Yes, it is just like a garden where the faded roses make place for the new ones. Did you look at her?'

'I could not fail to.'

'How did you find her?'

'The face of a Raphael virgin on the body of his Galatea, and such softness of voice!'

'Such a modest look!'

'Such propriety in her bearing!'

'And a refinement in what she says such as I have seen in no other young woman. That is what education does.'

'When there is good material there to start with.'

The Marquis left Mme de La Pommeraye at her door. Madame de La Pommeraye hastened to tell our two devout ladies how satisfied she was with the way they had played their roles.

JACQUES: If they carry on the way they've started, M. le Marquis des Arcis, even if you were the devil himself you'd never get out of it.

MASTER: I would very much like to know what their scheme is.

JACQUES: I wouldn't. It would spoil everything.

HOSTESS: From that day the Marquis became more assiduous in his visits to Mme de La Pommeraye, who noticed this without asking the reason. She never spoke first on the subject of the two devout ladies, but waited for him to bring it up, which the Marquis always did with impatience, and with badly simulated indifference.

MARQUIS: Have you seen your friends?

MME DE LA POMMERAYE: No.

MARQUIS: Do you know that is not very nice? You are rich and they are badly off. Do you not even invite them to eat with you occasionally?

MME DE LA POMMERAYE: I thought Monsieur le Marquis knew me a little better than that. Your love used to see good points in me. Today your friendship only sees my faults. I have invited them ten times, without once getting them to accept. They refuse to come to my house because of the most singular objections. And when I visit them I have to leave my carriage at the end of their road and go practically undressed, without rouge or diamonds. But you must not be surprised by their reserve. One false rumour would be enough to alienate the good will of a certain number of benevolent people and deprive them of their assistance. Marquis, it would appear that the price of doing good is great.

MARQUIS: Especially to church-goers.

MME DE LA POMMERAYE: Since the smallest pretext suffices for it to be withdrawn. If people knew that I was taking any interest they would soon say: 'Madame de La Pommeraye is their protector. They have need of nothing.' And that would be the end of their charity.

MARQUIS: Charity?

MME DE LA POMMERAYE: Yes, Monsieur, charity!

MARQUIS: You know them and they depend on charity?

MME DE LA POMMERAYE: Yet again, Marquis, I see that you do not love me any more and that a large part of your esteem has vanished with your love. Who told you that if these women depend on the charity of the parish it is my fault?

MARQUIS: Pardon, a thousand pardons, Madame, I am wrong. But what reason could they have for refusing the benevolence of a friend?

MME DE LA POMMERAYE: Ah! Marquis, we people of the world are a long way from understanding the delicate scruples of such timorous souls. They believe themselves unable to accept help from anyone indiscriminately.

MARQUIS: But that deprives us of the best way of making amends for our follies and dissipation.

MME DE LA POMMERAYE: Not at all. If I were to suppose that Monsieur le Marquis des Arcis were touched with compassion for them, what would there be to prevent him from offering his help through hands more worthy than his?

MARQUIS: And less sure.

MME DE LA POMMERAYE: Perhaps.

MARQUIS: Tell me, if I sent them twenty louis, do you think they would refuse it?

MME DE LA POMMERAYE: I am sure of it. And would their refusal be inappropriate, coming from a mother with such a charming daughter?

MARQUIS: Do you know that I have been tempted to go and see them?

MME DE LA POMMERAYE: I can well believe it. Marquis! Marquis! Be careful. Your compassion is rather sudden and rather suspect.

MARQUIS: Whatever it is, would they have received me?

MME DE LA POMMERAYE: Certainly not! With the brilliance of your carriage, your clothes, your servants and the charms of the young lady, it would not need more than that to set the neighbours gossiping and lead to the two women's downfall.

MARQUIS: I am upset, because that was certainly not my intention. Must I give up any hope of helping them or seeing them?

MME DE LA POMMERAYE: I think so.

MARQUIS: But if my help came to them through you?

MME DE LA POMMERAYE: I do not think that kind of help is disinterested enough for me to take responsibility.

MARQUIS: That is harsh.

MME DE LA POMMERAYE: Yes, harsh, that is the word.

MARQUIS: What an idea! Marquise, you are making fun of me. A young girl whom I have only seen once . . .

MME DE LA POMMERAYE: But one of the small number of girls that are once seen and never forgotten.

MARQUIS: It is true that faces like that stay with you.

MME DE LA POMMERAYE: Marquis, take great care for yourself, you are heading for great sorrows and I would prefer preserving you from them to having to console you. Do not confuse these women with the women you have known. You cannot tempt them, cannot seduce them, cannot go near them, they will not listen to you and you will never get what you want.

After this conversation the Marquis suddenly remembered that he had urgent business, got up quickly and left, looking very preoccupied. For quite a long period of time the Marquis hardly went a day without seeing Mme de La Pommeraye, but when he arrived he would sit down and stay silent. Madame de La Pommeraye would speak alone, and after a quarter of an hour or so the Marquis would get up and leave. After that he disappeared for maybe a month, at the end of which time he reappeared, but how sad, how melancholic, how dejected he looked. On seeing him like this, the Marquise said: 'What are you doing here! Where have you come from? Have you been all this time in a bawdy-house, or what?'

MARQUIS: My God, almost. My despair flung me into the most frightful debauchery.

MME DE LA POMMERAYE: What! Despair?

MARQUIS: Yes, despair! . . .

At this point he started pacing up and down without saying a word. He went to the windows, looked out at the sky, stopped in front of Mme de La Pommeraye, went to the door, called his servants to whom he had nothing to say, sent them away again, came back in and came back to Mme de La Pommeraye, who was working and appeared not to notice. He wanted to say something but didn't dare. At last Mme de La Pommeraye took pity on him and asked him: 'What is the matter with you? We go a whole month without seeing you, and then you reappear with a face like a corpse and prowl around like a soul in torment.'

MARQUIS: I cannot stand it any longer. I must tell you everything. I am struck to the quick by your friend's daughter. I have tried everything, everything, to forget her, and the more I have tried the more I have remembered her. I am obsessed by this angelic creature. You must do me a great favour.

MME DE LA POMMERAYE: What?

MARQUIS: I have to see her again and it must be through you. All my agents are in the field. The only thing the two women do is to go from their house to the church and from the church to their house. I have intercepted them on foot at least ten times and they have not even noticed me. I have waited at their door without success. At first their snubs made me debauched as a monk and then as devout as an angel. I haven't missed Mass for a fortnight. Ah! My friend! What a face! She is so beautiful!

Madame de La Pommeraye already knew all this.

'What you are telling me', she replied to the Marquis, 'is that, after you tried everything to get over it, you then tried everything likely to drive you wild with desire and succeeded in this.'

MARQUIS: Succeeded! I could not begin to tell you quite how much. Will you not take pity on me? Shall I not be indebted to you for the joy of seeing her again?

MME DE LA POMMERAYE: That will be difficult, but I will take care of it on one condition. That is that you leave these poor ladies in peace and stop tormenting them. I will not hide from you that they have written bitterly to me of your persecution. Here is their letter . . .

The letter which she gave the Marquis to read had been composed between the three women. It came as if from the daughter following her mother's instructions and they had contrived to make it honest, sweet, touching, elegant and witty – in short everything that would touch the Marquis' heart. So, on reading it he exclaimed at every word. There was not a sentence he didn't read twice. He was crying with joy and said to Mme de La Pommeraye: 'Admit it, Madame, one could not have written a letter better than that.'

'I admit it.'

'Every line fills me with admiration and respect for women of such character.'

'That is as it should be.'

'I will give you my word, only I beg you not to fail me on yours.'

MME DE LA POMMERAYE: In all truth, Marquis, I am as foolish as you are. You must have retained terrible powers over me. That frightens me.

MARQUIS: When will I see her?

MME DE LA POMMERAYE: I don't know. I must first find a way of arranging things without arousing suspicion. They can hardly be ignorant of your feelings.

Imagine how my complicity would appear in their eyes if they thought I was acting in concert with you . . . Marquis, between you and me, do I need to saddle myself with these problems? Does it matter to me whether you are in love or you are not in love, or whether you are delirious? Get out of your mess by yourself. The role you are asking me to play is too bizarre.

MARQUIS: My friend, if you abandon me I am lost! I will not speak to you about myself since that will offend you. But I entreat you on behalf of those touching and worthy creatures who are so dear to you. You know me: spare them from the follies of which I am capable. I will go to their house, yes, I will go there, I warn you of it. I will break down their door, and force my way past them. I will sit down and I don't know what I will say or do because I could do anything in the violent state I am in.

HOSTESS: You will have noticed, Messieurs, that from the beginning of this story, up to this point, the Marquis des Arcis has not said one word which was not like a knife thrust into the heart of Mme de La Pommeraye. She was bursting with indignation and rage and when she replied it was in a trembling, broken voice:

MME DE LA POMMERAYE: You are right. Ah! If only I had been loved like that, perhaps . . . But let's not speak of that . . . It is not for you that I will do this thing, but I flatter myself, Monsieur le Marquis, that you will at least allow me time.

MARQUIS: The least I can.

JACQUES: Ah! Madame! What a devil of a woman! Lucifer himself cannot be worse. I am trembling. I'd better have a drink to steady me . . . You will not leave me to drink alone?

HOSTESS: Well, I am not afraid . . . Madame de La Pommeraye said to herself: 'I am suffering, but I will not suffer alone. Cruel man. I do not know how long my torments will last but I will make yours last for ever . . .'
She kept the Marquis waiting more than a month for the encounter she had promised. She left him all this time to suffer, to become more obsessed, and under the pretence of making the length of his waiting more tolerable she allowed him to speak to her of his passion.

MASTER: And strengthen it in talking about it.

JACQUES: What a woman! What a devil of a woman! Madame, my fears are mounting.

HOSTESS: And so every day the Marquis would come and speak to Mme de La Pommeraye, who with her artful speeches succeeded in driving him to a peak of irritation, resolution and perdition. He found out about the birthplace, the education, the fortune and the misfortune of these two women. He came back to this all the time and never thought himself well enough informed or touched enough by the story. The Marquise pointed out how his feelings were becoming deeper and stronger and under the pretext of frightening him gradually got him used to considering what would be the final outcome of this process.

'Marquis,' she said to him, 'take great care for yourself. This passion will take you to great lengths. There may well come a day when my friendship which you now abuse so strangely, will not excuse me in your eyes, or in those of others. It is not as though even greater follies are not a daily occurrence. Marquis, I have grave suspicions that you will only obtain this girl on conditions which up to now have not been to your liking.'

When Mme de La Pommeraye believed the Marquis to be well set up for the successful completion of her plan, she arranged for the two women to come and have lunch at her house. She also arranged with the Marquis that he should come dressed for the country to put them off the scent. This was done.

They were on the second course when the Marquis was announced. The Marquis, Mme de La Pommeraye and the two d'Aisnons gave a convincing display of embarrassment.

'Madame, I have just returned from my estates. It is too late for me to return to my home and I am not expected there until this evening. I flattered myself that you would not refuse to invite me to luncheon.'

While he was speaking he had taken a chair and sat down to table. The table had been set in such a way that he found himself next to the mother and opposite the daughter. He thanked Mme de La Pommeraye for this thought-ful gesture with a wink. After the confusion of the first moment the two devout ladies became more relaxed. They talked and even laughed. The Marquis was full of attention for the mother and maintained an attitude of very reserved politeness with the daughter. The scrupulousness of the Marquis to say and do nothing which might frighten them away gave the three women a great deal of secret amusement. They were inhuman enough to make him speak for three whole hours on matters of devotion. Madame de La Pommeraye said to him: 'What you have been saying there is a marvellous tribute to your parents. One's first lessons are never forgotten. You understand all the subtleties of divine love as if you had never read anything other than the writings of Saint Francis of Sales. You haven't dabbled in quietism at some stage, have you?'

'I really don't remember any more.'

Needless to say, our two pious ladies made their conversation as graceful, witty, charming and sophisticated as they could. They touched in passing upon the subject of the passions and Mlle Duquênoi (for that was her family name) maintained that there was only one dangerous passion. The Marquis was of the same opinion. Between six and seven o'clock the two ladies retired in spite of all efforts to make them stay. Madame de La Pommeraye maintained with Mme Duquênoi that one should always place duty first, otherwise one would hardly spend a day whose sweetness was not embittered by remorse. Eventually, to the great regret of the Marquis, they were gone, leaving the Marquis alone with Mme de La Pommeraye.

MME DE LA POMMERAYE: Well, Marquis, you must admit that I am kind to you. Show me another woman in Paris who would have done as much for you.

MARQUIS (throwing himself on his knees): I admit it. There is no one like you. Your kindness leaves me speechless. You are my only true friend in the whole world.

MME DE LA POMMERAYE: Are you sure that you will always appreciate what I am doing for you as greatly?

MARQUIS: I would be a monster of ingratitude were that not the case.

MME DE LA POMMERAYE: Well, let's change the subject. What is the state of your feelings?

MARQUIS: The simple truth? . . . I must have that girl or I will die.

MME DE LA POMMERAYE: You will have her without doubt. The question is, on what basis?

MARQUIS: We will see.

MME DE LA POMMERAYE: Marquis! Marquis! I know you and I know them. It is obvious.

The Marquis did not show himself at Mme de La Pommeraye's for about two months and this is what he did in the meantime. He got to know the confessor of the mother and daughter. He was a friend of the little priest of whom I've already spoken. This confessor, after having brought up every hypocritical objection that might be raised against a dishonest intrigue, and after having sold for the highest possible price the sanctity of his ministry, finally agreed to everything the Marquis wanted.

The first villainy of this man of God was to alienate the benevolence of the parish priest and convince him that the two protégées of Mme de La

Pommeraye were depriving other parishioners who were more needy than themselves of the alms they were obtaining from the parish. His aim was to force them to do what he wanted through poverty.

Next he sought, through the confessional, to sow discord between the mother and the daughter. When he heard the mother criticize the daughter he exaggerated the faults of the daughter and increased the resentment of the mother. If the daughter complained of her mother he suggested that the power of fathers and mothers over their children was limited and that if the persecution of the mother went beyond a certain point it would not be impossible to withdraw the daughter from such tyrannical authority, and for her penance he would order her to come back to confession.

Another time he spoke to her of her charms, but in a frivolous manner. These were, he said, the most dangerous presents which God had given to a woman. He spoke of the great impression they had made on an honest man whose identity he did not reveal but which was easy to guess. From there he passed on to the infinite mercy of heaven and its indulgence for faults which certain circumstances made inevitable. He spoke of the weakness of human nature for which each of us finds excuse in himself. He spoke of the violence and the universality of certain feelings from which even the most saintly of men were not free. He asked her if she had ever experienced any desires, if her feelings ever spoke to her in dreams, if the presence of men did not trouble her. Next he brought up the question of whether a woman should give way to an impassioned man or resist him and so doom to death and damnation one for whom Christ's blood was spilled. And he did not dare decide for her. Then he sighed deeply several times, raised his eyes to heaven and prayed for peace to be brought to troubled souls. The young girl let him carry on. Her mother and Mme de La Pommeraye, to whom she faithfully reported all of the advice of her spiritual director, suggested fresh revelations she might make to him which were all designed to lead him on further.

JACQUES: Your Mme de La Pommeraye is a really wicked woman.

MASTER: That is easily said, Jacques. But where does her wickedness come from? From the Marquis des Arcis. Let him be what he swore he would be and what he should have been; then find fault with Mme de La Pommeraye. When we are on our way again, you will accuse her, but I will make it my business to defend her. As for this priest, this vile seducer . . . I won't attempt to defend him.

JACQUES: The priest is such a wicked man that this whole business will put me off going to confession ever again. And you, Madame Hostess?

HOSTESS: I shall continue my visits to my old parish priest who isn't the least bit curious and only ever hears what people say to him.

JACQUES: Perhaps if we drink to the health of your old parish priest?

HOSTESS: I'll take you up on that for he's a good man, who allows the boys and girls to dance on Sundays and feast days and lets the men and the women come here provided they don't come out drunk. To my parish priest!

JACQUES: To your parish priest!

HOSTESS: The three women were certain that very soon the man of God would risk giving a letter to his penitent, and this he did. But what a performance he made of it! He didn't know who it came from. He was certain, however, that it had come from some well-meaning charitable soul who had discovered how badly off the two ladies were and was offering help. He often passed on similar letters. He advised that since the girl was wise and her mother prudent she should open the letter only in her mother's presence. Mademoiselle Duquênoi accepted the letter and gave it to her mother, who straight away sent it to Mme de La Pommeraye. She, armed with the letter, summoned the priest, overwhelmed him with the reproaches he deserved and threatened to report him to his superiors if he caused any more trouble.

In the letter the Marquis exhausted almost his entire vocabulary in praise of himself, in praise of Mlle Duquênoi, painted his passion in all its violence, made drastic offers and even proposed a kidnapping.

After her lecture to the priest Mme de La Pommeraye called the Marquis to her and pointed out to him in the strongest terms how his conduct was little worthy of a man of the world and how much it could compromise her. She showed him his letter and protested that in spite of the tender friendship which united them she could not promise to withhold it from the hands of the law or from Mme Duquênoi if the daughter were involved in any scandal.

'Ah! Marquis,' she said, 'love has corrupted you. You were surely born under an evil sign since love, which inspires great actions, can only prompt you to such degrading ones. What have these poor women done to you that you should want to add ignominy to their poverty? Just because this girl is beautiful and wants to remain virtuous, do you have to become her persecutor? What right have you to make her hate heaven's greatest gift? What have I deserved, to be your accomplice in this? Come, Marquis, down on your knees and ask me to forgive you and give me your oath that you will leave my poor friends in peace.'

The Marquis promised her not to do anything without her permission but he had to have this girl, whatever the cost. The Marquis was anything but faithful to his word. The mother knew how things stood and he did not hesitate to address himself to her. He wrote admitting the wickedness of his plans and he offered a considerable sum of money by way of a token of what the future might bring. His letter was accompanied by a jewel box full of rich stones.

The three women held counsel. The mother and the daughter were of a mind to accept but this was not what Mme de La Pommeraye wanted. She reminded them of the promise they had given her and threatened to reveal everything. And so, to the great regret of the two devout ladies, the younger woman had to take off the diamond ear-rings which suited her so well, and the jewel case and the letter were returned with a reply full of pride and indignation. Madame de La Pommeraye complained to the Marquis about the unreliability of his promises. The Marquis excused himself by pointing out that it was impossible for him to ask her to carry out such a dishonourable errand.

'Marquis, Marquis,' Mme de La Pommeraye replied, 'I have already warned you and I repeat my warning. You have not got what you want but this is not the time to preach to you. That would be a waste of breath. There is nothing left to do.'

The Marquis admitted that he thought as she did and asked her permission to make one last attempt. This was to settle a considerable sum on the two women, to share his fortune with them, and to settle on them for life one of his town houses and another in the country.

'Go ahead,' said the Marquise, 'I forbid only violence. But believe me, my friend, when honour and virtue are real, their value to those who are fortunate enough to possess them is beyond price. Your new offers will not be any more successful than the previous ones. I know these women and I will stake my life on it.'

The new propositions were made. The three women again held counsel together. The mother and daughter waited in silence for the decision of Mme de La Pommeraye. She paced up and down for a while without speaking: 'No, no,' she said, 'it is not enough for my wounded heart.' And as soon as she announced her refusal the two women burst into tears, threw themselves at her feet and protested how terrible it was for them to reject an immense fortune which they could accept without any awkward consequences.

Madame de La Pommeraye replied harshly: 'Do you imagine that I am doing what I do for you? Who are you? What do I owe you? Why should I not send the two of you back to your brothel? If what is being offered is too much for you, it is not enough for me. Write down the reply I dictate to you, Madame, and I want to see it go off.'

The two women went away more frightened than sorrowful.

JACQUES: This woman has the devil in her. What does she want? What! Isn't the loss of half a great fortune punishment enough for the waning of love?

MASTER: Jacques, you've never been a woman, still less a respectable one, and you are judging with reference to your own character, which is not that of Mme de La Pommeraye. Do you want to know what I think? I'm very much afraid that the marriage of the Marquis des Arcis and a whore is written up above.

JACQUES: If it is written up above it will be.

HOSTESS: The Marquis soon visited Mme de La Pommeraye again: 'Well,' she asked him, 'what about your new offers?'

MARQUIS: Made and rejected. It has driven me to despair. I would like to tear this unfortunate passion from my heart. I would like to tear out my heart itself and I am not able to. Marquise, look at me. Do you not see certain similarities between me and this young girl?

MME DE LA POMMERAYE: Although I have not said anything to you I had noticed. But that's not the point. What have you decided to do?

MARQUIS: I cannot come to any decision. One minute I am seized with the urge to leap into a post-chaise and travel to the ends of the earth. The next I am left completely helpless, I cannot think straight, I go into a daze and I do not know what to do with myself.

MME DE LA POMMERAYE: I do not advise you to travel. It is not worth going as far as Villejuif just to come back again.[40]

The next day the Marquis wrote to the Marquise that he was leaving for his estates, he would stay as long as he could and he begged her to look after his interests with her two friends if the opportunity arose. His absence was short. He came back resolved to marry.

JACQUES: I feel sorry for this poor Marquis.

MASTER: I don't.

HOSTESS: On the way back he stopped at the door of Mme de La Pommeraye. She had gone out. On her return she found the Marquis stretched out in a large armchair, his eyes shut, deeply lost in thought.

'Ah, it is you, Marquis! The charms of the country did not detain you very long!'

'No,' he replied, 'I am happy nowhere and I have come back resolved to commit the greatest stupidity which a man of my rank, my age and my character could do. But it is better to get married than to suffer. I am getting married.'

MME DE LA POMMERAYE: This is a serious business and requires reflection.

MARQUIS: I have made only one reflection but it is a sound one. That is that I could never be more unhappy than I am.

MME DE LA POMMERAYE: You could be wrong there.

JACQUES: What treachery!

MARQUIS: Here at last, my friend, is a negotiation which, it seems to me, I can decently entrust to you. See the mother and the daughter. Question the mother, sound out the feelings of the daughter and tell them of my plan.

MME DE LA POMMERAYE: Gently, Marquis. I believed I knew them well enough for the dealings I had with them but since I am now concerned with your happiness, my friend, you must allow me to investigate further. I will make inquiries in their province of origin, and I promise you I will follow every step they take during the rest of their stay in Paris.

MARQUIS: Such precautions seem quite superfluous to me. Women who live in poverty and who are able to resist the bait I have held out to them can only be exceptional beings. With the offers I have made them I could have overcome a duchess, and anyway, did you not tell me yourself . . .

MME DE LA POMMERAYE: Yes, I said whatever you like, but, in spite of that, allow me to satisfy myself.

JACQUES: What a bitch, what a wicked, mad bitch! Why did he take up with such a woman?

MASTER: Why did he seduce her and then abandon her?

HOSTESS: Why did he stop loving her without rhyme or reason?

JACQUES (pointing to the heavens): Ah! Master! . . .

MARQUIS: Why do you not get married too, Marquise?

MME DE LA POMMERAYE: To whom, if you please?

MARQUIS: To the little Count. He is witty, of good family and has a large fortune.

MME DE LA POMMERAYE: And who will answer to me for his fidelity? You, perhaps?

MARQUIS: No, but it seems to me that one can easily do without a husband's fidelity.

MME DE LA POMMERAYE: I agree, but if my husband were unfaithful to me I might perhaps be eccentric enough to take offence and I am vindictive.

MARQUIS: Well then, you would avenge yourself, obviously. We would take a town house together and we'd make the most delightful foursome.

MME DE LA POMMERAYE: That is all very nice, but I am not going to get married. The only man whom I might perhaps have been tempted to marry . . .

MARQUIS: Was me?

MME DE LA POMMERAYE: I can admit it to you now without consequence.

MARQUIS: Why did you not tell me sooner?

MME DE LA POMMERAYE: From what has happened I did well not to. The wife you are going to have suits you in every way better than I would.

Madame de La Pommeraye made her inquiries with all the precision and rapidity she wanted. She produced for the Marquis the most glowing of testimonials, both from Paris and the country. She made the Marquis wait another fortnight so that he might take stock of himself once more. This fortnight seemed an eternity to him. At last the Marquise was obliged to give in to his impatience and his entreaties. The first meeting took place at the house of her friends. Everything was agreed. The banns were published. The Marquis gave Mme de La Pommeraye a superb diamond, and the marriage was consummated.

JACQUES: What a conspiracy! What a revenge!

MASTER: She is incomprehensible.

JACQUES: Deliver me from my worries about the wedding night, but up to this moment I do not see any great harm in it.

MASTER: Shut up, you fool.

HOSTESS: The wedding night went very well.

JACQUES: But I thought . . .

HOSTESS: Don't think. Just remember what your master told you . . .

And as she said that she smiled and as she smiled she passed her hand over Jacques' face and pinched his nose: 'It was the next day.'

JACQUES: The next day wasn't like the day before?

HOSTESS: Not exactly. The next day Mme de La Pommeraye sent the Marquis a note inviting him to go to her house as soon as he could on an important matter. The Marquis did not keep her waiting. When she received him her face expressed her indignation in all its violence. Her speech was not lengthy.

'Marquis,' she said to him, 'learn to know me. If other women valued themselves enough to show the resentment I feel, men like you would be less common. You acquired an honest woman whom you could not keep. That woman was me. She has avenged herself on you by making you marry someone who is worthy of you. Leave my house and go to the Hôtel de Hambourg in the rue Traversière where you will learn the filthy trade your wife and mother-in-law carried on for ten years under the name of d'Aisnon.'

It would be impossible to describe the surprise and consternation of the poor Marquis. He did not know what to think, but his uncertainty lasted only the time it took to go from one end of town to the other. For the rest of the day he did not return home but wandered the streets. His mother-in-law and his wife had some suspicion of what had happened. At the first knock on the door his mother-in-law fled to her apartment and locked herself in. His wife waited for him alone. As her husband approached she could read on his face the fury which possessed him. She threw herself at his feet, her face pressed against the parquet, silent.

'Get out, you unspeakable creature. Get away from me.'

She wanted to get up but she fell back down on her face again, her hands stretched out on the floor between the Marquis' feet.

'Monsieur,' she said to him, 'trample me underfoot, crush me, for I have deserved it. Do with me whatever you will, but spare my mother.'

'Get away from me!' repeated the Marquis. 'Get away from me! It is enough that you have covered me with shame. Spare me a crime.'

The poor creature stayed in the same position and did not reply. The Marquis was sitting in an armchair, his head cradled in his arms, half leaning forward against the foot of his bed and shouting at her from time to time without looking at her: 'Get away from me!'

The silence and immobility of the girl took him by surprise and he shouted at her even more loudly: 'Get out, do you hear me!'

Next he bent down and pushed her away heavily. Realizing that she was unconscious and almost dead, he took her round the waist and laid her down on a sofa. For a short while he stood looking at her with an expression which alternated between commiseration and anger. He rang and his valets came. Her maids were summoned and he told them: 'Take your mistress. She is ill. Carry her into her apartment and look after her.'

A few moments afterwards he secretly sent for news of her. They told him that she had come round from her first faint but that her swoons were following in rapid succession. They were so frequent and so long that it was impossible to say whether she would recover. One or two hours afterwards he again sent secretly to find out about her condition. He was told that she was suffocating and that there had come over her a kind of repeated choking which could be heard as far away as the courtyard. The third time, towards daybreak, they told him that she had cried a lot, that her gasping had calmed and that she appeared to be dozing.

The following day the Marquis gave orders for his horses to be harnessed to his carriage and disappeared for a fortnight without anybody knowing where he had gone. However, before going, he had made all the necessary arrangements for the mother and the daughter, and had given orders that Madame's commands were to be obeyed as if they were his own.

During this time the two women remained in each other's company hardly speaking, the daughter sobbing and occasionally crying out, tearing her hair and wringing her hands, the mother not daring to go near her or console her. One was the picture of despair, the other the picture of stubborn endurance. The daughter said to her mother twenty times: 'Mother, let us leave here, let us escape,' and as many times the mother rejected the idea, replying: 'No, my daughter, we must stay. We must see what happens. This man is not going to kill us.'

'I wish to God he had already done so,' said her daughter.

Her mother replied: 'You would do better to keep quiet than to speak like a fool.'

On his return the Marquis shut himself in his study and wrote two letters, one to his wife, one to his mother-in-law. The latter left the same day and went to a Carmelite convent in the next town, where she died a few days ago. Her daughter got dressed and dragged herself to her husband's apartment, to which he had apparently summoned her. At the door she threw herself to her knees.

'Get up,' the Marquis told her . . .

Instead of getting up she went forward to him on her knees. Her whole body was shaking. Her hair was dishevelled. She was bending forward, her hands by her side, her head raised up, her gaze fixed on his eyes and her face flooded with tears.

'I think I perceive', she said to him, a sob separating her every word, 'that your justly outraged heart has softened and that perhaps with time I will obtain mercy from you. Monsieur, I beg you, do not hasten to forgive me. So many honest girls have become dishonest wives that perhaps I will provide an example to the contrary. I am not yet worthy enough for you to come near me, but wait and only leave me with the hope of forgiveness. Keep me far away from you. You will see my conduct. You will judge it. I will be a thousand times too happy, a thousand times, if you deign occasionally to summon me! Mark out for me an obscure corner of your house where you will allow me to live. I will stay there without complaint. Ah! If only I could tear away from me the name and the title which I have been made to usurp, and then die afterwards. I would instantly give you such satisfaction. I have allowed myself through weakness, seduction, domination and threats to be led to an infamous action. But do not believe, Monsieur, that I am wicked. I am not since I did not hesitate to appear before you when you summoned me and I now dare to set eyes on you and speak to you. Ah! If you could only read the bottom of my heart and see how far away from me are my past faults, how the morals of those others of my kind are alien to me. Corruption alighted on me but did not gain hold. I know myself and will do myself justice on this point, which is that by my tastes, my emotions and my character I was born worthy of the honour of belonging to you. Ah! If I had only been free to see you. I would only have needed to speak one word and I believe that I would have had the courage. Monsieur, do with me what you want. Summon your people. Let them strip me naked and throw me into the street at night. I will consent to everything. Whatever destiny you are preparing for me, I will submit to it. Some remote part of the country, the obscurity of some cloister, would remove me forever from your eyes. Just speak and I will go there. Your happiness is not lost without hope and you will be able to forget me.'

'Get up,' the Marquis said softly, 'I have forgiven you. Even as I received the offence. I respected my wife in you. Not one word has left my lips which has humiliated her or at least of which I do not repent and I promise that she will not hear one more word to humiliate her, if she only remembers that one cannot make one's spouse unhappy without becoming unhappy oneself. Be honest, be happy, and make me the same. Get up, I beg you, my wife, get up and embrace me. Madame la Marquise, get up! You are not in your proper place! Madame des Arcis, get up!'

While he was speaking she had stayed where she was, her face in her hands and her head pressed between the knees of the Marquis, but at the words 'My wife', at the words 'Madame des Arcis', she got up sharply and threw herself on to the Marquis. She held him in her arms, half suffocated by sorrow and joy. Then she pulled away from him, threw herself to the floor and kissed his feet.

'Ah!' the Marquis said to her, 'I have told you that I have forgiven you and I can see that you do not believe a word of it.'

'It is necessary', she replied, 'that it be so and that I never believe it.'

The Marquis added: 'In all honesty I believe that I regret nothing and that this Pommeraye woman, instead of avenging herself, has done me a great service. My wife, go and get dressed while our luggage is being packed. We are leaving for my estates where we will stay until we can show ourselves here again without consequence for either of us.'

They spent nearly three years away from the capital.

JACQUES: And I bet that those three years went as quickly as a day and that the Marquis des Arcis was one of the best husbands and had one of the best wives in the world.

MASTER: I'd go along with you, but to be honest I do not know why because I was not at all happy with this girl during the course of the schemings between Mme de La Pommeraye and the girl's mother. Not one moment's fear, not the slightest sign of uncertainty, not the slightest remorse. I saw her lend herself to this long and horrible scheme without any repugnance. Whatever was wanted of her, she never hesitated to do it. She went to confession and went to communion, she played at religion and played along with its ministers. She seemed to me to be as false, as despicable and as wicked as the two others.

Madame, you tell a story quite well, but you are not yet skilled enough in dramatic art. If you had wanted us to feel for this young woman, you should have made her honest and shown her to us as an innocent victim forced to her actions by her mother and de La Pommeraye. She should have been forced, against her will, by the cruellest treatment, to participate in a series of hideous and continual crimes lasting a year. That was how the reconciliation of this woman with her husband should have been prepared. When one introduces a character on the stage the role of that character must be consistent. Now, I ask you, dear lady, is the girl who plots with our two scoundrels the same imploring wife we have seen at her husband's feet? You have sinned against the rules of Aristotle, Horace, de Vida and Le Bossu.[41]

HOSTESS: I don't follow any rules. I told you the story as it happened, without leaving anything out and without adding anything. Who knows what was going on at the bottom of this young girl's heart, and whether perhaps in the moments when she appeared to us to be acting in the most carefree manner she was not secretly consumed with sorrow.

JACQUES: Madame, this time I must agree with my Master, who will forgive me for it since it happens to me so rarely. I don't know about his Bossu or those other gentlemen he mentioned either. If Mlle Duquênoi, formerly d'Aisnon, had been a nice child it would have shown through.

HOSTESS: Nice child or not, she's still an excellent wife and her husband is pleased as a lord with her and wouldn't swap her for any other.

MASTER: I congratulate him for it. He has had more luck than wisdom.

HOSTESS: And as for me, I wish you a good night. It is late and I am always the last to bed and the first to get up. What a wretched trade. *Bonsoir, messieurs, bonsoir.* I promised, I can't remember why, that I would tell you the story of a preposterous marriage and I believe that I have kept my word. Monsieur Jacques, I don't think you will have any trouble sleeping – your eyes are more than half shut already. *Bonsoir*, Monsieur Jacques.

MASTER: Madame, is there no way we will hear of your adventures?

HOSTESS: No.

JACQUES: You have a terrible appetite for stories.

MASTER: That is true. They instruct me and amuse me. A good raconteur is a rare man.

JACQUES: And that is exactly why I don't like stories – unless I am telling them.

MASTER: You prefer speaking badly to keeping quiet.

JACQUES: That is true.

MASTER: And I prefer to listen to someone speaking badly than to nothing at all.

JACQUES: And that suits us both perfectly.

I don't know where Jacques, his master and their hostess had left their wits for them not to have been able to find even one of the many things which could be said in favour of Mlle Duquênoi.

Did this girl understand anything of the schemings of Mme de La Pommeraye before they reached their end? Would she not have preferred to accept the offers of the Marquis rather than his hand and have him as her lover rather than her husband? Was she not under the continual despotism and threats of the Marquise? Can one blame her horrible aversion for an unspeakable condition? And if one gives her credit for these feelings, could one expect very much more delicacy and scruple in the choice of means to extricate herself?

And, do you think, Reader, that it is any the more difficult to offer a defence of Mme de La Pommeraye? Perhaps you would prefer to hear Jacques and his master on that subject, but they had so many more interesting things to talk about that it is probable they would have neglected to talk about this one. Allow me therefore to discuss it for a moment.

You are furious at the mention of the name Mme de La Pommeraye; you are crying out: 'Ah! What a horrible woman! Ah! What a hypocrite! Ah! What a scoundrel!'

Do not exclaim, do not get angry, do not take sides. Let us reason. Every day blacker crimes than hers are committed but without any genius. You may hate Mme de La Pommeraye, you may fear her, but you will not despise her. Her vengeance is abominable but it is unsullied by any mercenary motive.

I did not tell you that she threw the beautiful diamond which the Marquis had given her back in his face, but she did, and I have it on the best authority. It wasn't a question of increasing her fortune or gaining honourable titles. If this woman had done as much to obtain for a husband the due rewards for his services, if she had prostituted herself to a minister, or even a first secretary, for some decoration or a regiment, or to the keeper of the register of benefices for a rich abbey, that would seem all too simple. Everyday experience would be on your side. But when she avenges a treacherous act you become indignant with her instead of seeing that her resentment only moves you to indignation because you yourself are incapable of feeling such deep resentment, or perhaps because you place almost no value on the honour of women. Have you reflected a little on the sacrifices Mme de La Pommeraye had made for the Marquis? There is no point in telling you that her purse had been open to him whenever required and that for several years he had no other home, no other table, than hers. You'd merely shake your head, but she had given in to his every whim, to his every taste, and in order to please him she had turned her life upside down. She enjoyed the highest esteem in society because of the purity of her morals and she had now lowered herself to the common rank. People said, when they saw she had accepted the attentions of the Marquis des Arcis, 'At last that wonderful Mme de La Pommeraye has become one of us . . .' All around her she had noticed ironic smiles and heard their jokes which often made her blush and lower her eyes. She had drained the cup of bitterness reserved for those women whose blameless conduct has for too long shown up the morals of other women around them. She had endured all the scandal and publicity by which society takes its revenge on those rash prudes who make a show of propriety. She was proud and she would have died of shame rather than show society the ridiculous spectacle of forsaken love following lost virtue. She was nearing the age when the loss of a lover cannot be made good. Her character was such that this event condemned her to boredom and solitude. A man will stab another for a gesture or a denial. Is it not permissible for an honest woman who has been lost, dishonoured and betrayed to throw the man who betrayed her into the arms of a courtesane? Ah! Reader, you are frivolous in praise and harsh in censure. But are you saying: 'It is more the way the thing was done than the thing itself that I reproach in the Marquise. I cannot accept such a long-lived resentment, an intrigue of lies and deceit lasting nearly a year.' But then, nor can I, nor Jacques, nor his master, nor their hostess. One does, however, forgive everything that is done in the heat of the moment and I can tell you that, if the heat of the moment means a short while for you and me, for Mme de La Pommeraye and women of her character it is a long time. Sometimes their heart continues for the rest of their life to feel the injury just as deeply as in the first moment, and what is wrong or unjust about that? I see in it nothing more than a less ordinary type of treachery and I would strongly approve of a law which condemned to the company of prostitutes whomsoever might have seduced and abandoned any honest woman. The common man to the common woman.

Meanwhile, while I have been expatiating, Jacques' master is snoring as if he had been listening to me, and Jacques, who has lost the use of the muscles in his legs, is prowling around the room barefoot in his nightshirt, bumping into everything in his way, eventually awakening his master, who said to him from behind his bed curtains: 'Jacques, you're drunk!'

'Or not far from it.'

'And what time do you intend to go to bed?'

'Soon, Monsieur. It's just . . . it's just . . .'

'It's just that what?'

'There's a little left in this bottle which will go off. I hate half-empty bottles. I'd remember in bed and I don't need more than that to stop me getting a moment's sleep. By God, Madame our hostess is an excellent woman and her champagne is excellent as well. It would be a shame to let it go bad. There, it will soon be covered up and then it won't go bad any more.'

And while he was babbling away, Jacques, in his nightshirt and bare feet, had knocked back two or three glasses without punctuation, as he used to say, that is from the bottle to the glass and from the glass straight into his mouth. There are two versions of what happened after he had put out the light. Some claim that he started to feel his way along the walls of the room without being able to find his bed and that he said: 'My God, it isn't there any more or if it is it must be written up above that I won't find it. One way or another I'll have to do without.' And then he decided to stretch out on some chairs. Others claim that it was written up above that he would trip over the legs of the chairs and that he would fall on to the floor where he stayed.

Tomorrow or the day after, when you have had time to consider more fully, you may choose whichever of these two versions suits you best.

Having gone to bed late and a little the worse for wear our two travellers overslept the next morning, Jacques on the floor or the chairs, according to whichever version you prefer, his master more comfortably in his bed. Their hostess came up and told them that the day would not be fine and that even if the weather allowed them to continue on their way they would have to choose between risking their lives in trying to cross the swollen streams on their way or being forced back, as had already happened to several men on horseback who'd chosen not to believe her.

The master said to Jacques: 'Jacques, what shall we do?'

Jacques replied: 'First we will have breakfast with our hostess. That will give us the answer.'

The hostess swore that this was a wise decision. Breakfast was served.

Now their hostess wanted nothing better than a cheerful time and Jacques' master would have been quite happy to join in but Jacques was beginning to suffer. He ate reluctantly, drank little, and did not speak. This last symptom was especially serious. It was because of the bad night he had spent and the bad bed he had spent it in. He complained of pains in his limbs and his hoarse voice indicated a sore throat. His master advised him to go to bed but he wouldn't hear of it. Their hostess offered to make him some onion soup. He asked for a fire to be lit in his room because he was feeling cold and for them to make him some tisane and bring him a bottle of white wine. This was done immediately. When their hostess was gone, Jacques was left alone with his master. His master went over to the window and said: 'What devilish weather!', looked at his watch to see what the time was, because it was the only one he trusted, took a pinch of snuff from his snuff-box and did the same thing hour by hour, saying every time: 'What devilish weather!', and then turning to Jacques and adding: 'This would be a good moment for you to carry on and finish the story of your loves! But one cannot talk well of love and other things when one is in pain. Listen, see how you feel. If you can carry on, do so. If not drink your tisane and sleep.'

Jacques claimed that silence was bad for him, that he was a talkative creature and the principal advantage of his present position and the one which mattered the most to him was the freedom it gave him to make up for the twelve years he had spent gagged in the house of his grandfather – on whose soul may God have mercy.

MASTER: Speak, then, since it gives us both pleasure. You had got up to some dishonest proposition or other made by the surgeon's wife. It was a question, I believe, of throwing out the surgeon in the château and installing her husband there.

JACQUES: I remember. But one moment, if you please. Let us imbibe.

Jacques filled up a large goblet with tisane, poured a little white wine into it and swallowed the brew. It was a recipe which he had got from his Captain and which M. Tissot, who had got it from Jacques, recommends in his treatise on common illnesses.[42] White wine, as Jacques and M. Tissot used to say, makes you piss, is a diuretic, enriches the bland flavour of the tisane and improves the tone of the stomach and intestine. When he had drunk his glass of tisane, Jacques continued. –

JACQUES: There I was, out of the surgeon's house, into the carriage, arrived at the château and surrounded by everyone who lived there.

MASTER: Did they know who you were?

JACQUES: Most certainly. Do you remember a certain lady with a pitcher of oil?

MASTER: Very well.

JACQUES: This woman was the messenger of the steward and the servants. Jeanne had extolled the act of commiseration I had performed towards her around the château. My good deed had come to the ears of the master of the château who had also heard of the kicks and punches with which I had been rewarded that night on the high-road. He had given orders for me to be found and brought to his château. There I was. They looked at me, asked me questions, and admired me. Jeanne embraced me and thanked me.

'Give him a comfortable room,' the master said to his people, 'and see that he lacks for nothing.'

Then he said to the surgeon of the house: 'Take good care of him.'

His instructions were followed to the letter. There now, Master. Who knows what is written up above? Tell me whether it was a good or a bad thing to have given away my money or whether it was a bad thing to have been beaten up. Without these two events M. Desglands would never have heard of Jacques.

MASTER: Monsieur Desglands, Seigneur of Miremont! You are at the château of Miremont? At my old friend's house, the father of M. Desforges, the King's Administrator for the province?

JACQUES: Exactly. And the young girl with the beautiful figure and black eyes . . .

MASTER: Is Denise, Jeanne's daughter?

JACQUES: The same.

MASTER: You are right. She is one of the most beautiful creatures to be found within a radius of fifty miles of the château. Most of the men who used to visit Desglands' château, including myself, tried everything possible to seduce her but all to no avail. There was not one of us who would not have committed great follies for her provided she committed a little one for him . . .

Here Jacques stopped talking and his master asked him: 'What are you thinking about, what are you doing?'

JACQUES: I am saying my prayer.

MASTER: Do you pray?

JACQUES: Sometimes.

MASTER: And what do you say?

JACQUES: I say: 'Thou who mad'st the Great Scroll, whatever Thou art, Thou whose finger hast traced the Writing Up Above, Thou hast known for all time what I needed, Thy will be done. Amen.'

MASTER: Don't you think you would do just as well if you shut up?

JACQUES: Perhaps yes, perhaps no. I pray on the off-chance, and no matter what might happen to me I would neither rejoice nor complain if I could keep control of myself. But I am inconsistent and violent and I forget the lessons or the principles of my Captain and laugh and cry like an idiot.

MASTER: And did your Captain never laugh or cry?

JACQUES: Rarely . . . Jeanne brought her daughter to me one morning and addressing me first she said: 'Monsieur, here you are in a beautiful château where you will be a little better looked after than at your surgeon's house. In the first days especially you will be wonderfully looked after, but I know servants, I've been one long enough. Little by little their zeal wears off, their masters will no longer think of you, and if your illness lasts you will be forgotten, and so completely forgotten that if you took it into your head to die of hunger you would succeed.

'Listen, Denise,' she said to her daughter, 'I want you to visit this good man four times a day, in the morning, at lunch time, at five o'clock and at supper time. I want you to obey him as you would me. That is an order, make sure you obey it.'

MASTER: Do you know what happened to poor Desglands?

JACQUES: No, Monsieur, but if the wishes which I made for his prosperity have not been fulfilled it is not for want of their being sincere. It was he who gave me to Commander La Boulaye who died on his way to Malta. And it was Commander La Boulaye who gave me to his elder brother, the Captain, who is now probably dead from the fistula, and it is this Captain who gave me to his youngest brother, the Advocate-General of Toulouse who went mad and was shut up by the family. It was M. Pascal, Advocate-General of Toulouse, who gave me to the Comte de Tourville who preferred to take a

...abit and let his beard grow rather than risk his life. It was the Comte ...rville who gave me to the Marquise du Belloy who ran away to ...on with a foreigner. It was the Marquise du Belloy who gave me to one of h.. cousins who ruined himself with women and went off to the Indies and it was that cousin who gave me to a M. Hérissant, a usurer by profession, who was investing the money of M. de Rusai, doctor of the Sorbonne who placed me with Mlle Isselin whom you were keeping as your mistress and who placed me with you, who will provide me with a crust of bread in my old age, as you promised, if I stay with you.[43] And there is not the slightest indication that we will separate. Jacques was made for you and you were made for Jacques.

MASTER: But Jacques, you went through a large number of houses in a very short time.

JACQUES: That is true. Sometimes they dismissed me.

MASTER: Why?

JACQUES: Because I was born a talker and all those people wanted silence. They are not like you, who would suggest I find another position if I shut up tomorrow. I have got precisely the vice which suits you. But what happened to M. Desglands? Tell me, while I pour myself some more tisane.

MASTER: You lived in his château and you never heard about his spot?

JACQUES: No.

MASTER: That story will be for the road. The other one is short. He made his fortune gambling. Then he attached himself to a woman whom you might have seen in his château, an intelligent woman, but serious, taciturn, unconventional and hard. This woman told him one day: 'Either you love me better than you love gambling, in which case you will give me your word of honour that you will never gamble again, or you love gambling better than me, in which case you will never speak to me again of love and gamble as much as you want.'
Desglands gave his word of honour that he would never gamble again.
'No matter how big or small the stakes?'
'No matter how big or small.'
They had been living together in the château which you know for around ten years when Desglands, having been called to town on business, had the misfortune to meet at his lawyer's one of his old gambling cronies who dragged him off to dinner in a gambling den, where he lost everything he

owned in a single sitting. His mistress was unyielding. She was rich and gave Desglands a small pension and left him for ever.

JACQUES: That's a shame. He was a good man.

MASTER: How's the throat?

JACQUES: Bad.

MASTER: That's because you are speaking too much and not drinking enough.

JACQUES: That's because I don't like tisane and I like speaking.

MASTER: Well then, Jacques, there you are at Desglands' château, near Denise, and Denise has been authorized by her mother to visit you at least four times a day. The hussy! Prefer a Jacques!

JACQUES: A Jacques! A Jacques, Monsieur, is a man like any other.[44]

MASTER: Jacques, you are wrong. A Jacques is not a man like any other.

JACQUES: He is sometimes better than another.

MASTER: Jacques, you are forgetting yourself. Get on with the story of your loves and remember that you are only and will never be anything other than a Jacques.

JACQUES: When we came across those rogues in the cottage, if Jacques hadn't been worth a bit more than his master . . .

MASTER: Jacques, you are insolent. You are abusing my kindness. If I was foolish enough to raise you from your proper place I can always send you back. Jacques, take your bottle and your pot of tisane and go downstairs.

JACQUES: You say what you like, Monsieur, I am comfortable here and I will not go downstairs.

MASTER: I tell you, you will go downstairs.

JACQUES: I am sure that what you say is wrong. What, Monsieur, after having accustomed me over ten years to live as your equal . . .

MASTER: It is my pleasure to put an end to all that.

JACQUES: After having put up with all my impertinence . . .

MASTER: I will suffer it no more.

JACQUES: After having seated me next to you at table, having called me your friend . . .

MASTER: You do not know the meaning of the word 'friend' when it is used by a superior to his inferior.

JACQUES: When everybody knows that your orders aren't worth a fig unless they have been ratified by Jacques; after your name and mine have become so well linked that one never goes without the other and everyone says: 'Jacques and his master . . .', all of a sudden you take it into your head to separate them. No, Monsieur, it will not be so. It is written up above that as long as Jacques lives, as long as his master lives, and even after they are both dead, people will still say: 'Jacques and his master'.

MASTER: And I tell you, Jacques, that you will go downstairs and you will go downstairs immediately because I order you to.

JACQUES: Monsieur, order me to do anything else if you want me to obey.

Here Jacques' master got up, took Jacques by the lapels and said gravely: 'Go downstairs.'
Jacques replied coldly: 'I will not go downstairs.'
His master shook him hard and said: 'Go down, you scoundrel, obey me.'
'Scoundrel if you wish, but the scoundrel will not go downstairs. Listen, Monsieur, what I have in my head, as they say, I have in my heels. You are losing your temper for nothing. Jacques is staying where he is and will not go downstairs.'
And then Jacques and his master, who had been restrained up to this point, both lost control at the same time and started shouting.
'You will go down!'
'I will not go down!'
'You will go down!'
'I will not go down!'
At this noise their hostess came up to see what it was all about but she didn't get an answer straight away since they carried on shouting.
'You will go down.'
'I will not go down.'
Then the master, with heavy heart, stalked up and down the room grumbling: 'Have you ever seen anything like it?'
The hostess, who was standing there in amazement, said: 'Messieurs, what's going on?'

Jacques did not move but said to the hostess: 'It's my master. He's gone off his head. He's mad.'

MASTER: Soft, you mean.

JACQUES: If you say so.

MASTER (to hostess): Did you hear that?

HOSTESS: He's wrong, but peace, peace. Speak, one of you or the other, and let me know what it's all about.

MASTER (to Jacques): Speak, you scoundrel.

JACQUES (to master): Speak yourself.

HOSTESS (to Jacques): Come along, Monsieur Jacques, speak. Your master has ordered you to and after all a master is a master.

Jacques explained the thing to their hostess. When she had heard it the hostess said: 'Messieurs, do you agree to accept me as arbitrator?'

JACQUES AND HIS MASTER (at the same time): Willingly, willingly, Madame.

'And will you promise me on your word of honour to carry out my sentence?'

JACQUES AND HIS MASTER: On our word of honour.

Then the hostess sat down at table and taking on the grave manner of a magistrate she said: 'Having heard the declaration of Monsieur Jacques and having considered the facts which would tend to prove that his master is a good, indeed a very good, in fact too good a master, and that Jacques is not a bad servant although sometimes subject to confound absolute and irrecoverable possession with passing and gratuitous concession, I hereby annul the equality which has been established between them by virtue of lapse of time and hereby recreate it simultaneously. Jacques will go downstairs and when he shall have gone downstairs he shall come back up again and there shall revert to him all the prerogatives he has exercised up to this date. His master shall tender his hand to him and shall say to him in friendship: "Hello, Jacques, I am pleased to see you again", and Jacques will reply: "And I, Monsieur, am delighted to return." And I forbid this business ever to be discussed by them or the prerogative of master and servant ever to be re-examined by them again. It is our wish that the one shall order and the other obey, each as best he can, and that there be left between that which the one can and that which the other must the same obscurity as heretofore.'

In finishing this judgement, which she had lifted from some work of that time published on the occasion of a similar quarrel when from one end of the kingdom to the other the entire country could hear the master crying to his servant: 'You will go down!', and the servant from his side shouting: 'I will not go down!',[45] 'Come along,' she said to Jacques, 'give me your arm without any more argument.'

Jacques cried out plaintively: 'It must have been written up above that I would go downstairs.'

The hostess said to Jacques: 'It is written up above that at the moment when any man takes a master he will go down, rise up, go forward, go backward or stay where he is without his feet ever being free to refuse the orders of his head. Give me your arm and let my order be fulfilled.'

Jacques gave his arm to their hostess but they had hardly passed the threshold of the room when the master threw himself on to Jacques and embraced him. Then he let go of Jacques to embrace the hostess and then both of them together saying: 'It is written up above that I shall never get rid of that character there and so long as I live he shall be my master and I shall be his servant.'

The hostess added: 'And as far as one can tell neither of you will be any the worse off.'

After the hostess had calmed their quarrel, which she took for the first of its kind when there had been more than a hundred like it, and reinstated Jacques in his former position, she carried on about her business and the master said to Jacques: 'Now that we have calmed down and are in a state where we can make clear judgements, will you not acknowledge it?'

JACQUES: I will admit that when one has given one's word of honour one must keep it, and since we gave our judge our word of honour not to come back to this business we must speak no more of it.

MASTER: You are right.

JACQUES: But without coming back on this dispute, could we not prevent a hundred more like it by means of some reasonable arrangement?

MASTER: I agree to that.

JACQUES: Whereas it is agreed: Firstly, considering that it is written up above that I am essential to you, that I know it, and that I know that you cannot do without me, I will abuse this advantage each and every time the occasion presents itself.

MASTER: But Jacques, no such agreement was ever made.

JACQUES: Made or not, that's how it has been for all time, is now, and ever shall be. Do you imagine that other men have not looked for a way to escape from this decree or that you are cleverer than them? Rid yourself of that idea and submit yourself to the rule of a necessity from which you cannot escape.

Whereas it is agreed: Secondly, considering that it is just as impossible for Jacques not to know his ascendancy over his master as it is for his master to be unaware of his own weakness and divest himself of his indulgence, it is therefore necessary that Jacques be insolent, and that for the sake of peace his master not notice. All of this was arranged without our knowledge, all of this was sealed by Fate at the moment when nature created Jacques and his master. It was ordained that you would have the title to the thing and I would have the thing itself. If you wish to oppose yourself to the will of nature you will only make a fool of yourself.

MASTER: But if that is right your lot is worth more than mine.

JACQUES: Who's arguing with you?

MASTER: Then if that is true I have only to take your place and put you in mine.

JACQUES: Do you know what would happen then? You would lose the title to the thing and still not have it. Let us stay as we are. It suits us both very well, and let the rest of our life be devoted to creating a proverb.

MASTER: What proverb?

JACQUES: Jacques leads his master. It will be said of us first but it will be repeated about a thousand others who are worth more than you or me.

MASTER: That seems to be hard, very hard.

JACQUES: My Master, my dear Master, you are shying away from a needle which will only prick you the harder. That is what has been agreed between us.

MASTER: What relevance has our consent got if it's a law of necessity?

JACQUES: A lot. Do you not think that it would be useful to know where we stand, clearly and precisely, once and for all? The only reason for all our quarrels up to now is that we had not accepted, for your part, that you would call yourself my master and, for my part, that I would be yours. But now that is all understood and all that remains for us is to carry on our way accordingly.

MASTER: Where the devil did you learn all that?

JACQUES: In the great book. Ah! Master, no matter how much a man may study, reflect and meditate on all the books in the world, he is nothing more than a minor scribe unless he has read the great book.

After lunch the sun came out. A few travellers assured them that the stream could now be crossed. Jacques went downstairs. His master paid their hostess very generously. At the door of the inn quite a large number of travellers who had been held back by the bad weather were getting ready to continue on their way. Among these travellers were Jacques and his master, the man who had made the ridiculous marriage and his friend. Those travellers who were on foot had taken their sticks and their bundles, others had got into their wagons or coaches and those with horses were mounted up drinking stirrup cups. Their gracious hostess had a bottle in one hand and was giving out glasses and filling them, not forgetting her own. They all made obliging remarks to her which she replied to with politeness and gaiety. Then they spurred their horses, waved goodbye and went off into the distance.

It so happened that Jacques, his master, the Marquis des Arcis and his young travelling companion were going the same way. Out of these four characters only the last one is unknown to you. He was barely twenty-two or twenty-three. His face showed that he was a person of great timidity. He carried his head a little inclined towards his left shoulder. He was quiet and showed hardly any knowledge of worldly ways. If he bowed he lowered the upper part of his body without moving his legs. When seated he had the peculiar habit of taking the tails of his coat and crossing them on his thighs, keeping his hands in the pockets, and also the peculiar habit of listening to whoever was speaking with his eyes almost shut. From this extraordinary bearing of his, Jacques figured him out, and moving close to his master's ear he said: 'I bet you that young man was a monk.'

'Why is that, Jacques?'

'You'll see.'

Our four travellers carried on together, talking about the rain, good weather, their hostess, their host and about the argument the Marquis des

Arcis had had about Nicole. This starved and filthy bitch kept wiping herself on his stockings and, after he had chased her away several times with his napkin to no avail, out of impatience he let fly a rather violent kick . . . And then all of a sudden the conversation turned to this singular attachment women have for animals. Everyone said what they thought. Jacques' master turned towards Jacques and said: 'And you, Jacques, what do you think?'

Jacques asked his master if he had ever noticed that no matter what poverty people lived in, even if they hadn't got enough bread for themselves, they always kept dogs. If he hadn't noticed that these dogs were always trained to turn circles, walk on their hind legs, dance, retrieve, jump into the air at the name of the king or the queen or play dead, and this training had made them the most unfortunate beasts in the world. From this he concluded that every man wants to command another and that since animals are immediately below the lowest classes of society which are ordered around by all the other classes, these get hold of animals so that they too can order someone around . . .

'And so,' said Jacques, 'everyone has his dog. The Minister is the King's dog, the First Secretary is the Minister's dog, the wife is the husband's dog, or the husband the wife's dog. Favori is so-and-so's dog and Thibault is the man on the corner's dog.

'When my master makes me speak when I want to be silent, which in all honesty happens rarely,' continued Jacques, 'or when he makes me silent when I want to speak, which is very difficult, or when he asks me to tell the story of my loves when I want to talk about something else, or when I have started the story of my loves and he interrupts me, am I anything other than his dog? Weak men are the dogs of the strong.'

MASTER: But, Jacques, I haven't noticed this attachment to animals only in the poor. I know many great ladies who are surrounded by packs of dogs, and that's without counting their cats, parrots and songbirds.

JACQUES: It makes them look ridiculous as well as those around them. They love nobody and nobody loves them and so they throw this emotion which they don't know what to do with to their dogs.

MARQUIS DES ARCIS: To love animals means to throw one's heart to the dogs. That is a singular interpretation.

MASTER: What they give to those animals would be enough to feed two or three of the poor.

JACQUES: Does that surprise you now?

MASTER: No.

The Marquis des Arcis turned his eyes on Jacques, smiled at his ideas, and then, speaking to his master, he said: 'That is a most extraordinary servant you have there.'

MASTER: A servant. You are too kind. It is I who am his. And he almost proved it to me this morning in due and established form.

While they were talking they arrived at the place where they were to spend the night, and took rooms together. Jacques' master and the Marquis des Arcis had supper together. Jacques and the young man were served separately. The master explained to the Marquis in four words the story of Jacques and his fatalistic turn of mind. The Marquis spoke of the young man who was with him. He had been a Premonstratensian and had left his abbey through a bizarre incident.[46] Some friends of the Marquis had recommended him to the Marquis who had made him his secretary while waiting for better things.

'That's funny.'

'What do you find funny about that?'

'I was speaking of Jacques. Hardly had we gone into the inn we have just left when Jacques whispered to me: "Monsieur, take a good look at that young man. I bet that he was a monk."'

'He guessed correctly, but I don't know how. Do you normally go to bed early?'

'Not usually, and this evening I am in even less of a hurry since we have only made half a day's travel.'

'If you have nothing more useful or agreeable to do I will tell you the story of my secretary. It's rather unusual.'

'I'll be glad to hear it.'

I can hear you, Reader, you are asking me: 'What about the story of Jacques' loves? . .'

Do you think that I am not as curious as you? Have you forgotten that Jacques loved to speak, and especially about himself, which is the normal obsession of people of his condition, an obsession which raises them from their debasement, which puts them on a pedestal and suddenly transforms them into interesting people? What do you think is the reason that the populace is attracted to public executions? Inhumanity? Well, you are wrong. The populace is not inhuman but if it could it would tear from the hands of justice the unfortunate man around whose gallows it gathers.

The man in the street goes to the Place de Grève so that he can see something which he can in his turn tell to others in his suburb. Whatever the scene it doesn't matter, just so long as it gives him a role to play, makes his neighbours gather round him, and makes them listen to him. Put on some exciting festival on the boulevard and you will see that the place of execution will be empty. The populace is hungry for something to look at and goes there because it enjoys seeing it and even more enjoys telling others about it afterwards. The populace is terrible in its fury but that does not last long. Its own poverty has made it compassionate and it turns its eyes away from the spectacle of horror which it has gone to see, is moved to pity and goes home crying.

Everything which I have just told you, Reader, I was told by Jacques. I admit it to you because I do not like to take the credit for the cleverness of others. Jacques knew neither the word vice nor the word virtue. He claimed that we were all born at a good or an evil hour. When he heard the words reward or punishment he used to shrug his shoulders. According to him reward was the encouragement of the good and punishment the fear of the wicked. How could it be otherwise, he used to ask, if we have no freedom and our destiny is written up above? He believed that a man follows his path towards glory or ignominy as ineluctably as a boulder with consciousness of its self might roll down the side of a mountain, and that if the series of causes and effects which form the life of a man, beginning at the first moment of his birth up to his last breath, were known to us, we would remain convinced that he had only ever done the inevitable.

I have often argued the contrary with him but to no avail and without success. What does one say to somebody who says: 'Whatever the sum total of the elements I am composed of I am still one entity. Now one cause has only one effect. I have always been one single cause and I have therefore only ever had one effect to produce. My existence in time is therefore nothing more than a series of necessary effects'?

Thus did Jacques reason in the manner of his Captain. The distinction between a physical world and a moral world seemed to him to be devoid of sense. His Captain had crammed into Jacques' head all these opinions which he had found in his Spinoza, whom he knew by heart. According to this system one might imagine that Jacques neither rejoiced in nor despaired of anything. But that was not, however, quite correct. He acted more or less like you and me. He thanked his benefactor so that he might do him more good and got angry with the unjust man. When people pointed out to him that this was like a dog biting the stone that hurt him, he would say: 'No, the stone that the dog bites will not correct itself but the unjust man is often corrected by the stick.'

Like you and me he was often inconsistent, and inclined to forget his principles, except, of course, in the moments when his philosophy dominated him and then he would say: 'That had to be so because it was written up above.'

He tried to anticipate misfortune and while he showed the greatest disdain for prudence he was always prudent. When misfortune struck he came back to his motto and was always consoled by it. Otherwise he was a good man, frank, honest, courageous, loyal, faithful, very stubborn, even more talkative and as upset as you and me at having started the story of his loves with hardly any hope of finishing it.[47]

And so I advise you, Reader, to submit yourself to the inevitable and in the absence of the story of Jacques' loves to make the best of the story of the Marquis des Arcis' secretary. Besides, I can see him, this poor Jacques, his neck wrapped in a large handkerchief, his gourd, hitherto full of good wine, now holding no more than tisane, coughing and cursing the hostess of the inn they had just left and her champagne, which he would not be doing if he only remembered that everything is written up above, even his cold.

And what is this, Reader? One love story after another! That makes one, two, three, four love stories I've told you and three or four more still to come. That is a lot of love stories. It is also a fact that since I am writing for you I must either go without your applause or follow your taste, and you have shown a decided taste for love stories. All of your works, whether in prose or verse, are love stories. Nearly all your poems, elegies, eclogues, idylls, songs, epistles, comedies, tragedies and operas are love stories. Nearly all your paintings and sculptures are no more than love stories. Love stories have been your only food ever since you existed, and you show no sign of ever growing tired of them. You have been kept on this diet and will be kept on it for a very long time to come, all of you, men, women and children, both big and small, and you will never grow tired of it. To be truthful it is really very strange . . . I wish that the Marquis' secretary's story was yet another kind of love story, but I am afraid that it is nothing of the kind, and you will be bored. Well, that is too bad for the Marquis des Arcis, too bad for Jacques' master, for you, Reader, and for me too.

'There comes a moment when nearly all young girls and young boys become melancholic. They are disturbed by a vague uneasiness which extends to everything and can find no consolation. They look for solitude. They weep. The silence of the cloister moves them and the image of peace which seems to reign in religious houses seduces them. They mistake the first movements of their developing emotions for the voice of God calling them and it is at the precise moment when nature is calling to them that they embrace a life which is contrary to the laws of nature. Their mistake does not last. The voice of nature becomes clearer and is heard and the prisoner falls into regrets, listlessness, swooning, madness or despair.'

That was how the Marquis des Arcis started.

'At the age of seventeen, disgusted with the world, Richard left his father's house to take the habit of a Premonstratensian.'

MASTER: A Premonstratensian? I am pleased at his choice. Their habits are white as swans and Saint Norbert who founded them left only one thing out of their constitutions . . .

MARQUIS: To give them each a two-seater carriage.

MASTER: If it wasn't already Cupid's custom to go naked he would wear the habit of a Premonstratensian. That order has the most extraordinary ways. You are allowed to have a duchess, a marquise, a countess, the wife of a president, a counsellor or even a financier, but not the wife of a bourgeois. No matter how pretty the shopkeeper's wife you will rarely see a Premonstratensian in a shop.

MARQUIS: That is what Richard told me. Richard would have taken his vows after two years in the novitiate if his parents had not expressed their opposition. His father insisted that he return to his house and that he should test his vocation by following all the rules of the monastic life at home for a year. And this pact was faithfully carried out on both sides. When he had spent the trial year under the eyes of his family Richard again asked to take his vows. His father said to him: 'I gave you a year so that you could finally make up your mind and I hope that you will not refuse me one for the same reason. All that I will agree to is that you spend that year wherever you please.'

While waiting for the end of the second period the Abbot of the Order took up Richard and it is during this interval that he became implicated in one of those intrigues which can only ever happen in monasteries.

There was at that time at the head of one of the Houses of the Order a Superior of extraordinary character. He was called *le père Hudson*. Father Hudson had the most attractive features, a large forehead, oval face, aquiline nose, large blue eyes, large handsome cheeks, a generous mouth, fine teeth, the most subtle smile and, on his head, a forest of white hair which added dignity to the attractiveness of his face. He was a man of intelligence, knowledge and gaiety, dignified in speech and manner, with a love of order and of work, but also a man of the most fiery passions and the most immoderate love of pleasure and women, a consummate genius for intrigue, the most dissolute morals and the most absolute despotism over his own House. When he was given charge of it, the House was blighted by ignorant Jansenism. The studies of the House were neglected, its temporal affairs were in disorder, religious duties were no longer fulfilled, the divine services were celebrated without proper respect and the surplus accommodation was occupied by dissolute lodgers. Father Hudson either won over or sent away the Jansenists, presided personally over the studies of the House, put the temporal affairs in order, reintroduced the monastic rule, expelled the scandalous lodgers and introduced regularity and propriety into the celebration of the divine offices, making his community one of the most edifying. But he himself dispensed with the austerity to which he subjected the others. He was not fool enough to follow this rule of iron under which he held his subordinates, who consequently were moved against Father Hudson with a fury which was all the more violent and dangerous for being secret. Every one of them was his enemy and spied on him. Every one busied himself secretly in order to penetrate the mystery surrounding his conduct. Every one of them kept his own record of Hudson's secret depravity. Every one of them was resolved to bring about his downfall. He couldn't make a move without being followed. He had no sooner planned some intrigue than it was known about. The Abbot of the Order had a house adjoining the monastery. This house had two doors, one of which opened on to the street, the other into the cloister. Hudson had forced the locks and this house had become the retreat for his nocturnal activities and the bed of the Abbot that of his pleasures. It was through this door which led into the street that when night had fallen he would personally bring into the rooms of the Abbey women of every condition. It was here that he would give his delicate supper parties. Hudson had a confessional and he had corrupted every one of his female penitents who was worth the trouble. Among these penitents there was a little confectioner who was well known in the quarter because of her coquettishness and her charms. Since he was not able to go to her house Hudson shut her up in his seraglio. Such an abduction did not take place without arousing the suspicions of her parents and her husband. They came to visit him. Hudson listened to them with an air of dismay. While these good people were explaining their sorrows to him the bell rang. It was six o'clock in the evening. Hudson bade them be silent, took off his hat, stood up, crossed himself generously and started off in a sincere and vibrant tone *'Angelus Domini nuntiavit Mariae . . .'*, leaving the father and brothers of the little confectioner ashamed of their suspicions to say to the husband as they were on their way down the stairs: 'My son, you're an idiot . . .'; 'Brother, have you no shame? . . . A man who says the angelus! A saint! . . .'

One winter's evening on his way back to his monastery he was accosted by one of those creatures who solicit passers-by. She seemed pretty. He followed her. Hardly had he gone into her house when the night watch arrived. This incident would have been the undoing of another man but Hudson was a cool customer and the incident won him the friendship and the protection of the Commissioner of Police. When he was brought into his presence this is what he said: 'My name is Hudson. I am the Superior of my House. When I arrived there everything was in disorder. There was no learning, no discipline, no morals. The spiritual life was neglected to the point of scandal and the neglect of temporal affairs threatened the imminent ruin of the House. I have reformed everything but I am a man and I preferred to address myself to a corrupt woman than to an honest one. You may now do with me what you will.'

The magistrate advised him to be more careful in the future, promised he would say nothing of the incident, and indicated a desire to get to know him better.

However, the enemies he was surrounded by had each individually sent to the General of the Order memoranda in which what they knew of Hudson's misconduct was exposed. Comparison of these records only increased their strength. The General was a Jansenist and consequently inclined to seek vengeance for the kind of persecution which Hudson had led against adherents of his belief. He would have been only too pleased to extend the reproach against one defender of laxism and the papal bull *Unigenitus* to the whole sect. Consequently he entrusted the different records of the actions and deeds of Hudson to two commissioners whom he secretly sent away to the Abbey with orders to verify these and obtain legally admissible evidence. He instructed them above all to show the greatest circumspection in the way they went about the business since it was the sole means of bringing about the downfall of the guilty party and removing him from the protection of the court and Mirepoix, in whose eyes Jansenism was the greatest of all crimes, and submission to the bull *Unigenitus* was the greatest of all virtues.[48] Richard, my secretary, was one of these two investigators. The two men left the novice house and were installed in Hudson's Abbey, where they secretly set about obtaining information. Before long they had gathered a list of more crimes than it needed to send fifty monks to the *in pace*.[49] Their stay had been a long one but their conduct had been so skilful that nothing had leaked out. Hudson, sly as he was, was nearing the moment of his undoing without the least suspicion. However, the newcomers' failure to pay court to him, the secrecy of their journey, their frequent discussions with the other monks and their journeys out, sometimes together, sometimes alone, the kind of people they visited and who visited them all caused him some anxiety. He watched them and had them spied on and before long the object of their mission became clear to him. He did not lose his self-assurance but busied himself in finding a way not of escaping the storm which was threatening him but of bringing it down on the heads of the two commissioners, and this is the extraordinary way he went about it.

He had seduced a young girl whom he held hidden in a little lodging in the Saint-Medard quarter. He went straight to her house and this is what he said to her: 'My child, everything has been discovered and we are lost. Before the week is out you will be locked up and I do not know what will become of me. But do not despair, do not cry, pull yourself together. Listen to me and do what I tell you. Do it well and I will take care of the rest.

'Tomorrow I am leaving for the country. During my absence go and find two monks whose names I shall give you,' and he named the two commissioners. 'Ask to speak to them in secret. When you are alone with them, throw yourself at their feet, beg their help, beseech their impartiality, beg their mediation with the General over whom you know they have so much influence. Cry, sob, tear out your hair, and while you are crying and sobbing and tearing your hair tell them all about us and tell them in the way which will inspire the most commiseration for you and the most horror of me.'

'What, Monsieur, do you want me to tell them . . .'

'Yes, you will tell them who you are, who your family is, that I seduced you, yes, seduced you, in the confessional, abducted you from your parents and shut you away in the house you are in now. Tell them that after having dishonoured you and thrown you into crime I have abandoned you in squalor. Tell them that you do not know what will become of you.'

'But, Father Hudson . . .'

'Either you will do what I have told you and what I am about to tell you or you will bring about your downfall and mine. These two monks will not fail to feel sorry for you, to offer their assistance, and ask for a second meeting which you will consent to. They will make inquiries of you and your parents and, since you will not have told them anything which is not true, they will not become suspicious. After the first and second meeting I will tell you what you have to do at the third. All that I ask of you is that you play your role well.'

Everything happened as Hudson thought it would. He went away on a second journey and the two commissioners told the girl to come to the monastery. They asked her to tell them her sad story again. While she was telling it to one, the other was taking down notes. They lamented over her misfortune and told her of her parents' distress, which was only too real, and promised her immunity for herself and prompt vengeance on her seducer but on condition that she would sign a declaration. At first this proposition appeared to revolt her. They insisted. She agreed. All that remained to be decided was the day, the hour and the place where the document could be drawn up, something which needed time and privacy . . .

'We can't do it here: if the Abbot came back and saw me . . . I wouldn't dare suggest my house . . .'

The girl and the two commissioners went their own ways, giving each other time to overcome these difficulties.

The same day Hudson was told of what had happened. He was overjoyed, nearing the moment of his triumph. Soon he would teach these callow youths what kind of man they were dealing with.

'Take your pen,' he said to the girl, 'and arrange a rendezvous with them in the place I will tell you. This place will suit them, I am sure, since it is a respectable house and the woman who occupies it has a very good reputation amongst the other lodgers and in the neighbourhood.'

This woman was, however, one of those secret schemers who pretend to be devout, who insinuate themselves into the best houses, affect a soft, friendly, ingratiating manner and abuse the confidence of mothers and daughters to bring them to dishonour. That was the use Hudson made of her. She was his procuress. But did he tell her or did he not tell her of his secret? That I do not know.

In fact the two envoys of the General accepted the invitation and were there with the young girl. The lady of the house withdrew. They had started taking down the evidence when a loud noise broke out in the house.

'Messieurs, who do you want?'

'We want Mme Simion.' (This was the lady's name.)

'You are at her door.'

They knocked loudly on the door.

'Messieurs,' the girl asked the monks, 'shall I answer?'

'Answer.'

'Shall I open the door?'

'Open it.'

The person who had spoken was a Commissioner of Police whom Hudson knew intimately. After all, whom didn't he know? He had told the man of his peril and told him what part to play.

'Aha! Aha!' said the Commissioner of Police, 'two monks, alone with a prostitute! She's not bad either.'

The girl was so indecently dressed that it was impossible to be mistaken about her profession or what she could have been doing alone with two monks, the eldest of whom was not yet thirty. They, however, protested their innocence. The Commissioner sneered and passed his hand under the chin of the young girl who had thrown herself at his feet and was begging for mercy.

'We are in a respectable house,' said the monks.

'Yes, yes, a respectable house,' said the Commissioner.

'We are here on important business.'

'We know what important business you had here. Speak, Mademoiselle.'

'Monsieur, these men are telling you the truth.'

The Commissioner, however, started to speak in his turn and as there was nothing in his report other than the pure and simple exposition of fact the two monks were obliged to sign it. On their way out they passed all the other tenants, who were on the landings outside their apartments. At the door of the house there was a large crowd of people, a carriage and constables of the watch, who put them into the carriage to the booing and shouting of the crowd. They had covered their faces with their cloaks and were deeply distressed.

The perfidious Commissioner shouted: 'Fathers, tell me, why do you frequent these places and these creatures? But nothing will come of this. I have orders from the authorities to hand you over to your Superior, who is a broad-minded and tolerant man and will not treat this business more severely than it deserves. I do not think that your order behaves in quite the same way as the cruel Franciscans. If it were them you were dealing with, by God I'd feel sorry for you.'

While the Commissioner of Police was speaking to them the coach started on its way back to the monastery. The crowd, which was still growing, surrounded them and people were running as fast as they could in front and behind. This is what they heard:

'What's going on?'

'Those are monks there.'

'What have they done?'

'They got caught in a brothel.'

'Premonstratensians in a brothel!'

'Yes, they're poaching the Carmelites' and the Franciscans' game.'

Then they arrived. The Commissioner of Police got down and knocked on the door. He knocked again, and then again. At last the door opened. The Superior was sent for. Hudson made them wait at least half an hour in order to create as big a scandal as possible. He appeared at last and the Commissioner whispered some words in his ear. The Commissioner appeared to be pleading and Hudson to be rejecting his intercessions harshly. Eventually, putting on a serious face and a firm manner, he said: 'I have no dissolute monks in my House. These people here are two strangers who are unknown to me. Perhaps they are two ruffians in disguise. You can do whatever you want with them.'

At this the door was shut. The Commissioner got back into the carriage and said to our two poor devils, who were more dead than alive: 'I have done everything I could for you. I would never have thought that Father Hudson was so harsh. Why the devil did you go to the prostitutes?'

'If the girl you found us with is a prostitute, it is not debauchery which led us to her.'

'Come on, fathers, you are talking to an old Commissioner of Police. Who are you?'

'We are monks and the habits we are wearing are our own.'

'Listen. Tomorrow you will have to explain your business. Tell me the truth. I may perhaps be able to help you.'

'We have told you the truth . . . But where are we going?'

'To the Petit Châtelet.'

'To the Petit Châtelet . . . To prison!'

'I'm afraid so.'

And it was there that Richard and his companion were led. But it was not Hudson's intention to leave them there. He had got into a post-chaise and gone back to Versailles, where he had managed to get an audience with the Minister, to whom he explained the business as it suited him.

'And so you see, Monseigneur, what one exposes oneself to by introducing reform into a dissolute House, and expelling heretics. A moment later and I would have been lost and dishonoured. But their persecution will not stop there. You will hear every single allegation by which it is possible to blacken the reputation of a good man. But I hope, Monseigneur, that you will remember that our General . . .'

'I know, I know, and I feel sorry for you. The services which you have rendered to the Church and your Order will not be forgotten. The Lord's elect have always been exposed to disgrace. They have suffered it. You must learn to imitate their courage. You may depend on the kindness and the protection of the King . . . Ah! monks, monks . . . I was once one and I know from experience what they are capable of.'

'Were the Church and State so fortunate as to see Your Eminence outlive myself, I would persevere without fear.'

'I will help without delay. Go now.'

'No, Your Eminence, no, I will not go without an express order . . .'

'To free those two bad monks? I do believe that the honour of your religion and your cloth has moved you to the point of forgetting your personal injuries. That is a very Christian act, and I am edified by it but not surprised, coming from a man such as you. This affair will have no publicity.'

'Ah, Monseigneur, my soul is overwhelmed with joy! That is the only thing I feared.'

'I will see to it.'

That same evening Hudson had the order for release and the next day Richard and his companion found themselves twenty miles from Paris at daybreak, under the conduct of a bailiff who brought them back to their Mother House. He also brought with him a letter which enjoined the General to desist from similar intrigues and to impose monastic discipline on our two monks. This incident threw Hudson's enemies into consternation. There was not one monk in his House who did not tremble under his gaze.

A few months afterwards he received the preferment of a rich abbey.

The General developed an intense hatred for him. He was old and he had every reason to fear that abbot Hudson might one day succeed him. He was very fond of Richard. 'My dear friend,' he said to him one day, 'what would happen to you if you fell under the power of that scoundrel Hudson? I am afraid for you. You have not yet taken your final vows. If you take my advice you will put aside your habit . . .'

Richard followed this advice and returned to his father's house, which was not far from Hudson's abbey.

Hudson and Richard moved in the same society and it was impossible that they should not one day meet. In fact they did meet. One day Richard was visiting the lady of a château situated between Châlons and Saint-Dizier, but nearer to Saint-Dizier than Châlons, and a stone's throw away from Hudson's monastery.

The lady said to him: 'Your old abbot is here. He is very likeable, but what kind of man is he underneath?'

'The best of friends and the most dangerous of enemies.'

'Are you not tempted to see him again?'

'Not at all.'

Hardly had Richard answered when they heard the noise of a coach entering the courtyard and saw Hudson get down, accompanied by one of the most beautiful ladies of the neighbourhood.

'Well, in spite of your wishes, you are going to see him again,' said the lady of the château, 'for here he is.'

The lady of the château and Richard went to meet Hudson and the lady who had got out of the carriage with him. The ladies embraced. As Hudson got close to Richard, he recognized him and cried out: 'Ah! Is that you, my dear Richard? You once tried to cause my downfall. I have forgiven you. You must forgive me for your visit to the Petit Châtelet and there's an end to it.'

'Father Abbot, you must admit that you were a terrible scoundrel.'

'Perhaps.'

'And if justice had been done it wouldn't have been me in the Châtelet but you.'

'Perhaps . . . But I think that I owe my new way of life to the dangers I ran then. Ah, my dear Richard, how it has made me reflect, and how I am changed.'

'That lady you arrived with is charming.'

'I no longer see such attractions.'

'What a figure!'

'I am indifferent to all that.'

'How well she looks.'

'Sooner or later one tires of a pleasure which one can take only on the apex of a roof in danger of breaking one's neck at any moment.'

'She has the most beautiful hands in the world.'

'I no longer have any use for them. A sensible person always returns to the real values of his calling, to the only true happiness.'

'And those eyes, and the sidelong glances they are giving you. You must admit that even you, who happen to be a connoisseur, can hardly ever have attached yourself to eyes more brilliant or more soft than that. What grace, what nobility and what dignity in her gait and her bearing.'

'I no longer think of such vanities. I read the Scriptures and meditate on the fathers of the Church.'

'And from time to time the perfections of this lady. Does she live far from Moncetz? Is her husband young?'

Hudson, tired of these questions, and quite convinced that Richard did not take him for a saint, said: 'My dear Richard, you are taking the piss, and you are quite right.'

My dear Reader, you must forgive me here for the lack of propriety of this expression and admit that here, as in an infinity of good stories, such as, for example, those of the conversation of Piron and the late Abbé Vatri,[50] the decent word would spoil everything.

– What's this conversation between Piron and the late Abbé Vatri?

Go and ask the editor of his works who hasn't dared write it down but won't need to have his arm twisted to tell you.

Our four protagonists had joined company again in the château. They ate well, and happily, and that evening they parted company promising to see each other again. But while the Marquis des Arcis was speaking with Jacques' master, Jacques for his part was not sitting in silence with the Marquis' secretary, who thought Jacques one of life's true originals. Such characters would be more prevalent if first of all education, and then afterwards the ways of the world, did not wear men down like pieces of money which lose their definition in circulation. It was late. The masters and their valets were warned by the clock that it was time to go to bed. And they followed its advice.

While he was undressing his master Jacques asked him: 'Do you like pictures?'

MASTER: Yes, but only verbal pictures, because when they are in colour on canvas, although I am as trenchant in my verdicts as any connoisseur, I will admit to you that I don't know anything about them at all and I would be very hard put to tell the difference between one School and another. I would take a Boucher for a Rubens or a Raphael and I would mistake a bad copy for the sublime original. I would pay a thousand écus for some daub worth six francs and six francs for something worth a thousand écus. And I have always bought paintings at the Pont Notre-Dame at the Gallery of a certain Tremblin, who in my youth was the dealer for those who hadn't much money or who wanted salacious stuff and who ruined the talent of Vanloo's young pupils.[51]

JACQUES: How was that?

MASTER: What has that got to do with you? Describe your picture to me and be quick about it because I am dropping with sleep.

JACQUES: Imagine yourself in front of the Fountain of the Innocents, or near Saint-Denis' gate – two accessories which will enrich the composition.

MASTER: I am there.

JACQUES: Picture, in the middle of the road, a carriage with a broken spring turned over on its side.

MASTER: I can see it.

JACQUES: A monk and two prostitutes have got out of it. The monk is running away as fast as he can, the coachman rushing to get down from his seat. The coachman's dog has escaped from inside the coach and set off in pursuit of the monk, whom he has caught by his tails. The monk is trying everything to rid himself of the dog. One of the prostitutes, dishevelled, and with her breasts showing, is splitting her sides laughing. The other prostitute, who has received a bump on her forehead, is leaning against the door of the coach holding her head in both hands. Meanwhile the populace of the town has gathered around. Street urchins run up shouting. The shopkeepers and their wives are all at their doors and other spectators are at their windows.

MASTER: What the devil! Jacques, your composition is well ordered, rich, pleasing, varied and full of movement. On our return to Paris take this subject to Fragonard and you will see what he could do with it.

JACQUES: After what you've confessed to me about your knowledge of painting, I can accept your praise without lowering my eyes.

MASTER: I bet that was one of the adventures of Hudson.

JACQUES: That is correct.

Reader, while these good people are sleeping, I would like to propose a little question for you to think about on your pillow. What would the child of Abbot Hudson and Mme de La Pommeraye have been like?

Perhaps an honest man?

Perhaps a scheming trickster?

You can tell me the answer tomorrow morning.

Morning has come and gone and our travellers have parted company because the Marquis des Arcis wasn't going the same way as Jacques and his master.

– So are we going to get back to the story of Jacques' love life?

I hope so, but I can tell you one thing for certain. The master knows what time it is, has taken a pinch of snuff and has already asked Jacques: 'Well, Jacques, your love life?'

Instead of replying to this question Jacques said: 'Isn't it amazing? From morning to night they speak badly of life and yet they still can't bring themselves to end it all. Could it be that life is not such a bad thing, all in all, or are they just afraid of a worse one to come?'

MASTER: I suppose it's a bit of both really. While we're on the subject, Jacques, do you believe in the life to come?

JACQUES: I neither believe nor disbelieve. I just don't think about it. I do my best to enjoy this one as an advance against future expectations.

MASTER: Well, I prefer to think of myself as a sort of chrysalis. I rather like to think that the butterfly – which is my soul – will one day manage to break out of its cocoon and fly away to divine justice.

JACQUES: What a charming image.

MASTER: It's not mine. I read it I think in a book by an Italian poet called Dante who wrote a work called *The Comedy of Inferno, Purgatory and Paradise*.

JACQUES: That's a strange subject for a comedy.

MASTER: By God, there are some good things in it though – especially in Hell. He shuts all the heretics in tombs of fire out of which spout flames which carry destruction far and wide. And he puts the ungrateful in niches where they cry tears that freeze on their faces. And the slothful in other niches where their life blood flows from their veins and is consumed by disdainful worms . . .[52]

But why the sudden outburst about our disdain for a life we are afraid of losing?

JACQUES: Because of what the Marquis' secretary told me about the husband of that pretty girl in the gig.

MASTER: Is she a widow?

JACQUES: She lost her husband on a trip they made to Paris and the wretch of a man wouldn't even hear mention of the sacraments. The lady of the château where Richard met the Abbé Hudson was given the job of putting his bonnet on.

MASTER: What do you mean by bonnet?

JACQUES: His christening bonnet, like they put on new-born babies.[53]

MASTER: I see what you mean. And how did she go about that?

JACQUES: They all gathered round the fire. The doctor took his pulse, which he found very weak, and went to sit down with the others. The lady in question went over to the bed and asked the deceased several questions in a calm quiet voice without speaking any louder than she needed to in order for him to hear every word she wanted him to. After that the conversation continued between the lady, the doctor and one or two others as follows:

LADY: Well, Doctor, how is Mme de Parme these days, tell us?[54]

DOCTOR: I've just come from a house where I was assured that she is so ill that they think it's hopeless.

LADY: But the Princess has always shown herself so devout. As soon as she felt herself in danger she asked to confess and receive the sacraments.

DOCTOR: The curé of Saint-Roch is bringing a relic to Versailles for her today, but it will arrive too late.

LADY: The Princess is not the only person to give that example. The Duke of Chevreuse did not wait until the sacraments were suggested to him when he was ill. He asked for them by himself and that gave great solace to his family . . .

DOCTOR: He is much better now.

ONE OF THOSE PRESENT: It is absolutely beyond doubt that the sacraments can't kill you . . . on the contrary even.

LADY: In all honesty one should attend to these things as soon as there is any danger at all . . . Sick people apparently have no conception of how hard it is for those around them and yet how indispensable it is to suggest these things to them.

DOCTOR: I have just left a man who asked me two days ago: 'Doctor, how am I?'
'Monsieur, the fever is bad and relapses are common.'
'Do you think that I will have one soon?'
'No, I am afraid only for tonight.'
'In that case I had better warn a certain gentleman with whom I have a

little personal business to attend to so I can finish it while I've still got my wits about me.'

He confessed and took the sacraments. I returned that evening and there was no relapse. Yesterday he was much better. Today he's almost completely out of it. And I've seen the sacraments have that effect many times in the course of my practice.

SICK MAN (to his servant): Bring me my chicken.

JACQUES: So they brought him his chicken. He wanted to cut it but didn't have the strength so they cut up the wing into small pieces. He asked for some bread and threw himself on it, tried to chew a mouthful, which he wasn't able to swallow and which he threw up in his napkin. He called for some wine and wet his lips with it and said: 'I feel fine.'

Half an hour after he had eaten his bread and drunk his wine he was no more.

MASTER: Yet the lady went about the business quite well . . . What about your love life?

JACQUES: What about the condition you agreed to?

MASTER: I understand – you are installed in the château Desglands and the old messenger Jeanne has ordered her young daughter Denise to visit you four times a day and look after you. But before we go any further, tell me, had Denise lost her virginity?

JACQUES: I don't believe so.

MASTER: What about yours?

JACQUES: Mine had long since vanished.

MASTER: So the story of your love life is not about your first love.

JACQUES: No, why should it be?

MASTER: Because a man loves the girl he loses his virginity to just as he is loved by the one whose virginity he takes away.

JACQUES: Sometimes yes and sometimes no.

MASTER: Well, how did you lose it, then?

JACQUES: I didn't lose it. I swapped it.

MASTER: Well, tell me something about this swap.

JACQUES: That would be like the first chapter of Luke's gospel – a litany of begats – from the first one up to Denise, the last.[55]

MASTER: Denise who thought she was taking it but wasn't.

JACQUES: And before Denise our two neighbours' wives.

MASTER: Who thought they were taking it and didn't get it.

JACQUES: No.

MASTER: For both of them to miss your virginity is none too clever.

JACQUES: Master, I can see from the way the right-hand corner of your mouth is twisting up and the way your left nostril is twitching that I may as well tell the thing with good grace as have you beg me for it. Just as I can sense my sore throat getting worse and know that the story of my loves will be long and I have hardly enough strength to tell one or two little stories.

MASTER: If Jacques wanted to give me very great pleasure . . .

JACQUES: How would he go about that?

MASTER: He would begin with the loss of his virginity. Do you want me to tell you why? It is because I've always been very partial to stories about that great event.

JACQUES: And why is that, if you please?

MASTER: That is because out of all the stories of the same type it is the only interesting one. All the other times are nothing more than insipid banal repetition. Out of all the transgressions of a pretty sinner I am sure that her father confessor is only interested in the first time.

JACQUES: My master, my master, I can see that your mind is corrupted and on your death bed the devil will probably appear to you in the same form as to Ferragus.[56]

MASTER: Well, perhaps he will. But I bet you were deflowered by some dreadful old bag from your village.

JACQUES: Don't bet on it – you'd lose.

MASTER: Was it your parish priest's housekeeper?

JACQUES: Don't bet on it – you'd still lose.

MASTER: It was his niece then?

JACQUES: His niece was seething with bad temper and piety, which are two qualities that go very well together but do not suit me.

MASTER: This time I think I've got it.

JACQUES: I don't think anything of the sort.

MASTER: It was one day when the fair was in town – or perhaps it was market day.

JACQUES: There wasn't any fair and it wasn't market day.

MASTER: You went to town.

JACQUES: I didn't go to town.

MASTER: And it was written up above that in some tavern you would meet one of those obliging young ladies, that you would get drunk and . . .

JACQUES: Actually I hadn't eaten and what has been written up above is that at the present moment you will tire yourself out with false conjecture. And that you will pick up a bad habit which you have corrected me of – a mania for guessing, and always wrongly.

As I stand before you now, Monsieur, I was once baptized . . .

MASTER: If you intend to start the loss of your virginity with your emergence from the font we're not going to get there very quickly.

JACQUES: But I had a godfather and a godmother just like anyone else. Master Bugger – the most famous cartwright in our village – had a son. Bugger the Father was my godfather and Bugger the Son was my friend. When we were about eighteen or nineteen we both of us at the same time fell for a little seamstress called Justine. She wasn't supposed to be particularly unyielding but she thought it right to establish her reputation by a first act of rejection and her choice for this fell on me.

MASTER: That is one of the strange things about women one can never understand.

JACQUES: The total living arrangements of the cartwright, Master Bugger my godfather, consisted of a workshop and a garret. His bed was at the back of the shop and Bugger the Son, my friend, used to sleep up in the loft which you got up to by a little ladder placed about half-way between his father's bed and the door of the workshop.

When Bugger my godfather was fast asleep Bugger my friend used to open the door of the shop and Justine would slip up the little ladder into the loft. The following morning at daybreak, before Bugger the Father was awake, Bugger the Son would come down from the loft, open the door again and Justine would slip out the way she had entered.

MASTER: To go off and visit some other bugger's loft, yours or another's.

JACQUES: Why not? Bugger and Justine got along quite well really, but their relationship had to run into trouble. That was written up above. And so it did.

MASTER: Because of the father?

JACQUES: No.

MASTER: Because of the mother?

JACQUES: No, she was dead.

MASTER: A rival, then?

JACQUES: No! No! And by all the devils that ever were, No! My Master, it is written up above that you will suffer from this for the rest of your days. For the rest of your life, I'm telling you, you'll try to guess things and guess wrong . . .

One morning while my friend Bugger – who was more tired than usual, either from the previous day's work or the previous night's pleasure – was sleeping softly in Justine's arms, a loud roar bellowed up from the foot of the little ladder.

'Bugger? Bugger? You lazy swine! The angelus has sounded. It's nearly half past five already, and there you are still up in your loft! Have you decided to stay there till noon? Do you want me to come up there and throw you down? Bugger! Bugger!'

'Yes, father.'

'And what about the axle that old bear of a farmer is waiting for? Do you want him to come ranting back here again?'

'His axle is ready and he'll have it in another fifteen minutes.'

I will leave you to imagine the terror of Justine and my poor friend Bugger the Son.

MASTER: I am sure that Justine swore never to come back to that loft and that she came back the same night. But how did she manage to get out that morning?

JACQUES: If you've decided that it's your duty to guess the rest then I'll stop now . . . Meanwhile Bugger the Son had leapt out of bed naked, trousers in one hand and jacket in the other. While he was getting dressed Bugger the Father was muttering between his teeth: 'Ever since he's been caught up with that little tramp everything's gone wrong. It's got to stop. This can't carry on any longer. I'm getting tired of it. It wouldn't be so bad if she was worth it, but a creature like that! My God, what a creature! Ah, if only the poor departed wife who was honour down to the tips of her fingers could see him like this, she would have taken the stick to him long ago and then scratched out the girl's eyes on her way out of High Mass right outside the church in front of everyone. Nothing would have stopped her! But I've been too kind up to now, and if they think I'm going to carry on like this they're making a big mistake.'

MASTER: And could Justine hear all this in the loft?

JACQUES: I'm sure that she could. Meanwhile Bugger the Son had gone off to the farmer, axle on his shoulder, and Bugger the Father had set to work. After a few strokes with the adze he was dying for some tobacco. He turned out all his pockets looking for his pouch. Then he searched around the side of his bed and didn't find it.

'It's that brat', he said, 'who's taken it again as usual, I suppose. I wonder if he's left it upstairs . . .'

And there he was going up into the loft.

A moment later he noticed that his pipe and his knife were missing and went back up again.

MASTER: What about Justine?

JACQUES: She had quickly gathered up all of her clothes and slid underneath the bed where she was lying on her stomach more dead than alive.

MASTER: What about your friend Bugger the Son?

JACQUES: When he had delivered, fitted and been paid for the axle he ran straight to my house, where he told me about the terrible predicament he was in. After I had laughed a bit I said: 'Listen, Bugger, go and walk around the village or somewhere. I'll get you out of it. I only ask one thing of you: that is to give me time . . .'

You're smiling, Master – what do you find so funny?

MASTER: Nothing.

JACQUES: My friend Bugger left. I got dressed because I hadn't got up, then I went to see his father, who no sooner set eyes on me than he let out a great yell of surprise and joy and said to me: 'Eh! Godson! Is that you there? Where have you come from and what are you doing here so early?'

My godfather Bugger was always very fond of me so my answer was quite open: 'It's not so much a question of where I've come from but more one of how I'm going to get home.'

'Ah! Godson, you're becoming a rake. You and Bugger make a right pair. You've spent the night out.'

'And that's not something you can discuss with my father.'

'And he's quite right too, Godson. But let's have some breakfast and see if the wine bottle can give us the answer.'

MASTER: Now there's a man with the right idea, Jacques!

JACQUES: I told him that I neither needed nor wanted anything to eat or drink but I was on the point of collapse from exhaustion. The old Bugger who'd been as good as the next man in his time said: 'I know, Godson. She was a pretty girl and you really went at it, eh? Listen. Bugger has gone out. Go up into his loft and get into his bed . . . but a quick word before he comes back. He's your friend. Next time you're alone with him you tell him from me I'm not pleased with him, not at all pleased. It's that little Justine – you know the one I mean, there's not a boy in the village who doesn't know her – who's debauched him. You'd be doing me a great service if you could detach him from that creature. Before, he was what you might call a nice lad – but ever since he made her unfortunate acquaintance . . .

'You're not listening to me. Your eyes are closing. Go on up and get some rest.'

I went up. I got undressed. I lifted up the blanket and the sheets and felt all around. No Justine. Meanwhile my godfather Bugger was muttering away downstairs: 'Children! Damned children! There's another one breaking his father's heart.'

Since Justine was not in the bed I suspected she might be underneath it. The loft was quite dark. I got down and ran my hands around, met one of her hands, grabbed it and pulled her towards me. Out she came from under the bed trembling. I kissed her, reassured her, and indicated that she was to go to bed. She clasped her hands, threw herself at my feet and threw her arms around my knees. I might not perhaps have been able to resist this mute scene if the loft had been lit, but when darkness does not scare people it makes them enterprising. And anyway I was still bitter about her earlier rejection of me. By way of reply I pushed her towards the ladder which led down to the workshop.

She let out a long cry of fear.

Bugger heard this and said: 'He must be dreaming.'

Justine fainted. Her knees gave way under her. In her delirium she said in a stifled voice: 'He's going to come . . . he's coming . . . I can hear him coming up . . . I'm lost!'

'No, no,' I replied in a muffled voice. 'Calm down, shut up, and get into bed.'

She persisted in her refusal. I held firm. She resigned herself. And then there we were the one beside the other.

MASTER: You traitor! You criminal! Do you know what crime you're about to commit? You're about to rape that girl. If not by sheer force then by force of terror. If you were to be brought before a court of law you would be punished with all the severity reserved for rapists.

JACQUES: I don't know whether I raped her or not. But I do know that I didn't do her any harm and she didn't do me any harm either!

At first she turned her mouth away from my kisses and whispered: 'No, Jacques, no . . .'

At this I pretended to get out of bed and go towards the ladder. She held me back and whispered in my ear again: 'I would never have thought you were so wicked. I can see it's no use asking you to have pity on me, but at least promise me, swear to me . . .'

'What?'

'That Bugger will never know.'

MASTER: And you promised, you swore, and everything went very well.

JACQUES: And then again very well.

MASTER: And then very well again?

JACQUES: Precisely. You speak like a man who was there himself. Meanwhile Bugger my friend, impatient, worried and tired of prowling around his house waiting for me, decided to go home to his father, who said angrily: 'You've been away a long time over nothing . . .'

Bugger replied even more angrily: 'Didn't I have to trim down both ends of that blasted axle which was too thick?'

'I warned you about that but you always want to do things your way.'

'Well, it's always easier to take a bit more wood off than to put it on again.'

'Take this rim and go and finish it over by the door.'

'Why at the door?'

'Because the noise of your tool will wake up your friend Jacques.'

'Jacques!'

'Yes, Jacques. He's upstairs resting in your loft. Ah! God I feel sorry for fathers. If it's not one thing it's another! Well, can't you move? Standing there like an imbecile with your head hanging, your mouth gaping and your arms akimbo isn't going to get the work done, you know.'

Bugger my friend was furious and threw himself at the ladder. Bugger my godfather pulled him back and said: 'Where are you going? Let the poor devil sleep. He's worn out. If you were him would you like to have your rest disturbed?'

MASTER: And Justine heard all that too?

JACQUES: As you hear me now.

MASTER: And what were you doing?

JACQUES: I was laughing.

MASTER: And Justine?

JACQUES: She had ripped off her coif and was tearing her hair. She was raising her eyes to heaven – or I assume she was – and wringing her hands.

MASTER: Jacques, you're a barbarian. You have a heart of stone.

JACQUES: No, Master, that's not true. I'm very sensitive really but I keep it in reserve for an occasion when I might need it more – 'And the foolish ones used of these riches prodigiously when they should have used of them sparingly and found they had none to use when they should have used of them prodigiously . . .'

In the meantime I got dressed and went down to Bugger my godfather who said to me: 'You certainly needed that. It's done you the world of good, that has. When you arrived here you looked like you'd just been disinterred. And now look at you! All pink and rosy like a baby fresh from the breast. Sleep is a marvellous thing! Bugger! Go down to the cellar and bring up a bottle so we can have breakfast. Now, Godson, will you eat with us?'

'Willingly.'

The bottle had arrived and been put on the work-bench. We were standing around. Old Bugger filled his glass and mine. Bugger the Son pulled his away and said in a fierce voice: 'I'm not thirsty so early in the day.'

'Don't you want a drink?'

'No.'

'Ah! I know what it is. Listen, Godson, Justine is in this somewhere. He went round to her house and she wasn't there. Either that or he found her with someone else. This sulking and taking it out on the bottle isn't natural, I tell you.'

JACQUES: I think you might have hit on it there.

BUGGER THE SON: Jacques, enough of your witticisms, appropriate or inappropriate. I don't like them.

BUGGER THE FATHER: If he doesn't want a drink we mustn't let that stop us. Your health, Godson.

JACQUES: Your health, Godfather. Bugger, my friend, have a drink with us. You're upsetting yourself over nothing.

BUGGER THE SON: I've already told you. I'm not drinking.

JACQUES: Bugger, if your father has hit on the truth, what the devil. You'll see her again, ask her about it and then you'll accept that you're wrong.

BUGGER THE FATHER: Leave him alone. Isn't it right that this creature should punish him for all the suffering he's caused me. There, one more glass and we'll get down to your business. I can see that I'll have to take you back to your father, but what do you want me to say to him?

JACQUES: Whatever you want. Whatever you've heard him say to you a hundred times before whenever he's brought your son home.

BUGGER THE FATHER: Let's go.

He left and I followed. We arrived at the door of my house and I allowed him to go in alone. Being curious about what Bugger the Father was going to say to my father, I hid in a corner behind a partition where I could hear every word.

BUGGER THE FATHER: Come on old chap, you can forgive him this time too.

'Forgive him? What for?'

'You're just pretending you don't know.'

'I'm not pretending. I don't know.'

'You're angry and you've got every right to be.'

'I'm not angry.'

'I'm telling you, you are angry.'

'If you want me to be angry with him that suits me fine but would you mind telling me what mischief he's been up to before I get angry.'

'All right, three times, four times, but it's hardly a habit. You find yourself with a crowd of young lads and girls, have a few drinks and a laugh, dance a bit. Time passes quickly, and before you know it you're locked out.'

Lowering his voice, Bugger added: 'They can't hear us. Tell me honestly. Were we any wiser than they are at their age? Do you know what a bad father is? A bad father is one who has forgotten the faults of his own youth. Tell me, did we never spend a night away from home?'

'And you tell me, Bugger old friend, did we never take up with girls our parents didn't like?'

'All right . . . So I shout louder than it hurts. Do the same.'

'But Jacques didn't spend the night away from home, at least not last night, I'm sure of it.'

'Oh well, if it's not that girl it's another one. Anyway the long and the short of it is you're not cross with the boy?'

'No.'

'And when I'm gone you won't ill-treat him?'

'Not at all.'

'You promise?'

'I promise.'

'Word of honour?'

'Word of honour.'

'Well that's that and I'm going home.'

Just when Bugger my godfather was on the doorstep my father tapped him on the shoulder and said: 'Bugger, my friend, there's something funny going on. Your boy and mine are a tricky pair of rogues, and I suspect they've put one over on us today. Time will reveal all, though. Goodbye, old friend.'

MASTER: And what was the end of the story for your friend Bugger and Justine?

JACQUES: As it should have been. He got very angry. She got even angrier. She cried. He softened. She swore I was the best friend he ever had. I swore to him that she was the most faithful girl in the village. He believed us and apologized and loved and valued us both all the more afterwards. And that's the beginning, the middle and the end of the loss of my virginity. Now, Monsieur, I should like you to tell me – what is the moral of this rude story?

MASTER: To show what women are like?

JACQUES: Do you need to learn that?

MASTER: To show what friends are like?

JACQUES: Have you ever believed that you had even one friend who would resist if your own wife or your daughter proposed her own undoing?

MASTER: To show what fathers and children are like?

JACQUES: Come on, Monsieur. Children have always fooled their fathers and been fooled by their own children. It has always been so and will be so evermore.

MASTER: These things you are saying are the eternal facts of life and cannot be emphasized too much. But no matter what the story you have promised to tell me after this one is about, Jacques, you may be assured that only an idiot would not find some lesson to be learned from it. So carry on.

Reader, there is something that is worrying me, and that is that I have honoured Jacques or his master with making reflections which belong to you by right. If that is the case you can take them back without Jacques and his master taking offence.

I believe that I have also noticed that the word 'Bugger' displeases you. I would like to know why. It is the real name of my cartwright's family. Their birth certificates, death certificates and marriage certificates are all signed 'Bugger'. The descendants of Bugger occupy the same workshop today and they are all called Bugger. When their children, who are all pretty, pass by in the street, people cry out: 'Look at the little Buggers!'

When you pronounce the word Boulle you remember one of the greatest cabinet-makers that ever lived. In Bugger's country no one pronounces the name Bugger without remembering the greatest cartwright in living memory. The Bugger whose name is on all the pious religious publications of the beginning of this century was related to him. If ever the great-grand-nephew of Bugger distinguishes himself the name will be no less imposing to you than that of Caesar or Condé.[57]

You see there's Bugger and Bugger like there's William and William. If I say simply William, that is neither William the Conqueror nor William the draper in the farce of Maître Pathelin.[58] The name William is neither heroic nor common. And it's the same with Bugger. Bugger without qualification is neither the famous cartwright nor one of his boring ancestors nor one of his boring descendants. In all honesty, how can a person's name be in good or bad taste? The streets are full of hounds called Pompey. So cast off your irrational false sense of propriety or I shall have to deal with you like Lord Chatham dealt with Parliament: 'Shh . . . ugar, Sugar, Sugar,' he said to them. 'What do you find so funny about that?'[59]

And as for me I say unto you: Bugger, Bugger, Bugger. Why shouldn't someone be called Bugger?

As one of his officers told General Condé, the thing is there's proud Buggers like Bugger the cartwright, good Buggers like you and me, and plain Buggers like a hell of a lot of others.

JACQUES: It was a wedding feast. Friar Jean had married one of our neighbour's daughters and I was a groomsman. I was seated at table between the two jokers of the parish. I looked like a right booby, but I wasn't as much of a fool as they thought. They asked me a few questions about what happens on wedding nights and I gave them some pretty dumb answers. They were splitting their sides with laughter and the wives of these two jokers shouted down from the other end of the table: 'What's the matter with you? You're having a good time over there.'

'It's just too funny for words,' one of them replied to his wife. 'I'll tell you about it tonight.'

The other wife, who was just as curious, asked her husband the same question and got the same reply. The meal continued. So did the questions and my stupid answers, the bursts of laughter and the surprise of the women. And then, after the meal the dance, and after the dance the nuptial bed for the happy couple, the giving away of the bride's garter and bed for me. And bed for the two jokers as well, who told the incomprehensible unbelievable fact to their wives that at twenty-two years of age, hale and hearty as I was, good-looking, alert and sound in mind, I was as pure, as pure as the day I came from my mother's belly. And then it was the turn of the wives to marvel as much as their husbands had done.

But the very next day Suzanne beckoned me: 'Jacques, have you nothing to do?'

'No, neighbour. Can I be of service to you?'

'I would like . . . I would like . . .' and as she said 'I would like' she squeezed my hand and looked at me in a singular way . . . 'I would like you to take our bill-hook and come with me to the common and help me to cut two or three sheaves because it's too hard for me all alone.'

'Certainly, Madame Suzanne.'

I took the bill-hook and off we went. On the way Suzanne let her head fall on to my shoulder, tickled my chin, pulled my ears and pinched my sides. We arrived. It was a sloping field. Suzanne stretched herself out at the top of the slope, her arms behind her head, her legs wide apart. I was beneath her cutting on the slope. Suzanne bent her legs drawing her heels up to her thighs. Since her knees were in the air her skirts didn't come down very far. I was still cutting away on the slope hardly looking where I was cutting and missing most of the time. At last Suzanne spoke: 'Jacques, you will finish soon, won't you.'

And I replied: 'Whenever you want, Madame Suzanne.'

'Can't you see', she half-whispered, 'that I want you to finish?'

So I finished, got my breath back and finished again. And Suzanne . . .

MASTER: Took away the virginity you never had.

JACQUES: That is true, but she wasn't fooled and smiled at me and said: 'Well, you certainly fooled my husband. God, you're a rogue.'

'What do you mean by that, Madame Suzanne?'

'Nothing, nothing. You know very well what I mean. But fool me again a few more times and I forgive you.'

I tied up her bundles, put them on my back and we came back, her to her house and me to ours.

MASTER: Without stopping on the way?

JACQUES: No.

MASTER: So it wasn't far from the common to the village?

JACQUES: No farther than from the village to the common.

MASTER: Wasn't she worth more than that?

JACQUES: Perhaps she would have been worth more to another man or on another day. Every moment has its price.

Some time after that Marguerite, the wife of the other joker, had some grain which needed milling and didn't have the time to go to the mill. She came to ask my father if one of his boys could go for her. Since I was the biggest she was sure that his choice would fall on me – which it did.

Marguerite left. I followed, loaded the sack on to the mule and drove it to the mill – alone. Her grain milled, we started on our way back – the mule and I – sadly, because I thought I would be left unrewarded for my pains. I was wrong. The road from the mill to the village passed through a little wood. It was there that I found Marguerite sitting by the roadside. Dusk was falling.

'Jacques,' she said to me, 'there you are at last! Do you know I've been waiting here for a whole interminable hour?'

– Reader, you are being far too pedantic . . . Very well, interminable hour is what a society lady would call it and damned hour is what Marguerite would call it.

JACQUES: Well, the water was low so the mill went slowly and the miller was drunk and no matter how hard I tried I just couldn't come back any quicker.

MARGUERITE: Sit down here and let's talk awhile.

JACQUES: Madame Marguerite, I'd like that . . .
And so there I was seated beside her to chat and all the time we were silent. So I said to her: 'Madame Marguerite, you're not saying anything to me and we're not chatting.'

MARGUERITE: It's just that I'm dreaming about what my husband told me about you.

JACQUES: Don't believe anything your husband told you. He's full of wind.

MARGUERITE: He told me that you've never been in love.

JACQUES: Oh well, yes, he's right about that.

MARGUERITE: What? Never in your life?

JACQUES: Never.

MARGUERITE: What! At your age you don't even know what a woman is?

JACQUES: Excuse me, I do, Madame Marguerite.

MARGUERITE: Well, tell me then, what is a woman?

JACQUES: A woman?

MARGUERITE: Yes, a woman.

JACQUES: A woman . . . wait a minute . . . it's a man . . . with skirts . . . a bonnet . . . and big tits.

MASTER: You villain.

JACQUES: The other one wasn't fooled by me and I wanted to make sure that this one was. On my reply Madame Marguerite burst into fits of laughter which seemed as if they would never stop. I was speechless and asked her what she found so much to laugh about. Marguerite said she was laughing at my innocence.

'Are you telling me that at your age you really don't know any more than that?'

'No, Madame Marguerite . . .'

At that Marguerite fell silent and I did the same: 'But, Madame Marguerite,' I said to her, 'we sat down here to chat and you haven't said a word and we're not chatting. Madame Marguerite, what's wrong with you? Are you dreaming?'

MARGUERITE: Yes I'm dreaming . . . dreaming . . . dreaming . . .

As she was saying 'I'm dreaming' her breasts were rising and falling, her voice growing weaker, her limbs trembling, her eyes closed, her mouth half open. She let forth a great sigh and I pretended I thought she was dead and started shouting in a tone of terror: 'Madame Marguerite! Madame Marguerite! Speak to me! Madame Marguerite, are you ill?'

MARGUERITE: No, my child. Leave me to rest a moment. I don't know what took me. It came on suddenly.

MASTER: She was lying.

JACQUES: Yes, she was lying.

MARGUERITE: I was dreaming . . .

JACQUES: Do you dream like that at night, next to your husband?

MARGUERITE: Sometimes.

JACQUES: That must frighten him.

MARGUERITE: He's used to it . . .

Marguerite came out of her faint little by little and said to me: 'I was dreaming that at the wedding night eight days ago my man and Suzanne's made fun of you and I felt sorry for you and then I felt all peculiar.'

JACQUES: You are too kind.

MARGUERITE: I don't like people being made fun of. I was dreaming that the first chance they get they would start all over again even worse. And that would make me even more angry.

JACQUES: But it would only need you to make sure that it would never happen again.

MARGUERITE: How?

JACQUES: By teaching me . . .

MARGUERITE: Teaching you what?

JACQUES: Whatever it is that I don't know which made your man and Suzanne's laugh so much, which they wouldn't do again.

MARGUERITE: Oh no! No! I know that you're a good lad and that you wouldn't tell a soul, but I wouldn't dare to.

JACQUES: And why not?

MARGUERITE: It's just that I wouldn't dare to.

JACQUES: Ah, Madame Marguerite, teach me, I beg you. I will be ever so grateful to you. Please teach me . . .

While I was begging her I was gripping her hands and she was gripping mine. I was kissing her eyes and she was kissing me on the mouth. By now it was quite dark so I said to her: 'I can see, Madame Marguerite, that you don't care about me enough to teach me. I am very hurt. Come on. Let's get up and go back.'

Marguerite became quiet. She took hold of one of my hands. I don't know where she put it but the fact is I cried out: 'There's nothing there! There's nothing there!'

MASTER: You scoundrel! You double-dyed scoundrel!

JACQUES: The fact is that she was terribly undressed and I was extremely undressed too. The fact is that I still had my hand where she didn't have anything and she had hers where the same wasn't quite true of me. The fact is that I found myself underneath her and consequently she found herself on top of me. The fact is that since I wasn't helping any she had to do all the work. The fact is that she gave herself to my instruction so wholeheartedly that there came a moment when I thought it was going to kill her. The fact is that I was as agitated as she was and not knowing what I was saying I cried out: 'Ah! Suzanne! You make me feel so good!'

MASTER: You mean Marguerite.

JACQUES: No, no. The fact is that I took one name for the other and instead of saying Marguerite I said Suzon. The fact is that I made Marguerite realize that it was not her who was teaching me on that day but Suzon who had taught me – a bit differently, it is true – three or four days earlier. The fact is that she said to me: 'What, it was Suzon and not me?'

The fact is that I replied: 'It was neither of you.'

The fact is that while she was all the time making fun of herself, Suzon, their two husbands, and throwing little insults at me, I found myself on top of her, and consequently she found herself underneath me, and while she was admitting that she enjoyed it a lot like that but not as much as the other way round she found herself back on top of me and consequently I found myself underneath her. The fact is that after some moments of rest and silence I found myself neither underneath nor on top of her and consequently she found herself neither on top of nor underneath me, because we were both on our sides, her head was bent forward and her two buttocks were stuck against my two thighs. The fact is that if I had not known so much, the good Marguerite would have taught me everything there was to learn. The fact is that we had a lot of trouble getting back to the village. The fact is that my sore throat has got much worse and there is no sign of me being in a position to talk for the next fortnight.

MASTER: And have you never seen these women since then?

JACQUES: On the contrary, more than once.

MASTER: Both of them?

JACQUES: Both of them.

MASTER: They didn't fall out together?

JACQUES: They were both useful to each other and they became better friends than ever.

MASTER: Women of our class would probably have done the same. But each woman to her man . . . Why are you laughing?

JACQUES: Every time I remember that little man shouting, swearing, foaming at the mouth, struggling with his head, his feet, his hands, his whole body, and ready to throw himself from the top of the barn at the risk of killing himself, nothing can stop me laughing.

MASTER: And who is this little man? Suzanne's husband?

JACQUES: No.

MASTER: Marguerite's husband?

JACQUES: No . . . Always the same, and it'll be the same as long as he lives.

MASTER: Who is he then? . . .

Jacques didn't answer his question and the master added: 'Just tell me who the man was.'

JACQUES: Once upon a time there was a child sitting at the foot of the counter in a laundry, and he was crying with all his might. The shopkeeper's wife, put out by his crying, said to him: 'Little man, why are you crying?'
'Because they want me to say "A".'
'And why don't you want to say "A"?'
'Because as soon as I say "A" they'll want me to say "B".'
As soon as I tell you the name of the little man I'll have to tell you the rest.

MASTER: Perhaps.

JACQUES: No, it's absolutely certain.

MASTER: Come along, my dear friend Jacques, tell me the little man's name. You're dying to, aren't you? Tell me for your own satisfaction.

JACQUES: He was a sort of dwarf, hunchbacked, gnarled, blind in one eye, with a stammer, jealous and lecherous, in love with and maybe even loved by Suzanne. He was the village priest.

Jacques resembled the child in the laundry as if they were two peas in a pod. The only difference was that ever since he had caught a sore throat one had the greatest difficulty to get him to say "A", but once he had started he would carry on by himself to the end of the alphabet.

JACQUES: I was in Suzon's barn alone with her.

MASTER: And you hadn't gone in there for nothing.

JACQUES: No. Then the priest arrived, lost his temper, started preaching and asked Suzon haughtily what she was doing alone with one of the most debauched boys in the village in the most isolated part of the farm.

MASTER: I can see that you had a reputation even then.

JACQUES: And well earned at that. He was really angry and added a few more even less flattering things to what he had said already. So then I got angry. From swapping insults it turned to blows. I grabbed a pitchfork and passed it between his legs — one prong through here and the other here — and then threw him into the hayloft, not more or less but exactly as if he were a bale of hay.

MASTER: And how high was this hayloft?

JACQUES: Ten feet at least. And he couldn't get down without breaking his neck.

MASTER: And next?

JACQUES: Next I undid Suzon's blouse, took her breasts, caressed them. She resisted a little. In the barn there was a pack saddle whose other uses were well known to us. I pushed her on to it.

MASTER: And pulled up her skirts?

JACQUES: I pulled up her skirts.

MASTER: And the priest could see all that?

JACQUES: As I see you now.

MASTER: And he shut up?

JACQUES: Certainly not, if you please. Barely able to contain his anger he started shouting 'Mmm . . . mm . . . murder! Fff . . . ff . . . fire! Ttt . . . tt . . . thief!' and then the husband whom we thought was far away ran in.

MASTER: I'm sorry about that. I don't like priests.

JACQUES: Then you would have been delighted if in front of his very eyes . . .

MASTER: Yes, I admit it.

JACQUES: Suzon just had time to get up. I adjusted my clothing and ran off and Suzon told me what happened later. As soon as the husband saw the priest perched on top of the hayloft he burst out laughing. The priest said:

'That's right, laugh, you fool.'

And so the husband laughed even more and asked who had perched him up there.

PRIEST: Lll . . . ll . . . let me ddd . . . dd . . . down!

The husband carried on laughing and asked how he should go about that.

PRIEST: Lll . . . ll . . . like I ggg . . . gg . . . got up here, www . . . ww . . . with a ppp . . . pp . . . pitchfork.

'Hell's teeth, you're right. That's what comes of having studied.'

So the husband took the pitchfork and presented it to the priest who straddled himself on it as I'd done with him. The husband then carried him round the barn on the end of it a few times singing a sort of plainchant while the priest was yelling: 'Lll . . . ll . . . let me ddd . . . dd . . . down you rrr . . . rr . . . ruffian!'

The husband said: 'Monsieur le vicaire, why should I not show you like this along all the roads in the village? They can't ever have seen such a pretty procession as this.'

However, the priest was let off with just the threat and the husband got him down. I don't know what he said to the husband next because Suzon ran away. But a little while later I heard: 'Www . . . ww . . . wretch, you ddd . . . dd . . . dare to sss . . . ss . . . strike a ppp . . . pp . . . priest. I exccc . . . cc . . . communiccc . . . cc . . . cate you. You will be ddd . . . dd . . . damned!'

It was the little man who was speaking and he was being chased by the husband, who was hitting him with the pitchfork. I arrived with a crowd of others. From a long way off the husband saw me, stopped his business with the pitchfork and said: 'Come here.'

MASTER: And Suzon?

JACQUES: She got out of it.

MASTER: Badly?

JACQUES: No. Women always get out of things well when they are not caught *in flagrante delicto* . . . What are you laughing at?

MASTER: At what makes me laugh, like you, every time I remember the little priest on the end of the husband's pitchfork.

JACQUES: It was not long after this incident, which my father heard about and also laughed at, that I joined up, as I have told you . . .

After a few moments of silence, or coughing, on the part of Jacques – according to some – or more laughter – according to others – his master turned to Jacques and said: 'And the story of your loves?'

Jacques tossed his head and did not answer.

How can a man of wisdom and morality, who fancies himself as something of a philosopher, amuse himself telling tales as obscene as this?

Well, firstly you must remember that these are not tales. It is a true story, and I certainly do not feel more guilty – and perhaps even less – when I write about Jacques' follies than Suetonius when he recorded for us the orgies of Tiberius. Moreover you read Suetonius without reproaching him. Why do you not frown at Catullus, Martial, Horace, Juvenal, Petronius, La Fontaine and so many others? Why don't you tell the stoic Seneca: 'We don't need to hear about the debauchery of your slave with his concave mirrors?' Why is it that you are only indulgent with dead writers? If you were to reflect a little on this partiality you will see that it is born of a false assumption. If you are innocent you will not read my work. If, on the other hand, you are depraved, you may read me without consequence. And then if you are not satisfied by what I say, open the preface to the works of Jean-Baptiste Rousseau and you will find my apologia.

Who is there amongst you who dares to criticize Voltaire for writing *La Pucelle*?[60] Nobody. So you have, therefore, two standards for assessing the actions of men.

– But, I hear you protest, Voltaire's *Pucelle* is a masterpiece.

So much the worse since people will read it more.

– And your *Jacques* is nothing more than a tasteless farrago of facts, some real, some imaginary, written without elegance and arranged without order.

So much the better: *Jacques* will be less read.

Whichever way you turn you are wrong. If my work is good it will please you. If it is bad it won't do you any harm. There is no book that is more innocent than a bad book.

I enjoy writing up under assumed names the follies I have seen you commit. Your follies make me laugh and my writings annoy you. To speak to you frankly, Reader, I find that you are the more wicked of the two of us. How satisfied would I be if it were as easy for me to protect myself from your calumny as it is for you to protect yourself from the boredom or the danger of my work!

Filthy hypocrites. Leave me in peace. Fuck away like unsaddled asses but allow me to say 'fuck'. I allow you the action. Allow me the word. You boldly use words like 'kill', 'steal', 'betray' all the time but only dare to pronounce that word under your breath. Might it be that the less you allow such supposed impurities to pass your lips the more they remain in your thoughts? And what has a thing so natural, so right and so necessary as sexual intercourse done to you that you should exclude the word for it from your conversation and imagine that your mouth, your eyes and your ears will be sullied by it?

It is a good thing that the expressions we use least, write least, and repress most are the best known and the most widely understood. Thus the proper term is as common as the word 'bread'. It is present in every age in every idiom. There are a thousand synonyms in all languages and it impresses itself in each of us without being expressed, without voice and without shape, and the sex which does the thing the most is the one which says the word the least.

I can still hear you exclaiming: 'Oh! What a vulgar man! Oh! What a cynic! Oh! What a sophist!'

Go on. Heap your insults on an estimable author who is always in your hands and whom I only translate here. To me the freedom of his style is almost the guarantee of the purity of his morals. It is Montaigne. *Lasciva est nobis pagina vita proba.*[61]

Jacques and his master spent the rest of the day without opening their lips. Jacques kept coughing and his master kept saying: 'That is a terrible cough.'

Then he would look at his watch to see what time it was without being aware of doing so, and then take a pinch of snuff without being aware of it. The proof of this is that he would do these things three or four times in a row in the same order. A moment afterwards Jacques would cough again and then his master would say: 'That's the devil of a cough you've got there! So you drank so much of our hostess's wine that you lost your voice. And last night with the secretary you weren't any more moderate. When you came up you were staggering and you didn't know what you were saying, and today you've stopped ten times and I bet that you haven't got a drop of wine left in your gourd.'

Then he would carry on muttering to himself, look at his watch and give his nostrils a treat.

I have forgotten to tell you, Reader, that Jacques never went anywhere without a gourd filled with the best wine, which used to hang from the pommel of his saddle. Every time his master interrupted him with a question which was a little long he would unfasten his gourd, throw back his head, raise the gourd above it and pour a stream of its contents into his mouth, only putting it back when his master had stopped speaking. I have also forgotten to tell you that in moments which required reflection his first impulse was to ask his gourd. Were it a matter of resolving a moral question, discussing an event, choosing one road rather than another, beginning, continuing or abandoning a transaction, weighing up the advantages or disadvantages of a political matter, a commercial or financial speculation, the wisdom or folly of a law, the outcome of a war, the choice of a room, or in a room the choice of a bed, his first word was, 'Let us consult the gourd', and his last word, 'That is the opinion of the gourd and my own.'

When his Destiny was silent in his head, it made itself known through his gourd. It was a sort of portable Pythian priestess, silent as soon as it was empty. At Delphi the Pythian priestess, her skirts pulled up, sitting bare-bottomed on the tripod, received her inspiration from the bottom upwards. Jacques, on his horse, his head turned towards heaven, his gourd uncorked with the neck inclined towards his mouth, received his inspiration from the top downwards. When the Pythian priestess and Jacques spoke their oracles, they were both drunk.

Jacques used to claim that the Holy Spirit had descended on the apostles in the form of a gourd and he used to call Pentecost the feast of the gourd. He even wrote a treatise on all the various types of divination, a profound treatise in which he gives preference to divination by Bacbuc, or by the gourd.[62] He contradicted, in spite of all the veneration he had for him, the curate of Meudon who consulted the divine bottle by its effect on the stomach. He used to say: 'I like Rabelais, but I prefer the truth to Rabelais.' He used to call him a heretical engastrimyth,[63] and prove in a hundred ways, each one better than the previous, that the true oracles of Bacbuc, or the gourd, could only be understood through the neck of a bottle. He included amongst the ranks of the distinguished followers of Bacbuc those who have during these last centuries been truly inspired by the gourd: Rabelais, La Fare, Chapelle, Chaulieu, La Fontaine, Molière, Panard, Gallet and Vade.[64] Plato and Jean-Jacques Rousseau, who recommended good wine without drinking it, are in his opinion two false followers of the gourd. In olden times the gourd had a few well-known sanctuaries, the Pomme de Pin, the Temple and La Guingette, a place of worship whose history is recorded elsewhere.[65] He gave the most magnificent description of the enthusiasm, the warmth and the fire with which Bacbucians or Périgourdians were and are still today filled, when, at the end of the meal, with their elbows on the table, the divine Bacbuc or the sacred gourd would appear and be brought down into their midst, would hiss, pop its cork and cover its worshippers in its prophetic foam. His manuscript is illustrated with two portraits beneath which appear the words: 'Anacreon and Rabelais, the former among the ancients, the latter among the moderns, sovereign pontiffs of the gourd'.

– Did Jacques use the expression 'engastrimyth'?

Why not, Reader? Jacques' Captain was a follower of Bacbuc. He might have known this expression and Jacques, who used to pick up everything he said, might have remembered it. But the truth is that 'engastrimyth' is my own word and the original text says 'ventriloquist'.

– That's all very nice, you are saying, but what about Jacques' loves?

Jacques' loves? Only Jacques knows about those, and there he is tormented by a sore throat which has reduced his master to his watch and his snuff-box – a privation which distresses him as much as you.

– What is to become of us?

My God, how should I know? This would now be an opportune moment to consult the divine Bacbuc or the sacred gourd, but her cult has declined, her temples are deserted. In the same way as the pagan oracles ended on the birth of our Saviour, so did the oracles of Bacbuc become silent on the death of Gallet. And so that was the end of those great poems, no more of those sublimely eloquent pieces, no more of those works stamped with the seal of drunkenness and genius. Everything is reasoned, measured, academic and flat. Oh divine Bacbuc! Oh sacred gourd! Oh divinity of Jacques! Come back amongst us . . .

There comes upon me, Reader, the need to talk to you about the birth of the divine Bacbuc, of the prodigies which accompanied her and followed her, of the marvels of her reign and the disasters of her retreat from society. And if our friend Jacques' sore throat continues and if his master stubbornly persists in silence you will have to make do with this story, which I will try and drag out until Jacques recovers and continues the story of his loves.

At this point there is a really deplorable gap in the conversation of Jacques and his master. Someday a descendant of Nodot or of the president of de Brosse or Freinsheimius or Father Brothier[66] will perhaps fill it and the descendants of Jacques, or of his master, the owners of the manuscript, will laugh a lot.

It would appear that Jacques, reduced to silence by his sore throat, suspended the story of his loves and that his master started the story of his own. This is only a conjecture, which I make for whatever it is worth. After a few perfunctory lines which announce the gap, one reads the words: 'There is nothing that is more sad in this world than to be a fool.'

Is it Jacques who offers this aphorism? Is it his master? This could become the subject of a long and thorny dissertation. If Jacques was not insolent enough to address these words to his master, was the latter frank enough to address them to himself? Whichever it was, it is evident, it is very evident, that it is the master who continues.

MASTER: It was the eve of her birthday and I had no money. However, the Chevalier de Saint-Ouin, my intimate friend, was never at a loss.

'Have you no money?' he asked me.

'No.'

'Well then, all we have to do is make some.'

'And do you know how that's done?'

'Of course.'

He got dressed. We went out and he led me through several remote streets until we reached an obscure little house where we went up a dirty little staircase to the third floor where I went into quite a spacious and strangely furnished apartment. There were, among other things, three chests of drawers, all three in different styles. Behind the middle one there was a large mirror with a cornice, too high for the ceiling, which was placed in such a manner that a good half foot of this mirror was hidden by the chest of drawers, on top of which there were goods of every kind, and two back-gammon boards. All around the apartment were quite good chairs of which there were no two the same. At the foot of a bed which had no curtains there was a superb day-bed and against one of the windows a brand-new birdcage without any birds in it. Against the other window there was a chandelier hanging on a broom handle, both ends of which were resting on the backs of two dilapidated rush chairs, and to the right and the left all around were pictures, some hanging on the walls, others stacked up.

JACQUES: That smells of shady deals a mile away.

MASTER: You've guessed it. And there we were, with the Chevalier and M. Le Brun – which was the name of our dealer in second-hand goods and usurer's broker – throwing themselves into each others' arms.

'Ah! Is it you, Monsieur le Chevalier?'

'Yes, it is me, my dear Le Brun.'

'But what has become of you? We haven't seen you for ages. Times are very sad, are they not?'

'Very sad, my dear Le Brun. But it's nothing to do with all that. Listen to me, I have something to say to you . . .'

I sat down. The Chevalier and Le Brun withdrew into a corner to talk. I can only tell you the few words of their conversation which I overheard . . .

'Is he good?'

'Excellent.'

'Adult?'

'Very much so.'

'And he is the son?'

'The son.'

'You do know that our last two affairs . . .'

'Speak more quietly.'

'And the father?'

'Rich.'

'Old?'

'Decrepit.'

LE BRUN (more loudly): Now look, Monsieur le Chevalier, I don't want to get involved any more. There are always unfortunate consequences. He is your friend. Fine! Monsieur has every appearance of being an honest man, but . . .

'My dear Le Brun . . .'

'I have no money at all.'

'But you know people.'

'But they are all scoundrels, complete tricksters. Monsieur le Chevalier, are you not tired of dealing with such people?'

'Necessity knows no law.'

'The necessity that's pressing you is a fine sort of necessity, a game, a hand of cards, some girl.'

'My dear friend! . . .'

'It's always me. I am weak as a baby, and then as for you, I do not know anyone whom you couldn't make break an oath. Well, let's ring so I can find out if Fourgeot is at home . . . No, don't ring, Fourgeot will take you to Merval.'

'Why not you?'

'Me, I have sworn that this abominable Merval would never again work, either for me or for my friends. You would be obliged to answer for Monsieur, who is perhaps, who is without doubt, an honest man, I would answer for you to Fourgeot, and Fourgeot would answer for me to Merval . . .'

Meanwhile his servant girl had come in and asked: 'Is it for M. Merval's?'

Le Brun said to his servant: 'No, it's for nobody's . . . Monsieur le Chevalier, I really can't, I can't.'

The Chevalier embraced him and caressed him: 'My dear Le Brun, my dear friend . . .'

I came nearer and joined my pleadings to the Chevalier's: 'Monsieur Le Brun, my good sir . . .'

Le Brun allowed himself to be persuaded. The servant who was smiling at this dumb show left and then reappeared in the twinkling of an eye with a little man with a limp, dressed in black, a cane in his hand, a stammer, a thin wrinkled face and a sharp eye.

The Chevalier turned to him and said: 'Come, Monsieur Mathieu de Fourgeot, we have not a moment to lose. Lead the way quickly . . .'

De Fourgeot did not seem to have heard him and was undoing a little chamois purse.

The Chevalier said to Fourgeot: 'Don't be silly, we'll look after that.'

I came closer and pulled out an écu, which I slipped to the Chevalier, who gave it to the servant girl, passing his hand under her chin. Meanwhile Le Brun said to Fourgeot: 'I forbid you to do it. You are not to take these gentlemen there.'

'Monsieur Le Brun, why not?'

'He is a trickster, a scoundrel.'

'I am well aware that M. de Merval . . . but forgive them that trespass . . . and then he's the only person I know who's got any money at the moment.'

LE BRUN: Monsieur Fourgeot, do as you please. Messieurs, I wash my hands of it.

FOURGEOT: Monsieur Le Brun, are you not coming with us?

LE BRUN: Me! God preserve me. He is a traitor and I will never again see him for the rest of my days.

FOURGEOT: But without you we won't get anything done.

CHEVALIER: That is true. Come along, my dear Le Brun, it is a question of helping me, and it is a question of obliging a gallant man who finds himself in straits. You will not refuse me. You will come.

LE BRUN: Go to the house of a Merval! Me! Me!

CHEVALIER: Yes, you. You will come for me.

Eventually, through our pleadings, Le Brun allowed himself to be borne away, and there we were, him, Le Brun, the Chevalier and Mathieu de Fourgeot on our way, with the Chevalier patting Le Brun's hand in a friendly manner and saying to me: 'He is the best of men, the most helpful man in the world, the best acquaintance . . .'

'I believe that M. le Chevalier would even persuade me to turn counter-feiter.'

And then there we were at Merval's house.

JACQUES: Mathieu de Fourgeot . . .

MASTER: Well! What are you trying to say?

JACQUES: Mathieu de Fourgeot . . . I mean to say that M. le Chevalier de Saint-Ouin knows these people by name and Christian name and that he is a trickster in league with all these other scoundrels.

MASTER: You may well be right . . .
You couldn't meet a man more kind, more civil, more honest, more polite, more human, more tender-hearted or more disinterested than M. de Merval. Having established to his satisfaction that I was not a minor and that I was solvent, M. de Merval looked positively affectionate and sad and said to us in a tone of deep compassion that he was profoundly sorry but he had been obliged that very morning to help one of his friends, pressed by the most urgent needs, and that he was absolutely without funds. Then, turning to me, he added: 'Monsieur, do not regret not having come here earlier. I would have been distressed to refuse you, but I would have done so. Friendship goes before everything else.'

We were all totally flabbergasted. There were the Chevalier, even Le Brun and Fourgeot, at the knees of Merval.

And M. de Merval said to them: 'Messieurs, you all know me. I like to oblige people and try not to spoil the services which I render by obliging people to plead for them. But, on my word, as a man of honour, there are not four louis in this house.'

And I, standing in the midst of these people, resembled a patient who has heard his death sentence.

I said to the Chevalier: 'Chevalier, let us go away since these gentlemen can do nothing.'

And the Chevalier drew me to one side: 'That is unthinkable. It is the day before her birthday. I have warned her, I tell you, and she is expecting a gallant gesture on your part. You know her. It is not that she is self-interested, but she is like all the others and does not like to be betrayed in her expectations. She may already have boasted to her father, her mother, her aunts, to her friends, and, after all that, to have nothing to show them, that is mortifying . . .'

And then he went back to Merval and pressed him even harder. Eventually, after letting himself be pestered at some length, Merval said: 'I have the softest heart in the world. I cannot bear to see people in trouble. I'm mulling things over, I've had an idea.'

CHEVALIER: What idea?

MERVAL: Why do you not take some goods?

CHEVALIER: Do you have any?

MERVAL: No, but I know a woman who will give you some, a good woman, an honest woman.

LE BRUN: Yes, who will give us baubles which she will sell to us for their weight in gold, from which we will recover nothing.

MERVAL: Not at all. There will be beautiful cloths, jewels in gold and silver, silks of every kind, pearls, a few precious stones. There will be very little to lose on her goods. She is a good creature who is content with little provided that she is given good security. And these are business goods which cost her very little. Anyway, why don't you see them? Seeing won't cost you anything . . .

I protested to Merval and to the Chevalier that I was not of a rank to engage in trade and that, even if this arrangement was not repugnant to me, my situation would not leave me time to benefit from it.[67] The kindly Le Brun and Mathieu de Fourgeot both said at the same time: 'What does that matter? We will sell for you. It is only half a day's work . . .'

And the rendezvous was set for that afternoon at the house of M. de Merval, who tapped me lightly on the shoulder and said in an unctuous and sincere tone of voice: 'Monsieur, I am delighted to help, but believe me, do not make a habit of borrowing money in this manner. It always ends in ruin. It would be a miracle if you were to find for a second time in this part of the world such honest people to deal with as Messieurs Le Brun and Mathieu de Fourgeot . . .'

Le Brun and Fourgeot de Mathieu or Mathieu de Fourgeot bowed and thanked him and told him that he was too kind, that they had simply tried until the present to carry on their little business in good faith, and there was no cause to praise them.

'You are wrong, Messieurs. Tell me, who has a conscience these days? Ask Monsieur le Chevalier de Saint-Ouin, who knows what I am talking about . . .'

And then there we were on our way out of Merval's house when he shouted to us from the top of the stairs to ask if he could count on us and summon his tradeswoman. We told him that he could and the four of us went off to have lunch in a neighbouring inn to pass the time until the appointment.

Mathieu de Fourgeot ordered lunch and ordered well. At dessert two street girls came over to our table with their hurdy-gurdys. Le Brun had them sit down. They were given something to drink, and encouraged to chatter and play. While my three guests were amusing themselves in teasing one of them, her friend, who was sitting next to me, said to me quietly: 'Monsieur, you are in very bad company here. There is not one of these people here whose name isn't on police files.'

We left the inn at the appointed hour and went to Merval's house. I forgot to tell you that our lunch had emptied the Chevalier's purse and my own and on the way there Le Brun told the Chevalier, who repeated it to me, that Mathieu de Fourgeot would require six louis for his commission, which was the least that one could give him, and that if he was satisfied with us we would have the goods at a better price and would easily recover this sum on their sale.

There we were again at Merval's house, where his merchant lady had arrived before us with her goods. Mademoiselle Bridoie, for that was her name, overwhelmed us with politeness and curtseys and then laid out before us her materials, cloths, laces, rings, diamonds and gold boxes. We took something of everything. It was Le Brun, Mathieu de Fourgeot and the Chevalier who fixed the prices of the goods, and Merval wrote them down. The total came to nineteen thousand, seven hundred and seventy-five pounds, for which sum I was about to make out my note when Mlle Bridoie curtseyed to me – because she never said anything without curtseying: 'Monsieur, do you intend to pay your notes when they fall due?'

'Of course,' I answered.

'In that case,' she replied, 'it makes no difference to you whether you give me a note or a bill of exchange . . .'

The word 'bill of exchange' made me turn pale. The Chevalier noticed and said to Mlle Bridoie: 'Bills of exchange, Mademoiselle! But bills of exchange circulate and there is no telling in whose hands they might end up.'

'You are joking, Monsieur le Chevalier. One does have some idea of the respect due to persons of your rank . . .' And then she curtseyed . . . 'One keeps this sort of document in one's wallet and only produces it on the due date. Here, look . . .'

And then another curtsey . . . and she took her wallet out of her pocket and read out a multitude of names of every state and condition.

The Chevalier had come over to me and said: 'Bills of exchange! That is all devilish serious. Consider what it is you are going to do. This woman seems honest to me, and then before it falls due you will be in funds, or I will be.

JACQUES: And you signed the bills of exchange?

MASTER: That is correct.

JACQUES: It is the custom of fathers when their children leave for the capital to preach them a little sermon. Do not frequent bad company, make yourself liked by your superiors through your assiduity to fulfil your duties, don't forget your religion, avoid girls of bad character and sharpsters, and above all never sign bills of exchange.[68]

MASTER: Well, what do you expect? I did the same as everyone else. The first thing I forgot was my father's lesson. There I was, well stocked in goods for sale, but it was money we needed. There were a few pairs of lace cuffs which were very beautiful. The Chevalier took some at cost price and said: 'There, that is already one part of your purchase on which you will lose nothing.'

Mathieu de Fourgeot took a watch and two gold boxes for which he was going to give me cash immediately. Le Brun took everything else on sale or return at his house. I put a superb set of jewels into my pocket along with the lace cuffs. It was one of the flowers in the bouquet which I was going to present. Mathieu de Fourgeot returned in the twinkling of an eye with sixty louis. He kept ten for himself and I took the fifty remaining. He told me that he had sold neither the watch nor the two boxes but that he'd pawned them.

JACQUES: Pawned them?

MASTER: Yes.

JACQUES: I know where . . .

MASTER: Where?

JACQUES: With the lady with the curtseys, la Bridoie.

MASTER: True. With the pair of lace cuffs and the rest of the set of jewels I also took a pretty ring and a gold plated box. I had fifty louis in my purse, and we were, the Chevalier and I, in the utmost good spirits.

JACQUES: That's all very well. There's only one thing in all this which intrigues me. That is the disinterestedness of M. Le Brun. Didn't he have any part of the spoils?

MASTER: Come along, Jacques, you are joking. You do not know M. Le Brun. I suggested to him that I should reward his good offices. He got angry with me and replied that I apparently took him for a Mathieu de Fourgeot, and that he had never asked for anything.

'Good old Monsieur Le Brun,' exclaimed the Chevalier, 'he's always the same. We would be embarrassed if you were more honest than us . . .'

And straight away he took out from amongst our merchandise two dozen handkerchiefs and a piece of muslin, which he asked him to accept for his wife and daughter. Le Brun started to contemplate the handkerchiefs which appeared so beautiful to him, the muslin which he found so fine. It was offered to him with such good grace and he had so close at hand the opportunity to repay our kindness through the sale of the goods which remained in his hands that he allowed himself to be won over. And then we were gone, going as fast as our carriage would take us towards the home of her whom I loved and for whom the set of jewels, the lace cuffs and the ring were destined. The present worked like magic. She was charming and tried on the set of jewels and the lace cuffs straight away. The ring seemed to have been made for her finger. We dined merrily as you can well imagine.

JACQUES: And you slept there?

MASTER: No.

JACQUES: It was the Chevalier, then?

MASTER: I believe so.

JACQUES: At the pace you were being led, your fifty louis did not last very long.

MASTER: No. At the end of a week or so we returned to Le Brun to see what the rest of our goods had produced.

JACQUES: Nothing or hardly anything. Le Brun was sad and spoke out against Merval and the lady with the curtseys and called them thieves, scoundrels, rogues, swore all over again never to have anything more to do with them and paid you seven to eight hundred francs.

MASTER: More or less. Eight hundred and seventy pounds.

JACQUES: If I know how to count at all – eight hundred and seventy pounds from Le Brun, fifty louis from Merval or de Fourgeot, the set of jewels, the lace cuffs and the ring, say another fifty louis, and that is what you recovered from your nineteen thousand seven hundred and seventy three pounds worth of goods. Heavens, that is honest. Merval was right. It's not every day one deals with such worthy people.

MASTER: You are forgetting the lace cuffs taken at cost price by the Chevalier.

JACQUES: That is because the Chevalier never mentioned them to you.

MASTER: Exactly. And the two gold watches and the watch pawned by Mathieu, you haven't mentioned them.

JACQUES: That is because I don't know what to say.

MASTER: Meanwhile the date of payment of the bills of exchange came.

JACQUES: And neither your funds nor the Chevalier's arrived.

MASTER: I was obliged to hide myself. My parents were informed. One of my uncles came to Paris. He sent a statement against all these rogues to the police. This statement was sent to a clerk and this clerk was a paid protector of Merval. They replied that since the matter was a civil case the police could do nothing. The pawnbroker to whom Mathieu had entrusted the two boxes issued a summons against Mathieu. I became involved in the action. The court costs were so enormous that after the sale of the watch and the boxes there still remained five or six hundred francs to pay.

You don't believe that, do you, Reader? But if I told you that an innkeeper in my neighbourhood died a short time ago and left two poor infant children. The bailiff went to the deceased's house and had the place sealed. Then the seals were removed, an inventory was made, and a sale took place. The sale produced nine hundred francs. Out of these nine hundred francs, after the costs of justice had been deducted, there remained two sous for each orphan, which they put into each child's hand and then led them both to the workhouse.

MASTER: That's horrifying.

JACQUES: And it's still going on.

MASTER: My father died while all this was going on. I paid off all the bills of exchange and came out of my retreat, and to give credit to the Chevalier and my lady-friend I must admit that they kept me more or less faithful company.

JACQUES: And there you were, just as struck on the Chevalier and your girlfriend keeping you on an even tighter rein.

MASTER: Why so, Jacques?

JACQUES: Why? Because, being the master of your own person, and the possessor of an honest fortune, they had to make a complete fool of you, a husband.

MASTER: Indeed, I think that was their project, but they didn't succeed.

JACQUES: You were very lucky, or they were very clumsy.

MASTER: It seems to me that your voice is less hoarse and you are speaking more freely.

JACQUES: It may seem so to you, but that is not the case.

MASTER: Could you not continue with the story of your loves?

JACQUES: No.

MASTER: Then is it your wish that I should continue with the story of my own?

JACQUES: It is my wish to stop here for a moment and raise the gourd.

MASTER: What! With your sore throat, you've filled your gourd?

JACQUES: Yes, but by all the devils that ever were, it's tisane. So I have no inspiration, I am a fool, and for as long as there is nothing but tisane in the gourd, I will remain a fool.

MASTER: What are you doing?

JACQUES: I am pouring the tisane away. I am afraid it will bring us bad luck.

MASTER: You're mad.

JACQUES: Wise or mad, I'm not leaving a drop in this gourd.

While Jacques was emptying out his gourd his master looked at his watch, opened his snuff-box, and prepared to continue the story of his loves. But, as for me, Reader, I am tempted to shut his mouth by showing him, in the distance, either an old soldier on a horse, his back stooped, coming towards them rapidly, or a young peasant girl, wearing a little straw hat and red petticoats, going her way on foot, or on a donkey. And why shouldn't this old soldier be Jacques' Captain or his Captain's friend?

– But he's dead!

You think so? And why shouldn't the young peasant girl be Suzon or Marguerite, or the hostess of the Grand-Cerf, or mother Jeanne, or even Denise, her daughter? A novelist wouldn't miss such an opportunity, but I don't like novels – except Richardson's. I am writing history: either this story will be interesting or it won't be interesting, but that is the least of my worries. My project is to be truthful and I have fulfilled it. So I will not have brother Jean return from Lisbon. That fat prior coming towards us in a gig with a pretty young lady sitting beside him will not be Father Hudson.

– But Father Hudson is dead.

You believe so? Were you at his funeral?

– No.

You didn't see him buried?

– No.

Then he is either dead or alive, as you please. It is entirely up to me whether or not I stop this gig and bring out of it along with the Prior and his travelling companion a series of events, the result of which would be that you would know neither Jacques' loves nor those of his master. But I disdain all these expedients. I can see that with only a little bit of imagination and style, nothing is easier to rattle off than a novel. But let us stick to the truth, and while we are waiting for Jacques' sore throat to go away, let us allow his master to speak.

MASTER: One morning the Chevalier seemed to me to be extremely sad. It was the day after we had spent a day in the country, that is, the Chevalier, his lady friend, or my lady friend, or perhaps his and mine, her father, her mother, her aunts, her cousins and me. He asked me if I had committed any indiscretion which might have alerted her parents to my passion. He informed me that her father and mother, alarmed by my regular visits, had questioned their daughter, that if I had honest intentions nothing was more simple than admitting them, that they would be honoured to receive me on those conditions, but if I did not explain myself clearly within a fortnight they begged me to stop these visits, which were being talked about and which were harming their daughter by keeping away from her advantageous parties who might present themselves were it not for fear of refusal.

JACQUES: Well then, Master, didn't Jacques smell it?

MASTER: The Chevalier added: 'Within a fortnight! That is quite a short time. You are in love and you are loved. In a fortnight, what are you going to do?'

I told the Chevalier straight away that I would give up.

'You're giving up! Don't you love her, then?'

'I love her a lot, but I have parents, a name, a position in life, ambitions, and I will never decide to bury all those advantages in the shop of a little bourgeoise.'

'Shall I tell them that?'

'If you wish. But, Chevalier, the sudden scrupulous delicacy of these people surprises me. They have allowed their daughter to accept my presents, they have left me alone with her a score of times, she goes to balls, gatherings, shows, walks alone in the fields and in the town with the first fellow who has a decent carriage and team to put at her disposal. They sleep soundly while people converse or play music at her house. You frequent the house whenever you please and, between you and me, Chevalier, when you are allowed into a house, anyone else can be brought there. Their daughter has a reputation. I do not believe and I do not deny all the things that people say about her, but you must admit that these parents might have taken it into their heads earlier to be punctilious about their child's honour. Do you want me to speak the truth? They have taken me for some kind of simpleton whom they have calculated they could lead by the nose to the feet of the parish priest. They've made a mistake. I find Mlle Agathe charming and I am infatuated with her, which is obvious, I believe, from the frightful expense I have incurred for her. I'm not saying that I won't continue in the same vein, but I must be certain, in that event, that I'll find her somewhat less unyielding in the future.

'It is not my intention to lose at her knees time, money and entreaties which I could put to much better use elsewhere. You will repeat these last words to Mlle Agathe, and everything which preceded to her parents. Our relationship must end, or I must be accepted on a new footing and Mlle Agathe treat me better than she has done up to now. When you introduced me to her house, you must admit, Chevalier, that you led me to anticipate a more responsive attitude than I've met with so far.'

'Heavens, I was a little deceived myself at first. Who the devil would ever have imagined that with her free and easy airs and manner the young scatterbrain would be a little dragon of virtue?'

JACQUES: What the devil! Monsieur, that's strong stuff. So you have been brave at least once in your life?

MASTER: There are days like that. I still had the incident of the usurers on my mind, my retreat in sanctuary because of the Bridoie woman, and more than all the rest the severity of Mlle Agathe. I was a little tired of being strung along.

JACQUES: And consequent on this courageous speech which you made to your friend the Chevalier de Saint-Ouin, what did you do then?

MASTER: I kept my word. I stopped my visits.

JACQUES: Bravo! Bravo! *Mio caro maestro!*

MASTER: A fortnight went by during which time I heard nothing except through the Chevalier who kept me faithfully informed of the effects of my absence on the family and who encouraged me to remain steadfast.

He said to me: 'They are beginning to be surprised and starting to look at each other and talk. They are asking themselves what reasons you might have for being displeased with them. The young girl is trying to be dignified and she is affecting an air of indifference which cannot conceal her pique, saying: "If we no longer see this gentleman it is apparently because he no longer wishes us to see him. Fine. That's his business." Then she does a pirouette, starts humming, goes over to the window and comes back again. But her eyes are red and everyone sees that she's been crying.'

'She's been crying!'

'Then she sits down, takes up her needlework, tries to carry on with it but can't. They make conversation, she remains quiet. They try to cheer her up, she goes into a temper. They suggest a game, a walk, the theatre, she wants to do something else and then the next moment she doesn't . . . Now what? You're getting upset! I won't tell you anything more.'

'But, Chevalier, do you think then that if I reappeared . . .'

'I think that you would be a fool. You must hold fast, you must have courage. If you come back without being called, you are lost. You've got to teach that lot some manners.'

'But what if I am not called back?'

'You'll be called back.'

'What if there's a long delay?'

'You'll be called back soon. Damn it, a man like you is not easily replaced. If you come back of your own accord, you'll get the cold shoulder, you'll be made to pay for your outburst and you'll be forced to accept whatever terms are imposed on you. You would have to submit to them, you would have to bend the knee. Do you want to be master or slave, and the most ill-treated slave at that? Choose. To tell the truth, your conduct has been a little cavalier and hardly seems the behaviour of a man who is head over heels in love. But what is done is done and you must make certain that you secure any possible advantage.

'She's been crying!'

'Well! So, she's been crying. It's better for her to cry than you.'

'But what if I am not called back?'

'You will be called back, I tell you. When I arrive I do not speak about you any more, as if you no longer existed. They turn the conversation and I allow them to turn it. Eventually they ask me if I've seen you. My reply is indifferent, sometimes yes, sometimes no. Then they talk about something else but do not take long to come back to your disappearance. The first word comes from the father or the mother or the aunt or Agathe herself: "After all the respect we showed for him! . . ." "The interest which we all took in that business he was recently involved in! . . ." "The friendship my niece showed for him! . . ." "The politeness I lavished on him! . . ." "All those protestations of affection which he made to us! . . ." "Who would ever trust men after that! . . ." "Who would ever open their house to visitors or put their trust in friends after a thing like that?"'

'What about Agathe?'

'Full of dismay, I assure you, all of them.'

'And Agathe?'

'Agathe took me aside and asked me: "Chevalier, do you understand anything of your friend's behaviour? You have assured me so many times that he loved me. You believed him without doubt, and why would you not have believed him – I believed him too . . ." Then she stopped, her voice changed and tears came into her eyes . . . Well! Now you're doing the same! I won't tell you any more, that's for sure. I can see what you want, but there's absolutely nothing doing. Since you were stupid enough to stay away without rhyme or reason I do not want you to compound it all by going back and throwing yourself on them. You must turn this incident to your advantage if you want to make progress with Agathe. She must be made to see that she does not hold you so securely that she might not lose you unless she makes more effort to keep you. After all that you have done, and still to be only on hand-kissing terms! Come now, Chevalier, put your hand on your heart, we are friends and you can, without being indiscreet, reveal yourself to me. Is it true that she's never granted you anything?'

'No.'

'You're lying, you're being discreet.'

'I would be, perhaps, if I had reason to, but I swear to you that I am not fortunate enough to be in such a position.'

'That is inconceivable, because, after all, you're not clumsy. What! Has she never had even the least little moment of weakness?'

'No.'

'Then it must have come without your noticing and you missed it. I fear that you may have been a little simple. Honest, delicate, tender people like you are prone to that.'

'But, what about you, Chevalier? Where do you stand?'

'Nowhere.'

'Have you never had any pretensions?'

'Quite the contrary, I assure you. They even lasted a long time, but you came, you saw, and you conquered. I noticed that she looked at you a lot and at me hardly at all, and took it as read. We have remained good friends and she confides her little thoughts in me and sometimes follows my advice, but for want of anything better I have accepted the role of subaltern to which you have reduced me.'

JACQUES: Monsieur, two points. The first is that I have never been able to tell my story without some devil or other interrupting me and yet you tell your story straight off. That's the way life goes. One person runs through life's thorns without pricking himself while another, no matter how hard he looks where he puts his feet, finds thorns even on the best path and arrives at his destination skinned alive.

MASTER: Can you have forgotten your philosophy? What about the great scroll and the writing up above?

JACQUES: The other point is that I'm still convinced that your Chevalier de Saint-Ouin is a great rogue, and now that he has shared your money with the usurers Le Brun, Merval, Mathieu de Fourgeot or Fourgeot de Mathieu and the Bridoie woman he is trying to lumber you with his mistress, all square and above board, of course, and in front of a notary and a priest, so that he can share your wife with you . . . Ahi! My throat! . . .

MASTER: Do you know what you are doing there? It is something very common and very impertinent.

JACQUES: I am certainly capable of it.

MASTER: You complain about being interrupted and yet you interrupt me.

JACQUES: That is the effect your bad example has had on me. Mothers want to have a good time and want their daughters to be well behaved, fathers want to be spendthrift and have thrifty sons, masters want . . .

MASTER: To interrupt their valets, interrupt as much as they want and not be interrupted.

Reader, are you not afraid of seeing here a repetition of the scene in the inn where one of them was shouting: 'Go downstairs!', and the other: 'I will not go downstairs!'?

Why should I not cause you to hear: 'I will interrupt!' 'You will not interrupt!'

What is certain though is that it only needs me to provoke Jacques or his master for the quarrel to be started and once that's happened who knows how it might end?

'Monsieur, I am not interrupting you, but I am conversing with you since you have given me permission.'

MASTER: All right, but that's not all.

JACQUES: What other impropriety can I have committed?

MASTER: You are anticipating the story-teller and taking away from him the pleasure he has promised himself by surprising you, so that, since you have guessed by a very misplaced and ostentatious show of wisdom what he was going to tell you, there is nothing left for him other than to shut up, so I am shutting up.

JACQUES: Ah! Master!

MASTER: God damn all clever men!

JACQUES: I agree. But you are not going to be so cruel . . .

MASTER: Admit at least that you would deserve it.

JACQUES: All right. But all the same, you are going to look at your watch to see what time it is, you will take your pinch of snuff, your bad temper will go away, and you will carry on with your story.

MASTER: The rascal can make me do whatever he wants . . . A few days after this conversation with the Chevalier, he came back to my house. He seemed triumphant.

'Well, my friend! Next time will you believe in my predictions? I told you so, we are the stronger and here is a letter from the little lady, yes, a letter, a letter from her.'

This letter was very touching, full of reproaches, pleadings *et cetera*. And so there I was, reinstated in their house.

Reader, you've stopped reading! What's wrong? Ah! I think I know. You want to see the letter. Madame Riccoboni would not have failed to show it to you.[69] And as for the letter which Mme de La Pommeraye dictated to her two saintly ladies, I am sure you regretted that. Although that letter was a lot more difficult to write than Agathe's, and although I don't have unlimited confidence in my talents, I believe I could have managed it, but it wouldn't have been original. It would have been like one of those sublime harangues of Livy in his 'History of Rome', or of Cardinal Bentivoglio in his 'Wars of Flanders'.[70] One reads them with pleasure but they destroy the illusion. A historian who imputes to his characters speeches they have not made can also supply them with actions they have not performed. I beg you, therefore, to do without these two letters, and carry on reading.

MASTER: They asked me the reason for my absence. I told them something or other. They accepted what I said and everything carried on as before.

JACQUES: That is to say that you continued your expenditure and your *amours* did not progress any further.

MASTER: The Chevalier asked me for news and seemed to become impatient.

JACQUES: And he actually really was becoming impatient, perhaps . . .

MASTER: Why so?

JACQUES: Why? Because he . . .

MASTER: Well, finish.

JACQUES: I'll be careful not to. That must be left to the story-teller.

MASTER: I am pleased that you are profiting from my lessons . . . One day the Chevalier suggested to me that we should go for a walk alone together. We went to spend the day in the country. We left early. We lunched at an inn and we had supper there. The wine was excellent and we drank a lot of it, chatting about government, religion and love affairs. Never had the Chevalier shown me so much trust, so much friendship. He told me the story of his whole life with the most incredible frankness, without hiding from me either the good or the bad. He drank. He embraced me. He cried with tenderness. I drank. I embraced him. And I cried in my turn. In all his past conduct there was only one single action with which he reproached himself, the remorse for which he would carry to his grave.

'Chevalier, confess your sin to your friend since that will give you comfort. Well, what was it then? Some peccadillo whose importance you are exaggerating through your own scrupulousness?'

'No, no,' cried the Chevalier, burying his head in his hands and hiding his face in shame. 'It is a foul deed. An unpardonable foul deed. Would you believe it that I, the Chevalier de Saint-Ouin, once deceived, yes, deceived, his friend?'

'And how did that happen?'

'Alas! Both of us used to frequent the same house, as you and I do. There was a young girl there, like Mlle Agathe. He was in love with her, but I was the one she loved. He ruined himself in expense for her, and it was I who enjoyed her favours. I have never had the courage to admit it to him but if we found ourselves together again I would tell him everything. This frightful secret which I carry at the bottom of my heart overwhelms me. It is a burden from which I absolutely must deliver myself.'

'Chevalier, you would do well to do so.'

'Do you advise me to do so?'

'Of course I advise you to.'

'And how do you think my friend would take it?'

'If he is your friend, if he is fair, he will find your forgiveness in his own heart. He will be touched by your honesty and your repentance. He will throw his arms around your neck. He would do what I would do if I were in his place.'

'Do you believe so?'

'I am sure of it.'

'And is that what you would do?'

'I have no doubt of it.'

At that moment the Chevalier got up and came towards me, tears in his eyes, arms open: 'My friend, embrace me, then.'

'What! Chevalier,' I said, 'is it you? Is it me? And that hussy Agathe?'

'Yes, my friend. I release you from your promise. You are free to do with me as you wish. If you think, as I do, that my offence is inexcusable, do not excuse me. Get up from here, leave me and never see me again without scorning me, and abandon me to my sorrow and my shame. Ah! My friend, if only you knew how much power the little minx had over my heart. I was born honest. Imagine how much I have had to suffer in the unworthy role to which I have lowered myself. How many times have I turned my eyes away from her to look at you, inwardly groaning at my betrayal and hers. It is extraordinary that you never noticed . . .'

Meanwhile I was completely petrified. I had hardly heard the Chevalier's speech. I cried out: 'Ah! Unworthy man! Ah! Chevalier! You, you, my friend!'

'Yes, I was, and I am still, since, in order to free you from the snares of this creature, I am revealing a secret which is more hers than mine. But what makes me really sorry is that you have received from her nothing to compensate you for all that you have done for her.'

Here Jacques started to laugh and whistle.

– But this is just like Collé's *Vérité dans le vin* . . .[71]

Reader, you don't know what you are talking about. You are so concerned with showing how intelligent you are that you end up being stupid. It is so little a case of *in vino veritas* that it is in fact the opposite – it is untruth in the wine. I have been rude to you. I am sorry and I beg your pardon.

MASTER: My anger subsided little by little. I embraced the Chevalier, who sat down again in his chair with his elbows on the table and fists clenched over his eyes. He did not dare to look at me.

JACQUES: He was so upset! And you had the kindness to console him!

(And Jacques carried on whistling.)

MASTER: It seemed to me that the best thing to do was to turn the thing into a joke. At every light-hearted word the downcast Chevalier said to me: 'There can be no other man like you. You are unique. You are worth a hundred times more than me. I doubt if I would have had the generosity or the strength to forgive you a similar wrong and you are treating it all light-heartedly. That is unheard of. My friend, what could I do that could ever make amends? . . . Ah! No, no, that is not the kind of thing one can make amends for. Never, never will I forget either my crime or your leniency.

Those are two deeds which are profoundly engraved on my heart . . . I will remember one so that I may detest myself, the other so that I may admire you and so that my affection for you will increase.'

'Come along, Chevalier, think no more of it. You are making too much of your action and mine. Let us drink. To your health. Chevalier, to my own health then, since you do not wish us to drink to yours . . .'

Little by little the Chevalier took heart. He then told me all the details of his betrayal, heaping upon himself the hardest epithets. He tore the daughter, her mother, her father, her aunts and her whole family to pieces and he showed them to be a bunch of rogues unworthy of me but only too worthy of him. Those were his own words.

JACQUES: And that is why I advise women never to sleep with people who get drunk. I despise your Chevalier hardly less for his indiscretion in love than for his treachery in friendship. What the devil! He had only to . . . be an honest man and tell you straight away . . . But listen, Monsieur, I still think he's a blackguard, a frightful blackguard. I no longer know how all this will end and I am afraid lest he cheat you again in being honest with you. Release me, release yourself quickly from the inn and the company of that man . . .

At this point Jacques picked up his gourd again, forgetting that it contained neither tisane nor wine. His master started laughing. Jacques coughed non-stop for nearly ten minutes afterwards. His master took out his watch and his snuff-box and carried on with his story, which I will interrupt, if you don't mind, if only to annoy Jacques by proving to him that it was not written up above, as he believed, that he would always be interrupted and his master would never be.

MASTER: 'After what you have told me I hope that you will never ever see them again.'

'Me, see them again! But what infuriates me is to go away without taking revenge. They have betrayed, manipulated and robbed a worthy man. They have taken unfair advantage of the passion and weakness of another worthy man – for I still dare to think of myself as such – to lead him into one abomination after another. They have exposed two friends to hate each other, perhaps to tear out each other's throat, because, after all, my dear friend, you must admit that, if you had discovered my unworthy conduct, you are brave and you might perhaps have felt such resentment at it that . . .'

'No, it would not have been as bad as that. Why should it? And for whom? Because of a deed which nobody could guarantee they might not commit? Is she my wife? And even if she were? Is she my daughter? No, she's a little guttersnipe, and you believe that for a little guttersnipe . . . Come along, my friend, let us forget all about that and drink. Agathe is young, lively, white, shapely, plump . . . with the firmest body? The softest skin? Making love to her must have been delightful and I imagine that the pleasure of being in her arms could hardly have left you much time to think of your friends.'

'It is beyond doubt that, if the charms of the person concerned and physical pleasure could mitigate the offence, no one on this earth could be less guilty than me.'

'Ah! Now then, Chevalier, I will backtrack a little. I withdraw my forgiveness and wish to impose one condition on pardoning your betrayal.'

'Speak, my friend, command me, tell me. Must I throw myself out of the window, hang myself, drown myself, plunge this knife into my chest . . .'

At that moment the Chevalier grabbed a knife which was on the table, pulled off his collar, opened his shirt and, wild-eyed, with his right hand placed the point of the knife on his left clavicle and seemed to be just waiting for my order to dispatch himself in the manner of the ancients.

'That's not what I meant, Chevalier, put the knife down.'

'I will not. I deserve it. Give me the signal.'

'Put that useless knife down, I tell you. I don't put such a high price on your pardon . . .'

However, the point of the knife was still hovering over his left clavicle. I grabbed his hand, snatched the knife away from him and threw it far away from me. Then, moving the bottle close to his glass and filling it full, I spoke to him: 'First of all let us drink and then you will know what terrible terms I am imposing for your forgiveness. So, Agathe is delicious then, voluptuous?'

'Ah, my friend, if only you knew like I do.'

'But wait. Let them bring us a bottle of champagne and then you can tell me the story of one of your nights. Charming traitor, your absolution comes at the end of the story. Go on, begin . . . Didn't you hear me?'

'I heard you.'

'Does the sentence seem too harsh to you?'

'No.'

'You are thinking.'

'I am thinking.'

'What did I ask you?'

'For the story of one of my nights with Agathe.'

'That's right.'

Meanwhile the Chevalier was measuring me from head to toe and saying to himself: 'Same size, more or less the same age, and although there are some differences there won't be any light and in her mind's eye she'll be expecting me and won't suspect a thing . . .'

'But, Chevalier, what are you thinking of? Your glass is still full and you haven't started.'

'I am thinking, my friend, I have thought it out. Everything is worked out. Embrace me. We will have our vengeance, yes, we will have it. It is a dastardly trick on my part, but, if it is unworthy of me, it certainly isn't unworthy of that little hussy. You asked me to tell the story of one of my nights, didn't you?'

'Yes, is that too much to ask?'

'No, but what if, instead of the story, I could get you the night itself?'

'That would be even better.'

(Jacques started whistling.)

At that the Chevalier took two keys out of his pocket, one small, the other large.

'The small one', he said to me, 'is the latch-key to the front door. The large one is for Agathe's dressing-room. There they are. Both of them are at your service. This has been my routine every day for about the past six months. Yours will be the same. The windows of her room are at the front, as you know. I walk up and down the street for as long as I see them lit up. A pot of basil placed outside is the agreed signal, and when I see that I go up to the front door, open it, go in, shut it behind me and go upstairs as quietly as I can. Then I turn down the little corridor which is on the right. The first door on the left of this corridor, as you know, is hers. I unlock this door with the big key and go into the little dressing-room which is on the right, where I find a little night candle, by the light of which I undress at my leisure. Agathe leaves the door to her bedroom ajar and I go through and go to her in her bed. Do you understand that?'

'Very well.'

'Since there are people all around us we keep quiet.'

'And then I imagine that you've got better things to do than talk.'

'If anything goes wrong I can always jump out of her bed and shut myself in the dressing-room. However, that has never happened. Our normal practice is to part around four o'clock in the morning. When pleasure or sleep keeps us later, we get up together. She goes downstairs and I stay in the dressing-room where I get dressed, read, rest and wait until I can safely appear. Then I go downstairs, say hello and embrace her as if I had just arrived.'

'Are you expected tonight?'

'I am expected every night.'

'And will you let me take your place?'

'With all my heart. I don't mind at all if you prefer the night itself to the story, but what I would like is . . .'

'Say it. There is hardly anything that I do not feel courageous enough to do to oblige you.'

'What I would like is for you to stay in her arms till daylight and then I could arrive and surprise you.'

'Oh, no, Chevalier, that would be too wicked.'

'Too wicked? I am not as wicked as you think. Beforehand I would get undressed in the dressing-room.'

'Come along, Chevalier, you have the devil in you. Anyhow it's impossible. If you give me the keys you won't have them any more.'

'Ah! My friend, you are so stupid!'

'Yes, but not all that stupid, it seems to me.'

'And why could we not go in together? You would go to Agathe and I would stay in the dressing-room until you gave a signal we agreed on.'

'My God, that is so absurd, so mad, that it wouldn't take much for me to keep this trick up my sleeve for one of the other nights.'

'Ah! I understand. Your plan is to take your revenge more than once.'

'If you agree.'

'Absolutely.'

JACQUES: Your Chevalier is upsetting all my theories. I thought that . . .

MASTER: You thought?

JACQUES: No, Monsieur, you may continue.

MASTER: We drank and we said a hundred extravagant things about the night which was coming, the following nights and the night when Agathe would find herself between the Chevalier and me. The Chevalier's mood changed back to one of delightful merriment and the subject of our conversation was hardly a sad one. He laid down for me rules of nocturnal conduct which were not all equally easy to follow, but after a long succession of well-spent nights I was sure of upholding the honour of the Chevalier on my first night, no matter how wonderful he maintained he was. And then there were endless details on the talents, perfections and facilities offered by

Agathe. The Chevalier combined the headiness of passion and that of wine with incredible skill. The hour chosen for our escapade or vengeance seemed to come all too slowly. Nevertheless we got up from table. The Chevalier paid. It was the first time he had ever done that. We got into our carriage. We were drunk, and our coachman and valets were even drunker than us.

Reader, what is there to prevent me from throwing the coachman, the horses, the carriage, the masters and their valets into a ditch? If the ditch scares you, what is there to prevent me from bringing them safe and sound into town where I could have their coach collide with another in which I could place some other young drunkards? Offensive words would be spoken, then a quarrel, swords drawn and a full-scale brawl. If you don't like brawls, what is there to stop me from substituting Mlle Agathe and one of her aunts for these young people? But there was none of that. The Chevalier and Jacques' master arrived in Paris. The latter took the Chevalier's clothes. It was midnight and they were underneath Agathe's windows. The light went out. The pot of basil was in its place. They went down to the end of the road and back again for the last time, the Chevalier rehearsing the drill with his friend. They went up to the door. The Chevalier unlocked it and let Jacques' master in, keeping the pass-key to the street door, and giving him the key to the corridor room. Then the Chevalier closed the door and went off. After this little detail, laconically related, Jacques' master carried on talking and said: 'The building was familiar to me. I went upstairs on tiptoe, opened the door into the corridor, shut it, and went into the dressing-room where I found the little night light. I undressed. The bedroom door was ajar. I went through and into the alcove where Agathe was still awake. I opened the curtains around her bed and at the same moment felt two bare arms throw themselves around me and pull me closer. I let myself go, got into bed, and was overwhelmed with caresses which I returned. There I was, the happiest man who ever lived, and I still was when . . .'

Here Jacques' master noticed that Jacques was sleeping or pretending to sleep and said: 'You are sleeping, you are sleeping, you scoundrel, at the most interesting part of my story . . .'

This was just what Jacques had been anticipating.

'Will you wake up?'

'I don't think so.'

'Why not?'

'Because if I wake up my sore throat might wake up as well and I think it would be better for both of us if we rested.'

And Jacques let his head hang forward.

'You'll break your neck riding like that.'

'Of course, if that is what is written up above. Were you not in Mlle Agathe's arms?'

'Yes.'

'Were you not happy there?'

'Very happy.'

'Well, stay there then.'

'Long may I stay there, you mean to say.'

'At least until I hear the story of Desglands' spot.'

MASTER: You are avenging yourself, you traitor.

JACQUES: What if I am, Master? After you have interrupted the story of my loves with a thousand questions and as many whims, without the least murmur on my part, can I not beg you to interrupt your own to tell me the story of Desglands' spot, that good man to whom I owe so much, who took me out of the surgeon's house at the very moment when, because of shortage of money, I knew not what was to become of me, and at whose house I met Denise, Denise without whom I would not have spoken one word to you this whole journey? My Master, my dear Master, the story of Desglands' spot. You may be as brief as you like and in the meantime the drowsiness which grips me and of which I am not the master will disappear and you may count on all my attention.

MASTER (shrugging his shoulders): In the neighbourhood of Desglands, there was a charming widow who had several qualities in common with a well-known courtesan of the last century. She was discreet by reason but libertine by temperament and regretted the next day the follies of the day before. She spent her whole life going from pleasure to remorse and remorse to pleasure, without the habit of pleasure lessening her remorse and without the habit of remorse lessening her taste for pleasure. I knew her towards the end of her life, when she used to say that at long last she had escaped from two great enemies. Her husband, who was lenient about the only fault which he could reproach her for, complained about her while she was alive and missed her for a long time after her death. He claimed that it would have been as ridiculous for him to prevent his wife from taking lovers as to prevent her from drinking. He forgave her the multitude of her conquests because of the discrimination she showed in her choice. She never allowed a stupid or wicked man to pay her court; her favours were always the reward of talent or probity. To say of a man that he was or had been her lover was to certify that he was a man of worth. Because she was aware of her inconstant nature she never pledged fidelity. She used to say: 'I have only made one false oath in my life, and that was the first.'

After the decline of those feelings she inspired or felt, friendship remained. Never was there a more striking example of the difference between probity and morality. One could not say that she had morals, but at the same time one had to admit that it was difficult to find a more honest person. Her parish priest saw her but rarely at the foot of his altar but he found her purse open at all times to help the poor. She used to say jokingly of religion and the law that they were a pair of crutches which were not to be taken away from those who had weak limbs. Women who feared their husbands being in her company desired their children to be so.

After Jacques had muttered from between clenched teeth: 'You will pay for that damned portrait', he added: 'Were you in love with this woman?'

MASTER: I would certainly have become so had not Desglands got there first. Desglands fell in love with her.

JACQUES: Monsieur, could it be that the story of his spot and that of his loves are so closely linked the one to the other that one cannot separate them?

MASTER: They can be separated. The spot is an incident. The story is the account of everything which happened while they were in love.

JACQUES: And did a lot of things happen?

MASTER: A lot.

JACQUES: In that case, if you are going to give each one the same length as you have given to the portrait of the heroine we won't get to the end of this much before Whitsun, and that will be the end of the story of your loves and mine.

MASTER: Well, Jacques, why did you sidetrack me then? . . .
Did you ever notice a little child at Desglands' château?

JACQUES: A wicked, stubborn insolent little valetudinarian? Yes, I saw him.

MASTER: He is the natural son of Desglands and the beautiful widow.

JACQUES: That child will cause him a lot of sorrow. He was an only child, which is good enough reason to be a scoundrel. He knew he was going to be rich, which is another good reason to be just a scoundrel.

MASTER: And since he is a valetudinarian, no one can teach him anything or dares to annoy him or contradict him on anything, which is a third good reason to be just a scoundrel.

JACQUES: One night the little lunatic started uttering the most awful cries. The whole house was in uproar. Everybody ran to him. He wanted his father to get up.
'Your father's sleeping.'
'It doesn't matter. He must get up. I want it. I want it.'
'He is ill.'
'It doesn't matter. I want him to get up. I want it. I want it.'
They woke up Desglands. He threw his dressing-gown over his shoulders and arrived.
'Well, my little man, here I am. What do you want?'
'I want you to make them come.'
'Who?'
'Everyone in the château.'
He made them come, masters, valets, guests, all the other habitués of the place, Jeanne, Denise, me with my bad knee, everybody except for one old crippled concierge who had been given a place of retirement in a cottage about a half a mile from the château. He wanted her to be fetched.
'But, my child, it is midnight.'
'I want it, I want it.'
'You know that she lives a long way away.'
'I want it. I want it.'
'And that she's very old and hardly able to walk.'
'I want it. I want it.'

JACQUES: The poor concierge had to come. She was carried, because she would as soon have eaten the road there as walked it. When we were all assembled he wanted to be got up and dressed. Then when he was up and dressed he wanted us all to go into the great drawing-room and he wanted to be put in the middle of us in his papa's great armchair. When that was done he wanted us all to take each other by the hand, which we did, and then we had to dance around him, and so we all started to dance around him. But it is the rest which is incredible . . .

MASTER: I hope you'll spare me the rest.

JACQUES: No, Monsieur, you will listen to the rest. If he thinks he can paint me a portrait four yards long with impunity . . .

MASTER: Jacques, I spoil you.

JACQUES: Too bad for you.

MASTER: You are cross about that long boring portrait of the widow, but I think you have paid me back sufficiently with the long boring story of the child's whims.

JACQUES: If that's your opinion carry on with his father's story, but no more portraits, Master. I hate portraits to death.

MASTER: Why do you hate portraits?

JACQUES: Because they are so unlifelike that if, by chance, one happens to meet the subjects, one does not recognize them. Tell me facts, repeat words to me faithfully, and then I will know what kind of man I am dealing with. One word, one gesture, has sometimes taught me more than the gossip of an entire town.

MASTER: One day Desglands . . .

JACQUES: When you are away I sometimes go into your library and take down a book, which is normally a history book.

MASTER: One day Desglands . . .

JACQUES: I skip all the portraits.

MASTER: One day Desglands . . .

JACQUES: Forgive me, Master. The mechanism was wound up and had to carry on until it had run down.

MASTER: Has it?

JACQUES: It has.

MASTER: One day Desglands invited the beautiful widow to dinner, together with a few neighbouring gentlemen. The reign of Desglands was in its decline and among his guests there was one towards whom the inconstant widow was beginning to be attracted. At table, Desglands and his rival were sitting next to each other opposite the beautiful widow. Desglands used all his wit to enliven the conversation. He addressed the most gallant remarks to the widow but she was distracted, paid no attention to him and continued to stare at his rival. Desglands was holding a fresh egg in his hand when he was overcome by a convulsive movement occasioned by jealousy. He clenched his fist and the next moment there was the egg squeezed from its shell and plastered all over the face of his neighbour, who made a movement with his hand. Desglands grabbed his wrist, stopped him and said in his ear: 'Monsieur, I consider the blow to have been struck.'

Then there was a profound silence. The beautiful widow felt ill. The meal was sad and brief. On leaving table the widow called Desglands and his rival into a separate room. She did everything which a woman could decently do to reconcile them. She begged, she cried, she fainted, quite genuinely. She clasped Desglands' hands, she turned to his rival with tears in her eyes.

To him she said: 'You love me.'

To the other she said: 'And you have loved me.'

To both of them: 'And you want to ruin me, to make me the scandal of the whole province, hated and despised by all! Whichever of the two of you takes the life of his enemy, I will never see him again. He can be neither my friend nor my lover and I vow that I will hate him until my dying day.'

Then she swooned again and as she swooned she said: 'Cruel men. Draw your swords and plunge them into my breast. If I see your arms around each other when I die, I will die without regret.'

Desglands and his rival stood motionless or helped her and a few tears fell from their eyes. The time finally came to part and the beautiful widow was taken back to her house more dead than alive.

JACQUES: Well, Monsieur! Why did I need the portrait you painted of this woman? Don't I now know everything mentioned in the portrait?

MASTER: The next day Desglands went to visit his fickle charmer and found his rival there. Mistress and rival were both surprised when they saw Desglands' entire right cheek covered with a large circle of black taffeta.

'What's that?' asked the widow.

DESGLANDS: Nothing.

HIS RIVAL: A gumboil.

DESGLANDS: It will go away.

After a moment's conversation, Desglands went, and on his way out he gave his rival a sign which was clearly understood. The latter followed him downstairs and they each went a different way down the street. They met behind the gardens of the beautiful widow where they fought. Desglands' rival was left lying on the field seriously, but not mortally, wounded. While he was being carried back to his house, Desglands returned to the widow's house. He sat down and they spoke again of the incident the day before. She asked him the significance of the enormous and ridiculous patch covering his cheek. He got up and looked at himself in the mirror. Indeed, he said to her, he did find it a little too big. Then he took a pair of scissors from the lady and took off the spot, made it a stitch or two smaller all round, put it back on again, and said to the widow: 'How do you find me now?'

'A stitch or two less ridiculous than before.'

'Well, that's something anyway.'

Desglands' rival got better. There was a second duel, victory again falling to Desglands; this happened again five or six times in a row. After every combat, Desglands reduced the size of his taffeta spot a little by trimming the edge down and put the rest back on his cheek.

JACQUES: And how did this little adventure end? When they carried me into Desglands' château my recollection is that he no longer had his black spot.

MASTER: No. The end of this adventure was the end of the beautiful widow. The long sorrow which it caused her completed the ruin of her weak and delicate health.

JACQUES: And Desglands?

MASTER: One day while we were out walking together he received a note which he opened and said: 'He was a very brave man, but I am unable to feel upset at his death . . .', and at that moment he tore from his cheek the remainder of the black circle which his frequent trimmings had almost reduced to the size of an ordinary patch. That is the story of Desglands. Is Jacques happy now? Might I now hope that he will either listen to the story of my loves or carry on again with the story of his own?

JACQUES: Neither.

MASTER: And why not?

JACQUES: Because it is hot, I am tired, this place is charming, and we will be shaded under these trees, where we will be able to rest in the cool air at the side of the stream.

MASTER: I agree, but what about your cold?

JACQUES: It is a hot cold and doctors do say that things are cured by their opposites.

MASTER: Which is true in matters moral as well as physical. I have noticed something quite peculiar. It is that there are hardly any moral maxims which could not be turned into medical aphorisms, and reciprocally hardly any medical aphorisms which could not be turned into moral maxims.

JACQUES: That has to be so.

They got down from their horses and stretched out on the grass. Jacques said to his master: 'Are you watching? Or are you sleeping? If you watch I will sleep. If you sleep I will watch.'
His master said to him: 'Sleep, sleep.'
'Can I count on it that you will watch, because this time we could have two horses stolen?'
His master took out his watch and snuff-box. Jacques prepared himself to sleep but every other second he kept waking up with a start, beating his two hands against each other in the air.
His master asked him: 'What the devil are you doing?'

JACQUES: I'm trying to get the flies and the midges. I wish somebody would tell me what's the use of these irritating creatures.

MASTER: Just because you don't know you think they're useless, do you? Nature made nothing useless or superfluous.

JACQUES: I can believe that because if something is it has to be.

MASTER: When you have too much blood or bad blood what do you do? You call a surgeon who relieves you of two or three basins of it. Well then! These gnats which you are complaining about are a cloud of little winged surgeons who come with their little lancets to sting you and draw off your blood drop by drop.

JACQUES: Yes, but at random, without knowing whether I've got too much or too little. Bring some starving wretch here and see if your little winged surgeons don't sting him. They are concerned with themselves. Everything in nature is concerned with itself, and with itself only. If it is harmful to others, then so what, as long as the thing is all right itself . . .

Next he beat the air again with both hands and said: 'The devil with your little winged surgeons!'

MASTER: Do you know the fable of Garo?[72]

JACQUES: Yes.

MASTER: What do you think of it?

JACQUES: Bad.

MASTER: That's easily said.

JACQUES: And easily proved. What if oak trees had pumpkins instead of acorns? Would that fool Garo have gone to sleep under an oak tree then? And if he hadn't fallen asleep under an oak tree, what difference would it have made to the safety of his nose if pumpkins or acorns fell from it? Give that to your children to read.

MASTER: A philosopher with the same name as you will not have that.

JACQUES: Well, everyone has his own opinion and Jean-Jacques is not Jacques.[73]

MASTER: Well, too bad for Jacques.

JACQUES: Who can tell unless he has read the last word on the last line on the page which he occupies on the great scroll?

MASTER: What are you thinking?

JACQUES: I am thinking that, although you were speaking to me and I was answering you, you were speaking without wanting to and I was answering without wanting to.

MASTER: And?

JACQUES: And? That we are nothing but two living and thinking machines.

MASTER: Well, at this moment what do you want?

JACQUES: My God, that doesn't make any difference. That only brings one more function of the two machines into play.

MASTER: What function is that?

JACQUES: May the devil take me if I can conceive of any function operating without a cause. My Captain used to say: 'Suppose a cause and an effect will follow. From a weak cause, a weak effect. From a momentary cause a momentary effect, from an intermittent cause an intermittent effect, from an impeded cause a reduced effect, from a cause that ceases a nil effect.'

MASTER: But it seems to me that I can sense within me that I am free in the same way that I sense that I think.

JACQUES: My Captain used to say: 'That may be true at this moment when you do not want to do anything, but what if you wanted to throw yourself off your horse?'

MASTER: I'd throw myself off.

JACQUES: Happily, without repugnance, without effort, as when you dismount at the door of an inn?

MASTER: Not exactly, but what does it matter so long as I throw myself off, and prove that I am free?

JACQUES: My Captain used to say: 'What! Can you not see that were it not for my contradiction you would never have taken it into your head to break your neck. It is therefore me who takes you by the foot and throws you out of your saddle. If your fall proves something it is not that you are free but that you are mad . . .' My Captain also used to say that the enjoyment of freedom which could be exercised without any motivation would be the real hallmark of a maniac.

MASTER: That is all too much for me. But in spite of your Captain and in spite of you, I believe that I want when I want.

JACQUES: But if you are now and have always been the master of your will, why don't you want to make love to some old bag at this moment, and why did you not stop loving Agathe all the times that you wanted to? My Master, one spends three quarters of one's life wanting without doing.

MASTER: That is true.

JACQUES: And doing without wanting to.

MASTER: Will you demonstrate that to me?

JACQUES: If you consent to it.

MASTER: I consent.

JACQUES: Then it will be done, but let us speak of other things . . .

After this nonsense and a few other words of the same importance they were silent and Jacques pushed up his enormous hat, which was an umbrella in bad weather, a parasol in hot weather and a hat in all weathers, the shadowy sanctuary under which one of the best brains which has ever existed would consult destiny on great occasions . . . When the edges of his hat were raised up his face was more or less in the middle of his body. When they were turned down he could hardly see ten feet in front of him, which had given him the habit of walking with his nose in the air and it is because of this that one could say of his hat: *Os illi sublime didit, caelumque tueri/ Jussit, et erectos ad sidere tollere vultus . . .*[74]

And so, as Jacques pushed up his enormous hat, looking far and wide around him, he saw a farmer who was belabouring one of the two horses harnessed to his plough, apparently to no effect. This horse, which was young and vigorous, had lain down in the furrow, and no matter how much the farmer shook his bridle, begged him, caressed him, threatened him, swore at him and beat him, the animal stayed stock still and stubbornly refused to get up.

After Jacques had mused for a while on this scene he turned to his master, whose attention had similarly been attracted.

JACQUES: Do you know what is happening over there, Monsieur?

MASTER: What would you wish to be happening over there other than what I already see?

JACQUES: Can you really not guess?

MASTER: No, but what's your guess?

JACQUES: My guess is, that there stupid proud useless animal is a town-dweller and because he is proud of his first condition as a saddle horse he despises the plough, and, in a word, it is your horse and also the symbol of Jacques here and so many other faint-hearted wretches like him who have left the countryside to go and bear livery in the capital and who would prefer to beg their bread in the streets or die of hunger than to return to agriculture, the most useful and honourable of occupations.

The master started to laugh, and Jacques, speaking to the farmer, who could not hear him, said: 'Poor devil. Beat him, beat him as much as you want. He's set in his ways now and you'll wear out more than one cracker on your whip before you inspire a little true dignity and some taste for work in that good-for-nothing . . .'

His master carried on laughing and Jacques, half out of impatience, and half out of pity, got up and walked over toward the farmer. He hadn't gone two hundred paces when he turned round to his master and started shouting: 'Monsieur, come here, come here. It's your horse, it's your horse!'

And it was indeed. Hardly had the animal recognized Jacques and his master when he got up of his own accord, shook his mane, whinneyed, reared and tenderly nuzzled his companion's muzzle.

Meanwhile Jacques, who was indignant, said from between clenched teeth: 'Scoundrel, wastrel, good for nothing. Is there even one good reason why I shouldn't give you twenty good kicks?'

His master, by way of contrast, was kissing him and had put one hand on his side and was softly patting his rump with the other, almost crying with joy, and he was saying: 'My horse, my poor horse, so I've found you once again!'

The farmer understood nothing of all this: 'I can see, Messieurs, that this horse used to belong to you but I do not own him any the less legitimately for that. I bought him at the last fair. If you want to take him for two thirds of what he cost me, you'll be doing me a great service because I can do nothing with him. When he has to be taken out of the stable he's the devil incarnate. When he has to be harnessed he's even worse, and when we arrive in the fields he lies down. He'd rather be beaten to death than pull anything or put up with a sack on his back. Messieurs, would you be so charitable as to relieve me of this accursed animal. He's a fine animal, but he's good for nothing other than prancing under a gentleman, and that's no use to me . . .'

They suggested a swap with whichever of the two others suited him best. He agreed and our two travellers came slowly back towards the place where they had rested, from where they watched with great satisfaction as the horse they had given the farmer acquiesced without repugnance in his new condition.

JACQUES: Well, Monsieur?

MASTER: Well! Nothing can be surer than that you're inspired. But is it by God or by the devil? I don't know which. Jacques, my dear friend, I am afraid you've got the devil in you.

JACQUES: And why the devil?

MASTER: Because you work wonders and your doctrine is extremely suspect.

JACQUES: And what connection is there between the doctrine one possesses and the wonders one works?

MASTER: I can see that you have not read Dom La Taste.[75]

JACQUES: And this Dom La Taste whom I haven't read, what does he say?

MASTER: He says that God and the devil both work miracles.

JACQUES: And how does one distinguish God's miracles from the miracles of the devil?

MASTER: By doctrine. If the doctrine is good the miracles are God's, if it is bad they are the devil's.

Here Jacques started whistling, then he added: 'And who will teach me, poor ignorant fellow that I am, if the doctrine of any particular miracle-worker is good or bad? Come along, Monsieur, let us mount up again. What does it matter to you whether your horse has been recovered by the work of God or Beelzebub? Will he go any the less well for it?'

MASTER: No. If, however, Jacques, you were possessed . . .

JACQUES: What cure would there be for that?

MASTER: The cure! That would be, until you were exorcized, to put you on holy water for your only drink.

JACQUES: Me, Monsieur, on water! Jacques on holy water! I would rather have a thousand legions of devils stay in my body than drink one drop, holy or unholy. Have you never noticed that I'm hydrophobic? . . .

– Ah, hydrophobic? Did Jacques say 'hydrophobic'?

No, Reader, no, I confess that the word isn't his own, but with such a severe critical attitude, I defy you to read a scene of any comedy or tragedy, a single dialogue, no matter how well it is written, without surprising the words of its author in the mouth of his character.

What Jacques said was: 'Master, have you never noticed that at the sight of water I turn rabid?'

Well, in speaking differently from him I have been less truthful but more brief. They got back on their horses and Jacques said to his master: 'You had got up to the point in the story of your loves where after you had been made happy twice you were getting ready perhaps to be made happy for a third time.'

MASTER: And all of a sudden the door from the corridor opened. The bedroom was invaded by a tumult of people. I saw lights and heard the voices of men and women all speaking at the same time. The curtains were pulled back violently and I saw the mother, the father, the aunts, the cousins and a Commissioner of Police, who said to them in a serious voice: 'Messieurs, mesdames, no noise. He has been caught red-handed. Monsieur is a gallant man. There is only one way to make good the wrong, and Monsieur will surely prefer to do it voluntarily than be forced to do it by the law . . .'

At every word he was interrupted by the father and the mother, who were heaping reproaches on me, by the aunts and the female cousins, who were berating in the most unrestrained terms Agathe, who had buried her head in the covers. I was stupefied and I didn't know what to say. The Commissioner turned to me and said in an ironic tone of voice: 'Monsieur, I can see that you are comfortable there but please be so good as to get up and get dressed . . .'

Which, of course, I did, with my own clothes, which had been substituted for those of the Chevalier. A table was pulled out and the Commissioner started to draw up the charge. Meanwhile it was taking four people to keep the mother held down and stop her from beating her daughter, and the father was saying to her: 'Gently, wife, gently, when you've finished beating your daughter it won't change things one bit. Everything will turn out all right.'

The other people were spread around the room on chairs in varying attitudes of sorrow, indignation and anger. The father was scolding his wife at intervals, saying: 'That's what happens when one doesn't watch over one's daughter's conduct.'

The mother replied: 'With such a good and honest appearance, who would have thought it of Monsieur? . . .'

The others were silent. When the police report had been prepared it was read out to me and since it contained nothing but the truth I signed it and went downstairs with the Commissioner, who asked me most politely to get into the carriage which was at the door, and from there I was led away in quite a large convoy straight to Fort-l'Evêque.[76]

JACQUES: Fort-l'Evêque! To prison!

MASTER: To prison. And then what an abominable court case. It was nothing less than a question of marrying Mlle Agathe. Her parents didn't want to listen to any arrangement. At daybreak the Chevalier appeared in my retreat. He knew everything. Agathe was devastated. Her parents were enraged. He had been subjected to the most cruel reproaches because of the perfidious acquaintance he had introduced to them. It was he who was the primary cause of their unhappiness and their daughter's dishonour. The poor parents were a pitiful sight. He had asked to speak to Agathe alone, which he eventually – though not without difficulty – succeeded in doing. Agathe had almost torn his eyes out. She had called him the most odious names. He had been prepared for it and he waited for her fury to subside, after which he tried to bring her to a more reasonable frame of mind.

'But this girl said one thing,' added the Chevalier, 'to which I do not know the answer: "My father and my mother surprised me with your friend. Should I tell them that when I was sleeping with him I thought I was sleeping with you?"'

He replied: 'In all honesty, do you think that my friend could marry you?'

'No,' she said, 'it is you, you unworthy wretch, who ought to be condemned to do so.'

'But,' I said to the Chevalier, 'it only needs you to get me out of the mess I am in.'

'And how could I do that?'

'How? By explaining things as they are.'

'I have threatened Agathe I would do so, but I certainly will not. It is by no means certain whether it would be of any use to us, but it is absolutely certain that we'd be completely dishonoured. And anyway it's your fault.'

'My fault?'

'Yes, your fault. If you had approved the trick I suggested to you, Agathe would have been caught between two men and the whole thing would have finished in derision. But things didn't work out like that and now it's a question of getting out of this mess.'

'But, Chevalier, could you explain to me one small thing. That is how my clothes were returned to me and yours put in the dressing-room. My God, I've thought about it a lot but it is a mystery which totally baffles me. It made me suspect Agathe a little because it occurred to me that she might have discovered the ruse and there was some kind of connivance between her and her parents.'

'Perhaps you were seen going up. What is certain is that you were hardly undressed when my clothes were sent to me and yours asked for.'

'It will all come clear in time . . .'

While we were busy, the Chevalier and I, grieving, consoling ourselves, accusing ourselves, insulting ourselves and begging each other's pardon, the Commissioner came in. The Chevalier turned pale and left abruptly. This Commissioner was a good man, as some of them are, and reading over the police report at his home remembered that in earlier times he had studied with a young man who had my name. It occurred to him that I might perhaps be a relation or even the son of this old college friend, as was in fact the case. His first question was to ask me who was the man who had run away as he came in.

'He didn't run away,' I told him, 'he went out. He's my close friend, the Chevalier de Saint-Ouin.'

'Your friend! You have a nice friend there! Do you know, Monsieur, that he is the man who came to warn me? He was accompanied by the father and another relation.'

'Him!'

'Himself!'

'Are you absolutely sure of this?'

'Absolutely sure. What did you call him again?'

'The Chevalier de Saint-Ouin.'

'Ah! The Chevalier de Saint-Ouin, that's it. And do you know what your friend, your intimate friend the Chevalier de Saint-Ouin, is? A crook. A man on record for a hundred dirty tricks. The police only leave that type of man free to walk the streets because he can sometimes be useful to them. They are rogues and informers on rogues and are apparently more useful in the harm they forestall or reveal than dangerous by that which they do . . .'

I told the Commissioner my sad story exactly as it had happened. He didn't see it in any the more favourable light because nothing that could exculpate me could be adduced or proved in any court of law. However, he undertook to call the girl's father and mother and grill her, to inform the magistrate and to neglect nothing which might help to justify me. But he warned me all the same that if these people were well counselled the authorities could do little.

'What! Monsieur le Commissaire, do you mean I will be forced to marry her?'

'Marry her! That would be very harsh, and that wasn't what I was concerned about, but there will be damages, in this case, considerable . . .'

But Jacques, I think there is something you want to say to me . . .

JACQUES: Yes. I wanted to say to you that you were actually more unfortunate than me who paid for it but didn't get my night's worth. All the same I think I'll have heard it all if she turns out to be pregnant.

MASTER: Don't drop the idea yet. The Commissioner told me that a short while after my arrest she had come to see him and made a declaration of pregnancy.

JACQUES: And there you were, the father of a child.

MASTER: Whom I haven't done badly by.

JACQUES: And whom you didn't spawn.

MASTER: Neither the protection of the magistrate nor all the steps taken by the Commissioner could prevent this affair from following the course of justice. But, as the girl and her parents were of bad repute I didn't end up marrying in prison. I was sentenced to a large fine to pay the costs of the childbirth and also to provide for the maintenance and education of a child which issued from the actions and deeds of my friend the Chevalier de Saint-Ouin, of whom he was the portrait in miniature. It was a bonny boy to whom Mlle Agathe gave birth without any problems between the seventh and eighth month and who was given over to a good nurse whom I have paid every month until this day.

JACQUES: And what age is Monsieur your son now?

MASTER: He will soon be ten. I have left him in the country all this time and the schoolmaster there has taught him to read and write and count. It is not far from where we are going and I am taking the opportunity to pay these people what is owing to them and to take him away and put him to a trade.

Jacques and his master spent yet another night on the road. They were too close to the end of their journey for Jacques to take up the story of his loves again, and anyway his sore throat was far from better. The following day they arrived.
– Where?
On my word of honour, I don't know.
– And what did they have to do at wherever they were going to?
Whatever you like. Do you think that Jacques' master told everyone his business? Whatever it was, they did not need to stay for more than two weeks.
– Did it end well or did it end badly?
That is what I still don't know. Jacques' sore throat cleared up because of

two cures which he had an aversion to: diet and rest.

One morning the master said to his valet: 'Jacques, saddle up and bridle the horses and fill up your gourd because we have to go you know where.'

It was no sooner said than done and there they were on their way towards the place where for the last ten years the Chevalier de Saint-Ouin's son had been looked after at the expense of Jacques' master. Some distance from the resting-place they had just left the master addressed the following words to Jacques: 'Jacques, what do you think of the story of my loves?'

JACQUES: There are strange things written up above. There's one more child made, God knows how. Who knows what role the little bastard will play in the world? Who knows if he wasn't born for the happiness or the destruction of an empire?

MASTER: I say no. I will make a good turner or a good clock-maker out of him. He will get married and have children who will turn the chair legs of this world in perpetuity.

JACQUES: Yes, if that is what is written up above. But why shouldn't another Cromwell come out of a turner's shop? Didn't the man who had his King's head cut off come out of a brewer's shop? And aren't people saying today . . .

MASTER: Let's leave all that. You are better now. You know the story of my loves. In all conscience you cannot get out of carrying on the story of your own.

JACQUES: Everything is against it. Firstly the short distance we've got left to travel. Secondly I've forgotten where I was. Thirdly I have the devil of a premonition . . . that this story will not be finished, that this story must bring us bad luck, and that I will have no sooner started when it will be interrupted by a favourable or an unfavourable event.

MASTER: If it is favourable, so much the better.

JACQUES: I agree, but something tells me that it will be unfavourable.

MASTER: Unfavourable! So be it, but whether you speak or not, will it happen any the less?

JACQUES: Who knows?

MASTER: You were born two or three centuries too late.

JACQUES: No, Monsieur, I was born at the right time like everyone else.

MASTER: You would have been a great augur.

JACQUES: I do not know precisely what an augur is, nor do I particularly want to.

MASTER: It is one of the important chapters in your *Treatise of Divination*.

JACQUES: That's true but it is so long since I wrote it that I can't remember a word. Monsieur, listen. This is what knows more than any augurs, prophetic geese or sacred hens of the Republic of Rome. It is the gourd. Let us consult the gourd.

Jacques took his gourd and consulted it at length. His master took out his watch and snuff-box, saw what time it was, took his pinch of snuff, and then Jacques spoke.

JACQUES: It seems to me at present that I see Destiny less darkly. Tell me where I was up to.

MASTER: The château of Desglands. Your knee was a little better and Denise had been ordered by her mother to look after you.

JACQUES: Denise was obedient. The wound in my knee had almost closed up. I had even been able to dance on the night of the child. However, every now and then I would suffer the most unheard-of pain. It occurred to the surgeon in the château, who knew a little more than his colleague, that these attacks, which returned so suddenly, could only have as their cause the fact that a foreign body had stayed in the flesh after the extraction of the bullet. Consequently he came into my bedroom early one morning, brought a table over to my bed and when my bed curtains were opened I saw that this table was covered in surgical instruments . . . Denise was sitting at the head of my bed, crying hot tears. Her mother was standing up with her arms crossed and looking sad. The surgeon took off his jacket, rolled up his sleeves and took a lancet in his right hand.

MASTER: You are frightening me.

JACQUES: I was frightened too.
'Friend,' the surgeon asked me, 'are you tired of being in pain?'
'Very tired.'
'Do you want it to finish and keep your leg?'

'Of course.'

'Then put it outside the bed so that I can work on it more easily . . .'

I held out my leg. The surgeon put the handle of his lancet between his teeth, took my leg under his left arm, held it firmly in place, took his lancet again and put the point into the opening of my wound, making a wide deep incision. I didn't turn a hair, but Jeanne turned her head away and Denise screamed and felt ill . . .

At this point Jacques stopped his story and took another pull at his gourd. His halts became more frequent as the distances became shorter, or, as the geometricians say, they were in inverse proportion to the distances. He was so precise in his measurements that although the gourd was full on leaving it was always exactly empty on arrival. The Department of Bridges and Highways would have made an excellent odometer of him, and each pull he took from the gourd usually had its own sufficient reason. This time it was to bring Denise back from her faint and to recover from the pain of the incision the surgeon had made in his knee. When Denise had recovered and he was comforted he continued.

JACQUES: This enormous incision revealed the bottom of the wound out of which the surgeon pulled with his tweezers a very small piece of cloth from my breeches which had stayed there and whose presence was causing my pain and preventing the complete healing of the wound. After this operation my health got better and better, thanks to the attentions of Denise. There were no more attacks and no more fever. My appetite returned and I slept and grew stronger. Denise bandaged me with precision and infinite gentleness. You should have seen the cautiousness and dexterity of hand with which she used to undo my bandage, the fear she had of causing me pain, the way she used to bathe my wound. I used to be sitting on the edge of my bed and she would have one knee on the floor. My leg would rest on her thigh which I sometimes used to press a little. I used to have one hand on her shoulder and watch her do all this with a tenderness which I believe she shared. When my bandaging was finished I would take her two hands and thank her. I did not know what to say to her. I did not know how I could express my thanks. She would stand there, her eyes lowered, listening to me without saying anything. Not a single pedlar passed through the château from whom I did not buy something for her. Once a neckerchief, another time a few lengths of calico or muslin, a golden cross, cotton stockings, a ring, a garnet necklace. When my little present had been bought my problem was to offer it and hers to accept it. At first I would show her the thing and if she liked it I would say: 'Denise, I bought it for you.' If she accepted it, my hand used to tremble when I gave it to her, as did hers when she took it. One day, no longer knowing what I could give her, I bought her some garters. They were made of silk and brightly figured in red, white and blue. That morning before she arrived I put them on the back of the chair which was next to my bed. As soon as Denise saw them she said: 'Oh, what pretty garters.'

'They are for my lover,' I replied.

'So you have a lover, Monsieur Jacques?'

'Of course, haven't I already told you?'

'No. She's very attractive, I suppose?'

'Very attractive.'

'And do you love her a lot?'

'With all my heart.'

'And does she love you too?'

'I have no idea. These garters are for her and she has promised to grant me a favour which will drive me mad, I think, if she grants it to me.'

'What favour is that?'

'It is that I will put on one of these two garters with my own hands . . .'

Denise blushed, misunderstood what I had said and thought the garters were for someone else. She became sad and made blunder after blunder, looked for everything she needed for my bandage without finding it when she had it under her nose the whole time, knocked over the wine which she had warmed, came close to my bed to bandage me, took hold of my leg with a trembling hand, undid my bandage all wrong and then, when she had to bathe my wound, she had forgotten what she needed for the task and had to go and look for it. She bandaged me, and as she was bandaging me I saw she was crying.

'Denise, I do believe that you are crying. What's wrong with you?'

'Nothing.'

'Has somebody hurt you?'

'Yes.'

'What nasty man has hurt you?'

'You.'

'Me?'

'Yes.'

'How did that happen? . . .'

Instead of answering me she looked at the garters.

'Oh,' I said to her, 'is that what made you cry?'

'Yes.'

'Denise, don't cry any more. It is for you that I bought them.'

'Monsieur Jacques, is that true?'

'Very true. So true that here they are.'

As I said this I gave her both of them but I held one back and as I did so a smile appeared under her tears. I took her by the arm and drew her closer to my bed, took one of her feet which I put on the edge, and raised up her skirts as far as the knee where she held them down with both hands. I kissed her leg and attached the garter which I had held on to, and hardly had I put it on when Jeanne, her mother, came in.

MASTER: That was an annoying visit.

JACQUES: Perhaps yes, perhaps no. Instead of noticing our emotion she only saw the garter which her daughter had in her hands.

'That's a pretty garter,' she said, 'but where's the other one?'

'On my leg. He told me that he'd bought them for his lover and I imagined that they were for me. Now that I've put one on I have to keep the other one, isn't that right, Mother?'

'Ah! Monsieur Jacques, Denise is right. One garter doesn't go without the other, and you wouldn't want to take back the one she is wearing.'

'Why not?'

'Because Denise wouldn't wish it, nor me either.'

'Well, let's settle it. I'll put the other one on in your presence.'

'No, no, you can't do that.'

'Then let her give them both back to me.'

'She can't do that either.'

But now Jacques and his master are at the edge of the village where they were going to see the Chevalier de Saint-Ouin's child and his foster-parents. Jacques fell silent.

MASTER: Let us sit down and pause a while here.

JACQUES: Why?

MASTER: Because, by all appearances, you are nearing the end of the story of your loves.

JACQUES: Not quite.

MASTER: When you get as far as the knee there's not much farther to go.

JACQUES: Master, Denise's thigh was longer than many another girl's.

MASTER: Well, let's get down anyway.

They dismounted. Jacques got down first and attended rapidly to the boot of his master, who had no sooner put his foot on the stirrup when the strap became undone and our horseman was thrown backwards and would have landed heavily on the ground if his valet hadn't caught him in his arms.

MASTER: Well, Jacques! So that is how you look after me! It wouldn't have taken much for me to have broken a rib or an arm or cracked open my head or even been killed.

JACQUES: What a terrible misfortune that would have been.

MASTER: What did you say, you scoundrel? Just you wait, I'll teach you to speak . . .

And after he had wound the lash of his whip twice around his wrist, the master set off after Jacques, who ran around the horse bursting with laughter while his master was swearing, cursing, foaming with rage, also running round the horse, vomiting forth a torrent of invective against Jacques. This went on until the two of them, both worn out and dripping with sweat, stopped each on the opposite side of the horse from the other. Jacques was panting and still laughing. His master was also panting and giving him furious looks. They waited to get their breath back, when Jacques said to his master: 'My Master, will you not admit it now?'

MASTER: Well, what do you want me to admit, you dog, you wretch, you scoundrel, other than the fact that you are the most wicked of all valets and that I am the most unfortunate of all masters?

JACQUES: Has it not been clearly demonstrated that most of the time we act without willing to? Come now, put your hand on your conscience and tell me, did you will any of the things you have said and done for the last half hour? Were you not my marionette, and would you not have carried on being my puppet for a month if I'd wanted you to?

MASTER: What, it was a game?

JACQUES: A game.

MASTER: And you were waiting for the straps to come undone?

JACQUES: I had prepared them.

MASTER: And your impertinent reply was premeditated?

JACQUES: Premeditated.

MASTER: And that was the string you'd tied to my head to throw me around as you wished?

JACQUES: Just so.

MASTER: You are a dangerous ruffian.

JACQUES: Say, rather, that I am a subtle reasoner, thanks to my Captain, who once played the same trick on me.

MASTER: But what if I had hurt myself?

JACQUES: It was written up above and in my precautions that such a thing would not happen..

MASTER: Come, let us sit down. We must rest.

As they sat down Jacques cried: 'A plague be on the fool.'

MASTER: You are speaking of yourself, I presume?

JACQUES: Yes, for not leaving an extra pull in the gourd.

MASTER: There's no point in regretting it. I would have drunk it because I'm dying of thirst.

JACQUES: A plague again on the fool for not having left two.

The master begged him to take their minds off their tiredness and their thirst by continuing his story. Jacques refused and his master sulked. Jacques let him sulk, but at length, after he had protested against the misfortunes which would happen to him, Jacques carried on again with the story of his loves.

JACQUES: One feast day the lord of the château was away hunting.

After these words he stopped dead and said: 'I cannot do it. It is impossible for me to continue. It seems to me that yet again the hand of Destiny is on my throat and I can feel it tighten. For God's sake, Monsieur, allow me to stop.'

MASTER: Very well, stop, and go and ask at the first cottage over there where the foster-parents live.

It was the last house. They went there, each of them leading his horse by the reins. At that moment the door opened and a man appeared. Jacques' master cried out and drew his sword and the other man did the same. The two horses were frightened by the clashing of swords and Jacques' horse broke away from its reins and ran free. At the same moment the gentleman his master was fighting fell dead on the spot. The peasants from the village rushed up. Jacques' master jumped nimbly into his saddle and rode away as fast as he could. They grabbed hold of Jacques, tied his hands behind his back, and brought him in front of the local judge, who sent him to prison. The dead man was the Chevalier de Saint-Ouin, whom Fate had led, on that very day, along with Agathe, to their foster-parents. Agathe was tearing her hair out over her lover's corpse. Jacques' master was already so far away that he was lost from sight. Jacques mused as he was led from the judge's house to the prison that it was, it had to be, written up above.

And as for me, I'm stopping because I've told you everything that I know about these two people.

– What about the story of Jacques' loves?

Jacques must have said a hundred times that it was written up above that he would not finish the story and I can see, Reader, that Jacques was right. I can see that this annoys you. Well then, carry on his story where he left off and finish it however you like. Or, if you'd rather, go and see Mlle Agathe. Find out the name of the village where Jacques is in prison, go and see Jacques and question him. He won't need to be coaxed to satisfy you. It will relieve him of his boredom. Following the written record, which I have good reason to hold suspect, I might perhaps supply what is missing here. But what use would that be? One can only interest oneself in that which one believes to be true. However, since it would be imprudent to make any final decision without a detailed examination of the conversations of Jacques the Fatalist and his master, the most important work which has appeared since Francois Rabelais' *Pantagruel*, and the life and times of *Compère Mathieu*,[77] I will re-read these memoirs with all the concentration and impartiality of which I am capable. And after a week I will give you my definitive judgement – definitive, that is, until I retract it because someone more intelligent than me has shown that I'm wrong.

A week has gone by. I have read the memoirs in question and out of the three additional paragraphs which I find in the manuscript I own, the first and the last appear to me to be original, and the middle one has obviously been interpolated. Here is the first one, which supposes a second gap in the conversation of Jacques and his master.

One feast day, while the lord of the château was hunting and the other residents had gone to Mass at the parish church, which was a good quarter of a league away, Jacques got up. Denise was sitting beside him and they were both silent and seemed to be sulking. In fact they were sulking. Jacques had done everything he could to persuade Denise to make him happy. And Denise held fast. After this long silence Jacques was crying hot tears and he said to her in a harsh, bitter voice: 'You don't love me.'

Disappointed, Denise got up, took him by the arm, led him to the edge of the bed and said: 'So, Monsieur Jacques, I don't love you. Well then, Monsieur Jacques, do with the unfortunate Denise whatever you want.'

And as she said these words she burst into tears, was choking with sobs.

Tell me, what would you have done if you were in Jacques' place?

– Nothing.

Well, that is precisely what he did. He brought Denise from the bed to her chair, threw himself at her feet, wiped the tears which were running from her eyes, kissed her hands, consoled her, reassured her, believed that she loved him dearly and left it to her love to choose the moment to reward his own. This behaviour deeply touched Denise. One might perhaps object that if Jacques was at Denise's feet he could hardly wipe her eyes unless the chair was extremely low. The manuscript doesn't say, but this seems a plausible assumption.

Here is the second paragraph, which has been copied from *The Life and Times of Tristram Shandy*, unless the conversation of Jacques the Fatalist and his master predates this work and the good minister Sterne himself is the plagiarist, which is something I do not believe, because of the particular esteem in which I hold Mr Sterne, whom I distinguish from the majority of men of letters of his nation whose quite frequent custom is to steal from us and then insult us.

Another time it was morning and Denise had come to bandage Jacques. Everyone was still asleep in the château. Denise came near to Jacques, trembling. When she reached Jacques' door she stopped, uncertain whether to go in or not. She entered, trembling, and stayed for quite a long time beside Jacques' bed without daring to open the curtains. Still trembling, she opened them quietly, and said good morning to Jacques. She asked about the night he had spent and his health and she was still trembling. Jacques told her that he hadn't slept a wink and that he had suffered and he was still suffering from a terrible itching on his knee. Denise offered to comfort him and took a little piece of flannel. Jacques put his leg out of the bed and Denise started to rub below the wound with her flannel, first with one finger, then two, then three, then four, then her whole hand. Jacques watched her do this, drunk with love. Then Denise started to rub her flannel on the wound itself, the scar of which was still red, first with one finger, then two, then three, then four, then her whole hand.

But it wasn't enough to have cured the itching under the knee and on the knee. It still needed to be cured above the knee where he could feel it all the more sharply. Denise put her flannel above his knee and started rubbing there quite firmly, first with one finger, then two, then three, then four, then her whole hand. Jacques had not stopped looking at her and his passion reached such a point that, no longer being able to resist, he threw himself on Denise's hand . . . and then kissed her . . . hand.

But what leaves no doubt at all as to the fact that this is a plagiarism is what follows. The plagiarist adds the following exhortaton: If you are not satisfied with what I have revealed to you of Jacques' loves, Reader, you may go away and do better – I consent to it. But however you go about it I am sure you will conclude as I have.

– You are wrong, insidious slanderer. I will not conclude as you have. Denise was a good girl.

But who has told you otherwise? Jacques threw himself on her hand, and then he kissed her – on the hand, that is. You are the one with the corrupted mind who doesn't understand what he is being told.

– Well! And he only kissed her hand?

Of course. Jacques had too much sense to take advantage of the woman he wanted to make his wife and prepare for himself a lifetime of poisonous suspicions.

– But in the previous paragraph it says that Jacques tried everything to persuade Denise to make him happy.

Apparently that is because at that time he didn't want to make her his wife.

The third paragraph shows us Jacques, our poor Fatalist, with his hands and his feet in irons, stretched out on the straw, at the bottom of some dark dungeon, recalling all the principles which he could remember of his Captain's philosophy, and not very far away from reaching the conclusion that he would perhaps one day regret his humid, foul-smelling dark dwelling, where he was fed on black bread and water and had to defend his feet and hands from the attacks of mice and rats. We are told that, in the middle of these meditations, the doors of his prison and dungeon were broken down and that he was given his liberty along with a dozen brigands and found himself enrolled in the gang of the outlaw Mandrin.[78] Meanwhile the mounted constabulary who had been tracking his master found him, arrested him and put him in custody in another prison. He got himself released through the good offices of the Commissioner, who had served him so well in his first adventure, and had been living in retirement in Desglands' château for two or three months when chance returned to him a servant who was almost as essential to his happiness as his watch and his snuff-box. There was not a single time that he took a pinch of snuff, nor a single time that he looked to see what time it was, that he didn't say with a sigh: 'What has become of my poor Jacques?'

One night Desglands' château was attacked by Mandrin's gang. Jacques recognized the residence of his benefactor and his mistress, interceded and preserved the château from being plundered.

We then come to the passage which describes the pathetic details of the unexpected encounter of Jacques, his master, Desglands, Denise and Jeanne.

'Is that you, my friend?'

'Is that you, my dear master?'

'How did you come to be with these people?'

'And how is it that I find you here? Is that you, Denise?'

'Is that you, Monsieur Jacques? How you made me cry!'

Meanwhile Desglands shouted out: 'Bring glasses and wine quickly. He has saved all our lives.'

A few days afterwards the old concierge of the château died. Jacques secured his place and married Denise, with whom he occupied himself in raising disciples of Zeno and Spinoza, loved by Desglands, cherished by his master and adored by his wife, for thus was it written up above.

It has been claimed that his master and Desglands fell in love with his wife. I do not know if this is true but I am sure that at night he used to say to himself:

If it is written up above that you will be cuckolded, no matter what you do you will be. If, however, it is written up above that you will not be cuckolded, no matter what they do you won't be. So sleep, my friend.

And he slept.

NOTES

———◆———

1. A Belgian village, site of a French victory in 1745 over a combined force of English, Dutch and Imperial troops.

2. The surgeon, like other country surgeons who appear in *Jacques*, would seem to be a barber-surgeon, occupying a relatively humble position in the medical hierarchy of the period and dealing with minor surgical interventions.

3. French military successes of 1747 and 1756 respectively.

4. Saint Roch, traditionally invoked by plague victims, is sometimes represented as a pilgrim, but is most often recognizable by a sore or boil on his thigh. It is not known whether Diderot was thinking of any particular representation of the saint.

5. This anecdote refers to the Marquis de Castries, wounded fighting in Westphalia in 1762. Dufouart and Louis were prominent French surgeons of the period.

6. This phrase has become a catch-phrase in French, but Diderot's reference to Harpagon is inaccurate, since the words are spoken by Géronte in Molière's *Les Fourberies de Scapin*, and not by Harpagon in *L'Avare*.

7. Pontoise and Saint-Germain are small towns situated close to Paris, and no doubt chosen to contrast with the more exotic and far-away places of pilgrimage, Loreto and Compostella.

8. Lieutenant-governor is an approximate translation of 'lieutenant-général', which, by the eighteenth century, refers to a magistrate appointed by the king and responsible for the administration of justice in and around a fairly important town. This suggests that the town of Conches referred to is the one in Normandy.

9. The reference is to *Le Philosophe anglais ou Histoire de Monsieur Cleveland*, a very popular novel by the Abbé Prévost, published between 1731 and 1739 and often cited in the eighteenth century as an example of the extravagant adventure-novel.

10. Diderot greatly admired Richardson for his realism. Regnard was the best-known writer of comedies in the generation after Molière, while

Sedaine, a contemporary whom Diderot much admired, was a successful writer of comedies and light-opera librettos.

11. The poet has been identified as one Viguier, who published a collection of verse in 1765. Pondicherry was a French possession on the east coast of India, and a prosperous commercial centre in spite of the effects of Anglo-French conflict in India during the eighteenth century.

12. Horace, *Ars poetica*, ll. 372–3, *Mediocribus esse poetis/Non homines, non di, non concessere columnae* ('Neither gods, men nor columns allow poets to be mediocre'). The columns referred to were used for advertising new literary works.

13. Carmelites who followed the reformed rule of Saint John of the Cross. They went barefoot (or rather wore sandals) as a sign of their commitment to a life of austerity.

14. A reference to the earthquake of 1 February 1755, and indirectly, perhaps, to Voltaire's *Candide*.

15. Aesop's master was Xanthos.

16. Diderot refers here to the *gardes de la Ferme*, that is, to the agents of the great organization which was contracted to levy some of the most important taxes for the kings of France. The system of tax-farming was open to considerable abuse, led to widespread smuggling and tax evasion, and was greatly disliked.

17. Charles le Pelletier, who died in 1756, was widely known for his piety and charitable work.

18. Niccolo Fortiguerra (1674–1735) was the author of *Ricciardetto*, a burlesque version of Ariosto's *Orlando furioso*. Richardet and Ferragus are characters in Fortiguerra's work. The continuator of *Don Quixote* is Luis Aliaga, who published his continuation under the name of Alonso Fernandez de Avellaneda.

19. It is not known to whom Diderot might be referring here. The Invalides is the establishment founded by Louis XIV for the relief of old and infirm soldiers.

20. *The Reluctant Doctor*, by Molière, Act I, scene 1. The original of Gousse is supposed to be one Louis-George Goussier.

21. Both Prémontval and the Pigeons have been identified. It is worth noting, however, that Prémontval had to leave France because of his anti-Christian views, rather than for the reasons given by Diderot.

22. A well-known surgeon of the period. Rousseau refers to him in his *Confessions*.

23. In the pre-Revolutionary currency, there were twenty *sous* to the *livre*

(pound) or *franc* (the terms were often but not always interchangeable). The *écu* was a silver coin worth three or six *livres*, and the *louis* a gold coin worth twenty-four *livres*. The wages of daily paid workers are reckoned to have been between ten and twenty *sous* per day.

24. 'He who goes slowly goes safely . . . he who goes safely goes far.'

25. Voltaire had objected to the vulgarity of *cul-de-sac*, *cul* having the sense of 'bottom', but some of the connotations of 'arse'. French usage followed Voltaire, and *impasse* replaced *cul-de-sac* to indicate a dead-end.

26. Prison situated to the south of Paris.

27. The eminent critic Jacques Proust, in a recent critical edition of *Jacques*, suggests that there is here an allusion to a well-known belief that a heavy hand with the seasoning is a sign of a woman in love.

28. This order is the famous *lettre de cachet*, which allowed for arrest and detention without trial for indefinite periods. It could easily be used to secure private and personal ends, as in the episode Diderot relates, and came to be seen as one of the most flagrant abuses of the *ancien régime*.

29. The comte de Saint-Florentin, later duc de La Vrillière, was a favourite of Louis XV and became minister of the royal household. He was held to be somewhat too free in issuing *lettres de cachet*.

30. Goldoni's play *Le Bourru bienfaisant* was written in French and first performed on 4 November 1771. Diderot had been accused, many years earlier, of plagiarizing Goldoni, and this may explain the reference to Goldoni here.

31. A well-known Genevan doctor who enjoyed a high reputation among the intelligentsia of Diderot's generation.

32. An untranslatable pun. *Jason* in French is close to *jaser*, 'to chatter'.

33. Claude-Louis de Regnier, comte de Guerchy.

34. In other words, the clergy.

35. A *tripot* was primarily a gambling-den, often maintained with some pretence of respectability by a woman of quality, and equally often functioning as a brothel.

36. In eighteenth-century French usage, the term *abbé* does not always mean 'abbot', but may indicate a priest without specific ecclesiastical duties. It often has pejorative connotations, implying venality, immorality, and lack of belief and vocation.

37. Respected seventeenth-century French churchmen. Dangerous from the anti-Christian perspective of Jacques' Captain because likely to foster a favourable attitude to the Christian religion.

38. Jansenism, in its seventeenth-century origins, was both a theological tendency, marked by its claim to return to a stricter understanding of certain aspects of the Church's teaching (particularly on human nature and divine grace), and a rigorist reaction to what were perceived as laxist tendencies in the Church. These, often associated with the Jesuits, came to be referred to as Molinism, after the Spanish Jesuit Molina. It is fair to say that by the second half of the eighteenth century the great issues that had animated controversy in the seventeenth century had in large measure ceased to be of primary importance. Jansenism was petering out into various forms of opposition to the Church hierarchy or to ultramontanism, while Molinism in turn came to mean little more than anti-Jansenism. Madame de La Pommeraye's dismissive reference may be seen as indicative of her own indifference to matters religious, but also as representative of much of public opinion.

39. A school for the daughters of the nobility was established by Louis XIV's second wife, Madame de Maintenon, in the convent of Saint-Cyr in 1685. More important, perhaps, is the fact that this is one of several examples of Diderot's teasing the reader; here, by drawing attention to the 'romantic' possibilities offered by the hostess's own life-story and at the same time refusing it to the reader.

40. A town which was only five miles from Paris.

41. This list of writers of poetics is taken from the title of a work by the abbé Batteux, but typically, Diderot replaces the last author, Despréaux, by Le Bossu merely for the sake of an untranslatable pun – *bossu* meaning 'crooked' or 'hunch-backed' in French.

42. Another doctor of Swiss origin admired by Diderot.

43. No one has satisfactorily established whether this list refers to historical persons, nor is it obvious that the effort would be worthwhile.

44. The quarrel between Jacques and his master takes on an added historical and political resonance when one remembers that a *jacques* was the traditional term of contempt for the French peasant.

45. This passage is probably an allusion to the political conflict between the monarchy and the *parlements* – particularly that of Paris – in eighteenth-century France. The *parlements* were the great courts of justice of the kingdom. The *parlementaires*, the great hereditary magistrates of these courts, claimed to be the defenders of the fundamental laws of the kingdom, and used their power to withhold ratification of royal decrees in order to assert their importance.

46. Premonstratensians were an order of regular canons founded by Saint Norbert in 1120. They had a reputation for social exclusiveness.

47. A passage which well illustrates the difficulty that the reader has in deciding on what level to take the philosophical issues advanced in the book.

48. On Jansenism and laxism, see note 38. The Papal Bull *Unigenitus* was promulgated in 1713. It condemned a number of propositions in a work by the Jansenist Quesnel, and was fiercely opposed for a further fifty years or more. The bishop of Mirepoix had much influence with Louis XV and was hostile to Jansenism.

49. An *in pace* is a monastic prison cell.

50. Piron was a celebrated wit who died in 1773, and whose works were edited by a rather prudish gentleman called Rigoley de Juvigny. The abbé Vatri was a near-contemporary of Piron and a classical scholar.

51. This reference reflects Diderot's preoccupation with the commercial pressures that lead artists to betray their talent.

52. The image of the chrysalis and the butterfly is from the *Purgatorio*, Canto X, ll. 124–6. The references to the heresiarchs, to the treacherous (rather than ungrateful as Diderot terms them) and to the slothful ('vile' is closer to Dante) come from the *Inferno*, Cantos IX, XXXII and XXXIII respectively.

53. The sense of this remark becomes clearer when one learns that from the word for christening cap or bonnet (*béguin*), French has formed the verb *embéguiner*, with the secondary meaning of 'to persuade someone to accept a foolish idea or belief'. Jacques' meaning is violently anti-Christian.

54. Madame de Parme was the eldest daughter of Louis XV. She died in 1759; the duc de Chevreuse in 1771.

55. The genealogy occurs in the first chapter of Matthew's gospel.

56. Ferragus, in Fortiguerra's *Ricciardetto*, is castrated for attempting to rape a nun. As he lies delirious on his death-bed, Lucifer appears before him, taunting him with the evidence of his lost virility.

57. The reference is to the prince de Condé, one of the greatest French generals of the seventeenth century.

58. *La Farce de Maître Pathelin*, written in the 1460s.

59. William Pitt, the Elder, made the speech in the House of Commons in 1759.

60. Jean-Baptiste Rousseau was accused of writing obscene and slanderous verses. He defended himself in a 1712 edition of his works. Voltaire's mock-heroic epic poem *La Pucelle* ('The Virgin') plays on the theme of Joan of Arc's virginity and its preservation.

61. Montaigne, *Essays*, book III, chapter 5. The Latin quotation is from

Martial's epigrams, book I, no. 4, l. 8, and means, 'Our page is licentious, but our life pure.'

62. Bacbuc is the name given to the 'sacred bottle' in Rabelais. The following pages are very much a celebration of the Rabelaisian tradition as Diderot seems to have understood it. The consultation of the bottle is to be found in the *Cinquième livre*, chapter XLV.

63. The same as ventriloquist, i.e. stomach-speaker.

64. The authors that Diderot lists here share – by reputation, at least – a more or less philosophical tendency to epicureanism.

65. The Pomme de Pin was a well-known meeting-place of poets in the seventeenth century, frequented in particular by Chapelle, Molière and La Fontaine. The Temple was the meeting-place of poets such as La Fare and Chaulieu, who established a prevailing tone of easy hedonism.

66. Editors and annotators of classical authors.

67. The clearest indication that Jacques' master is a nobleman. With a few local exceptions, the nobility could not engage in work or trade personally.

68. In contrast to the simple promissory note, the bill of exchange was a commercial transaction, and therefore made one liable to more stringent prosecution and penalties if one failed to honour it on the due date.

69. Madame Riccoboni was particularly noted for her success with the epistolary novel, which was very popular in the latter half of the eighteenth century.

70. Cardinal Guido Bentivoglio (1579–1644), historian and papal nuncio in France.

71. That is, *in vino veritas* – 'in the wine is truth'. Charles Collé was a successful song-writer and comic author. This play was first staged in 1747.

72. La Fontaine, *Fables*, book IX, 4. Garo asks why God didn't give the mighty oak a fruit of appropriate size, such as the pumpkin. While he takes a nap under an oak, an acorn falls on his nose, prompting Garo to the conclusion that, after all, God organizes things for the best.

73. The reference is to Jean-Jacques Rousseau who, in his *Emile* (book II), condemns La Fontaine's fables as unsuitable for children.

74. Ovid, *Metamorphoses*, book I, ll. 85–6. The quotation should read *Os homini sublime dedit caelumque videre/Iussit et erectos ad sidera tollere vultus* ('He placed man's countenance on top of his body, and enjoined him to look at the sky and to raise his face to the stars').

75. Carmelite who published a series of letters during the 1730s in which

he sought to prove that the miracles that the Jansenists claimed were occurring in their community might be of diabolical inspiration.

76. It is not clear why Jacques' master should be taken to what was primarily a debtors' prison.

77. *Le Compère Mathieu* (1766–73) was a bawdy and picaresque novel by an ex-priest called Dulaurens.

78. Brigand who developed an almost legendary reputation. He died in 1755.

Discover more about our forthcoming books through Penguin's FREE newspaper...

Penguin
Quarterly

It's packed with:

- exciting features
- author interviews
- previews & reviews
- books from your favourite films & TV series
- exclusive competitions & much, much more...

Write off for your free copy today to:
Dept JC
Penguin Books Ltd
FREEPOST
West Drayton
Middlesex
UB7 0BR
NO STAMP REQUIRED

READ MORE IN PENGUIN

In every corner of the world, on every subject under the sun, Penguin represents quality and variety – the very best in publishing today.

For complete information about books available from Penguin – including Puffins, Penguin Classics and Arkana – and how to order them, write to us at the appropriate address below. Please note that for copyright reasons the selection of books varies from country to country.

In the United Kingdom: Please write to *Dept. JC, Penguin Books Ltd, FREEPOST, West Drayton, Middlesex UB7 0BR*

If you have any difficulty in obtaining a title, please send your order with the correct money, plus ten per cent for postage and packaging, to *PO Box No. 11, West Drayton, Middlesex UB7 0BR*

In the United States: Please write to *Penguin USA Inc., 375 Hudson Street, New York, NY 10014*

In Canada: Please write to *Penguin Books Canada Ltd, 10 Alcorn Avenue, Suite 300, Toronto, Ontario M4V 3B2*

In Australia: Please write to *Penguin Books Australia Ltd, 487 Maroondah Highway, Ringwood, Victoria 3134*

In New Zealand: Please write to *Penguin Books (NZ) Ltd,182–190 Wairau Road, Private Bag, Takapuna, Auckland 9*

In India: Please write to *Penguin Books India Pvt Ltd, 706 Eros Apartments, 56 Nehru Place, New Delhi 110 019*

In the Netherlands: Please write to *Penguin Books Netherlands B.V., Keizersgracht 231 NL–1016 DV Amsterdam*

In Germany: Please write to *Penguin Books Deutschland GmbH, Friedrichstrasse 10–12, W–6000 Frankfurt/Main 1*

In Spain: Please write to *Penguin Books S. A., C. San Bernardo 117–6° E–28015 Madrid*

In Italy: Please write to *Penguin Italia s.r.l., Via Felice Casati 20, I–20124 Milano*

In France: Please write to *Penguin France S. A., 17 rue Lejeune, F–31000 Toulouse*

In Japan: Please write to *Penguin Books Japan, Ishikiribashi Building, 2–5–4, Suido, Tokyo 112*

In Greece: Please write to *Penguin Hellas Ltd, Dimocritou 3, GR–106 71 Athens*

In South Africa: Please write to *Longman Penguin Southern Africa (Pty) Ltd, Private Bag X08, Bertsham 2013*

READ MORE IN PENGUIN

A CHOICE OF CLASSICS

Netochka Nezvanova Fyodor Dostoyevsky

Dostoyevsky's first book tells the story of 'Nameless Nobody' and introduces many of the themes and issues which dominate his great masterpieces.

Selections from the Carmina Burana
A verse translation by David Parlett

The famous songs from the *Carmina Burana* (made into an oratorio by Carl Orff) tell of lecherous monks and corrupt clerics, drinkers and gamblers, and the fleeting pleasures of youth.

Fear and Trembling Søren Kierkegaard

A profound meditation on the nature of faith and submission to God's will, which examines with startling originality the story of Abraham and Isaac.

Selected Prose Charles Lamb

Lamb's famous essays (under the strange pseudonym of Elia) on anything and everything have long been celebrated for their apparently innocent charm. This major new edition allows readers to discover the darker and more interesting aspects of Lamb.

The Picture of Dorian Gray Oscar Wilde

Wilde's superb and macabre novel, one of his supreme works, is reprinted here with a masterly Introduction and valuable Notes by Peter Ackroyd.

Frankenstein Mary Shelley

In recounting this chilling tragedy Mary Shelley demonstrates both the corruption of an innocent creature by an immoral society and the dangers of playing God with science.

READ MORE IN PENGUIN

A CHOICE OF CLASSICS

The House of Ulloa   Emilia Pardo Bazán

The finest achievement of one of European literature's most dynamic and controversial figures – ardent feminist, traveller, intellectual – and one of the great nineteenth century Spanish novels, *The House of Ulloa* traces the decline of the old aristocracy at the time of the Glorious Revolution of 1868, while exposing the moral vacuum of the new democracy.

The Republic   Plato

The best-known of Plato's dialogues, *The Republic* is also one of the supreme masterpieces of Western philosophy, whose influence cannot be overestimated.

The Duel and Other Stories   Anton Chekhov

In these stories Chekhov deals with a variety of themes – religious fanaticism and sectarianism, megalomania, and scientific controversies of the time, as well as provincial life in all its tedium and philistinism.

Metamorphoses   Ovid

A golden treasury of myths and legends, which has proved a major influence on Western literature.

A Nietzsche Reader   Friedrich Nietzsche

A superb selection from all the major works of one of the greatest thinkers and writers in world literature, translated into clear, modern English.

Madame Bovary   Gustave Flaubert

With *Madame Bovary* Flaubert established the realistic novel in France while his central character of Emma Bovary, the bored wife of a provincial doctor, remains one of the great creations of modern literature.

A CHOICE OF CLASSICS

John Aubrey	**Brief Lives**
Francis Bacon	**The Essays**
George Berkeley	**Principles of Human Knowledge and Three Dialogues between Hylas and Philonous**
James Boswell	**The Life of Johnson**
Sir Thomas Browne	**The Major Works**
John Bunyan	**The Pilgrim's Progress**
Edmund Burke	**Reflections on the Revolution in France**
Thomas de Quincey	**Confessions of an English Opium Eater**
	Recollections of the Lakes and the Lake Poets
Daniel Defoe	**A Journal of the Plague Year**
	Moll Flanders
	Robinson Crusoe
	Roxana
	A Tour through the Whole Island of Great Britain
Henry Fielding	**Amelia**
	Jonathan Wild
	Joseph Andrews
	Tom Jones
Oliver Goldsmith	**The Vicar of Wakefield**

READ MORE IN PENGUIN

A CHOICE OF CLASSICS

George Herbert	**The Complete English Poems**
Thomas Hobbes	**Leviathan**
Samuel Johnson/	
James Boswell	**A Journey to the Western Islands of Scotland** and **The Journal of a Tour to the Hebrides**
Charles Lamb	**Selected Prose**
Samuel Richardson	**Clarissa**
	Pamela
Richard Brinsley	
Sheridan	**The School for Scandal and Other Plays**
Christopher Smart	**Selected Poems**
Adam Smith	**The Wealth of Nations**
Tobias Smollett	**The Expedition of Humphrey Clinker**
Laurence Sterne	**The Life and Adventures of Sir Launcelot Greaves**
	A Sentimental Journey Through France and Italy
Jonathan Swift	**Gulliver's Travels**
Thomas Traherne	**Selected Poems and Prose**
Sir John Vanbrugh	**Four Comedies**

READ MORE IN PENGUIN

A CHOICE OF CLASSICS

Leopoldo Alas	**La Regenta**
Leon B. Alberti	**On Painting**
Ludovico Ariosto	**Orlando Furioso** (in 2 volumes)
Giovanni Boccaccio	**The Decameron**
Baldassar Castiglione	**The Book of the Courtier**
Benvenuto Cellini	**Autobiography**
Miguel de Cervantes	**Don Quixote**
	Exemplary Stories
Dante	**The Divine Comedy** (in 3 volumes)
	La Vita Nuova
Bernal Diaz	**The Conquest of New Spain**
Carlo Goldoni	**Four Comedies (The Venetian Twins/The Artful Widow/Mirandolina/The Superior Residence)**
Niccolò Machiavelli	**The Discourses**
	The Prince
Alessandro Manzoni	**The Betrothed**
Emilia Pardo Bazán	**The House of Ulloa**
Benito Pérez Galdós	**Fortunata and Jacinta**
Giorgio Vasari	**Lives of the Artists** (in 2 volumes)

and

Five Italian Renaissance Comedies
  (Machiavelli/**The Mandragola**; Ariosto/**Lena**; Aretino/**The Stablemaster**; Gl'Intronati/**The Deceived**; Guarini/**The Faithful Shepherd**)
The Poem of the Cid
Two Spanish Picaresque Novels
  (Anon/**Lazarillo de Tormes**; de Quevedo/**The Swindler**)

READ MORE IN PENGUIN

A CHOICE OF CLASSICS

Honoré de Balzac	**The Black Sheep**
	The Chouans
	Cousin Bette
	Eugénie Grandet
	A Harlot High and Low
	Lost Illusions
	A Murky Business
	Old Goriot
	Selected Short Stories
	Ursule Mirouet
	The Wild Ass's Skin
Marquis de Custine	**Letters from Russia**
Corneille	**The Cid/Cinna/The Theatrical Illusion**
Alphonse Daudet	**Letters from My Windmill**
René Descartes	**Discourse on Method and Other Writings**
Denis Diderot	**Jacques the Fatalist**
	Nun
	Rameau's Nephew and **D'Alembert's Dream**
Gustave Flaubert	**Bouvard and Pecuchet**
	Madame Bovary
	The Sentimental Education
	The Temptation of St Anthony
	Three Tales
Victor Hugo	**Les Misérables**
	Notre-Dame of Paris
Laclos	**Les Liaisons Dangereuses**
La Fontaine	**Selected Fables**
Madame de Lafayette	**The Princesse de Clèves**
Lautrémont	**Maldoror** and **Poems**

A CHOICE OF CLASSICS

Molière	The Misanthrope/The Sicilian/Tartuffe/A Doctor in Spite of Himself/The Imaginary Invalid
	The Miser/The Would-be Gentleman/That Scoundrel Scapin/Love's the Best Doctor/Don Juan
Michel de Montaigne	Essays
Marguerite de Navarre	The Heptameron
Blaise Pascal	Pensées
	The Provincial Letters
Abbé Prevost	Manon Lescaut
Marcel Proust	Against Sainte-Beuve
Rabelais	The Histories of Gargantua and Pantagruel
Racine	Andromache/Britannicus/Berenice
	Iphigenia/Phaedra/Athaliah
Arthur Rimbaud	Collected Poems
Jean-Jacques Rousseau	The Confessions
	A Discourse on Equality
	The Social Contract
Jacques Saint-Pierre	Paul and Virginia
Madame de Sevigné	Selected Letters
Stendhal	Lucien Leuwen
Voltaire	Candide
	Letters
	Philosophical Dictionary
Emile Zola	L'Assomoir
	La Bête Humaine
	The Debacle
	The Earth
	Germinal
	Nana
	Thérèse Raquin